SPECIAL MESSAGE TO READERS

THE ULVERSCROFT FOUNDATION
(registered UK charity number 264873)
was established in 1972 to provide funds for research, diagnosis and treatment of eye diseases. Examples of major projects funded by the Ulverscroft Foundation are:-

- The Children's Eye Unit at Moorfields Eye Hospital, London
- The Ulverscroft Children's Eye Unit at Great Ormond Street Hospital for Sick Children
- Funding research into eye diseases and treatment at the Department of Ophthalmology, University of Leicester
- The Ulverscroft Vision Research Group, Institute of Child Health
- Twin operating theatres at the Western Ophthalmic Hospital, London
- The Chair of Ophthalmology at the Royal Australian College of Ophthalmologists

You can help further the work of the Foundation by making a donation or leaving a legacy. Every contribution is gratefully received. If you would like to help support the Foundation or require further information, please contact:

THE ULVERSCROFT FOUNDATION
The Green, Bradgate Road, Anstey
Leicester LE7 7FU, England
Tel: (0116) 236 4325

website: www.foundation.ulverscroft.com

AURORA'S PRIDE

Aurora Pettigrew has a loving family, a nice home, a comfortable life. She's waiting for the right man to offer marriage, and the man for her is Reid Sinclair, heir to the Sinclair fortune. But Reid's mother is against the match and unearths a secret that will tear Aurora's world apart. Unwilling to bring shame on her family, and needing answers, Aurora moves to York. By chance, she reconnects with a man from her past, and before he leaves with the army to war in South Africa, he offers her security through marriage. Aurora knows she should be happy, but the memory of her love for Reid threatens her future. When tragedy strikes, can Aurora find the strength to accept her life and forget the past?

ANNEMARIE BREAR

AURORA'S PRIDE

Complete and Unabridged

MAGNA
Leicester

First published in Great Britain in 2017 by
Knox Robinson Publishing
London

First Ulverscroft Edition
published 2020
by arrangement with
Knox Robinson Publishing
London

A catalogue record for this book is available
from the British Library.

ISBN 978–0–7505–4754–3

Published by
F. A. Thorpe (Publishing)
Anstey, Leicestershire

Set by Words & Graphics Ltd.
Anstey, Leicestershire
Printed and bound in Great Britain by
T. J. International Ltd., Padstow, Cornwall

This book is printed on acid-free paper

With special thanks to the wonderful members
of Historical Fiction Critique Group.
What would I do without you all?
Thanks also to Dana and the team at
Knox Robinson!

1

Yorkshire, 1898

Aurora sipped the delicately perfumed tea. Over the rim, she watched their neighbor, Julia Sinclair, chat idly to her mother, Winnie. Despite the outward appearances of two older women enjoying a high tea, Aurora felt the undercurrents simmering in the room.

For the past three years, most Tuesdays she and her mother took a leisurely walk through the gardens and across the lawns dividing the two properties of the Sinclairs and Pettigrews. And on each visit, Mrs Sinclair did her best to assert her prominence over her 'lower' neighbor. Aurora wished her mother would stand up to her, but it wasn't in her nature. Winifred Pettigrew was as affable as a puppy and as kind as an elderly grandmother to anyone who ever gained her acquaintance. But with each Tuesday tea, Aurora grew more and more attuned to Mrs Sinclair's belief that the Pettigrews were beneath her.

Years of living side by side, their families' children growing into adulthood together, the shared events and celebrations did nothing in Mrs Sinclair's eyes to close the social gap. The Sinclairs were old money, the Pettigrews were new. That was the difference. It was a difference which could never be ignored by Mrs Sinclair and suddenly, or at least in the last year or so, she had made it clear that the gap was widening as her boys started looking for wives. Aurora and her two younger sisters, Bettina and Harriet, were not for the Sinclair boys, the heir and spares to a large and impressive fortune.

Aurora gazed around the room, noting the new Chippendale piece on the far wall and above it a recently bought painting, a Constable perhaps? If it had been anyone else's house she would have gone to study it more closely but she hated adding to Julia Sinclair's conceit. Over the years Mrs Sinclair had redecorated and removed nearly all traces of the previous mistress' touches in the Hall. It was, in fact, a shrine to her own taste and judgment, which Aurora grudgingly admitted was rather fine, but Mrs Sinclair's attitude was such that she knew it and therefore her boasting ruined all pleasure of visiting the Hall.

Her mother nibbled a small triangle of light pastry filled with lemon curd and almonds. 'Your cook has outdone herself today, Julia.'

Mrs Sinclair briefly touched her immaculate hair, the color of coal and gathered up in wind-defying twists. As always she wore the finest of gowns, designed by the best Paris designers had to offer. 'My *cook* has gone. In her place I've employed an Italian chef, Moretti, a wonderful man I found working in one of London's best restaurants.'

Aurora smothered a giggle. 'You lured an Italian to the countryside near Leeds?'

'I think lured is a somewhat extreme word, my dear.' Julia's mouth thinned in irritation. 'He is an older man, who found the fast pace of a busy restaurant no longer suited him.'

'An Italian chef? How very interesting.' Mother peered at the pastry in her hand. 'Though I did think your previous cook was a rare talent, too. Hadn't she been at the Hall for many years?'

'A simple cook is not enough, Winnie. One must have the best and my chef is exactly that. You could improve in that area yourself, I'm sure. Shall I look into the situation for you?'

Aurora stiffened at the slight, giving the older woman a direct look. 'Mrs Pringle suits us rather well.'

'Indeed.' Mrs Sinclair gave a subtle sniff and raised a slender finger to the hovering maid to pour more tea, 'You do know, dear Winnie, that Reid is currently home from London?'

'He's home?' Aurora's eyes widened. She hadn't known and stared at the doorway as if she expected him to walk through it. Quickly looking down at her teacup, she hid a smile. He was home.

'He's been dreadfully busy. You know how industrious he is.' Mrs Sinclair paused to select a petite finger length cucumber sandwich. 'Of course, he's never too busy for our circle of friends in London.' She ate carefully, delicately. 'Naturally he is much sought after . . . ' She gave Aurora a subtle glance. 'Many a debutante desires the Sinclair heir as a husband.'

'And has he settled on one?' her mother asked innocently, unaware of Aurora's intake of breath.

'I do believe there is a special lady who has

caught his eye. Always a closed one is my darling Reid. I suppose being the eldest of four sons has taught him to be careful with his secrets in case the boys tease him.'

'Someone tease Reid?' Her mother's eyes widened at the absurdity of the idea.

'Is-is Reid at home today or out riding?' Aurora grimaced as her voice squeaked. She listened for any evidence he might be close by. Why hadn't he been to see her?

'He's probably with his father and occupied with estate business.' Julia's guileless smirk didn't hide the coldness of her manner. 'He has no need to waste his time sipping tea with the ladies. You know how he is. I do fear business will overtake his life. He has such a passion for it.' She frowned. 'I do wish he wouldn't be so zealous about things.'

'He is a dear boy.' Winnie took a macaroon. 'Dreadfully polite and so interesting. He once spoke to me on matters of some trade he was overseeing that quite confused me.' She chuckled at her own limitations. 'He now knows I have no head for commerce.'

'No self-respecting lady should, Winnie dear.' Mrs Sinclair tutted.

'I don't believe that.' Aurora couldn't help but speak out. 'Many women, high ranking women, run estates and properties. If their husbands have died they must learn to guard their children's inheritance.'

'Surely that task should be left to trustees.'

'Why? Why shouldn't a wife or mother control her own destiny?' Aurora glanced from her

4

mother, who blinked rapidly, to Mrs Sinclair, whose eyes narrowed with distaste.

'Did you hear that Amelia Williams from Grange Way is to be married in June?' Winnie broke the strained silence. 'The groom is from Manchester would you believe. I do so like summer weddings.'

'I did hear, yes. We are invited, as I expect you are. I think this coming year will see many weddings.' Their hostess preened. 'I expect an engagement announcement from Reid any day now. Obviously, it won't be to someone in this district. No doubt she will be a London beauty, perhaps even linked to nobility. He mixes in those circles, you see, so it would be suitably natural for him to choose from such exalted society.'

Aurora tensed, the blow hitting her hard between the breastbone. She wanted to block her ears. None of it was true. Reid was hers. The fragile porcelain handle of the teacup snapped in her hand and the last few drops of her tea spilled down her sprigged gown and to the Turkish rug on the floor.

'Oh!' Mrs Sinclair jumped up as though the hounds of Hell had been let through the door, while Aurora's mother quickly used a napkin to dab at the stain.

'Has it burnt you, my dear?' Her mother's worried tone brought Aurora back from the jolt Julia's words had caused.

'No. I'm fine, Mother.' She stared at her hostess. 'I beg your pardon, Mrs Sinclair, for breaking your piece.'

'Please, think nothing of it. It wasn't a favorite set at all.' Julia Sinclair was all smiles, though her ice blue eyes were hard as marble as she directed a maid to clean up the mess.

No, we don't deserve to drink from a favorite set, Aurora fumed. Unable to take any more of their neighbor, she reached for her mother's elbow. 'We must go, Mother. I need to change.'

With apologies and promises to see each other at the harvest festival on Saturday, they departed from the magnificent Sinclair Hall, its sandstone brick mellow from years of weather. Aurora escaped across the wide flat lawns skirted by well-tended garden beds flowering in a late rush summer bloom. A male peacock strutted out from beneath a large sycamore tree, opening his beautiful fanned tail for the hens to notice and Aurora grimaced. Julia even had regal birds to show off.

'Aurora, do slow down, my dear.'

'Sorry, Mother.' Once through the wooden gate leading to their own less illustrious grounds, Aurora let out breath, not realizing she had held it. Her head pounded and it wasn't caused by the evening storm building in the distance. She vowed that this would be the last Tuesday tea she would attend. Bettina and Harriet at sixteen and fifteen were old enough to go, she'd done her penance. But it wasn't the afternoon tea, or even Mrs Sinclair's superior attitude that plagued her. It was the news that Reid was looking for a wife that had shattered her world as easily as a spoon shattered the top of an egg.

Reid married. How would she bear it?

'As you know I do not like being uncharitable, but I do believe Julia was rather smug today.' Winnie sighed as they entered the front entrance of their warm red brick house, which although only half the size of Sinclair Hall, was filled to the brim with love and laughter. It may not have the expensive items Julia boasted, or the years of history the Hall claimed, but the house was comforting, like a warm blanket on cold winter's night.

'Mother, she is always smug. It is her character.' Aurora gave her hat and gloves to Tibbleton, their butler. How could she act normally after today? She wanted to go hide somewhere and think and grieve and try to imagine Reid, her tall handsome Reid, standing with another on his arm. No, surely not. He wouldn't do it to her. He knew her feelings.

'Now, darling, that is not nice.'

'And neither is she,' Aurora snapped, pouring her anger into Reid's mother, a worthy recipient. 'I cannot stand how-' She turned as her sisters came rushing down the staircase.

'Mother! Aurora!' They chorused as one.

'Really, girls. Do not shout.' Mother smiled her thanks to Tibbleton and sailed forth into the withdrawing room, which had none of the formality the Hall possessed, but instead was haphazardly arranged with bits of furniture. Many a visitor has had to remove a bonnet, a newspaper, or sewing from a chair before sitting down. Winnie waited for her two younger daughters to be seated with a patience her family adored. 'Now, what is your news?'

7

'We've been invited to Captain Lee's harvest ball next week.' Bettina gushed. 'It's been hastily arranged.'

'Why yes, he only returned home from the continent last week.' Their mother quickly went to her small mahogany secretary on the far wall and sat down on the plush red velvet chair placed before it. 'I'll check my diary. Really, the Captain should know better . . . '

'The Captain is without a female to guide him in such matters, Mother.' Aurora smiled, liking the genial old army captain, who, since the death of his wife and more recently his widowed daughter, lived alone at Sommervale Lodge a few miles to the south of them.

'We will go, of course,' their mother muttered, writing in her diary. 'Your father greatly admires the Captain.'

'Talking about me again?' Josiah Pettigrew strolled through the doorway, his tall thin frame commanding the room.

'Husband, you are home early.' At once on her feet, Winnie rang the bell pull beside the unlit fireplace.

'My meeting finished early.' He kissed his wife and daughters in turn and then sat on the leather wing-backed chair at a right angle to the fireplace. 'Like most of the businessmen of Leeds, we were happy to escape the town before the storm broke. Ah, Tibbleton, a drink before I go to my study, if you please.'

The butler, standing at his post by the door, immediately went to the drinks cabinet near the front window and the conversation resumed about the Captain's ball. However, the discussion of possible guests and entertainment was lost to Aurora as Mrs Sinclair's words circled her head again like a shark menacing a school of fish.

Reid, Reid, Reid.

What was she to do? Ignore the talk of a boastful mother? Seek out Reid?

She stood hovering, anxious to get out of the room and her tea stain was the perfect excuse. In her bedroom she was glad Hilda, the maid she shared with her sisters, wasn't about. She needed solitude to think, to plan.

Sitting on the window seat, she drew her knees up to her chin and stared down at the peaceful stables below. Two years ago, on her eighteenth birthday, Reid Sinclair had kissed her. It hadn't been a chaste birthday kiss, but a kiss given by a man to a woman. From that moment she had understood everything. Their secret looks, the lingering of their hands in greeting, the shared seating at functions, the soft smiles, the unspoken promises of the previous summer had all become clear. Without a significant word spoken, they both knew what was in the other's hearts.

Or at least she had thought so.

In the two years since that magical day he kissed her, their time alone had been limited. Reid had spent more and more time in London, learning how to manage his family's empire. He'd spent a mere six weeks at home each year and the longed for question she expected him to ask her had never been uttered. They had danced together and attended the same dinner parties, but he always seemed preoccupied. They hadn't found the chance to be alone for any length of time.

Had she made more of the situation than was warranted?

Did Julia speak honestly about Reid and a possible engagement? Had he changed his mind about her?

Aurora groaned and banged her forehead on her knees as thunder rolled over the roof. They sky was streaked with swirling angry gray clouds. As yet no rain fell and the atmosphere grew tight, expectant.

Why would Reid treat her so cruelly? She raised her gaze to the distant hills on the stormy horizon, ignoring the sudden gale which tossed the tree branches and battered birds flying home to roost. Had she imagined what was between her and Reid? Did she romanticize the situation to suit her own needs? She shook her head. No. What she felt for Reid, a pure love, had been reflected in his eyes, his manner. She was certain she hadn't been alone in what she felt in her heart.

But what to do? He had arrived home and the first she knew of it was at the tea. Why hadn't he called as he usually did? Why didn't he join them for tea if he was in the house? He'd done so many times before. He'd always eat the jam tartlets, as they were his favorites.

Then the thought she didn't want to dwell on came to the fore to taunt and bully her. What if his feelings had changed? What if he didn't want to see her? What if he no longer felt anything for her? What if he was promised to another? There had never been a spoken agreement between them. He had never mentioned a future together. It had all been in looks and gestures. If he'd been serious wouldn't he have talked to her father?

So many unanswered questions made her head ache worse. There was much she didn't understand and was confused about. Tears threatened and she blinked rapidly to deny their release. She must see him. She had to know if his mother was right. Scrambling over to her desk, she tried not to think of what she'd do if he'd found another. Scratching the pen across a piece of paper, she wrote the note and then rang for her maid.

2

The dancing couples swirled around the floor, the women's skirts flaring out like opened umbrellas of every color. The small orchestra swelled the room with music, drowning out the need to talk should the dancers even wish to. Aurora smiled automatically at her partner, Philip Sampson, a local Leeds bachelor with a belly the size of a keg. He was a friend of the family, but not a prospective suitor, even if he didn't know it.

As they swung around in time to the music at the edge of the dancing area, Aurora scanned the onlookers for Reid. He was here tonight at Captain Lee's ball, for she had seen him earlier talking to acquaintances. He'd been avoiding her, she was sure and her spirits plummeted. She had danced with every man in the room, some twice over, but not once with Reid. His three brothers who, after years of growing up together were like her own brothers, had plucked her from her chair the minute the music started after dinner and she'd laughed with them as they trotted around the room. But of Reid she'd seen very little.

She longed to join the gaiety of the night, but a week of hurt and anger robbed her of the ability to enjoy the ball as she should. The note she wrote to Reid last Tuesday was never answered. The harvest festival given in their small village at the weekend had been attended by all of his family except him. It left her in no

12

doubt that he avoided her now. In silent agony she dragged herself through each day, hoping her parents or sisters wouldn't guess her heartache. But then, how could they? No one knew of her attachment to Reid, of the love she carried for him.

'Thank you, Miss Pettigrew. A delightful dance.' Philip bowed as the last notes died and led her to her mother, who sat on a cream sofa with an elderly neighbor.

Once Philip left, Aurora turned towards the open doors leading into the next room. 'I'm in need of some refreshment, Mother. I shan't be long.'

'Very good, my dear.' Her mother waved her away and resumed her conversation.

At the refreshment table, Aurora waited for a footman to pour her a small glass of punch. She smiled and nodded to those she knew, pretending to be having a wonderful time, when all the while her stomach was tangled in knots of misery. The simple beauty of the flower decorations, the sumptuous food and the attentions of the single men were lost to her.

'Is your dance card full, Miss Pettigrew?'

With her heart banging in her chest, she slowly turned her head to gaze up at Reid. Her pulse slowed then sped up again. 'And what if it is, Mr Sinclair?'

'Then I would be aggrieved to have missed a dance with you.' His blue eyes so like his mothers, but much warmer, kinder, smiled down at her.

'You only have yourself to blame, sir, since the

13

night is nearly over.' She nodded her thanks to the footman and took her drink.

'Perhaps a stroll in the gardens then? It's not too cold.'

'It has rained for a week. Do you wish for me to ruin my gown and slippers?' She stepped away from the table and him. The forced civility made it easier for her to be near him. She'd treat him like a stranger and see how he liked that!

'And such a beautiful gown it is, but nothing compared to the beauty of its wearer,' he murmured, following her.

Her teeth clenched at his comment. The Reid she knew never spoke such trite compliments. Her new pale blue gown was very becoming and she spent hours readying herself for tonight because he would be here. Yet now, it all felt wasted. The night hadn't gone as planned. In the past they had danced numerous times, sat together, ate together, and laughed together. Only tonight none of that happened. He looked the same, still dashing, lithe, powerful, compelling, but not the man she knew and loved. Not her Reid. Not her best friend. The one who talked to her for hours about any subject under the sun. Something in his manner told her he was holding back. Was he protecting her or himself?

Without realizing it, they'd walked to the corner of the room, half shaded by a large potted palm.

'I've missed you, Aurrie.'

She glanced up at him. His intense look made her shiver with awareness. She studied his handsome face. It wasn't a classical face, his nose was a little crooked from a fall he took from his horse as a boy and his dark brown hair never sat straight, but kicked out over his collar if grown too long, but to her, he was perfect. 'Have you?'

'You believe I lie?' He frowned, shocked, then a smile lifted the corners of his mouth.

'I'm not sure what I believe any more. I rarely see you.'

'I'm sorry for that.' He sighed deeply. 'Much keeps me occupied in London.'

'I'll wager it does.' Anger, her constant companion this week, swelled again. 'Society down there is far superior to ours in the country. Is it not?'

Reid stepped closer, his manner gentle. 'What is wrong, Aurora?'

'Were you too busy to answer my note last week?'

'What note?'

'What note indeed.' She gulped down the fruity punch to hide the hurt clawing at her. Seeing him again was a bittersweet pleasure. Something had changed between them, distance and time had taken its toll. She no longer felt close to him and grieved at the loss.

'I've hardly been at home since I arrived. Every day has been taken up with activities and arrangements. My father — '

'We live just across the lawn, Reid.' She stepped back, putting space, and more, between them. 'But of course it is not a mere lawn that divides us, isn't it?'

His eyes narrowed, a clear sign she knew well of his growing frustration and annoyance. 'What on earth do you mean?'

'And ignoring me tonight has that been intentional too?'

'Aurora! There you are!' Bettina hurried to her, all smiles for Reid, but quickly dragging Aurora by the hand. 'Come, you have been awfully lacking. Your dance partners have been queuing up for the last three dances. Mother refuses to apologize to another disappointed young man and sent me to find you. Excuse us, will you Reid?'

'Certainly.' He bowed, his eyes assessing.

Aurora was glad to be away. Why had she allowed her emotions to get the better of her? Why didn't she stay calm and gracious? Instead of rekindling his affections as she had hoped to do, she'd acted like a spitting cat. Full of despair, she was quickly engulfed in a circle of willing partners and for the remainder of the night, she neither spoke to nor saw Reid again.

In the carriage on the way home, she stared out of the window at the approaching dawn. The shell pink of the sky was advancing on the gloom of the night. Her feet ached and her satin shoes were ruined from dancing, but none of it mattered when her mind only dwelt on her strange relationship with Reid. Repeatedly she tried to put him from her mind, to think of some other man who could fill his shoes, but it was useless. She hadn't imagined their closeness all these years. Surely he hadn't played her for a fool? Someone to casually toss aside when no longer needed? No. Reid wasn't that type of man or friend. So what did that leave her to consider? What was the truth of it all?

'Well, I am ready for my bed indeed,' her mother said, sighing.

'It was a wonderful night.' Bettina closed her eyes, a smile lifting her lips while Harriet dozed against their father's shoulder.

Her mother shifted in her seat and stifled a yawn behind her hand. 'Julia finally revealed Reid's intended's name, a Miss Hermione FitzGibbon from down south, lands in Kent, close to a Sinclair property, or something like that.'

'How exciting,' Harriet said, turning to Aurora, her yellow ribbons and curls now lank and in disarray. 'Did he mention his news to you? You two have always been close. You must be happy for him?'

Aurora stared, a silent cry opening her mouth. Anguish filled her heart.

'I think Julia is being a little premature, dearest,' Josiah murmured. 'John Sinclair mentioned nothing to me about the matter, and if an imminent engagement was to be announced, then surely he'd have spoken of it.'

'Perhaps they wish to keep it quiet for a while longer, though no one in Julia's presence was in any doubt of the news, she talked all night of it.' Her mother's gloved hand covered another yawn.

'Well, do not speak of it yourself until it is confirmed and acknowledged, my dear, we don't want to be accused of spreading gossip.'

A heavy weight pressed on Aurora's chest making it difficult to breathe. Inside the carriage the only sound was the creaking of the springs and the carriage wheels rumbling over the road towards home. Denial screamed inside her head, but outwardly she kept calm. No one knew what this news meant to her and she would keep it that way. She wanted to cry, rage, beat something hard, but instead, she gazed out as the sky lightened to a pearl gray and acted as if everything was as it should be.

Later that morning, Aurora skipped the late breakfast and ordered for her mare, Princess, to be saddled. She rode out beyond the fields at the back of the house, those that also bordered the Sinclair property. The weak autumn sun brightened the countryside while a stiff cool breeze swayed the uppermost branches of the ash and beech trees. Leaves the color of amber and russet fluttered and swirled to the ground, carpeting the grass and crunching under Princess's hoofs.

The fresh smell of recent rain enveloped the land and Aurora had a hard job keeping Princess steady. She sensed the mare's need to gallop and after a few minutes of pulling at the reins, she let the horse have its head and canter over the fields — scattering sheep and jumping hedges. After a few minutes of pace, which Aurora enjoyed just as much as the mare, she reined in Princess and turned her back the way they'd come.

Usually, when at home, Reid rode early with his brothers before breakfast. She was counting on them doing so today, despite the ball ending only hours earlier. She had to make amends for her waspish conversation of last night and learn the truth of his engagement.

She guided Princess out through the small coppice at the edge of their boundary and rode on into Sinclair lands. A small stream ran at the bottom of a long slope and from the top, she spotted Reid and his brother Tom walking their horses along the water's edge. With a nudge of her knee, she sent Princess down to meet them.

Both brothers smiled in greeting as she joined them. Tom, always the charmer, reached out to take her hand. 'This is a nice surprise. I expected all fair maidens to be abed after last night.'

She beamed at Tom, a younger version of his older brother, only with the gray eyes of his father. 'Some of us are made of sterner stuff, Tom Sinclair. You should know that by now.' She did her best to ignore the way her heart skipped at the sight of Reid.

'Yes, with you I should. You could easily have been a man, Aurora.'

'Is that a compliment?' She grinned into his boyish laughing face. At twenty one, Tom was athletic, gregarious and aware of his own good fortune in looks and family. She loved him like a brother, as she did the two other Sinclair boys, James and Edward.

'Of course. Though I confess I'm rather glad you are a woman. Your tennis game is good enough without you hitting like a man to beat me every time we play.' His laughter sounded loud in the fresh stillness of the morning. At their appearance, a rabbit broke cover of the undergrowth and fled across the fields, white tail bobbing.

'Will you return and have breakfast with us, Aurora?' Reid asked, steering his large bay around an outcrop of rock. He wore simple riding clothes, a dark tweed jacket and pale trousers tucked into high boots that strained across his thighs as he rode.

'Thank you. I would like to.' She averted her gaze from his thighs and the strong hands that lazily held the reins. How many times had she gone riding with Reid and never once felt all hot and bothered at seeing him astride his horse. Yet, this morning, when she looked at him, her skin felt as though she stood too close to a fire. Straightening her back, she smiled at Tom and chatted with him about nothing in particular all the way to the Hall. If Reid thought her rude, then so be it. She couldn't let him see her flushed face.

The breakfast room at the Hall caught the morning sun and the household was up and about as they entered. The aroma of bacon and coffee filled the air. Black-frocked maids, their white aprons starch to a stiff brilliance, refilled platters with smoked herring and kidneys, eggs and black pudding.

'Ah, Aurora. How wonderful.' John Sinclair rose from his chair as did his sons Edward and James before they resumed their seats and hungrily attacked their meal.

Mrs Sinclair spied her over her teacup. 'Delightful indeed. Were you out riding?'

'Yes.' Aurora glanced down at her deep blue

riding habit, hoping it didn't have mud on it. She sat on the chair Reid held for her. 'Thank you.' Tessa, a maid Aurora had known for years, filled her cup with tea with a smile, and Ben, the footman set a small rack of toast in front of the place setting he'd quickly laid out when she walked in.

'Did you enjoy yourself last night, Aurora?' Mr Sinclair said, his gaze flicking over the newspaper at his elbow, an indolent smile playing on his lips. The Sinclair men were stamped with John's noble-shaped head and straight nose. They all had differing shades of his thick dark brown hair, with Reid's being the darkest.

'I did, yes.' She added sugar to her tea, aware of Mrs Sinclair's cold stare on her.

'Danced with every man there I'm sure.' Edward grinned, a fork loaded with egg half way to his mouth. 'I know I got two dances with you. How many did you get James?'

'Three was it, Aurora?' James spread marmalade on his toast, his eyes full of good humor.

She chuckled self-consciously. 'I've no idea, I lost count.'

'And yet I didn't get one.' Reid rested back against his chair, his face unreadable as he stared at her. His long fingers played with a teaspoon.

Mrs Sinclair straightened, her smile brittle. 'I'm sure you were not short of partners, darling. Besides, dancing isn't for all.'

The men quickly switched the conversation to the last agricultural fair of the year to be held next month and the subject of horseflesh and bulls was of no interest to Aurora.

21

Wiping her mouth with a linen napkin, Mrs Sinclair then stood. 'If you are finished Aurora, perhaps you'd join me in the morning room. I'm certain discussion of animal husbandry holds no interest for you.' Her tone made it perfectly clear to Aurora that she knew exactly why she was there.

Aurora rose, her breakfast reluctantly abandoned. Spending time alone with Julia would be a punishment too detestable to tolerate. 'Actually, I should return home, Mrs Sinclair. My mother will be wondering where I've got to. Thank you for breakfast. Good day to you all.' She nodded to the men.

'I'll escort you.' Reid casually left the table to come around to her side as farewells were said.

Mrs Sinclair took her elbow and called over her shoulder, 'Reid, have Aurora's horse brought around to the drive. Oh, and will you collect my shawl from the chair in the drawing room?' She steered Aurora towards the front of the house as Reid, wearing a bemused expression, disappeared on his errand. Leaning close like a conspirator, the older woman grimaced. 'Poor Reid. He's at a loss without his lady love. Doesn't quite know what to do with himself. But I believe he'll return south shortly to be with her. You will be kind to him while he is lovelorn, won't you, Aurora?'

The warmth left Aurora's face, but she was saved from answering as Reid joined them at the front door that was being opened by the Sinclair butler, Matthews. They stood on the steps while the groom brought her mare around to the front.

22

'Shall we simply lead her across the lawn?' Reid asked her as he took the reins from the groom.

'Very well.' With a brief smile at his mother, Aurora stepped out alongside of him through the gardens, Princess following behind. They walked for a few minutes without talking, each absorbed in their own thoughts.

Once out of sight of the house, Reid took her elbow. 'I never received your note.'

Her step faltered. 'It is no longer important.'

'But it must have been?'

She shook her head, wondering how to broach the subject of his impending engagement. Suddenly she hadn't the courage to voice it. She didn't want him to acknowledge that he loved another. It was easier to suffer in silent ignorance.

Reid walked along, head bowed. 'I am to return to London soon.'

Her breath caught. So it was true. She closed her eyes in agony as pain pierced her.

'Would you write to me?'

'Why?' She swallowed past the lump in her throat.

He stopped and looked at her, puzzled. 'Why? Because I thought it would be nice. I thought — '

'You thought I would want to listen to your engagement plans?' She grabbed the reins from him. 'You thought wrong, Reid Sinclair!' She marched away with Princess, furious tears clouding her vision.

'Aurora!'

23

'Go away, Reid.' She quickened her step, but he easily caught up with her.

'What engagement?'

'I don't know. You tell me. Your mother goes to great pains to mention it as often as possible.'

He ran his hand through his dark hair making it stand upon end. 'I'm not engaged.'

'But you soon will be, is that it?' she spat. Then, seeing his shocked face, willed herself to calm down, to act mature.

'Not that I'm aware of.' He placed his hands on her shoulders and let out a breath. 'There is a young lady who has become . . . fond of me.'

Pride made her stiffen and blink back the threatening tears. 'I don't want to know.'

'Listen to me.'

'No!'

'Hermione's family have been corresponding with Mother. They want a union.'

'I'm very happy for you then.'

His grip tightened. 'They want it, not *me*.'

'And are you a boy to be told what to do and whom to marry?' Frustration was replacing the pain and she held on to it for it was better to be angry than cry in front of him.

'Of course not.' His expression hardened. 'I will inform Mother that her plans to join Hermione and me are fruitless. I want none of it.'

'Then why did you allow it to go so far?'

'It kept Mother from pestering me day and night. Foolish of me I know, but at the time it seemed easier with everything else I was doing. Father and I have great plans to expand some of

24

our business interests. It's all I have been focusing on.' Her shoulders drooped, helpless against the hot emotion searing through her body. 'I didn't want to believe it.'

He lifted up her chin with a fingertip. 'As if you could believe it.'

'You've been away so long. I wondered if what had happened . . . between us . . . our special friendship . . . was all my imagination.' Embarrassed, she lowered her lashes to hide her feelings.

'Special friendship?' He grinned and the small dimple in his left cheek that she loved so much appeared. 'You know how much you mean to me.'

'No, I don't. I didn't know what you felt. How could I when nothing has been said?'

'Then let me show you.' Slowly he lowered his lips to lightly touch hers. As soft as a butterfly's quiver he kissed her mouth, her nose, her eyes and then came back to linger over her lips once more. 'See now? That is a small hint of what I feel for you.'

She nodded, swaying against his chest, inhaling his scent of soap and of horse leather and wool. 'I had always hoped. Prayed . . . '

After another sweet, tender kiss, they continued walking arm in arm. Reid held Princess's reins again. 'Father has started a new venture. It means I must travel a lot since he's decided to invest in some North American companies. I will be away all winter touring America.'

'But you'll be back in the spring or summer?' She looked up at him, her arm around his waist drawing him ever closer to her side. How would she bear to be parted from him again after what they just shared?

'Yes. I promise. And then we'll make plans for our future. Will you wait for me, my beautiful girl?'

'I'll wait.'

'And tomorrow we'll spend the day together, just you and me.'

'Yes.' She smiled, feeling light with happiness. Reid Sinclair wanted her. A grin escaped and she fought the urge to skip and sing and shout it out to the world. They stopped at the gate and shared a kiss that grew more demanding with each second. The muscles of his shoulders tensed under her fingers as he deepened the kiss and she gloried in the intimate act. She had waited all her life for this moment.

★   ★   ★

From an upstairs window, Julia looked down on the tender scene and her fingers clenched into fists so tightly her nails dug half circles into her palm. That her darling son had lowered himself to consort with a Pettigrew made her irate, but that the chit could now use this embrace as some sort of promise made her furious. She knew something was up the moment she intercepted that little minx's note. Over her dead body would her adored firstborn marry into that family. The Pettigrews were trades people. Josiah had built the family fortune on the strength of his mining and warehouse interests. She

26

grimaced, watching the couple below and their lingering parting. No doubt Josiah's people were common laborers or shopkeepers before his rise to riches. Well, they were definitely not good enough for her Reid.

She thought back to the first time she met the Pettigrews, not long after their ugly house was built right beside her own park! It was bad enough at the time that the Sinclair's were even to have such close neighbors and John, damn him, had found nothing untoward about it. He claimed the Hall had more than enough land as it was to take care of, and selling some of it to invest in other areas a wise decision his late father had made. Julia believed differently. It was degrading to have others living just three acres away. True, ancient trees on the border sheltered both houses from the other's view, but the principle was the same. None of her friends had close neighbors in the country. Nor had any of them married into a family who didn't greatly care for land ownership, but who instead gained money from other opportunities. Trust her to pick the only wealthy man in England who preferred stocks and shares to solid ground investments. John's lack of interest in his estates verged on the ridiculous. Despite being born at the Hall he was a town man, like his father before him. Thank heavens Reid enjoyed the estate and would ensure it survived. She had no doubt that John would sell off more land if Reid hadn't dissuaded him.

Movement below brought her attention back to Reid and the *situation*. When she first met

Winnie Pettigrew, she knew at once of their class difference. Winnie had mentioned they'd arrived from York, although Josiah's family were originally from Manchester. So why, if one side came from York and the other from Manchester did they end up near Leeds? More than once over the years she had tried to pry information from Winnie, but the woman closed up when their conversations turned to families. She knew about Josiah's family, he'd spoken of them to John, and about his rise in fortune. But why did Winnie tactfully change the subject whenever she asked about her parents or siblings? Did Winnie have something to be ashamed of, or to hide? Were they running from something or someone? Did her family have debts or unsavory characters? There had to be something unmentionable, otherwise Winnie would speak of them. So what was it?

Julia wracked her mind for Winnie's maiden name, which she was sure she'd mentioned once. B . . . B-something. Baird? Barker? Burton? Barton! Yes, Barton. She silently congratulated herself on having a quick and retentive brain. Winnie Barton from York. She turned to her silent French maid hovering at her back. 'Gavet, send for my carriage. I wish to go into Leeds on business.' She glanced back at the couple standing by the gate in the distance and grimaced.

3

'I am so tired of this snow.' Bettina collapsed onto the blush red sofa beside the roaring fire. She'd just spent an hour playing the piano. 'Why do we still have snow in the first week of April? It's spring for heaven's sake and last week was so pleasant.'

'We cannot control nature. Besides, it is only a light dusting.' Aurora sighed, her attention wandering from the Jane Austen novel she held. She'd read *Sense and Sensibility* more times than she cared to count over the years, but she had nothing new to read since finishing *Dracula*, which hadn't been to her taste. The low clouds and white landscape beyond the window made not only the day gloomy, but also everyone in the house. Her mother was laid low with a chest cold and her sisters were bored and irritable.

'Let us ask Mrs Pringle if we can make shortbread again.' Harriet threw down her pen. She was practicing her German by writing letters in the language to people who didn't exist.

'I'm sure Mrs Pringle has more pressing things to do in the kitchen than pay attention to you two.' Aurora closed her book and went to stand by the window that showed a white world. 'The snow has stopped. I think the sun is trying to come out. Shall we go for a walk?' As she spoke the clouds parted just enough for a streak of pale sunshine to appear and coat the drive.

'It's too cold.' Harriet pouted, playing with the red ribbon in her curls.

'Come, we'll go to the kitchen. Mrs Pringle will be glad of our company.' Bettina grabbed Harriet's hand. 'After all, it's not as if we have dinner guests this week so her menus will be rather mild and she will have plenty of time to spend with us. We'll bake something for Mother to make her feel well again.'

'She'd like a nice cup of tea sent up,' Aurora added.

'Will do.' Bettina pulled Harriet after her and their chatter followed them down the hallway.

Alone, Aurora pulled out of her pocket Reid's latest letter, which had arrived two days ago from New York. Throughout the long cold winter months, she'd been kept hopeful by his letters that spoke of his regard and love for her. Her family knew she received some of them, but others arrived when the family were out and she'd been able to secret them off the silver platter on the hall table before anyone was aware. They thought Reid wrote to her as a friend, if they saw the number of letters he sent and their contents, they would soon know otherwise.

His latest news was about coming home in May. She closed her eyes in sweet anticipation of seeing him again. This year would be *her* year. She'd be engaged to a man she adored and loved and, if she had her way, by Christmas she'd be married to Reid. They'd spend their honeymoon celebrating the dawning of the last year of this century. Who knew, perhaps in the new century, she would be bringing into the world the next generation of Sinclairs.

She opened the letter and read again;

Dearest darling Aurri,

I'm writing this from my rooms overlooking the Hudson River and I hope you receive this in full health. I'm tired of writing letters to you, darling, I want to hold you in my arms. I've been away from you too long.

Father is keen for me to extend our business interests . . .

The muted crunch of carriage wheels on the drive drew her attention. The Sinclair carriage came to a stop as Tibbleton opened the doors. Julia Sinclair stepped down looking splendid in a day dress of striped blue and white with a matching blue hat trimmed with fur.

Sighing, Aurora straightened her skirt of pale green. In comparison to Reid's mother she felt like a poor cousin. Tucking her letter into her pocket, she rose and waited for Tibbleton to announce their guest. Aurora placed a polite smile on her face in welcome.

'How is your dear mother?' Mrs Sinclair stepped into the room and kissed the air at the side of Aurora's cheek. 'Is she better?'

'Not as yet, Mrs Sinclair. She is still abed.'

'Oh, dear that is rather sad news.' She glanced around the large parlor with a distinctive air of someone who has seen something unpleasant.

'Mr Sinclair and the boys are well?' Aurora waved her to a seat. 'I've not seen them for some weeks. They should be coming north for Easter soon.'

'No. They are staying in London with John. I'll be travelling down south on Saturday to be with them and I will stay there for a month or so to await Reid's home coming.'

'Lovely.' Aurora's smile became strained. 'What date does Reid return? Is it May?'

'Yes, and we are expecting some wonderful news then about Reid and Miss FitzGibbon.'

'Really?' She pretended to be interested; all the while she wanted to scream it wasn't so.

Mrs Sinclair perched on the very edge of the chair as though she didn't want to soil the fine material of her dress. 'Absolutely. Reid might be across the water, but he and his lady have been in constant touch.'

Aurora took a deep breath and strove for calmness. The poor woman lived in a dream. 'It is Tom's birthday in the summer. Will there be a large celebration?' She congratulated herself on acting normal and steering the conversation to a safer topic.

'I believe so. And I hope it will be a double celebration. A birthday and an engagement.' Julia's stare didn't waver.

'I see.' Trying to keep her composure, Aurora fiddled with a vase of freshly picked daffodils. Like the tide, Mrs Sinclair was unstoppable.

'Oh, yes. Nothing would please me more than to see Reid marry Miss Fitzgibbon and to soon hold his child in my arms.'

The barb struck home as was intended and Aurora couldn't remain silent another minute. She roamed around the room, itching to wipe the smug look from the other woman's face.

'Reid has been writing letters to me, did you know?'

'Well, naturally he would, dear. You are like a sister to him.' Mrs Sinclair rose and made for the door. 'Now, I must not delay another moment. I shall call again when your mother is well enough for visitors. Good day.' She was gone from the room and outside to her carriage before Aurora could say another word.

'Damn her!' Aurora gave the back of the sofa an unladylike punch.

★   ★   ★

By mid April the lingering snow had melted, allowing the spring flowers to bloom in all their glory in the bright sunshine. It seemed the countryside had suddenly sprang into life. Gorse and blackthorns were in blossom on the edge of the fields, as were the crab apple and other fruit trees in the small orchard behind the house. The air appeared filled with butterflies as wall and garden whites flittered from flower to blossom, jostling for position with the bees. Primroses bloomed in the shelter of the hedges and in the coppice bluebells were thick in number.

The girls could hardly be contained inside now the worst of the weather had departed and spent hours outside painting warblers, swallows and house martins which were busy with nests and fledglings. Each day Aurora took to riding the lanes and tracks in the countryside around her home, happy to be away from the confines of the house and the instructions of her mother, who was doing her best to teach her the home duties of a mistress. Sometimes her sisters joined her, but other times Aurora rode alone. After a winter of being cooped up indoors, she was glad to be out breathing the warm air and feeling the sun on her face.

Riding Princess along the road that led to village, she allowed her mind to go blank as she rocked gently in time to the mare's slow gait. Finches darted in the flowering hedgerows and a lark sang from the trees bordering the road. High above on a wind current a kestrel hovered, scouring the fields for rodents.

Further ahead a carriage came around the bend in the road. Aurora checked Princess and guided her to the grass verge as the carriage came closer. It wasn't until the vehicle had nearly passed that she recognized the driver, who raised his whip to her in salute.

'Good day, Benson,' she called, wondering if the Sinclair carriage was empty or if one of the boys had come home. A dark head popped out of the carriage window and her stomach flipped as Reid held up his hand in greeting.

'Reid!'

'Stop, Benson.' Reid had the door open and was stepping down before the carriage completely halted. He ran to her as she dismounted.

For a long moment they simply stood and stared at each other. It had been over seven months since they were last in each other's arms. Reid turned and waved the carriage on. 'I'll walk with Miss Pettigrew, Benson.'

'Very good, sir.'

They waited for the carriage to disappear behind another turn in the road before touching or speaking. She noticed he'd changed a little; his face was leaner, his eyes not so full of promise and excitement like they used to be. He looked tired, worn, and older.

Reid took her gloved hands and kissed the back of them. 'I have missed you every day.'

'And I you.'

'I'm glad.'

'Thank you for your letters. I lived for their arrival.'

'And I for yours.'

She stepped closer and wrapped her arms around his neck, her heart bursting for love of this man. 'Kiss me, *please*.'

He pulled her tight against him and kissed her soundly, deeply, exploring the shape of her lips and mouth as though to reacquaint himself. Out of breath they managed to draw apart to stare into each other's eyes.

'When did you get home? I thought it would be weeks yet?' She sensed something was wrong by the sadness in his eyes and her stomach clenched in fear. 'What is it?'

'I had to come home sooner than planned. Mother cabled me from London. My father . . .' Reid drew in a deep breath. 'He has had a heart seizure.'

'I didn't know!' She held him close. 'Oh, my darling. When?'

'Two weeks ago, just before Easter. He is weak, but alive and gaining some spirit back. The doctor says he might not make a full recovery and he could have another seizure at any time or he could live for years. I have never seen my father reduced as low as this. It's taken the fight from him . . . I'm not ashamed to admit I am scared.'

'Oh, Reid. I'm sorry to hear it, really I am.'

'My ship docked in Southampton a few days ago and I haven't had a moment's rest since. I headed straight to Kensington. I feel like I have been travelling for years and I'm exhausted. Mother is distraught and my brothers unsure of what to do or how to react.' His smile was brief, troubled. 'And I missed you.'

'It must be terrible for you all.' She cupped his cheek, aching for him in his unhappiness. As natural as breathing they fell into step and, collecting Princess, headed for home.

'I'm not going to be here long, my love.' He smiled gently, tucking her arm into his, leading the mare. 'Just today and tonight, I'm afraid. Tomorrow I must leave for London again. I'm only here because my father was anxious about some important papers in his study and insisted I and no one else retrieve them for him. You know how the sick can be. They worry over the slightest thing. The doctor made it very clear that we had to do all we could to ease father's stress and anxiety. So, I said I would leave immediately. Mother wanted to send Tom, but Father insisted on me going and I was only too glad because it meant I could see you. I'm afraid Mother is quite annoyed with me, and poor Tom, he thinks Father does not trust him on such an errand.' A long sigh escaped him. 'He got dreadfully drunk and didn't come home until the next morning. Now Mother is furious with everyone. I believe she uses anger as a shield when things are out of her control. I happily made my escape, but I worry about leaving Father.'

'You did the right thing to ease his worry.' Aurora shivered, glad Julia and all the upset was happening in London and not next door. 'I'm sorry it is due to tragic circumstances, but I am so pleased you are here.'

'I've been away longer than I expected, Aurora.' He stopped and took her in his arms again, holding her tight. 'Too many months have gone by since we were last together. I wish I had never gone to New York, but I had no choice in the matter. And now . . . '

'I understand.' She kissed him, loving the feel of being openly affectionate towards him. 'Do you think your family will have to remain in London for long?'

'For some months. Father is in no state to travel and everything is unsettled. He is acting strangely, as though he feels his time is short and therefore he must work harder and quicker to complete his plans. I do not mind he puts it all on my shoulders, but no matter how hard I try he expects me to do more.' He drew in a deep breath and looked out over the crop growing fields.

Aurora saw in his eyes all the stress and anxiety inside him. 'Then it will be another separation for us?'

'I'm sorry.' He kissed her gently as if in apology. 'We'll have to put our plans for the future on hold.'

'Yes . . . ' She tried not to be selfish, but her heart cried in disappointment. She'd waited long enough for Reid. For once she would like to have something of her own. A husband, a home, a baby. She was nearly one and twenty and ready to forge a life with the man she loved.

'I know it will be hard.' He threaded his long fingers through hers.

'Forces are against us it seems.' They turned and walked on, much to Princess's annoyance as she'd found a patch of new spring grass to nibble.

Reid hugged her close as they walked. 'But not forever. Soon we will be together.'

Sighing, she shook her head. 'I do not think it will be easy, Reid. Your mother is set on you marrying Miss FitzGibbon. A Pettigrew isn't good enough for you or her family.'

He stopped and stared in amazement at her. 'Nonsense. Mother adores you all. Our families have been friends for years.'

'She wants someone better for you. She told me.'

He tilted his head, studying her with a frown. 'She told you that you weren't good enough for me?'

'Not in those precise words, but yes, she implied it.'

'I think you are mistaken. Besides, my mother will not select my bride for me.' A gate led into a field and Reid opened it, then grabbing her hand, they sneaked behind the hedge, leaving Princess to munch the grass in the ditch.

Anything Aurora was about to say flew from

her mind as Reid grasped her to him and kissed her until she could barely remember her own name. His hands spanned her waist, pulling her against him, deepening the kiss until her senses reeled with the essence of only him. Unreservedly she kissed him back, wondering briefly if she was doing it correctly. She arched into him, not knowing what she wanted more of, but instinctively knowing she could only get it from him.

A passing cart made them pull apart. Shakily, they smiled at each other and grinned with the intoxicating knowledge of what they had shared. When it was safe, they went back onto the road and Reid reclaimed the mare.

'I'm not being much of a gentleman, Aurrie. Kissing behind bushes like a youth isn't my way of courting you. I'm sorry we cannot be open about it. I will speak to your father soon. It's just the timing is all wrong at the moment.'

'I understand.' Aurora absentmindedly stroked Princess's soft nose. Although she did understand, she was dreadfully frustrated that their relationship couldn't be acknowledged. 'You'll come to dinner tonight? You don't want to spend the evening alone.'

'An evening with you is exactly what I need. Perfect.' He kissed her gloved hand.

She smiled and they strolled along the road, chatting quietly as lovers do about nothing and everything. At the entrance to the drive leading to her home they paused, not daring to touch in case they were seen.

'About seven o'clock then?'

He gazed into her eyes. 'Seven.'

Aurora walked Princess down the drive, her spirit so light she thought she would fly.

'Aurora!' She turned to see Reid running down to her. 'I cannot wait until tonight to see you, we have such a short time. Come to the Hall in an hour, we'll spend the afternoon together.'

'I will.' She rose onto her toes, wanting to kiss him, but Jimmy, the groom, came around the side of the house to take her mare. Aurora grinned at Reid and hurried inside to find her mother and sisters in the parlor. 'Oh Mother, I bumped into Reid Sinclair on the road.'

Her mother put down her sewing. 'Did you really? Have all the family returned from London?'

'No, they still remain there. Mr Sinclair has had a heart seizure.'

Winnie gasped, a pale hand going to her throat. 'Heaven save us. John Sinclair?'

Aurora told them the news and about the dinner invitation and prided herself on not letting an ounce of emotion color her words.

'Well, of course Reid must come to us and have dinner. He cannot be alone tonight.' Winnie stood, the movement causing her to cough. 'I am not fully myself yet, but as a friend and neighbor we must do our duty in times of need. I shall consult Mrs Pringle.'

'Yes, Mother.' Aurora turned for the hall. 'I shall bathe I think. I've been riding for a good while. I promised Reid I'd go and spend the afternoon with him, to take his mind off things, you understand.' She spun from the room in excitement and took the stairs at a run. She wanted to be her best for Reid. How many chances would she get to visit him without his family nearby, without his mother casting her cold glares?

That evening, after a magnificent lazy afternoon with Reid where they spent hours touching, whispering and simply being together, Aurora stood in front of the long mirror and studied her reflection. She couldn't wear one of her best gowns, her mother would think it ostentatious on such a simple private occasion and it would make her appear to be trying too hard for Reid's attention. Though God knows it was true, she did want his sole attention, but she'd have to act nonchalant. She'd chosen a soft pale cream silk with wisps of lace an even paler shade of cream at her throat and sleeves. Hilda had scooped her hair up in a casual knot at the back of her head. Small diamond earrings were in her ears and a silver diamond pendant necklace around her throat.

Her stomach twisted with tension as they gathered in the parlor to wait for Reid's arrival. Why, she didn't know. Their guest was Reid, her Reid. But something felt different tonight. This evening her family would be able to properly talk to him alone, perhaps for the first time. Her father could judge him man to man and when the special day came that Reid asked him for permission to marry her then her father would know and like him, not as John Sinclair's eldest son, but for himself.

41

Her cheeks glowed when she thought of the afternoon spent kissing and laughing, darting through the Hall's orchard, blossom scent heavy on the air. Although Miss FitzGibbon had stayed in the back of her mind, she refused to mention her again and spoil what time they had together. Reid told her about New York and North Carolina where he'd also spent time. Captivated, she listened to his tales of all he experienced and the plans he had for expanding the Sinclair empire. They made plans to go to America together, to travel the world, to be together for always. Perhaps tonight he would even speak to her father about marriage? No, she must not rush him.

Downstairs, waiting in the drawing room, Aurora sipped the sherry her father gave her. She wavered between excitement of seeing him to dread, for in the morning Reid would be gone again. However, the moment Reid entered the room, the tension left her as his warm smile encompassed them all, but only she saw the twinkle in his blue eyes meant for her as they went into dinner.

Mrs Pringle, Aurora was certain, had cooked a marvelous meal, but later she knew she wouldn't be able to name a single dish. Her whole focus was Reid, but also, strangely enough, on her family too, as they chatted and discussed things so easily, so naturally. Aurora felt as though Reid had always sat at their table, been one of them, been in her heart. It was beautiful to watch him, listen to him, to hear his views on events. She cared not a whit about Britain and Egypt ruling the Sudan or anything else that her father and Reid discussed, but she took the opportunity to learn more about the man she loved.

It was as their spoons were scraping up the last of their dessert pudding that it happened — the incident that made Aurora sit up and take notice. Bettina, unbeknown to the rest at the table, except Aurora who sat directly opposite her, was surreptitiously gazing at Reid beneath lowered lashes. A fine blush tinged Bettina's cheeks and she smiled widely at anything Reid said, her gaze following his movements.

Sipping from her wine glass, Aurora watched her sister for another five minutes, her mind racing. If her sister, young and naïve, could be attracted, obviously deeply engrossed, in Reid, and see him as a man and perhaps a possible suitor, then so could any other young woman. Miss FitzGibbon flashed into her mind again, the stranger whose mere name made Aurora's teeth clench. With his mother on Miss FitzGibbon's side, encouraging, plotting, how would Aurora stand a chance when he was back in London?

She tried to think rationally. Reid had told her Miss FitzGibbon meant nothing to him, but he had the force of his mother working against him and he wasn't even aware of it. Aurora must secure his attention, his affection. But how? Soon he would be back down south and prey to his mother's scheming. She had to do something that would never allow him to think of another woman, something that would show him she was the one for him.

Tom's books.

Heat invaded her cheeks at the thought of them. A little over a year ago, Tom had found her in the Sinclair library during a New Year's celebration. Always the one for mischief, Tom had drunk a little too much and laughingly led her by the hand to a small step ladder. He urged her to climb it and reach for a red leather bound book on the top shelf. To her shock and curiosity he flipped through the book, which depicted graphic sexual poses of couples. Apparently there were similar such books on that top shelf. Two days later, a parcel was sent to her and when she unwrapped it, three of those books fell out of the paper with a card saying, *Enjoy!* She'd seen through Tom's joke of course. The next day, she boldly walked over to the Hall to hand them back to him in front of his father, who, obviously knowing the contents raised his eyebrows at his wayward son. She left them with a smile on her face. But now, the taunting sketches clamored in her brain, making her hot under her clothes.

'Aurora?'

She looked up at her mother, blinking back to focus. 'So sorry, Mother.'

'Do you feel unwell? You look flushed.'

'Not at all.' She rose from her chair. 'But if you could excuse me for just a moment.' Before her courage deserted her she left the dining room and hurried into the parlor and over to her mother's secretary. The note was simple. However, she knew getting it into Reid's hands wasn't going to be. While they had tea and coffee in the parlor, the note was tucked into her bodice, a constant reminder of what she was about to do.

As they said farewell to Reid at the end of the night, Aurora was frantic she wouldn't be able to give him the slip of paper, then, just as he headed out the door, she stepped forward and shook his hand to wish him and his family well. She left the note in his palm and to his credit Reid showed no reaction except to tuck his hand into his trouser pocket.

Once the door closed behind him, their mother turned and kissed each of her daughters' cheeks. 'Bedtime, girls.'

They chorused goodnights to their parents and Aurora followed her sisters upstairs. The two girls still shared a room, but as the eldest Aurora had her own.

'I believe Bettina has formed an attachment to dear Reid,' Harriet giggled as they reached the landing.

'Take that back!' Bettina blushed, her gray eyes wide in horror.

Harriet ran into their bedroom, laughing. 'I knew it was true.'

'I have no such thing.' Bettina chased her, furious. 'I swear I don't.'

'Stop it the pair of you.' Aurora stood in the doorway, wanting to slap them for their childishness.

'It's true.' Harriet defended, kneeling on the bed. 'I watched her and she was gazing at him all night. Poor Reid.'

Bettina grabbed for her again and missed as Harriet rolled away. 'You're horrid and I'll not forgive you.'

Cheekily, Harriet slipped over to the dressing

table and picked up a silver hairbrush. 'I'm only warning Aurora, after all, she is the one closest to him, always has been. Haven't you, Aurrie?'

Bettina grew even redder. 'She is wrong. I — '

'Be quiet, both of you.' Aurora hissed, stepping into the room and shutting the door. 'Reid has much more pressing problems than worrying about possible romances. His father is extremely ill.' She turned to Harriet. 'You, sister, show a lack of maturity and respect.' She glanced at Bettina, who nodded smugly. 'The pair of you should be ashamed of yourselves, acting like schoolgirls. It's time you grew up.'

'Aurora, I — '

She held her hand up to silence Harriet's petty argument. 'Have either of you noticed Mother's cough tonight? How pale she was?'

'She's been sick.' Bettina stepped over to Harriet, their natural closeness bringing them together when anything unpleasant happened.

'And she hasn't got over it.' Aurora lowered her voice. 'The cough lingers and she hardly ate at dinner. She hasn't regained her good health. I think we should concentrate our efforts on her and not some silliness.'

Straightening her shoulders, Bettina, the more sensible of the two, raised her chin. 'Yes, of course, you are right, Aurrie. Mother's well-being should be at the forefront of our minds.'

'Indeed it should.' Aurora opened the door and after bidding them goodnight went into her own room. Hilda had closed the curtains and turned back her bed sheet, but she wouldn't be sleeping for a while yet. Aurora pushed the curtains aside and stared out into the moonlit night. What would Reid think of her note?

A tap on the door had her spinning around and her mother walked in, smiling. 'Yes, Mother?'

'I thought I would come and say good night again and make sure you are all right. You were quiet tonight.' She held out her hand and when Aurora took it, she felt the coldness of it.

'I'm fine, Mother, I promise you.'

'Shall I help you undress?' Her mother stepped behind her to undo the buttons of her gown and unhitch her corset before replacing the garments with a linen nightgown.

Although getting undressed wasn't in her plans, Aurora sat on the stool in front of the dressing table without protest. Her mother unpinned her hair and began to brush it in long even strokes. 'You seemed a little out of sorts tonight, my dear.'

'Did I?' Aurora asked her mother's reflection in the mirror. 'I'm sorry.'

'Is something troubling you?' Her mother's eyes, a light green hazel, were so different to Aurora's dark brown ones.

'No, not at all. Except perhaps your health.'

'My chest cold lingers. It is nothing.' Her mother's hand holding the ivory brush paused. 'You would tell me if something was the matter, wouldn't you?'

'Of course.' Aurora smiled briefly.

Her mother gazed at her for some time and then kissed the top of her head. 'Good. Then I shall leave you in peace. Sweet dreams, dearest girl.'

'Good night, Mother.' When the door closed, Aurora let out a long breath. Lying to her mother tasted like acid on her tongue.

While the clock in the hall struck midnight, Aurora quietly slipped out of the side door near the conservatory and headed for the wood beyond the stables. A cloudless sky allowed the full moon to light the countryside in silver and gray, stretching shadows equal to the sun.

Silence cloaked Aurora as securely as the long, thick woolen shawl she wore over her nightdress. Her plans to stay dressed in her dinner gown had been thrown aside when her mother entered her bedroom, and dressing again without Hilda's help was not possible, so the nightgown was hidden beneath the shawl. On her feet were stout walking boots. Not a glamorous look by any means. Besides, what did it matter what she wore, the night's pewter darkness would hide her clothes. And really, Reid might not even come to meet her. Though in her heart she knew he would. The kisses they shared this afternoon proved he found her desirable. Now she had to act on it and secure the future.

Was she mad to contemplate this wanton move, this seduction? What if he rejected her, thought her fast and loose? He'd have every right to. Would he want a bride who he'd already touched? Would he think she was some kind of immoral woman not worthy of his name? Her step faltered as doubts rose.

'Aurora.' His whisper from behind a horse chestnut tree reached her like an invisible rope, pulling her towards him. 'I prayed you wouldn't change your mind.' Reid enveloped her in his arms, his warmth a comfort, his male closeness exhilarating.

'Oh, Reid.' She snuggled into him. 'I didn't know what to do.'

'I know, sweetheart.'

She clutched at the smooth material of his black coat. 'You'll be gone in the morning and I don't know when I'll see you again. This . . . this seems desperate, I know, but . . . '

'I know, sweetheart.' He nuzzled his cheek against hers and she felt the beginnings of his beard. 'I'll write.'

'Writing isn't enough. I want to be with you.'

'And you will, soon, I promise.' His hold on her tightened. 'When Father is well again, which hopefully will be soon, I'll return from London. We'll spend the summer together. And I'll speak with your father about us.'

'But it could be months before your father is fit enough for you to leave him.' Frustration grew in her voice and she pressed harder against him. She cupped his face in her hands and brought his head down so she could kiss him, stamp herself on him.

'Aurora, my darling . . . ' As though she had given him permission, he deepened the kiss, using his tongue to open her mouth so he could plunge within. His groans made the fire in the pit of her belly gather strength.

Whispering her name, he scattered kisses down her throat, tugging the shawl off her shoulders. For a moment he stilled. 'You have your nightdress on.'

She ducked her head in embarrassment at his surprise. 'Yes, I hadn't intended to, but mother came into my room and helped me undress for bed . . . '

'Then you . . . ' He pushed the shawl down so that it hung from her arms and low on her back. His hands lightly traced the contours of her shoulders, waist and hips through the linen material. She shivered at the intimacy of his touch. Using the thumb and first finger on his right hand he undid the blue silk ribbon at her throat and the nightgown gaped open a few inches on her chest. She heard his soft suck of breath. He kissed the bared skin. Slowly, his hand slipped into the opening of her nightgown and found the softness of her breast. Her nipples hardened at his caress and she gripped his shoulders as the power went from her legs.

'Reid . . . ' She moaned, tilting her head back when his head lowered and he sucked at her nipple through the material. She'd never felt such sensations rippling through her body as she did at that moment. Her legs buckled and she sank to the damp grass of the wood, pulling Reid with her.

'Aurora, no . . . ' Reid knelt beside her, holding her in his arms. 'This isn't, I mean, I can't . . . '

'I'm yours, Reid, forever.' She pushed herself against him, wanting the closeness of him.

'Yes, but — '

'No buts.' She kissed him hard. 'We are to be married, yes?'

'Well, yes, but not for some time. We — '

'Then if we are to be married we can *be* married tonight.' She took his hand and placed it on her breast. 'Let me be your wife for this night and always.'

His hand caressed her and his breathing grew shallow. 'You don't know what you're asking. We've done too much all ready.' He tried to laugh, to make light of it. 'You're too tempting, Aurrie. I need to go.'

She flicked her tongue out to taste along his top lip. Urgency filled her and it was too powerful to resist. 'Stay. I beg you.'

'This will change everything.'

'Only for the better. I will be yours and you will be mine. How can that be wrong?' Aurora slipped her hands beneath his coat and ran them down his stomach, tugging at his shirt as they went. A pulsing need throbbed in her loins, surprising her by its force.

As if he could take no more, Reid made a noise in the back of his throat as he shrugged off his coat to lay it on the grass. Aurora laid down into its warmth, for the night air was cool, and held out her arms for Reid to join her.

He lay alongside her and gathered her into his arms. He kissed her thoroughly, the needs of his body overthrowing his commonsense words. She had won this battle over Julia. Reid would be hers and his mother wouldn't be able to do a thing about it.

When Reid drew up the hem of her nightdress, all thoughts of his mother dispersed like water on sand. His hand found the top of her drawers and untied the string while he kissed her neck. His breathing grew heavy, matching her own. It was like she had a fever tearing through her body and it consumed her, hot and needy, dulling her mind, but sharpening her senses. Her touch, taste and smell were magnified, focused only on his body. She was helpless against it.

She raked off his shirt, hearing the fine material tear. The sight and touch of his naked chest in the moonlight sent her mind spinning. Drawing her fingernails down his spine to his buttocks, she heard his harsh intake of breath and gloried in the power she held.

The cold air touched the delicate skin of her inner thighs as Reid pulled off her drawers, exposing her to his gaze. In the darkness she couldn't see his expression, but when he touched her most secret of places, he was light and gentle. She shivered in anticipation.

'Are you completely sure, Aurora?' he whispered on a ragged breath.

'Absolutely.' And she was. Her doubts had flown the minute he returned her first kiss. She loved this man. Wanted this man. And tonight she would become his woman, his wife in all but name.

4

How did she do it? Day after day, since that magical night in the woods, Aurora had pretended to be her normal self, but nothing was normal anymore. Reid returned to London four weeks ago and since then she had received only two letters from him, a brief note when he arrived at his family's townhouse in Kensington and another short letter four days after that. She'd written twice a week and received no reply. Where were his affirmations of love now?

Frustrated, she sat on the grass, leaning her back against the warm stone wall surrounding one of the Sinclair fields. Newborn lambs bleated and skipped about their mothers, their tails nearly wagging off when they took milk. How tranquil the scene, the countryside basking in late May sunshine. Wildflowers of heartsease, daisies and red campion swayed in the slight breeze, while the pink flowers of the clover carpeted the ground. Blackbirds, thrush and chaffinches flew idly from tree to tree, busy with their chicks. In her heartache none of it soothed her. The pride she felt over her beautiful home, her land, her people, paled into insignificance against the sting of rejection she carried.

Reid wasn't callous. Surely he wouldn't use her and then disregard her? But then she had acted so wantonly he must doubt the respect he once held for her. She'd given him her body. She had lain on the grass with him like a common strumpet. Only it hadn't been that base. She had surrendered her whole self to him, her body, heart and mind. Offering him her love was a gift, a promise of what their future held. Had she been wrong to do it?

Of course she had! She had been stupid.

Perhaps what she had given wasn't enough. Or had it been too much? Should she have tempted him, but withheld the prize of her virtue? No. She shook her head, knowing that wouldn't have worked either.

She scratched her arm where a fly bothered her and tried to be mature and worldly about it all. Reid was his own man. If he wanted to write to her, he would. If he wanted to abandon her, he would. He did only what he pleased. However, Mrs Sinclair and her scheming was at the back of her mind. Would Reid listen to his mother, bend to her wishes? Anger curled inside Aurora, hot and painful.

One letter. One letter full of love and promises was all it would take to ease the ache. She felt so lonely without him. This was worse than when he was in America for seven months. One letter from him would banish the demons preying on her mind. His life couldn't be so full of activity that he couldn't spare five minutes to write a few lines. He must know how she'd be waiting to hear from him. Her fist clenched at the grass, tearing it from the soil, staining her fingers green. She wanted to slap him for abandoning her, for not speaking to her father, for not being here now!

An anguished cry escaped her before she could stop it. A sudden sound from the other side of the wall made her jolt upright and hurriedly smoothed down her fawn skirt.

'Well there.' Tom leaned over the wall to grin down at her. 'Miss Pettigrew.' He nimbly climbed over the stones and jumped down beside her.

'Good morning, Tom.' Her heart skidded in her chest. A Sinclair. Were they all home? Was Reid with him? 'How are you?'

'Fit, as you see. I can tell you are well.' He rested back and turned his face up to the sun and closed his eyes. 'What a beautiful day.'

'Yes, I agree.' She glanced sideways at him. 'When did you arrive home?'

'Last night.'

'The whole family?'

He opened one eye and peeked at her. 'Alone. They remain in Kensington, except for Edward and James who are at Oxford.'

'Oh.' She swallowed her disappointment. 'Is your father improving?'

'Little by little.' He closed his eye and waved his hand dismissively. 'You know how it is.'

'Yes.' And she did. Her mother still battled the cough from Easter and lately became short of breath at times. 'So why are you home?'

'I have been sent to home in disgrace, dear Aurora.' His tone was flat, matching his expression.

Surprised by his admission, she stared at him. 'What have you done this time?'

Tom shrugged lazily. 'Several things. I drink

too much, gamble too much and fail exams too much, the usual things. You know how I am. Oh and I begot a bastard, it seems.'

Aurora jerked at his frankness. 'Heavens, Tom.'

'Heavens, *Tom*,' he mimicked, eyes still closed.

She heard the hurt in his voice. 'Talk to me. It might help.'

'I doubt it.'

'Why not give it a try and see?'

He lowered his head and gazed at her. 'You're the first person who actually wants to listen. Everyone has been quick to shout, to demand, to accuse, but no one wanted to listen.'

She smiled and took his hand. 'You're like a brother. Of course I will listen.'

Sucking in a deep breath, he looked across the fields, his eyes losing focus. 'A simple story it is. Boy meets girl. Boys likes girl. Girl gets pregnant. Boy accused. Boy sent away.'

'Is it ever that simple?' she asked quietly, feeling sorry for him. He acted like a little boy in need of a thrashing and a cuddle.

'No.'

'Are you sure you are the father?'

'Yes.'

'You won't be made to marry her?'

'Mother refuses to allow it. The girl, Alice, is a baker's daughter. Mother is beside herself with disgust. It is all right for one to dally with the lower orders but one must never think to marry one. I think Mother would rather see me dead than to marry beneath her standards.'

Julia Sinclair. Would that woman never stop

meddling! Resentment flared and Aurora bit back a stinging retort. 'Do you love this girl, Alice?'

Tom bent his head and plucked a blade of grass. 'I don't, no. I like her a lot. We had fun, but I feel no more than that, and thankfully neither does she. Alice knew the possible cost of her actions and that marriage was never an option. And yet, despite Mother, I would marry her for the sake of the child, but Alice doesn't want it. And, after dealing with Mother, who could blame her? There is another man she has her eye on, an assistant in her father's shop.'

'What will happen to her then?'

'Mother has paid her a large sum of money and spoken to her family. Alice will marry the apprentice and it will all be tidied up to prevent embarrassment to both parties.' He sighed and the young, spoilt, fun-loving Tom Sinclair was replaced by another person, a man who, for perhaps the first time, knew the price of consequence.

'So you have been sent home.' She squeezed his hand in sympathy.

'Yes. Mother insisted upon it. I swear she has become even more . . . demanding during this past year. It is though she cannot stand to see her boys grow up and make decisions of their own. She's impossible.' He snorted and shook his head. 'Lord, I'm the eternal bad son, Aurrie. I even talk against my mother.'

'You're not bad, not at heart.' She raised her eyebrows wryly at him. 'I know you, remember? I've known you for years and you are far from

57

bad. Naughty, yes. High-spirited, yes. Spoilt, yes. Mischievous, yes.'

'Hold on!' He raised his hands in surrender. 'Jolly, you'll have me in tears next. I don't need any character assassinations, thank you. My mother is the queen of them.'

'Your mother should mind her own business.' She clapped her hand over her mouth as soon as she'd spoken.

Tom threw his head back and laughed loudly. 'How right you are, Aurrie.'

'I should keep my opinions to myself.' The last thing she wanted to do was show how much she disliked of his mother.

'And what a dreary place the world would be if we all did that.'

'What do you plan to do?'

'I've joined the army, or rather, my father bought me a commission and forced me to go. He hasn't left his sickbed, but with Mother's help, managed to organize it.'

'The army?' She tried not to sound as sad as she felt.

'Yes. I don't mind actually. I want adventure and this will provide it. Though *they* believe it will be a punishment, something to knock some sense into me. But I'll prove them all wrong, Aurrie. I will be a success. That would show them wouldn't it?'

'You'll be leading soldiers into battle on a white charger before you know it!' She laughed, trying to lift the dangerous tension in his body. He seemed as coiled as a spring.

He jumped up and held out his hand to help

her to her feet. 'Come on. I'm starving. Shall we have luncheon on the terrace?'

They strolled along the lane between the fields towards the Hall, relaxed and easy with each other as always. Aurora brushed away another hovering fly. 'I want to get you something for your birthday next month.'

'You'll be the only one to do so. Although Reid might buy me something, he usually does. However, Mother says I'm not to have a celebration, another punishment, you see. Though I am permitted to invite a few friends for a small dinner party before the army claims me.' He sniffed his disgust at the notion. 'I'll tell you another secret. On that subject I will do as I wish. I will have a party and invite half the county if I bloody well please. Forgive my language.' He gave her a saucy wink.

'If you do that your mother will — '

'Have a paroxysm? Most likely.' He took her hand and swung it high between them. 'A man is only two and twenty once, is he not? And for my coming of age last year it was a jolly boring affair at the Savoy. Mother invited all her tedious acquaintances and hardly any of my own friends.' He twitched his shoulders as if to be rid of an irritant. 'Therefore, I mean to have the time of my life this year. And hopefully I can cause a cartload of trouble before my banishment into the regiment. I hope we'll be posted somewhere exotic like Africa or the West Indies. There's trouble and strife everywhere. Imagine the sights I would see!' He did a jig down the lane and she laughed at his antics.

'Could I come too? I want to see elephants and giraffes!' She ran after him in the sunshine and pushed the thoughts of Reid to the back of her mind. For a little while she wanted to be young and careless and think of nothing but the next minute, the next hour, and with Tom for company she'd be assured of a fun day.

★ ★ ★

Julia, descending the staircase of her Kensington townhouse, noticed the footman sorting through the letters near the front door. Her step slowed as she watched him put the mail in three different piles on the silver platter. He looked up as she left the last step and she disarmed him with a curt smile. 'I'll see to the post, Rogers.'

'Yes, Madam.' He bowed.

She looked at the other platter sitting alongside its twin. It was empty and she fought a moment's panic. 'Has the mail gone out?'

'No, Madam. I am on my way shortly. I was just checking for any last minute letters.' He indicated the small leather satchel on the floor by the door.

'Let me see those.' She waited for Rogers to open the satchel and hand her the bulk of envelopes. Julia read through them and found the last one to be addressed to Aurora. 'Oh, here it is. This one can go later. I need to add to it.' The letter was slipped into her skirt pocket. 'Thank you, Rogers.'

'Ma'am.' He bowed slightly and left immediately.

Julia turned to the arrivals platter and flicked through her husband's correspondence, but none of it was of interest, and her own small pile would wait until later. She flipped through the envelopes addressed to Reid and found the one she wanted. Aurora's handwriting was familiar now. With a slip of her hand, the letter went into her skirt pocket to join the other and she hurried into her private morning room beyond the stairs.

At her desk, she quickly opened the letter and read the contents. A small smile played on her lips as she read of Aurora's puzzlement as to why Reid had stopped writing to her. The plan was working. Now, she had to act on it.

★   ★   ★

Aurora rode Princess into the stable yard behind the house and dismounted. Jimmy rose from where he sat on a low stool in the sun, polishing the harness and gathered Princess's reins. 'Thank you, Jimmy.'

'A good ride, Miss?'

'Very much so.' She gave him a smile and turned for the house. She'd just spent another day with Tom, as she had numerous times during the last two weeks. This morning, they'd ridden out to one of Tom's friend's house for morning tea and then on the way back, stopped at an inn situated beside a small river. They'd drunk ale from jugs, ate juicy meat pies with thick gravy and sat in the sunshine laughing and talking.

The hours flew by when with him and he helped her to ignore Reid's neglect. At times she wished she could unburden to Tom about Reid and the love she felt for him, but what good would it do? Tom didn't know Reid's thoughts on the issue. And actually speaking of the whole affair made her feel vulnerable and rather stupid. What she had done was the silliest of mistakes and she would bear the condemnation in silence.

Walking into the back of the house, she paused in the dimness of the boot room to allow her eyes to adjust after the brightness of outside. Her head throbbed a little. She felt awfully tired and hoped she wasn't coming down with a head cold or had too much sun. Thankfully, the corridor leading to the front of the house was deserted and much cooler than the June heat.

'There you are, Miss.' Dotty, the young parlor maid hurried down the hallway, relief altering her worried expression.

'What is it?' Aurora sighed. Dotty had a habit of getting on her nerves with her flighty, panicky ways.

Dotty wrung her apron in her hands. 'Well, Madam and the Misses are out visiting and it's Mr Tibbleton's day off, you see . . . '

'And?'

'Mrs Sinclair has arrived. I didn't know . . . '

Aurora didn't hear the rest of Dotty's prattle as her mind and her stomach whirled in unison. Julia here? She felt more ill than ever.

'So, I've put her in the parlor, Miss, and was off to get some tea.'

'Thank you.' Aurora took a deep breath and let it out slowly. Polite chatter with Julia? Could she do it feeling as defenseless as she did? The damned woman knew exactly how to torment her. She glanced up the staircase to where the haven of her bedroom beckoned, but duty made her step in the direction of the parlor.

She straightened her shoulders, and head held high, strode into the room. Mrs Sinclair stood by the front window, watching the drive. She turned, obviously expecting the maid, and her eyes widened. 'Good afternoon, Mrs Sinclair. I didn't realize you were back from London.'

'You!' Her sharp blue eyes narrowed. 'I have been here for five minutes. I am a busy woman and do not tolerate being kept waiting.'

Aurora gave her a cynical glare, doubting it was that long. 'I apologize, but we were not informed of your visit. My mother and sisters are out, I'm afraid, and I was riding.'

Mrs Sinclair's rigid stance reeked disapproval. 'With my son.'

'Yes, as a matter of fact.' Aurora smiled, enjoying the satisfaction of upsetting the older woman. How had she known she was with Tom? Did she have spies all over the county? 'We had a lovely day together.'

'Wasn't setting your cap at the eldest Sinclair enough for you?' Julia's top lip curled. 'Have you whored yourself to Tom as well?'

Aurora gasped and stumbled back as though struck.

A triumphant blaze lit Julia's eyes. 'You think I wouldn't know?'

'What do you know?'

'Everything your pathetic, yet detailed, letters revealed.'

Putting one hand to her mouth, fighting the nausea that rose to choke her, Aurora reached out for something solid to support her and found the back of her mother's chair. 'You read my letters?'

'Of course. Nothing happens in my house that I don't know about.'

'They were private letters!'

'Oh, yes, you are shocked I can see.' Julia smiled cruelly. 'You must understand Aurora that anything concerning my sons concerns me. Did you think I would not know how many letters you and Reid have been sending? How would such a thing go unnoticed?'

'You had no right. They were personal.'

'Everything my sons do is of great importance to me and the Sinclair family. They are mine, and worthless chits like you will never usurp my position in their lives.'

'You cannot control them, they are men.'

Julia gave a mocking laugh. 'Men or not, I rule this family. No other woman will change that. My boys rely on me totally for they know I have their best interests at heart. I would kill for them.'

A shiver of fear ran down Aurora's spine at the coldness of Julia's tone. 'You are evil to do this.'

'I protect my family.' She lifted one elegant shoulder as if the topic was trivial. 'But, by the time I'm finished with you, this particular matter will seem very unimportant.'

Confused, Aurora stared. 'What-what do you mean?'

'I'll get to that later. First, I want you to

understand that you will never marry Reid, or indeed any of my sons.'

'I — ' A tap on the door preceded Dotty, carefully carrying a tray of tea things. Aurora waited until the maid set the tray down with a slight thump and apologizing left the room again, before allowing herself to gulp in air.

Mrs Sinclair, as calmly as though she was Aurora's dearest friend, unashamedly poured two cups of tea. She didn't hand Aurora one, but instead took her own and sat down with a contented expression. 'Now, let me tell you what I know. And believe me it is quite a lot, more than you can guess. And more than I bargained for.'

Feeling sick and afraid, Aurora inched to the next chair and gently lowered herself onto the edge of it. She could tell by the other woman's air of arrogance that she had something vital to say and that it was going to hurt her.

'Is this tea fresh? I told your mother to order a special brand I found made in the wild mountains of China. A unique blend not well known, but of a supremely high quality.' Julia glared at the offending teapot on the tray as though it contained sludge from a riverbed. 'Never mind.'

Aurora watched Reid's mother, the woman who, if things turned out the way she hoped, would be her mother-in-law and a chill of unease rippled through her.

'So, you think yourself in love with my Reid, is that so?' Mrs Sinclair stared at her with a raised arched eyebrow. 'And he in love with you? How silly you are, my dear. He used your body. Men do it all the time. That doesn't mean a marriage or ever after love. Your mother should have explained that to you.'

Aurora swallowed back a retch. Her cutting words dirtied their relationship, made it impure.

'But then your mother is hardly the one to advise you on such subjects, with the history she hides.' The other woman sipped the tea and wrinkled her nose.

Dazed, Aurora grimaced. 'I don't know what you mean.'

'Naturally. How could you when it is a secret? I've only just found out myself. I wasn't expecting such a surprise.'

'Found out what?' she whispered, not wanting to know and wishing the vile woman would leave her home.

'Your mother has a sister, doesn't she?'

'Yes . . . '

'A sister she never sees. One you have never met. Is that true?'

She nodded, though it hurt her neck to do so. She ached in every tensed muscle. Even her teeth hurt as they clenched together, waiting for the poison to be spilt, which it would be. Aurora could see it in Mrs Sinclair's manner, the pleasure the other woman experienced in distressing her.

Mrs Sinclair picked at a piece of fluff on her skirt. 'The last time your mother saw her sister Sophia, was when you were a mere three weeks old.'

'How do you know this?' Aurora tried desperately to think of anything her mother said about her sister, but her mind went blank. And why was Julia Sinclair talking about an aunt she didn't know? This was about her and Reid.

'I hired a man to investigate your family.'

'You did what?' She gaped, shocked. It took several moments for her to believe what she said. 'Why?'

'Because I saw your growing intimacy with my son and I didn't want him becoming more enamored of you than he already was. I needed information to show him that you weren't worthy enough to be linked with the Sinclair family. You have no pedigree, my dear.' Mrs Sinclair put down her teacup and stood. 'However, I discovered more than I bargained for, I must admit. After reading your silly letters to him and his to you,' she paused to stare at Aurora as she walked towards the window, 'oh yes, I stopped letters from him reaching you too.' She carried on to the window and looked out. 'I must commend you on your letter writing. I was much entertained by your declarations of love. Still, they were all for nothing.'

Aurora waited for her to continue but when she didn't, she worried that perhaps Julia had lost her reason. One minute she was talking about stopping her letters, then about her aunt and then about her and Reid again. Was the strain of John's illness causing her mental health to suffer? Aurora took a calming breath. She found a glimmer of strength and clung to it. 'I'm sorry if you have felt deceived by Reid and I. We planned to tell both families about our relationship once his father regained his health.'

'I think not. The information I paid for is going to be very useful to me.'

'Whatever information you have found will not matter to us. I love Reid and he loves me. We will be married.'

Turning from the window, Julia's face showed her abhorrence. 'No, you will not.'

'Why are you doing this?' Aurora cried, irritated and upset. 'Why can't you let us be happy?'

'Because my son will become a great man, a man wealthier than even his father is now. He has the acumen for business and moneymaking that most men would sell their souls to have. I will not let him and all that go to waste.'

'Let him?' Aurora snorted with a bravado she didn't feel. 'He is his own man.'

'Not where the family is concerned. His family means everything to him. He is completely devoted to us and the Sinclair empire. He worships his father and will do nothing to hurt him. I won't allow Reid to lower himself by marrying a common slut like you.'

'I am not a slut.'

'Yes, you are. Haven't you proved it?' Mrs Sinclair raged. 'Haven't you acted just like your mother!'

'My mother?' Aurora jerked to her feet to defend herself and her mother from this foul woman. 'Of what are you accusing my mother?'

'Which one?'

Puzzled, her head throbbing like a beaten tambourine, she gazed at the other woman, wondering which one of them was mad.

Julia laughed, a light tinkling sound. 'You don't know what I am talking about, you poor stupid creature.'

'Perhaps you will enlighten me then?' Aurora scorned, wanting nothing more than to rake her nails down the awful woman's face.

'Gladly.' She glanced out the window and then back to her. 'Your real mother is Sophia Barton, younger sister to Winifred Barton Pettigrew.'

All warmth drained from Aurora's face. 'You're mistaken. You lie. You're insane.' She watched Julia cross to a leather bag left near the door, open it and pull out a large envelope, which she then flung onto the tea tray.

'Read it for yourself. It's all there. Every detail. For money your *mother* told all.' She screwed her nose up in disgust. 'You are bastard born to Sophia. She ran from her parents' home in disgrace when they found out she was with child. Winnie and your father, who were married by this time, found her alone, penniless. Sophia gave them her baby. You.'

'No . . .'

'True.' Julia unhurriedly tugged on her gloves. 'And that is why you, a bastard, will never marry Reid, or any of my sons. I will tell Reid of this when I return to London tonight. He will know you for what you are and put the family before you, my dear, count on it.' She reached inside her reticule and withdrew a slip of paper. 'I brought evidence of another kind.' She held it out for Aurora.

Taking it in shaking hands, Aurora gazed at her. 'What is it?'

'A letter I found on Reid's desk, not finished. Read it.'

Opening out the sheet of paper Aurora saw

Reid's handwriting and her heart constricted.

My darling,

Soon, it will be possible for us to be together. There are things I must do, arrangements I've made in haste, which have now prevented me from declaring myself fully to your father.

Be patient my dearest Hermione . . .

Aurora swayed, light-headed, dying inside. How was all this possible? How could something so shocking, so *wrong* be true? 'He doesn't love her,' her words came out low, scratching her throat.

'Love has nothing to do with it, Aurora. By marrying Miss FitzGibbon he is doing what is best for the family.'

Aurora crushed the letter in her fingers and it dropped to the floor. 'You must hate me very much to do all this. My parentage, Reid . . . '

'Actually, I don't.' Julia gave a little nod. 'You are extremely attractive and smart. You have courage and grace. Under other circumstances, such as you being higher born, I would have probably tolerated you for a daughter-in-law. But it isn't to be. I will protect my family against scandal and harm to the death. You, my dear, threaten them with both by pursuing Reid. I will not allow it. My family is all that I care about. I'm sorry if this news upsets you, or that I had to go to such lengths to protect what is mine. I hope you understand it isn't personal, not really.'

'But he loves me. I know he does. And I love him.'

'Any current affection he feels for you will pass in time, especially when he has a wife and family to think about.' Julia headed for the door. 'As will you one day.'

'How can you do this?' Bile rose threatening to choke her. 'You will hurt him too.'

'Only in the short term.'

'Please don't tell him about my birth,' Aurora begged, desperate. 'I will be the best daughter-in-law I can for you, I promise. You'd not regret allowing us to marry.'

'Put it out of your head for once and forever, my dear. Reid is not yours and never will be.' Pausing by the door, Julia turned back and sighed as though she was tired of this game. 'All right, I'll not reveal your circumstances to anyone if you distance yourself from Reid. But if you refuse to accept my warning, then I will let all this become public and I will embellish the tale greatly. Are you selfish enough to harm your mother and sisters, your father's interests, especially after all they've done for you by taking you in? Stay away from Reid or I will shame you and your family without a second thought.'

Aurora believed Julia would do exactly as she said. The steeliness in Julia's voice, the iciness in her eyes confirmed the words. She found it difficult to breath.

5

After the loathsome woman left, Aurora remained standing. Reluctantly, her gaze was drawn to the papers on the tea tray. How innocent they looked. Yet, the words written inside had changed her life forever. She eased onto the sofa slowly, moving as though the slightest jerk would dissolve her fortitude. Numbness descended on her as she reached over and pulled out the papers from the envelope, three sheets in all. She skimmed the opening address to Julia by the man she'd hired but faltered in reading when the name *Sophia Barton* leapt out at her.

The hired man had found one Sophia Barton working in a public house, The Yellow Moon. He recorded the details of his first meeting with Miss Barton and how he followed her back to her lodgings in Walmgate, York. He again spoke to her the next day as she left to go to work. For the information she gave him, confirming her background and past, he paid her the sum of fifty pounds.

Aurora closed her eyes at this. Her real mother had offered up all the sordid details for money. Had she done the same with Aurora, her baby? Given her to Winnie for money? In her heart, she knew the answer.

Carriage wheels on the drive brought her head up. Her mother and sisters had returned home. Suddenly the papers in her hands felt dirty, tainted. She stuffed them in the envelope and folded it into her skirt pocket. The paper bulged in the pocket and she frantically patted it down as out the window her mother step down from the carriage.

Her mother. She had two.

How could Aurora face her? How to pretend that life remained as it was an hour ago, when all she had to worry about was the lack of Reid's letters? The thought of Reid pierced the deadening fog surrounding her. Never would he be hers. She knew that clearly. She could not be his wife now. She could not fight Julia because she would lose. Her family would lose.

'Aurora, dearest.' Her mother breezed into the room, Bettina and Harriet following, smiling, talking and carrying several parcels.

'Did you have a nice morning?' Aurora pasted a tight smile on her face, wondering how she could be so calm when inside felt like an inferno was building in her chest. She stared at Winnie Pettigrew as though seeing her for the first time. Why hadn't she told her the truth years ago? Why live this lie?

'I bought a new hat, Aurrie.' Bettina busily unpacked a white hatbox and held up a pink-feathered creation. 'Isn't it lovely?'

'Very much so.' Aurora rose. 'I'll have a proper look later, but I've a bit of a headache at the present and might lie down for an hour.'

'A headache, my dear?' Her mother was full of concern. 'I hope you're not coming down with something. I pray I haven't passed on my cold to you.'

'I'll be fine, really.' No, I won't be, she silently cried. She would never be well again.

She went straight to bed and stayed there for the rest of the day, her mind alternating between denial and acceptance of all that Julia Sinclair told her. She read the papers repeatedly until she knew every word by heart. For a while she cried and then slept, only to wake and agonize over what to do with this new knowledge that had destroyed her life.

Hilda brought up a tray of soup and buttered bread, but Aurora couldn't eat. She lay in bed watching the night crawl over the countryside, thinking, crying, even praying. She pretended to be asleep when her mother peeked in and again later when her father did so, too. However, sleep was far from her mind as the night drew on until dawn pinked the sky. Finally, as the sun rose above the tree tops she fell into a fitful doze.

When Aurora woke late morning she felt feverish and lethargic. On sitting up, she dry retched, which made her head throb intolerably. She wondered if she was dying and hoped she was. Could bad news kill you? Could the fact that your whole life was changed for the worse make you so ill you could die within days? She prayed it was so. For living with the knowledge her true mother had given her up, that she was a bastard, that she'd never marry Reid now would surely murder her.

She sank down into the pillows at the same time a knock preceded the door opening and her mother stepped into the room.

'Darling, you've slept through breakfast.'

'I'm sorry.'

Her mother's smile faded and her eyes grew wary. 'Are you still ill?'

'I think I might have caught something,' Aurora lied, although in truth she felt terribly unwell, but it had nothing to do with a cold.

'I'll call the doctor.'

'No, please don't. There is nothing he can do. I'm certain a day in bed will be all I need.'

Winnie felt her head. 'Hmm . . . You're a little hot but also pale.'

'I didn't sleep very well.'

'I'll look in on you again after church.' Her mother kissed the top of her head. 'Shall I send a tray up?'

She nodded. 'Tea would be lovely.'

'Yes. Good. Try to rest, my dear.'

The door closed on her mother and Aurora turned onto her side to stare at the wall, but the movement made her heave again and she rushed for the basin on the dresser. The dry retching exhausted her even more. Her body ached as though she'd fallen down a flight of stairs. Perhaps she had caught a cold. It was the last thing she felt she could cope with, but at least it meant she could stay in bed and hide from the world.

Hilda brought the tea tray in and then opened the curtains to allow the sunshine to flood the bedroom. 'It's a beautiful hot June day, Miss, the kind I like.'

Aurora nodded, wincing at the light.

'The Mistress says you're not feeling the best.' Hilda fussed with the clothes hanging over a chair at the end of the bed. 'Do you wish to stay in bed or sit in the garden?'

'I might go downstairs later.'

'That's grand, Miss.' Hilda took away the clothes ready for the laundry and closed the door behind her.

Aurora eyed the tea tray dubiously. For some reason the sight of tea and toast made the nausea rise again. Once more she dashed for the basin to retch until her stomach hurt in protest. She groaned and wiped her mouth. Perhaps she really was sick? Wearily, she trudged over to the window. In the stable yard below, Jimmy was checking Princess's hooves. The pull of a long enjoyable ride was strong, but her stomach wasn't and it won the battle.

Sighing, Aurora plodded back to bed and settled amongst the sheets. Inevitably, her thoughts turned to the information Julia had told her. Sophia Barton. Her real mother. The one who gave her up. Did Sophia ever think of her? Did she keep in contact with her sister and ask about the baby she abandoned?

Aurora thought about the few times her mother had mentioned her sister and realized precious little had been revealed. There was so much she didn't know. So much she needed to know. For one thing, who was her real father?

Tiredness made her shuffle further down the bed and plump up the pillows. She closed her eyes, still thinking of the faceless woman who gave her life.

When she opened her eyes again, the small carriage clock on the mantelpiece showed she'd slept for an hour. Feeling a little better, Aurora threw back the covers and quietly washed and dressed, her movements slow and deliberate, not wanting to be sick again. She placed a napkin over the offending tea tray and decided to take it down to the kitchen and have a glass of cold water instead. The room was closing in on her. She needed fresh air, sunshine and somewhere to think. Her head felt like it was full of wool stuffing.

Mrs Pringle, glad to see her up out of bed, made a fuss, as did Dotty and Hilda, but Aurora sensed their unease. Mrs Pringle kept glancing at the back door and Dotty chatted too loudly.

'Is something the matter, Mrs Pringle?' Aurora asked, edging to the back door.

'Not at all, Miss.' The older woman made a great show of sieving flour.

Aurora glanced around the large warm kitchen and peeped into the scullery. 'Where's Fanny today?'

'Outside, Miss,' Dotty blurted.

'Dotty Marsh shut your gob.' Mrs Pringle threatened her with her sieve. 'Get about your business or you'll be scrubbing pans for a week, my girl.'

'Mrs Pringle?' Aurora questioned, sensing something wasn't quite right in the homely kitchen which the cook ruled.

'It's nowt, Miss. Fanny's eaten something that doesn't agree with her, that's all.' The cook nodded sagely.

'From this kitchen?'

'Eh, no!' The wise look was replaced by an

offended tone. 'Never from my kitchen!'

Needing fresh air herself, Aurora gave them a quelling look, letting them know she didn't believe a word of it and went outside into the morning sunshine. She found Fanny by the water pump. The young woman had just finished washing her face and neck.

'Fanny.'

'Oh, Miss.'

Aurora studied her, and noticed the paleness of her pretty face. She looked exactly how Aurora felt only an hour ago. 'You are ill?'

'Oh, Miss.' Fanny repeated, tears welling in her red eyes to drip slowly down her cheeks.

'Whatever is the matter?'

'I have to stop working here, Miss, and I really like it here.'

'Why must you stop?'

Fanny hiccupped on a sob. 'I'm to have a baby, Miss,' she whispered, horror in her voice. 'I'm so sorry.'

'A baby?' Stupefied, Aurora stared at her. 'But you're not married, Fanny.'

At this, the maid wailed into her hands and Aurora could have slapped herself at her own stupidity. Awkwardly, for she had never held a servant before, she hugged the young woman to her and patted her shoulder, suddenly feeling very much older than the maid although she knew they were the same age. 'How do you know you're to have a baby?'

'I've missed my monthlies, Miss. Twice.' She wailed harder. 'And then this morning I was sick and Mrs Pringle caught me and made me tell. I

78

should never have lain with him. Bloody sweet talker he was. Beg your pardon, Miss.' Fanny straightened, gathering control again. 'I told him, I did. I told him I wasn't someone who'd do it. But well, it was my birthday and I got drunk on cider and he was saying such nice things to me . . . and I went and did it, didn't I? And now I'm to have Jimmy's baby and he says we can get married. I don't want to bloody marry him!' Tears slipped over her lashes again and she wiped them away angrily. 'I'm such a stupid cow.'

The breath left Aurora as if someone had punched her hard between the ribs. Half of what Fanny said didn't register but two things did. Missed monthlies and being sick. Aurora thought of when she last had her monthly curse and couldn't remember. Panic gripped her. When? Dash it, when?

'I'd best go in now, Miss.' She wringed her hands, eyes sad. 'Mrs Pringle says she'll inform your mother today.' Fanny started walking back to the kitchen only to turn at the door. 'Thanks for listening Miss and for not judging me too harshly. I made a mistake, that's all. Jimmy and I will be all right. He's nice enough and I've made him happy. I hope you can come to the wedding, Miss.'

In a daze, Aurora watched the door close behind Fanny and she slumped against the trough beneath the pump. A baby? Surely not. How could she be? She only went with Reid once. It took more than once for a baby didn't it? Her mother said she and father were married

79

for two years before Aurora came along . . .

But Winnie wasn't her mother.

A cold shiver rippled over her skin raising goosebumps. A baby. No. She was jumping to conclusions. Her body was reacting to her news.

But what if she was . . .

Black spots appeared before her eyes. She felt a funny sensation creeping up her neck. Suddenly the ground rose up to hit her in the face and all went black.

★　★　★

'I won't take no for an answer, Aurora.' Her mother paced the bedroom, stopping only to cough with every other step. 'Imagine how scared we were on coming home from church and being told you had collapsed outside.' Her hand fluttered to her throat as she convulsed into another fit of coughing.

Alarmed by her mother's frailness, Aurora struggled to get out of bed. 'Mother, please sit down.'

Her mother drew breath and put up a hand to keep Aurora still. 'You had to be assisted to bed! We are lucky Donaldson found you when he did. What if he'd been digging in the garden on the other side of the house for hours? You'd have been lying there . . . I should never have gone to church but stayed with you and called Doctor Hedley.'

'I simply fainted, that's all.' Aurora picked at the edge of the sheet. The house had been in an uproar for the last hour ever since her family returned from church to the news that the gardener had found her on the ground. The doctor had been called and he was now washing his hands at the basin behind her pacing mother. In fact, out of the two of them, her mother looked the one who was in need of Dr Hedley's services more than Aurora.

Dr Hedley turned, as if attuned to Aurora's thoughts. 'Mrs Pettigrew, I insist you rest. You are not yet fully recovered yourself.'

'I am perfectly — '

He held up his hand to silence her. 'My word is final, Madam. Now please go and lie down. Your daughter is in no danger, but I can see you are. Do you wish to have a relapse?'

'No, Doctor,' her mother replied meekly. She, and the whole family, was in awe of this wise worldly man who had been their doctor since they moved to this house.

'Right then.' He took her elbow and assisted her out of the room. 'I shall come and examine you in a moment.' He closed the door and walked to Aurora's bedside. A sympathetic smile softened his gray eyes. 'Now then, Miss.'

Aurora braced herself for what he was to tell her.

'Have you been with a man? You know the context of what I mean?'

She nodded, a guilty blush heating her cheeks.

'And do you understand the consequences that can come from such a union?'

She nodded again, feeling like a small child caught licking sugar off her fingers. A knot in her throat made it hard to swallow.

'I must say I am surprised at you, Miss Aurora. I never expected you to behave in that way.'

'I'm sorry.'

He rubbed the back of his neck beneath his short gray hair, his expression full of concern. 'Don't apologize to me, my dear. It is your parents who will need the apology. You are with child.'

The words hit like death blows.

'Please do not tell my parents,' she whispered, already feeling their pain and disappointment. How could she bear to bring such hurt to them?

'Are you sure it wouldn't be kinder to you, and them, for me to be the bearer of bad tidings?'

'No. I'm not ready.'

'And the father? Will he marry you?'

She shrugged. Would he? Probably. Yes. Yes, he would. He loved her, she knew that, despite Hermione FitzGibbon being the perfect bride for him. But if she was honest, her feelings for him had altered after reading his unfinished letter to Hermione. Doubts of his commitment rose to mock her. Perhaps he always intended to marry Miss FitzGibbon? How could she know for certain? She didn't know anything anymore.

And what of her background? She was a bastard. Did she want him to marry her for the child, knowing it might ruin him? His mother threatened to shame her family. Did she want to be the one who brought the wrath of Julia Sinclair down on their heads? Or be the one who made Reid a laughing stock because his wife was illegitimate and he had to marry her for the sake of the child? Would he care? Would she? She didn't know and the questions and uncertainty was making her feel sick again.

'Your color has gone again. I'll leave you to lie quietly.' Dr Hedley patted her arm. 'I'll come back tomorrow, though my visit will be more about your mother than you. She needs bed rest. Her chest is not good.' He collected his bag and made for the door. 'We can have another talk tomorrow. Good day.'

After the door closed, Aurora laid back against the pillows. Her hands drifted down to lay on her flat stomach. A baby. It didn't seem real. A moan seeped out between her clamped lips. What on earth was she to do? She badly wanted to talk to someone, but who? Not her mother or father, and definitely not her sisters. She had no one. No close friends. The odd acquaintances she met at dinners and parties had never amounted to close friendships. Her sisters and the Sinclair boys had been enough for her, but it was those very people who couldn't share her secret. Sadly, she realized there wasn't one person she could unburden to. Hot tears burned behind her eyes, but she fought them, instinctively knowing that if she cried now, she'd never stop. No one could know her secret. She was alone.

She must have drifted off to sleep because the next thing she woke to a darkened room. Out the window the sun was slowly setting, showering the countryside with a soft golden tan. A low fire glowed in the small grate in the corner of the room, not that Aurora felt cold. The door opened and her mother peeped around the door.

'Oh, darling, you are awake.' She came to the bed and kissed Aurora's cheek. 'How do you feel?'

'Better,' she lied. Everything that had been safe and hers was now insecure and alien.

'Good.'

Not able to bear thinking about Reid, she focused on her mother. 'Are you rested, Mother?'

'I'm much improved. Dr Hedley left me some medicine to ease my cough.' She smiled and indeed appeared to have some color in her face. She had changed for dinner and the warm burgundy gown didn't hide the fact she'd lost considerable weight since becoming ill at Easter. 'You must have something to eat, dearest. Mrs Pringle tells me you've had nothing since yesterday. No wonder you fainted.'

'Silly me,' Aurora whispered with a small smile.

'I'll send up a tray for you. Perhaps some broth and a little bit of chicken?'

'That would be nice.' Aurora reached for her mother's thin hand and held it tight. She felt time was slipping away from her and she could do nothing to hold it back. 'May I ask you something?'

'Of course.'

'Why do you never speak of your parents or sister?'

Her mother's eyes widened. 'Where did that notion come from?'

'I was just lying here, thinking about things, that's all.' Aurora shrugged one shoulder, trying

84

to act as though none of it meant a great deal. 'I don't remember much about them.'

'Your grandparents died within six months of each other when you were about five or six. I loved them very much, but when I married your father we lived in Manchester and then came here. My parents enjoyed a quiet life north of York. Father was very involved with the church once he retired from being a schoolmaster. My mother was delicate. She had relatives in Cornwall and would sometimes go there for the warmer climate.' She smiled in remembrance. 'I went there once as a child.'

'And your sister? Where does she live?' Aurora hated being so sneaky but she needed information.

'Sophia always . . . um . . . moved around a lot.'

'Oh? Why?'

Her mother cleared her throat. 'She . . . she was a lady's companion to a rich woman who liked to travel. We lost touch . . . '

'How sad.'

'Yes. We were close at one time. That is how life can be at times, full of twists and turns.' Her mother stepped away and their hands broke contact. 'Now I'll organize that tray for you.' She coughed all the way out of the room.

Aurora stared at the closed door, knowing that to tell her parents she was with child would break them. She'd done exactly the same thing as her real mother. Was she dreadfully wicked for loving one man, a man who she believed would marry her? Is that what her mother had done too?

85

Leaving the bed she went to the drawer of her dresser and from under her handkerchiefs took out the papers Mrs Sinclair gave her. Once more she read the details. Sophia Barton worked in a public house. Shame filled Aurora. A public house! That meant Sophia was poor, working class. Was she married? Did she have other children?

A headache built behind Aurora's eyes. There was too much to think of and worry about. She wished it would all go away. The sun slipped lower and dusk descended. Sitting on the window seat, her thoughts returned to the mother she never knew she had. What did Sophia look like? Did she look like her? Did Sophia ever wonder about the baby she gave away? Aurora glanced down at her stomach. Now she would know what Sophia felt. But would she choose the same path?

6

A week later, most of it spent crying and worrying in her room, Aurora felt well enough in mind and body to rejoin the family. She knew she'd been a coward. Hiding would solve none of her problems, but for a little while it had given her the opportunity to lick her wounds. Now she had to gather her strength for the ordeal ahead. Despite all the anxiety, she'd dwelt more on Sophia Barton than she had on Reid. She loved him, she knew that, but losing him hadn't been as painful as finding out about her parentage. She could deal with a broken heart, she could even ignore the fact she was with child, but she couldn't cope with the ghost of Sophia, an unknown woman, her mother, the one who gave her away.

Heavy summer rainstorms had drenched the countryside while she stayed indoors but the sun was out as she made her way downstairs mid morning on Saturday. The house was quiet and after searching the rooms she found her father in his study, writing.

'Father.' Aurora tapped lightly on the opened door.

'Darling, come in.' He dropped his pen and walked around the desk to hug her. 'You're up and about. Excellent, excellent.'

His loving attention brought tears to her eyes. She was going to hurt this wonderful man and her heart grieved already. She swallowed back the ever present tears. 'Where is everyone?'

'Out, my dear. Shopping in Leeds, I take it, for Bettina's birthday next weekend.' He sat again behind his desk and Aurora drifted over to the window.

'It is a lovely day outside.'

'That it is. We should be out in it while it lasts.' He took his glasses off and wiped them with a soft felt cloth, his smile tender and loving as he gazed at her. 'Your mother will be so happy to see you up and about.'

'I might go for a ride. Princess will be missing me.' She didn't add it might be the last time she ever did.

'Indeed she will my pet, but are you strong enough?'

'Oh yes. Fully recovered.' She smiled to reassure him. Actually, the odd morning had her retching still, but once she was over that, she found nothing much else was wrong with her and she'd regained her appetite again.

'That is good news. Everyone has been so worried. Young Tom has been here daily to see you.'

She winced at the mention of Tom. 'I didn't mean to cause such trouble.'

'You can't help being ill, can you?' He sat behind his desk again. 'Well, you enjoy your ride, darling. Perhaps I'll meet you for some lunch. About one o'clock? We'll have it in the garden, what do you say?'

'I'd like that. I'll make sure I am back in time.'

The soft lushness of summer seeped into

Aurora, soothing her as she rode the lanes around the house. A part of her still felt fragile but she knew she must overcome it. Slowly she was gaining some of her old self back. The blow of Sophia, the baby, and losing Reid had beaten her badly, but life kept moving forward whether she wanted to go with it or not. She had important decisions to make and being holed up in her bedroom wasn't going to help. However, riding Princess with the warm sunshine on her back, her mind went blank and she just enjoyed being outside again. The time would come later for resolutions.

After her ride, she lunched with her father. It'd been a long time since she spent time alone with him. His pleasant intelligent conversation was relaxing as they sat in the shade beneath a chestnut tree at the side of the house.

Her father filled his pipe bowl with tobacco as Dotty cleared away the debris of their ham salad lunch. 'You didn't eat much, my love.'

Folding her napkin, Aurora flashed him a brief smile. 'I wasn't very hungry.' She reached for the teapot. 'More tea?'

'Yes, thank you.' Her father lit his pipe and sat back, crossing one leg over the other. 'I received a letter from John Sinclair this morning.'

Aurora, absentmindedly watching a butterfly drift over the roses, felt her heart turn over in her chest. 'Oh? Is he well?'

'He's had a few setbacks. Had a bad case of pneumonia, poor fellow, which hasn't helped his recovery.' Josiah sucked on his pipe. 'He's asked me to watch his boys for him.'

She sat up, giving him her full attention. The grip on her teacup tightened. 'Why?'

'Young Tom is having his birthday bash tonight, you see. One he's arranged himself from what I've heard. I take it he's invited most of his Oxford pals. I dread to imagine the state of the Hall by morning.'

'Are none of the family coming home to share in his celebrations?' Despite everything, she was dying to hear news of Reid.

'Not that I'm aware of, which is sad really. The boy is a bit wild, but harmless, I think. His banishment is a touch harsh in my opinion. No doubt the army will sort him out though.'

'I agree . . . ' She slumped back against the chair. 'Poor Tom.'

'Well, I might pop over later tonight and check they aren't smashing the furniture, but apart from that I'll leave them to it.'

'Yes, I don't think Tom will thank you for interfering.'

'Speaking of birthdays, after Bettina's it is your big celebration. Twenty One.' He sucked on his pipe thoughtfully. 'How the years have flown.'

'Are you glad you had me, Father?'

'Of course!'

'Never regretted not having a son?'

'Not really.' He waved his pipe in the air. 'I suppose if I'm honest I'd have liked someone to leave the businesses to, but you girls will provide me with grandsons, I'm sure. I may have more of those than I need.' He laughed at his own joke.

'So you never lamented having a girl as your first child?' she persisted.

'Why should I? You've grown into a beautiful, intelligent young woman, Aurora. I couldn't be more proud of you.'

She smiled, but felt that more could have been added to that last sentence. Or was she imagining it? She was very confused about so many things, she didn't know what to think or feel anymore. One thing was for certain though, he'd not be proud of her once he heard her news. She sighed deeply, wishing with all her heart she could go back in time and change things.

Later, Aurora spent an hour with her mother and sisters listening to their shopping stories and of who they met while in Leeds. Watching Bettina and Harriet giggle and fuss over new gloves and the latest fashions, she wondered if she'd ever been that childish at their age. They were acting like ten year old girls while she felt old, so very old.

Straight after their evening meal, Winnie, exhausted, went to bed. Their father took himself off to his study to read while the girls sorted out invitation replies to Bettina's birthday garden party. Taking advantage of the mild summer evening, Aurora slipped out of the house and strolled through the gardens. She breathed in the fragrances of the flowers, which were heavy on the still balmy air.

She was no closer on deciding what to do. Every time she considered her situation and tried to think of a solution her head pounded as though a madman was using her brains as a drum. She'd received no communication from

Reid, not that she expected to with Julia guarding the post. He didn't know of the torture she endured, but somehow she wished he'd instinctively know she needed him and come charging to her rescue. Why hadn't he come home to the Hall? What kept him in London all this time? Didn't he need her as much as she needed him? Wasn't he curious as to why he hadn't received any letters from her? Or had his mother told him something to discourage him?

Through the trees came the sound of music and raucous laughter. It came as no surprise to her to find herself walking across the lawns separating the two properties. She wanted to wish Tom a happy birthday.

Before she reached the side drive of Sinclair Hall, another burst of laughter reached her. Aurora hesitated on hearing men chanting, urging someone to do something. She slipped down the side of the house to peek through one of the drawing room windows. Inside, a group of young men were lounging around, drinking, eating from a buffet. They all looked so full of energy and fun. A grin lifted her lips as she spotted Tom. He jumped up on another fellow's back and was riding him like a horse to the joyous shouts of the others.

'Oh, I say.'

Aurora whipped around guiltily to stare at James Sinclair. 'James!'

'Aurora!' He slapped his thigh and laughed. 'What are you doing here?'

'I thought to come to wish Tom many happy returns of the day, but seeing his friends, and the

92

party well underway, I'd best leave it.'

'You do right, Aurrie.' James made a comical expression. 'It's not very suitable for a lady's company in there, I'm sorry to say.'

Just then, there came a high pitched stream of laughter that could only belong to a female. Aurora raised her eyebrows at the youngest Sinclair. 'No ladies, you say?'

James went beetroot red. 'Well . . . ' He pulled at his collar. 'Those gels aren't ladies . . . '

Aurora blushed too, as she caught his meaning. 'Oh, I see.'

'Tom planned them as er . . . entertainment.' He cleared his throat growing even redder.

Embarrassed, Aurora stepped away from the window and out onto the drive. 'I'll get along home then.'

'I can call for Tom to come out and see you, if you wish?'

'No, please.' She held her hand up to stop him. 'I'll speak to him tomorrow.'

'Hah! He'll not be awake until the evening I should imagine, not after tonight. And he'll have a sore head, knowing Tom. Reid has no chance to rein him.'

'Reid?' She gasped, her hand going to her chest as her heart thumped. 'Reid is here?'

'We all came up together this afternoon.' James stared at her with a frown. 'Perhaps we should have called on you . . . '

Aurora tried to pull herself together. Poor James must wonder what was wrong with her. 'I-I am sure you've been busy with guests arriving.'

'We have indeed, but we managed to have a brief luncheon together with just us brothers.' A pleasing softness came into his hazel eyes. 'We've not been together for some time, well not since Tom was sent up here and Reid has been in Kent.'

'I see.' The brightness of the day faded. Reid in Kent, where Miss FitzGibbon lived.

'And Reid was bursting to tell us his news.'

'News?'

'Why yes. He's getting married apparently. He told us he's planning on being married by the end of the year. Isn't that marvelous?'

'Absolutely.' Her wooden tone was lost on him as he continued.

'It took us all by surprise, though Mother will be delighted. She's wanted this for a good while.'

'Did-did Reid say who the lucky lady was?'

James scowled and peered down at his shiny boots. 'He refused to mention her name. He was very happy and wanted to tease us by not revealing her name. He did say we knew her, but he wasn't saying more until he'd proposed. We tried everything we could to find out who it was.'

'I . . . I believe it could be . . . Miss FitzGibbon?'

James's eyes widened. 'I say, you could be right in that, Aurrie. We said her name, but Reid wouldn't acknowledge or deny it. But Miss FitzGibbon has been a regular visitor to our home in Kensington and Reid to her home while in Kent.'

'She must be the one then. I'd best go now . . . ' Aurora stumbled backwards, away from James, away from the happy noise coming from the house, away from the source of pain that was lancing her heart like a doctor lanced a boil.

'Jolly good. I'll tell Tom you called, Aurrie.' James waved and headed along the drive as it curved behind the back of the house.

Aurora glanced through another window and saw Reid enter a room, a brash young woman came up to him and kissed him on the mouth, her red-painted nails clawed at his waistcoat buttons as she wrapped one leg around his. The woman reached for a wine glass, sipped from it and then placed it to Reid's lips. She licked his neck. Laughing, they left the room arm in arm.

Gagging, Aurora turned and fled across the lawn not stopping until she reached the dividing gate. Here she paused for a second to stifle a sob and unlatch the gate, before she raced off again to the small wood beyond the stables. She collapsed to the ground, crying so hard she thought she would die from the gaping hole inside her. Her eyes began to swell and her nose streamed as though she had a bad cold, but she couldn't stem the tears fast enough. They flowed, seemingly leaked out of her every pore until she feared she'd drown in them. She couldn't breathe or think and when an inhuman wail escaped her, she clapped her hands over her mouth in deadening despair that she was losing her mind.

Reid.

Why had he gone with that woman? Despite what she saw, she wanted Reid more at this moment than at any other time. She needed him to hold her, to tell her it would be all right. However, even in her misery she understood Reid would never be hers. Julia had won. Aurora could never tell him of the child, of her parentage. Their relationship was over, as was her life as she knew it.

The night closed in around her, the darkness like a blanket that kept her safe before the crying finally eased, leaving her exhausted and dizzy, but that was better than the sobbing which took all her breath. She rested her head against a tree and stared up without really seeing the leafy silvery canopy above. Only when the numbness in her legs became unbearable, did she come back to the distressing present.

Feeling as old as time, she staggered to her feet, wincing as the blood circulated down to her toes again. An owl hooted and somewhere in the distance a fox barked, its eerie sound carrying in the quiet.

Aurora didn't remember entering the house, nor climbing the staircase. Somehow she had done it and now, standing in the middle of her bedroom, she felt a stranger amongst her own things. She didn't belong here. Not now. Everything was different. The life course she believed was hers, being a member of her family, marriage to Reid, was a sham. But then, where did she belong?

A lamp had been lit on the dresser and in the dim golden light she looked around the room and felt nothing. She was dead inside. Dead to her belongings, this room, this house and the people in it. Dead to the whole world in fact.

She drew out a piece of paper from her drawer and began to write.

Dear Mother and Father,

This letter will come as a shock to you, and I'm sorry that I am to cause you pain but I feel this is something I must do.

I am leaving to find my real mother, Sophia Barton. It does not matter how I know about her but now that I do, I believe I should seek her out.

How long this will take me, I do not know, but I beg you not to try and find me. I will send word of my progress. To cover my absence, perhaps you could tell our friends that I have gone on holiday to Europe or something to that effect. I'll leave that for you to decide.

I hold you both and my sisters in great affection.

After adding her name, she folded the letter into an envelope and propped it on her pillow.

Slowly, methodically, she began to pack.

7

The deafening noise of the trains competed with the whistles and calls from the stationmaster. Smoke and steam hissed upwards towards the large steel dome of York's train station. People jostled Aurora; all eager to get where they were going, unlike her. She side-stepped an overflowing luggage cart and then did it again to avoid colliding with a small child who'd let go of his mother's hand. She heard the elegant woman chastising him as she grabbed his hand again.

Leaving the station, Aurora went out onto the busy street. Although she'd been to large cities before, mainly Leeds and Manchester and on one occasion to London, she wasn't used to the constant throb of noise that assaulted her from every direction. When shopping with her mother in Leeds she went from their carriage straight into the subdued tasteful surroundings of the milliner's shop, the dressmaker's shop, and the haberdashery before spending a peaceful half hour in a dainty tearoom her mother frequented each week. A visit to the tomb-like silence of the library usually completed the day and then they'd casually drive home. All this was very different to her experience on a cramped morning train and now the hectic pace of midday York traffic, which whizzed past her at alarming speeds.

A yell from a driver high up on a carriage seat

made her jump and step back onto the pavement. Crossing the street seemed a hazardous idea. How did people do it? In fact, how did anyone live in a city permanently? The snort from one of the horse pairs pulling a large wagon full of kegs from a brewery gave her a jolt. She read the brewery name emblazoned on the side of the wagon and speculated whether it would be going to The Yellow Moon. She had no idea where the public house Sophia worked at was situated in the sprawl of York. She only had a basic address. Walmgate.

Hitching her suitcase more comfortably in her hand, she headed down the road away from the station. She'd have to ask directions from someone. What looked to be shops loomed further ahead, but from around the corner of the next street stepped a policeman.

'Excuse me.' Aurora stopped him.

'Yes, Miss?' The policeman, tall with kind eyes gave her a smile.

'I need directions to Walmgate, please.'

His face altered and he frowned. 'Nay, Miss. Walmgate, you say?'

'That's correct, yes.'

'You'll not be wanting to go there, Miss. It's a right old . . . er . . . that is to say it's not fit for decent ladies, such as yourself, to be in those parts.' He swallowed audibly.

'But I must. There is someone I need to see.'

He studied her for a moment and saw the determination in her eyes. 'Very well then.' He gave her the directions, but as she went to leave him he spoke again. 'You'd do well to be away from there before nightfall, Miss. It's not safe.'

'Thank you. I will.' She nodded and hurried away before she forgot his instructions on where she needed to go. Her suitcase grew heavier as she traversed the streets, which became narrower and meaner in appearance with each turn of a corner. She didn't want to dwell on the policeman's comment of the area. She wasn't stupid, she knew there were poor people and dangerous parts of cities, but she'd never ventured into one of those areas until now. And she hoped she had the nerve to withstand it.

Her feet aching, and no doubt blisters growing on her heels with every step, Aurora walked along Hope Street, a dirty, soot-covered tenement, where houses stretched in a never-ending row, she doubted the wisdom of her plan to see Sophia. Escaping into the early dawn, leaving the safety of her home and family, she'd not focused on the end result. All she knew was that something had to be done. She had to take some action in sorting out the mess that her life had become. Begging a lift off a dairy farmer driving his cart to Leeds as the night sky turned creamy orange had been easy. So had catching the six o'clock morning train to York. But now as she neared the bleak and miserable exterior of The Yellow Moon, the misgivings of this idea swarmed her head.

The public house sat in the middle of Hope Street, but also on a corner of a narrow alley that even in the middle of the day was dark and menacing. Aurora glanced up at the building and her spirits sank even further. The decayed and peeling advertising on the walls matched the neglected look of the spotted dingy green paint of the doors and window frames. Thick dark glass fitted in the middle of each of the two front doors hid the interior from her gaze, as did the drawn blinds on the windows. No sound came from within.

Now she was here she didn't know what to do. Did one just knock on the door of a public house?

Turning from the doors, she took in the street. Terraced housing, their doors leading straight onto the pavement, dominated the view up and down. The overcast sky seemed to sit immediately on the dull slate roofs as though trying to press the houses into the earth. A brown, matted dog relieved itself against a wall across the street and Aurora jumped when a shriek pierced the air from an upstairs window to the right of her. One by one the noises of the street entered her head, filling her ears. A door banged, a baby cried, a man yelled. There came the sound of water being thrown from a bucket, the sliding of a window opening or closing, she didn't know which. Bottles rattled, a rug was thumped against a wall, a child shrieked.

She noticed the people of the street for the first time. Two slatternly women stood on their doorsteps chatting. A man lounged against a pole smoking a pipe. Another woman swept her steps while another leaned out of a window and blasted the air with foul language directed at one of the boys playing marbles in the gutter. Barefoot, ragged children played in groups, one of boys and the other of girls. The soft thwack of a skipping rope kept a perfect rhythm to the little girls chanting as they ran in and out of the twirling rope.

Aurora blinked and wiped her eyes with one hand. She felt as though she was coming out of a dream, no, a nightmare. This foreign world scared her. What was she doing here? Why had she come? She must have been out of her wits.

A big woman, with breasts that hung down and sat on her wide waist, walked over to her. 'Eh, lass, you lookin' for summat?'

'I . . . I . . . ' Aurora stared at the stained apron stretching around the woman's middle. Her stomach churned.

'You lost p'haps?' Her kindly face smiled to reveal missing front teeth.

Light-headed, Aurora focused on the woman's gaping mouth, but it was no use. A gradual blackness came over her and she gladly accepted it.

★   ★   ★

Sophia Barton left her lodgings in the filthy squalor that was Edinburgh Yard. After picking her way through a stinky, mucky cut leading to a bigger and dirtier alley, she then turned right and walked up Hope Street. She'd just had a blazing row with her latest man, Con, and now she had to go to work and put up with more leering drunken men until the bar closed late tonight. She was getting too old for this lark. How she hated her life!

She'd thrown Con out, sick of his whining and drunken antics, sick of his lazy habits and excuses when he didn't get up for work. She didn't have to put up with any of it. She'd been her own woman for over twenty years, she didn't need him or anyone, and she'd told him so when she'd kicked his skinny arse down the steps and thrown the bits of clothes he owned down after him.

At the front of the pub she noticed a noisy gathering, and her shoulders sagged. Today, she didn't want to deal with anyone else's problems. She didn't want to patch up a battered woman, or listen to some old drunk's tales of younger days. For once, she simply wanted to forget she lived in this squalor, do her work and then return to the flea-infested hovel that was her home and fall into a dreamless sleep. Couldn't she have that today? Was it so much to ask for?

Women stood about chatting nineteen to the dozen, and that gave their kids a perfect opportunity to misbehave and act like hooligans. The pub wasn't even open yet so it couldn't be a brawl surely?

What the hell was going on?

Pushing her way through the women, earning herself an elbow jab from one nasty piece for her trouble, Sophia made it to the centre of the action and stopped dead. Flo O'Neil was squatting on the ground, holding a slender stranger in her pudgy arms.

'What's happening, Flo?' Sophia bent to get a closer look, which was difficult, as Flo had the girl squashed into her body like a baby suckling.

'Nay, I'm not sure. One minute I'm asking if this lass here was lookin' for someone, an' the next minute she's fallin' to the ground.' Flo's chins wobbled as she shook her head in amazement of it all.

'She's not from these parts, that's for sure,' Ida McDonnell tutted.

Sophia glanced up at the tall thin woman dressed in black, a nasty crone who had nothing good to say about anything before addressing the rest of the crowd. 'Have any of you seen her before?' Shakes of head and negative mumbles were her reply.

'She's stirring.' Flo patted the girl's cheek.

Sophia stepped closer, noting the good cloth of her dress, the fine hat knocked askew. For some reason a shiver passed down Sophia's back. She swallowed as the young woman turned her face away from the heaving bosom of Flo and opened her eyes.

The blood drained from Sophia's face. And for the first time in her life she wished a faint would be lethal enough to release her from this world. She stared into the dark brown eyes of her daughter. Of that she had no doubt for weren't they the mirror of her own? The girl even had her shaped face. She was, in fact, a younger version of herself. And she was *here*!

'What we going to do with her?' Ida muttered, revulsion on her face as though the girl was scum off the street. Others nodded in agreement and rumbles of discord sounded.

Sophia wanted to laugh hysterically at them. Here they were in one of the worst areas of York and the girl on Flo's arms wore black silk that would have cost more than most of these women's husbands earned in a year. Yet, they were stiff and unyielding as though she'd brought the plague.

'I'm quite all right.' The girl, the *young woman*, struggled to her feet with Flo's help. The crowd stepped back, unused to having a member of the middle class in their territory and were united in their suspicion of her.

Sophia sighed resignedly, knowing exactly what they were thinking. Hadn't she been on the receiving end of it herself many years ago? Hadn't she spent years of making excuses why she didn't speak or act like they all did in these parts? Convent educated she had told them, a lady's maid was another lie. No one knew her sister was wealthy, nor did they know she'd given up a baby — a baby who'd grown into this pretty thing in Flo's arms.

'What's your name, lass?' Flo's gentle question had them all eager to listen for the answer.

'Aurora Pettigrew.'

Stifling another gasp that her daughter was really before her, and she hadn't imagined it, Sophia momentarily closed her eyes, hoping to find the strength she'd need to get through this day. Why had she come here?

'Aur-Arr-Auro . . . What a pretty name. Now then, luv,' Flo rubbed Aurora's arm. 'What you doing about 'ere?'

'I've come to find someone.' Aurora's gaze left Flo and looked directly at Sophia. 'I've come to find Sophia Barton.'

All heads turned to Sophia and she felt her cheeks grow warm. 'You'd best come inside then, hadn't you?' Sophia barged through the crowd and down the alley to the back of the pub, not knowing if the girl followed or not. She had the keys today because Big Eddie, the publican, was at the brewery for a meeting. The numerous keys on the ring didn't help her shaking fingers, but she finally found the correct key and unlocked the door.

Inside the scullery-come-storage room, she turned to find Aurora standing on the step behind her, suitcase in hand, hat knocked askew.

'Come in then, if you are.' Sophia didn't mean to bark it like an order, but her heart galloped wildly like she'd run for ten miles. She led the way through a curtained door into a large kitchen. It was empty and cold and silent. 'Mrs Flannigan will be in shortly and make some tea. She's the cook here. The pub serves meals, you see. Mrs Flannigan's a good cook.' She banged some pots around, filled the kettle, anything to keep her hands busy. 'The men enjoy her hotpots. She makes them fresh on the day and doesn't use the scrag ends of meat like others do.' Sophia closed her mouth, hating the fact she was rambling, but she was so nervous she couldn't think straight. What was the girl doing here?

'You are Sophia.' The girl, Aurora, asked quietly, standing by the door. 'You must be shocked to see me?'

Sophia faced the range, taking the poker she knocked out the cold ashes as if she wanted to

106

do them serious harm. 'I can't think why you are here.'

'I found out about you.'

'Obviously.'

'So it is true. You are my mother?'

'No, Winnie is your mother. I just gave birth to you.' She straightened and replaced the poker on its stand. 'I never expected Winnie to tell you.'

'She didn't.'

Nonplussed, Sophia turned to the large table dominating the middle of the room, but it was bare and didn't afford her something to do. How did she find out about her? Then she remembered the man, the fifty pounds pushed into her hands when she spilled out her past in a fit of pique. Oh, God help her.

She spun around to the aprons hanging on a hook at the back of another door. In frenzied movements she tied on a white apron and then opened the door. 'This leads through to the bar.'

She hurried up the dark passageway and pushed open another door into the wide space of the bar room. Spilt beer and stale smoke assaulted her nostrils as it did every time she started a new day at work. Would she ever get used to it?

Aware of the girl entering the bar room behind her, Sophia rushed around the chairs and tables to pull back the old, moth eaten, dark red velvet curtains at each window, flooding the room with weak light. She pushed up the sash windows to allow fresh air to flow in and the sounds of the street outside were, for once, comforting and very normal.

'I'm sorry if my coming here has upset you.'

She turned to face her daughter, *her daughter*! The idea still was too hard to believe. Again she felt the need to laugh hysterically. 'Then why did you come?'

'I had to see you.'

'Well, now you have, so you can go.' She steeled herself from the pain that clouded the girl's eyes.

'But I thought — '

'There is nothing for you here.'

A ghost of smile appeared on her pale beautiful face. 'There is nothing for me anywhere now.'

'Go home.'

'I cannot.'

'Why?' Although she didn't want to know. She didn't want to be involved in this young woman's life, a life so far removed from her own, yet a life she once had . . .

'I cannot return home because I am with child.'

Sophia swayed and gripped the back of a wooden chair for support. Lord in heaven, history had repeated itself.

'I'm sorry.'

She glared at the girl, hating her for dragging up a past she had successfully buried. 'Go home.'

'I told you I cannot.'

'The father won't or can't marry you, I gather?'

'No.'

'Look, Winnie will understand. She did before.'

'With you.'

'Yes, with me.'

'I can't do it to them. They'd be so disappointed.'

'They'll deal with it. They must be frantic with worry. You did leave a note, didn't you?'

'Yes. I told them I had found out about you and I was going to find you.'

'Did you give them my address?'

'No. I won't return to them, but I did promise to send letters to reassure them I am all right.'

'You can't stay here.' She hardened her heart against the desolate look on the girl's face. She hadn't given her baby up to Winnie for nothing. It had broken her heart when Winnie and Josiah left with her baby, but she'd done it because she wanted her child to have a better life than she could give her. She wasn't going to let the silly fool ruin all that she had sacrificed!

'Do you know of somewhere I may go?'

'What? Like a fallen women's home or something?'

'I-I don't know.'

'No, you don't know much about anything, do you?' Sophia snapped. 'What possessed you to come here, to me? I've got nothing for you. I work as a barmaid and live in lodgings. Go home.'

The girl bent and picked up her suitcase. 'Forgive me for disturbing you.' She turned and walked out of the bar room.

Against her better judgment, Sophia followed her into the kitchen. 'Do you have money?'

'A little, yes.'

'Then buy a train ticket back to Leeds, or wherever it is you live.'

The girl's head bowed and she went through to the scullery. Sophia fought the urge to say more.

At the back door the girl stopped and looked back at her. 'Who was my father?'

She stiffened at the question. 'Nobody.'

'Nobody?' Tears welled in her daughter's eyes.

'That's right. Just some fellow I met. Can't even remember his name or what he looked like.' She took a deep breath, ashamed at the lies that rolled so easily off her tongue. She remembered everything about Alexander Finchley, a good-looking friend of her uncle's who stayed with the family one spring.

'Goodbye then.'

'Go home, please.' She begged, taking a step towards the child, the piece of her she had painfully given up so many years ago.

'And shatter their lives? I don't think so. I won't do it to them. I'll make my own way.'

'How, for God's sake?' Fear filled her. The girl wouldn't survive it and if she did what kind of life would she have? *One like mine*, a voice whispered inside her head and her stomach constricted.

'I'll work it out.' The girl opened the back door. 'You did.'

'Wait!' Sophia rushed to her side and stood dithering a few feet from her. 'Listen . . . I . . . er . . . would you like a cup of tea before you go?'

Relief flooded the girl's face. 'That-that would be nice. Thank you.'

Sophia hurried into the kitchen to throw paper twists into the range and wood kindling. Striking a match she lit the fire and fed it more slivers of wood before placing the kettle on the hob. 'When did you last eat?'

'Yesterday . . . ' The girl sat at the table, her suitcase by her side. So neat and tidy, Sophia's heart dipped at the sight of her. 'It's all been a bit of a blur actually.'

'I'll make you a sandwich.' With her back turned, Sophia busied herself at preparing the tea and a light meal. It gave her the excuse not to make conversation. She didn't know what to say anyway. Discussing shared experiences of running away didn't seem the sensible thing to do and that's all they had in common. When the silence dragged on and the food prepared, Sophia turned around and found the girl asleep, her head lying back in an uncomfortable position.

She took the opportunity to properly look at the young woman her baby had grown into and felt the stirrings of an old buried love in her breast. Softly, she walked over to her and hesitantly lifted her hand to lightly touch her cheek. The girl, *Aurora*, looked so fragile. Shadows bruised the skin under eyes. Her full lips were turned down even in sleep. Her beauty seemed so delicate. How would she cope with bringing a child into the world? Why wasn't she home safe and adored? Anger flared at the unknown man who'd brought her girl down. Thoughts hurtled around in her head. Part of her was annoyed at being in this situation, but the other, traitorous, half was overjoyed to see and be near her baby again.

Aurora stirred, her hand coming up to rub her neck, which no doubt had cramped from the unwelcome position of her head. Sophia jumped away and quickly focused on arranging the sandwich and tea on the table.

'How rude of me to fall asleep.' A blush crept up Aurora's neck, giving her some color at last.

'Carrying a baby makes you tired. Have some tea.'

'Thank you.'

'Look, I have to open up this place soon. Why don't you rest here a bit and then later I'll take you back to my place and you can stay there tonight.' Now what on earth had made her say that! She wanted to take the words back, say she didn't mean them.

'Oh, thank you.'

'Well, it's just until you get yourself sorted out.' Sophia spun away and marched into the bar room, cursing herself for being all kinds of a fool.

8

While Mrs Flannigan poured her another cup of tea, Aurora listened to the hubbub of noise coming through from the bar at the front of the building. She'd been sitting at the table for the whole afternoon and felt stiff and achy. Mrs Flannigan, a widower in her sixties, kept up the flow of talk while she cooked and Aurora was grateful for it because it prevented her from thinking too hard about the craziness of being here with her real mother.

The woman, Sophia, hurried into the room, her face flushed. Locks of her chestnut hair, a bit darker than Aurora's, had slipped from its bun and whipped about her face as she gave Mrs Flannigan more orders for hotpots.

Aurora hadn't spoken to her much since the bar opened because Sophia had to serve the customers. But they smiled shyly at each other every time Sophia came into the kitchen. Aurora was sorry to have disrupted Sophia's life, but she needed to see her, identify her as the one who gave her life. And now that she had, she couldn't think what to do next. The future stretched out depressingly long and frightfully scary.

All three of them turned when the back door opened and in from the scullery walked a large barrel-shaped man.

'Ho, what's this then?' He beamed in Aurora's direction. 'A visitor?'

'Big Eddie, this is . . . this is a friend of mine, Aurora Pettigrew,' Sophia blurted, looking guilty. 'I hope you don't mind her staying here for a bit. I'll take her home shortly, but I'll be back in a flash.' She turned to Aurora. 'This is Eddie Minton, the landlord. We call him Big Eddie.'

Big Eddie's assessing gaze roamed over Aurora. He tilted his head to one side to study her and thrust out a large meaty hand. 'Pleased to meet you, Miss.'

She shook his hand, liking him instantly. 'And you, Mr Minton.'

'Call me Big Eddie, lass, everyone else does. I never answer to Mr Minton unless I'm in trouble.' His laughter boomed out, filling the room. He hung up his coat and hat. 'Smells good, Mrs Flannigan. Is it busy out there, Soph, my love?'

'Not yet, just the regulars, but it's early.'

'Aye.' He went to walk through to the bar, but paused in the doorway. 'Take the lass off home, she looks done in.'

'Thanks, Big Eddie, I will.'

'If it's quiet later, you can knock off a bit early like.'

'Ta, Eddie.' The color in Sophia's cheeks heightened and she lowered her head as if ashamed. 'Get your things . . . Aurora.'

Aurora allowed Sophia to usher her out of the door and into the evening dusk. The street seemed busier than before and Aurora stared at the number of men and women about.

'Day shift has finished. People are on their way home from work,' Sophia said, as though reading her thoughts.

'Oh, I see.'

Sophia strode down the street carrying Aurora's suitcase. 'Don't expect anything fancy. I've had to work for the last twenty years and can only afford what my pay provides, which isn't much.'

'Of course.' Aurora walked faster to keep up with her, especially when Sophia turned into a dark alley and then again into a narrow cut. She held her breath as the stink from open drains and piles of rubbish filled the area. From the cut they walked into a large square bordered on all sides by three storey buildings, with each side having its own narrow passageway. In the middle of the square were the privies and the one tap, which serviced the area, so Sophia said as they hurried along.

Aurora stared around in horror at the dismal sight. Everything was gray, dirty and dreadfully bleak. Revulsion at the way people lived here stirred up the contents of her stomach and she clapped a hand over her mouth.

'It's not pretty is it?' Sophia stood at the bottom of a steep wooden staircase that climbed up round the outside of the building. 'This is what happens to you when you leave the security and comfort of your home. You end up in places like this. Do you understand that now?'

Aurora stared at her, upset by the hardness in Sophia's eyes. Before she could say anything, Sophia went up the stairs and using a key hung on a string from around her neck, opened the last door on the small platform. Aurora looked up at the next landing above where two small children stood watching her.

'Well, are you coming in?'

Hitching up her skirts, Aurora crossed to the open door and stepped inside Sophia's home. The gloominess of the evening light didn't help to give the room a comforting feel. On the right a worn sofa sat opposite an unlit fireplace, which also served as a small cooking range. To the left was a double bed covered with a dark red blanket and at the end of it was an old battered trunk. A small table and two chairs hugged the far corner next to a rail from which hung clothes. Mould covered the top half of the walls, which once might have been white but now were a dull mud color. Aurora shuddered.

'Yes, this is what you can amount to.' Sophia said from near the fireplace. 'See why you need to go home? Anything is better than this.'

A scream rent the air from above. Aurora jerked around thinking they were being attacked.

Sophia laughed hollowly. 'That's Minnie upstairs, likely her Barney is giving her a black eye as he does every week.' She bent and put a match to the papers and odd bits of wood in the grate. 'Close the door so I can get this fire to draw.'

Heart thumping in her chest, Aurora moved into the room and closed the door behind her, shutting out the weak light.

'I've not got much in to eat. A bit of bread and some pickled onions, but there's tea. I usually eat at the pub.' Satisfied the fire would burn, Sophia straightened. 'You can sleep on the bed, I'll take the sofa.' She made for the door. 'I'll be home

116

after midnight, but I'll take my key, so lock the door. You'll be safe enough though. No one bothers me.'

Her dread of being alone in this God forsaken place kept her immobile in the middle of the floor. Aurora watched Sophia leave and the door close again. From somewhere in the building a baby cried and Aurora stifled the urge to join in. Crying wouldn't help her, crying didn't solve anything. And as much as she wished to be safe at home in her own bedroom right at this minute, it wasn't possible. It'd probably never be possible again and so she had to make the best of it.

She looked at the bed, and despite its sagging appearance the sheets seemed clean. Besides, she couldn't imagine Sophia sleeping in a dirty bed. She might be part of the working class now, but Sophia still carried a manner about her that indicated she'd been brought up as a lady. Too tired to think clearly and too despondent to care, Aurora climbed onto the bed fully dressed and pulled the red blanket over her. All she wanted to do was sleep and never wake up.

★ ★ ★

A loud bang and laughter woke her. The room was in darkness and for a moment Aurora couldn't remember where she was. Scraping outside made her scramble up in the bed and stare in terror at the door being unlocked. Soft laughter and low murmuring carried to her and suddenly the door sprang open. Two people

117

toppled in and landed on the floor in a fit of high giggles. The stink of alcohol filled the room.

'Christ, Soph, couldn't you wait until we got to the bed?' The male voice sent shivers down Aurora's back.

'What? You've . . . you've never d-d-done it . . . on the floor before, lover?' Sophia hiccupped and giggled again.

'I've done it everywhere, my honey,' the man slurred, then belched loudly.

Horrified, Aurora, her eyes now adjusted to the night, watched as the man lying on top of Sophia on the floor began undressing her as they kissed greedily, noisily. She didn't know whether to get up and alert them of her presence or hide under the blanket and pretend she didn't exist. But what if they got up onto the bed, what would she do then? Her fingers gripped the blanket up to her chin. She opened her mouth to speak but the man moaned and she scooted to the furthest corner of the bed.

'Hurry up, Fred, I'm desperate for it.' Sophia groaned huskily. 'It's been months. Con was useless.'

'I'm coming, sweetness, wait for me.' The man stripped his trousers down to his boots, his buttocks white in the pale light spilling from the doorway. 'Open wider, my sweet. Ah, that's it.'

Revolted, but unable to turn away, Aurora watched them rut like animals on the bare wooden floor. Their grunts filled her head until she wanted to scream.

'Oh, shitting hell!' The man raised himself on his hands and abruptly slapped Sophia's cheek.

'Wake up you stupid drunken bitch, I'm not finished!'

Aurora jerked with a half shout, before covering her mouth with the blanket, but it was too late. The man swung around.

'Oh, it's the long lost daughter. Me ears have bled from her talking about you all bloody night. Crying into her beer, she was.' He kicked off his trousers properly and stood up as though it was the most natural thing in the world to stand there naked. 'You're the reason why Miss Stuck-up Sophia was drunk earlier than normal tonight.'

'Please, go away.' Aurora inched further away from him, her back pressed hard against the cold damp wall.

'I've been wanting to get into her drawers for months and she's kept me at arm's length, but not tonight.' He bowed regally. 'So thank you, dear girl.'

'Just go away.' Her gaze darted to Sophia who hadn't moved.

The man, his features hidden in the shadow of the room, glanced over his shoulder at the woman on the floor. 'She won't wake up until morning. Likes her gin as well as ale, does Madam Sophia. It helps her forget how low she's become.'

'I'll . . . I'll see to her.'

'Yes, indeed you will, but before I go, how about I see to you, hey?'

'What?' Aurora froze. 'You need to leave.'

'Soon, petal, soon.' He lunged for her and, caught in the blanket, she couldn't escape him.

He pushed her down and ripped the blanket from her. She screamed, but he pressed his hand against her mouth and nose and she twisted, unable to breathe. 'Quiet now, Missy. Just enjoy it. I'm hard as nails and it'll be over in a minute. You're no virgin I've been told, so you know what to expect.'

The more she struggled the angrier he became. Swearing, he flipped her over onto her stomach and tore her dress down along the buttons. The ripping sound drove her into a frenzy and she thrashed about, lifting her head to give a blood curdling scream.

'Shut up!' His fist connected with the side of her head. Pain made her reel. She cried out again, but he pushed her head into the pillow and smothered all sound. Frantic with the need for air, she lashed out but he was behind her, pulling up her dress, his hands under her drawers reaching to touch her most sacred place. With no air, she felt the blackness coming over her, then suddenly the pressure was off her head. She lifted up and sucked in air as the man fell down beside her, a look of surprise on his face. She screamed again.

'Stop it, Aurora, stop it!' Sophia dropped the heavy iron pan onto the bed and huddled her close to rock her in her arms. 'It's all right now. It's over. It's over.'

She gripped Sophia's blouse and sucked in air, but couldn't get enough and panicked.

'Calm down. Breathe slowly. Come on, steady now. I've got you.' Sophia's crooning voice helped to settle her enough to find the air she

120

needed to fill her lungs. She breathed deeply, eyes closed to block out the man lying crumpled next to them.

'Come over to the sofa.' Sophia stood, cradling her close.

Painfully, Aurora sat on the sofa too stunned to cry, just thankful to be breathing. She was dimly aware of Sophia moving about behind the sofa near the bed. There was a thump and Aurora turned to find Sophia dragging the man by his ankles across the floor and out the door. She stopped and grabbed his trousers and threw them over his crotch before picking up his ankles again. She dragged him out onto the landing and, with sickening repeated thuds, down the stairs. Aurora heard her vomit at the bottom of the stairs, but refused to move to help.

Five minutes later, Sophia returned and busied herself lighting the sole lamp and starting a new fire. 'I'll put the kettle on.'

Aurora stared into the budding flames as they curled around balls of newspaper and licked the broken pieces of a timber plank. In twenty four hours her world had turned upside down for the second time and she didn't think she could cope with it. She felt dirty, confused, frightened and terribly alone.

'A nice fire and a cup of tea will soon sort you out.'

'I don't want sorting out,' Aurora stated coldly. She raised her gaze up to the disheveled, disgusting woman who had borne her. 'I want nothing from you.'

'Listen, I'm sorry about what happened.'

Sophia wrung her hands together. 'It got out of hand. I had too much to drink. I didn't mean for it to happen.'

'What have you done with him? Is he dead?'

Sophia glanced worriedly at the door. 'I don't know.'

'Didn't you check?' Fear made her tremble. How was this happening? She glanced at the door expecting the police to knock at any moment.

'There wasn't time. I had to get him out and away.'

'But if he is dead they will know it was you. People would have seen you leave the . . . the public house together.'

'I'm sure he's not dead, just knocked out.' Sophia shifted from spot to spot, her expression haunted. 'God, why did this have to happen!' She paced the floor in front of the fire. 'This is all your fault.'

'Mine?' Wide-eyed Aurora stared at her.

'Yes. If you hadn't come here I would never have been upset enough to drink as much as I did. If I hadn't been so drunk I'd never let slimy Fred Godfrey anywhere near me, let alone brought him back here. God almighty!' She pulled at her hair and groaned as if in agony, wiping her hands down her skirts as if to rid them of muck. 'Why did you come here?'

Unfazed by her *mother's* anguish and feeling amazingly calm, Aurora stood. It was as though a weight had been lifted off her. She felt beyond pain, beyond caring. 'I certainly didn't come here to be raped, that I can tell you.' She crossed over to her suitcase placed at the end of the bed and opened it. She took out a short-waist jacket to cover her ripped dress and put it on, and then picked up her case.

'What are you doing?' Sophia frowned, her hands clutching at her skirts, the ends of which were inches deep in filth from the pub and yard.

'I'm leaving. It's what we both want.'

'No. You can't. It's the middle of the night.'

'I don't care.' And she didn't. She didn't care about anything or anyone and she doubted if she ever would again. She simply wanted to walk and keep on walking until hopefully she died.

'Aurora, don't be silly. Stay until morning.' Sophia moved towards her, but Aurora jerked back and so she stopped and held up her hands in apology. 'Sit back down and have a cup of tea. It'll be morning soon.'

'I'll go now.'

'It's not safe!'

Aurora laughed mockingly. 'And it's safe here?'

'Look, just sit down. Please.'

The desperation in her voice left Aurora cold. 'I should never have come. You are right. There is nothing for me here.'

'No, please, Aurora, we can talk.'

'Good bye.' She opened the door, but Sophia dragged at her arm.

'No, Aurora. I won't say goodbye to you again.' Tears ran down Sophia's face. 'It broke my heart to do it the first time. I'll not do it again. You're my baby.'

'I'm nobody to you.' She looked at her without

pity or feeling. How could she when she was hollow inside? 'I must go.'

Sophia flung herself to the trunk at the end of the bed. 'Wait, wait!' She pulled out clothes and items that rolled on the floor. 'Here, have this!' Sophia thrust at her a large leather pouch. 'I want you to have this.'

'No.' Aurora recoiled. 'I'll not take anything from you.'

'Don't be bloody stupid!' The pleading had gone from Sophia and was replaced by anger. 'Be sensible and think. You have to learn to take what is offered if you're going to survive. How do you think I endured all these years alone?' She shoved the bag into Aurora's hand. 'There's a lot of money in there. Money I've been saving for years so I could get out of this life and away from this area.'

'I'll not take it.'

'Yes, you bloody will.' Sophia stood hands on hips. 'It's too late for me now, but if you won't go home, then at least start a new life with something. It'll be enough for you to rent a few decent rooms or sail to a new country.'

'No, I — '

'Think of the baby if nothing else. Start again somewhere nice. Don't end up like me . . . ' A sob broke from Sophia and she buried her face in her hands.

Aurora gazed at her bent head with its unwashed hair, the bowed trembling shoulders. She wanted to shake this woman, who wasn't anything like she had imagined. But what had she imagined her to be? Soft and loving like

124

Winnie? She didn't know. Only, never had she dreamed she'd be a cold-faced drunken whore. Was this what her own life would become?

Sophia gulped and wiped her eyes. 'I'm sorry for everything. You must think I am worthless, perhaps I am. One mistake ruined my life. I don't want that to happen to you. Why do you think I gave you up? I didn't want you at first, I admit that, but, but afterwards . . . I wanted something better for you, the kind of life I had before . . . before — '

'Before you had me.'

'I am not a bad person, please believe me.' Desperation filled Sophia's brown eyes. 'I drink sometimes to forget, to ease the pain. I sometimes will lay with-with a man to remember what it is like to be held and caressed, to be wanted and not be alone for a short time. I can't help being lonely, sad.' Another sob broke free from her. 'I'm sorry if that shames you, but it is the truth. I never wanted to be this way, to end up like this.'

Aurora turned away. She stepped out onto the landing, feeling something bite her leg. She itched under her clothes and shuddered to think of fleas on her. A tomcat yowled and she saw two rats run across the yard. Such a hateful place. How could anyone live here and not go mad? She thought of her mother, Winnie, of how distressed she would be to know her sister lived in these dire circumstances.

Taking a deep breath, Aurora looked back at Sophia, standing in the dim light dejected, crushed. 'Is there enough for two?'

125

Sophia's head wrenched up. 'What?'

'I said is there enough money for the two of us.'

'You want me to come with you?'

She shrugged, not really caring either way, but deep inside she knew she couldn't leave with this woman's hard-earned money. 'If you want to. It's the only way I'll take your money.' She watched the emotions and indecision flitter over Sophia's face, then she nodded, a look of determination in her eyes.

'Yes. Yes, I'll come with you.'

9

They decided to stay in the room until morning. Although wary of each other, they discussed what they should do and London seemed the obvious choice. There, they could easily find work and accommodation, or at least they believed so. Now they'd had time to calm down, Sophia wanted to stop and say good-bye to Mrs Flannigan and Big Eddie. They had been good to her and she couldn't leave without thanking them. Aurora agreed, though the thought of the despicable Fred Godfrey and what happened to him made her want to run from the place immediately. Thankfully, there was no evidence of Fred as they left the building.

Being early, Big Eddie was asleep in his rooms above the pub, but Mrs Flannigan was in the kitchen cutting up meat for her hotpots. 'I'll go up and get him, Soph, lass. Sit yourselves down and have a sup.'

Five minutes later Big Eddie stomped into the kitchen, his hair standing on end and the top buttons of his shirt undone. 'What's this Mrs Flannigan says about you sodding off, lass?'

'Sorry, Big Eddie. I know it's short notice.'

'It's no bloody notice at all,' he boomed, gratefully accepting the cup of tea Mrs Flannigan placed before him. 'What's the bloody rush?'

Sophia glanced at Aurora. 'This is my

daughter. She needs my help.'

Big Eddie and Mrs Flannigan looked from one to the other. 'That explains some of it then.' He sipped slowly, watching them over the cup rim. 'She looks like you.'

'Yes,' Sophia whispered. 'Only much prettier.'

'Where you heading to?'

'London.'

'London?' Big Eddie banged down his cup, slopping his tea. 'Nay lass, that's no place to go.'

'We'll get work there.'

'You've got work here.' He frowned, scratching his beard growth. 'I might be able to give the young miss here a couple of shifts, if she can pull her weight.'

'Thanks, Big Eddie, but she's having a baby and . . . well . . . ' Sophia blushed and wrung her hands as though it was all her fault.

An awkward silence descended in the kitchen, broken only by Mrs Flannigan's rhythmic chopping.

'Listen, I've an idea.' Big Eddie reached for the teapot and refilled his cup. 'Me sister Aggie was telling me last week at me Uncle Bert's funeral, that me Aunty Ethel was in a bit of bother because Uncle Bert has property and stuff that she didn't know much about.' He took a quick sip. 'Anyroad, I went and saw her last Monday morning and offered to help her out, like, and on Tuesday we met with the solicitors.'

Aurora had not been interested in anything being said, but now lifted her head to listen more closely.

'So, this solicitor chap tells me Aunty that

Uncle Bert had some terraced houses in a small lane off George Street. And I know for a fact one of those is empty because he mentioned they were all rented but one. How about I see if you can rent it?'

'George Street?' Sophia screwed up her nose.

Big Eddie sat his large frame back in his chair and the timber joints squeaked in protest. 'Nay, I know it's not Buckingham bloody Palace, but it's better than nowt. Two up and two down it is. A sight better than the hovel you're in, that's for sure.'

Aurora watched Sophia consider it, and for one fleeting moment she wanted to say no thank you and leave. But the thought left as quickly as it came and she remained in the numb, passive state that she liked where she didn't have to think or feel. After days of making the most important decisions in her life that got her to this point, she was happy to let others take control.

'Think about it, lass,' Big Eddie spoke softly. 'George Street isn't far and you can still work here. I'll make sure the rent is low enough for you to manage on. Me aunt put me in charge of the whole terrace.'

Sophia turned to her. 'What do you think?'

'Whatever you want.' She shrugged, not really caring. What did any of it matter if she lived here or London or the wilderness of Africa? Her life was over. The plans and dreams she had of her future with Reid had gone. All that remained was a half existence with strangers.

'Well, it might be worth a shot.' Sophia nodded. 'We can continue to save and then one day perhaps move somewhere nicer.'

'What about Fred Godfrey?' Aurora murmured. If Fred was dead then Sophia would be a murderer. Would she be an accomplice? A shiver of fear brought her out of her frozen state. The thought of her parents reading about her in a newspaper filled her with terror.

'What's this about Fred?' Big Eddie peered at them.

Sophia quickly told him the story, her hands shaking around the teacup.

Big Eddie stood. 'Right, I'll go see what's happened to him then. I know where he lives. Stay here, I'll be back as soon as I can. I'm not letting Fred sodding Godfrey be the reason I lose my best barmaid.'

Finishing her tea, Aurora watched him shrug on his coat and leave by the back door. A wave of drowsiness settled on her. She wasn't only physically tired, but mentally as well. She couldn't remember the last time she had a decent night's sleep.

'Why don't you go upstairs for a few minutes rest?' Sophia said tenderly.

'I don't think so.' She straightened in the chair.

'I just thought — '

'No, thank you.' The curtness in her voice made Sophia turn away. Aurora rubbed her head, weary of it all. If she had the strength, she would have cried. No, she would have got up and walked away, walked all the way home if possible. She squashed that thought immediately. There was nothing at home for her, except to bring heartache to her family.

She must have dozed in the end, for she was suddenly awake to the sound of voices. Big Eddie and Sophia stood at the end of the table talking softly. 'What's happened?'

'Nothing.' Sophia smiled, the relief in her eyes. 'Fred is alive.'

'Good.' Her neck ached and Aurora rolled her shoulders to ease the stiffness from them. The clock above the range showed she'd slept for over an hour.

'While you were sleeping, Eddie and I got a few things from Edinburgh Yard. We borrowed a cart from a friend of Eddie's. We thought we could go to the house today. Are you happy with that?'

'Whatever you wish.' Aurora followed them out and around to the front of the pub to see a cart piled with odds and ends from Sophia's room. Her own suitcase nestled amongst it all.

'Sit up with the driver, lass.' Big Eddie hoisted her up before joining Sophia on the end of the cart and they set off along Hope Street. Flo and Ida stood on their doorsteps and gave them a wave while whispering behind their hands.

Within ten minutes they halted before a short terrace off George Street. The row of five houses on each side were identical to the other. At the end of the cobbled lane was a high brick wall, on the other side of which, Big Eddie told them, were the backyards of the other tenements in the next street. He directed the cart driver to the end of the short lane to the last house on the left. A green painted door was peeling, so too was the white paint from the windowsill beside it and the one above.

Aurora was conscious of the doors opening to the other houses, of curtains twitching and curious faces peeking out with avid interest. The driver helped her down, an older man who hadn't spoken to her once. She waited with Sophia while Big Eddie found the right key to open the door from the numerous others he had on a large steel ring.

With trepidation, she entered the narrow dark hallway of number nine. Big Eddie filled the confined space, and she was thankful when he opened the first door on the left and stepped into the small square parlor. She winced at the mould on the ceiling and walls. Dead ashes filled a poky fireplace and the dirty window facing the lane kept out the weak sunlight. The floorboards were uneven and held not a scrap of carpet. The place smelt musty and damp.

'Let's see what the back room is like.' Big Eddie put false merriment into his voice and led the way down the passageway into the kitchen. 'It has a range.' He beamed, as though that would make living here the height of luxury.

'And a scullery.' Sophia injected another positive note, but Aurora couldn't hide her revulsion and shuddered.

'Out the back is the lav,' Big Eddie peered out of a tiny filthy window. 'It's all paved, so no mud. There's a coal house too and a gate leading into a cut that runs along the back of these houses and into George Street.' He turned and rubbed his hands together. Despite it being summer the house was freezing cold as if it had never felt the warmth of the sun or a fire. 'Shall we go upstairs?'

The rooms above repeated the worn, uncared for appearance of downstairs. Two rooms of the same size and containing the same amount of mould and dampness.

Once downstairs again, Big Eddie went out to help the driver unload the cart while Aurora and Sophia stood in the front room staring at what was going to be their home.

'I'm sorry it's not much,' Sophia muttered, wiping a hand across the top of the mantelpiece and finding it covered in thick dust and mouse droppings.

'Does it matter?' Aurora gazed out of the window not seeing the dirty lane and houses beyond, but thinking of the comfortable home she'd left behind, of Reid and his smiles, the laughter in his eyes. All of it was gone now. She turned to Sophia, pushing away those memories. 'Besides, it's better than being on the street. I could easily have ended up there. I ran away without enough money to see me through. Stupid really.'

'You weren't thinking straight, that's all.'

'No.' She stopped when the men brought in the iron bed and heaved it up the steep staircase.

'We'll have to share the bed, if that's all right. Until we can buy a new one.' Sophia went to the door. 'When the shops open in the morning we'll go out and buy some things for the house, to make it more homely.'

Aurora turned away to stare blindly down at

the ashes in the grate. Homely? She would have laughed if it hadn't been so tragic.

★   ★   ★

Reid nodded to Tibbleton, the Pettigrew's butler, handed him his hat and walked into their drawing room. His gut churned in anticipation of seeing Aurora again, but he was also very nervous, like a boy on his first day at boarding school. Why hadn't she returned his letters? He didn't understand what went wrong, but he meant to find out. They had planned a future together, so why was she giving him such silence? Had she changed her mind or found another? He could hardly believe such a thought though when she'd been so passionate towards him and the instigator behind their lovemaking. Was that the problem? She had regrets about that night? Was she too embarrassed to face him? He had to talk to her, let her know he loved her no less for giving him her body. He only loved her more in fact.

'Reid, my dear, do come in.' Winnie Pettigrew smiled, but immediately coughed into a hand-kerchief. 'Do forgive me.' She took a sip of water from the glass on the table beside her.

'How are you, Mrs Pettigrew?' he asked, though he could see her struggle to breathe normally. He was taken aback by her paleness and the loss of weight since he last saw her. The dark blue of her dress seemed to make her face bloodless. A blazing fire burned even though outside the sun shone brilliantly. He sat as far

134

from it as was polite.

'Oh, this silly cough stays with me.' She waved her white handkerchief in frustration. 'Did Tom's little party go well?'

'Indeed. Though it turned into a bigger party than I had been led to believe.' He smiled, still feeling the tired after effects. He'd drunk too much the night before last and didn't go to bed until long past dawn. He slept the day away because of it, but it had been many months since he'd felt able to relax and enjoy himself. Yesterday, he had attended to estate business for his father and now he was free to spend time with Aurora. 'Tom and his friends are still about, and extending the party over days instead of one night. The staff spends each morning righting the house again. I shall have to stop it soon, and be cursed because of it.'

'Oh dear. It is well and good your mother isn't here to see it.'

'If Mother had been here there would have been no party at all.' Reid looked around the neat peaceful room. He always felt at home in the Pettigrew's house. A warm atmosphere filled each room, something that his mother's expensive decorations failed to achieve.

'I'm sorry Josiah isn't home today. He's taken the girls into Leeds with him. They will shop and he has some business to attend to.'

'What a shame. I had thought to go for a ride and hoped Aurora would like to join me? She has gone with them?'

A nerve twitched in Winnie's eyelid. She began to cough violently, so much so that he got up to help her and offer a glass of water. Minutes passed before she had recovered her breath. She looked paler and drawn. 'I'm sorry, Reid. I am not fit for company I'm afraid.'

'I will take my leave then. Will you tell Aurora that if she wishes to go for a ride later to let me know? I must return to London tomorrow.'

'Actually, Aurora is not here. She . . . she has gone to stay with one of Josiah's aunts near Manchester.' Winnie didn't meet his eyes and she started coughing once more.

He tried to hide his surprise. 'But James saw her the day before yesterday.'

'She left early this morning. Josiah took her to the station for the early train.' Her cheeks flushed bright red and she coughed again.

'Will she be away long?' He swallowed the disappointment burning in him. He had missed her by hours!

'I'm not sure. Josiah's aunt is of an age where she enjoys and needs company while she travels. Aurora might stay with her for some months. I think they might go to Europe . . . '

'Europe?' He blinked, appalled to think of Aurora being away for so long. How could Aurora leave without telling him, without seeing him? Why didn't she send him a note to explain what she was doing?

Feeling something wasn't quite right, Reid left the house and strode across the gardens towards the dividing gate between the properties. He swore inwardly. His father's illness and business concerns had kept him in the south far longer than he expected, too long. Damn it! Why didn't he come straight away when she stopped sending her letters? What kind of fool was he to make love to her and then leave her for months on end! Now it was too late. She probably thought he had used her.

He dry washed his face in weary frustration. He hadn't wanted to go back to London without seeing Aurora, and asking her why she didn't return his letters. However, it was unexpectedly much more complicated than that. Why hadn't she left him a message? And if only James had told him she was at the house on the day of the party and not forgotten to mention it until the following morning.

He smashed his fist into his thigh. If Aurora had changed her mind about him then he wanted to know the reason why!

10

A door banged somewhere in the street and Aurora jumped. She'd been awake for a few minutes listening to the rain. She turned her head and stared at Sophia fast asleep beside her. She hadn't heard her come in after finishing work last night, although she tried to stay awake in case of a repeat performance with another Fred Godfrey. But the continual tiredness she felt now meant her night vigil only lasted a couple of hours before sleep claimed her.

The cold bedroom was dimly lit by the gray morning light. Aurora hurriedly relieved herself in the pot and then dressed, which included putting on her shoes and coat for warmth. She left the room and went downstairs. The fire had gone out in the kitchen overnight and there was no paper or kindling to relight it, not that she knew how to, really. She'd never made up a fire in her life.

Sophia had bought a few food essentials yesterday evening, but the sight of the pickled onions, hard bread and cheese was unappealing and with no tea to warm her, the swell of hot tears rose. She couldn't do it. She couldn't stay here!

She sat on the wooden chair brought from Edinburgh Yard and hugged her coat tighter about her, staring around the ghastly kitchen. It was nothing like the spotless cleanliness of the big warm kitchen at home. There was no Mrs Pringle to cook her bacon and kippers, or eggs and toast. There was no fire and newspaper, no mother to smile at her, no father to discuss matters with. She even missed Bettina and Harriet's squabbles over which hats they'd wear that day. If only she could go back to that night in the woods. As much as she adored Reid, she wished with all of her heart that she hadn't taken that final step with him. If she wasn't with child she could be home now, maybe not happy, but at least safe and with her family.

'You're up I see.' Sophia came into the kitchen carrying the piss pot that she emptied down the drain in the back yard. Raindrops glistened on her brown tumbling hair when she returned. 'Has the fire gone out?'

'Yes.'

'Hmm.' Sophia searched around the kitchen. 'Did we use all the paper lighting it last night?'

'Yes.'

'I remember, it kept going out, didn't it? I must have used enough paper and wood to start a dozen fires.' She laughed, but it sounded forced in the stillness of the chilly kitchen.

'I'm going back to bed.' Aurora left her without another thought.

Sophia followed her up the hallway. 'I promised Big Eddie I'd go in early today to help him with the accounts, but I thought we could get a few things this morning first.'

'I don't care,' Aurora climbed the stairs, wishing Sophia would just go away and not come back. No matter how hard she tried, she couldn't

139

accept this house as her home or Sophia as her mother.

'Well, we could leave it until tomorrow, if you want? And then go together before I start my shift.'

Aurora closed the bedroom door on her and crawled into the bed still warm from their bodies. She snuggled down and closed her eyes. She didn't care if she never woke up.

Knocking brought her out of a dreamless sleep. She groaned and turned over, ignoring the noise. It was quiet for a few moments and then the knocking started up again. She kicked at the restraining blankets and realized she still wore her shoes and coat. Pushing her straggly hair back from her face, she left the bed and went downstairs. The incessant knocking boiled her patience. She yanked open the door and glared at the young woman on the step. 'What?'

'Oh!' Alarmed, the woman stumbled back, one hand on her swollen stomach. 'I'm sorry.'

Seeing her condition, Aurora's inherent good manners made her instantly contrite. 'Forgive me. I didn't mean to startle you. You woke me.'

The young woman, with striking light blue eyes stared unblinking. 'Er . . . I'm your neighbor, from across the road.' She waved behind her, indicating the opposite doorway painted cheery red. 'I-I thought I'd pop by and say welcome to the lane.'

'Thank you.' Though she didn't feel grateful at all. The rain had stopped, but the gray sky hung low as though ready to send down another deluge. The houses seemed to huddle together

140

dank and grubby and it did nothing to lighten Aurora's spirits.

'Me name's Lily, Lily Bradshaw, but I'm still known as Lily Middleton too. I wasn't married long you see . . . '

'Pleased to meet you, Mrs Bradshaw. I'm Aurora Pettigrew.' She felt embarrassed by her unkempt appearance and hid behind the door, while trying to pat down her hair and straighten her rumpled blouse.

'I'm home alone during the day, so if you need anything, just pop along.' Lily smiled, transforming her thin face into something quite lovely.

'Thank you.'

'Would you like to come over and have a cup of tea? I've just made a current cake.' At that moment Aurora's stomach grumbled in response and Lily laughed lightly. 'Me dad has the same response to me cooking.'

Aurora couldn't help but return her friendly smile. 'I would like that, however I . . . ' Again, she put a hand up to her ruffled hair. 'I'm not fit for company.'

'Nay, don't worry about that. You'll only be sitting in me front room, not on ceremony for the queen, God bless her.'

'I don't know.' Aurora peeked up the lane, noting that the miserable weather kept people indoors.

'I've got a nice fire going.'

The cold and moisture from the house seeped through her clothes and Aurora nodded. Tentatively, afraid the neighbors would see the state of her, she hurried across the cobbles with

Lily, her face warm from embarrassment, knowing that her clothes were creased and she hadn't washed in a long while. 'Please excuse my appearance. I'm not looking my best. We haven't any water or . . . '

'I told you, it's fine.' Lily dismissed her concerns and ushered her past the red painted door and into number 10. At once Aurora sensed the difference between the two houses. Lily's home, though sparingly furnished, was warm and bright. White washed walls, greenish brown carpet, cheap paintings, ornaments on the polished sideboard, lace curtains at the window, a cheerful fire and a well-worn sofa and chair created a snug feel.

'Please sit down.' Lily gestured to the chair by the fire, one hand tucking up her black hair which had escaped from its bun. 'I'll bring in the tea things.'

Aurora sat and stared around. Two miniatures, a man and a woman enclosed in small wooden frames, stood in pride of place on the mantelpiece. A black shawl lay over the corner of the sofa and a few books and a newspaper were on the floor by the chair she sat on.

'Here we are.' Lily placed the tray on a small table near the fireplace. 'It's not much, I'm afraid.'

'It's better than I could make myself.'

'It's nice having new people in the lane.'

'You have a nice home.'

Pouring out the tea, Lily glanced up with a shy smile. 'Me mam was a proud woman. She lived here all her life and woe betide anyone mucking

142

up her house. Me Dad learned that lesson soon after marrying her.'

'So you live here with . . . ' She accepted the teacup, noticing hers was the only one with a saucer.

'Just me Dad now, he's called Noah Middleton. We lost Mam two years ago.'

'I'm sorry. And your husband?'

The light died from Lily's eyes. 'I lost him four months ago. He worked on the river barges.'

'How awful for you.' Aurora sipped her tea, savoring the sweetness. Sophia always forgot to buy sugar because she didn't use it herself, but Aurora missed having sugar in her tea.

'It was and still is hard to think of meself married and widowed within months.'

Aurora wondered how Lily's husband died, but etiquette prevented her from asking. She knew from one discussion with her father that two rivers, the Ouse and Foss, were like veins splitting the city of York and via them trade and industry thrived.

Lily brightened. 'And your family? I saw a lovely-looking woman leave your house this morning.'

'Oh . . . er . . . that is my-my . . . ' Aurora swallowed past the lump in her throat. 'That is my mother, Sophia.' There she had said it out loud for the first time. It felt wrong, foreign on her tongue. She put down her teacup, frantic that Lily would ask more questions. 'I'm sorry. I really must go. I . . . er . . . '

'Oh, that is a shame.'

'Thank you for the tea.' Aurora scuttled to the

door, her face aflame once more with shame.

'Just knock if you need anything. The door's always open,' Lily called after her as she ran across the cobbles and into number nine. She shut the door and leaned against it. Oh God. Her hands shook. In fact she trembled all over.

The smell of damp filled her nose and she shivered. The dark recess of the passageway depressed her and for a wild moment she wanted to run back to the warmth of Lily's house. Instead, she climbed the stairs, took off her coat and shoes and went to bed. Perhaps she could sleep her life away.

When she woke again the bedroom was completely dark. Confused, it took her a minute to readjust to where she was. Grabbing her coat and shoes she made her way downstairs to find the front room just as cold and dark as the bedroom. She walked into the kitchen and was surprised to find a cheery fire burning and the subtle smell of something cooking. On the table was a note.

On the stove is some of Mrs Flannigan's hotpot. There is enough wood to last the night and I brought home a candle and some tea leaves. In the morning we might go shopping.
Sophia

Aurora spied a box of utensils on the floor and quickly unpacked it and set the table for herself. She added more wood to the fire and gloried in the heat radiating out, although if she moved only a few feet from the stove, the intense cold soon sent her back to the fire. In spite of it being summer this house was permanently cold. She lit the candle for extra light and took the pot off the hotplate. From a chipped bowl, she ate her simple meal. Reading the remains of the newspaper Sophia had used to light the fire provided a diversion from her dismal surroundings while she ate.

After two cups of tea and a belly full of delicious meaty hotpot, she felt more herself. Her scalp itched for the need of washing and probably lice, but the bucket of water in the scullery was nearly empty and she had no idea how to get more. A child shouted from somewhere in the lane and there was an answering crack and a yell from a man. The darkness outside and the rain hitting the window made her aware how alone she was. They didn't have a clock and so unable to tell the time, she wondered how long it would be before Sophia came back.

The house creaked and suddenly scared, she decided to go back to bed. Despite sleeping most of the day and evening she was still tired and after her meal, the biggest she'd eaten in days, and the cups of tea, she felt replenished for the first time in a long while, but the sluggishness of her mind remained and all she wanted to do was curl up into a ball and hide.

* * *

The routine of sleeping most of the day and night became normal for Aurora as the days drifted by without affecting her. Most times

145

when she woke, Sophia was at work and a note would be on the table. Aurora ate whatever food was supplied and then returned to bed. She lost track of time and days. Sometimes she'd hear knocking on the door, but ignored it. Other times the sounds of the neighbors and street noise would disturb her and she'd listen to people going about their normal routines, but never once did she want to join them. She didn't wash or change her clothes. Her hair became matted and lank. She used the piss pot and left it for Sophia to empty, not caring about the stink. The bedroom became her world, her hell, and Sophia's growing mutterings mostly went unheard and unanswered.

By the morning of the end of the second week, the periodic rain ceased and the skies cleared to a brilliant blue. Aurora woke and stared around the room washed in sunlight. She jumped and smothered a scream at the sight of an enormous rat sitting in the corner, its beady black eyes staring back at her. Terrified, she huddled in the bed, wondering if Sophia was in the house. She opened her mouth to call out, but the rat ran out of the bedroom door.

The thought of getting out of bed and going downstairs with a rat loose in the house petrified her, but she needed to use the pot and her stomach grumbled for food.

Gathering her courage, she dragged on her coat that she'd thrown over the end of the bed the night before and slipped her feet into her shoes. Inch by inch she crept downstairs, her eyes wide looking for any evidence of the vermin. She found Sophia downstairs cooking bacon on the stove. At some point she'd cleaned the little kitchen window and sunlight streamed in, banishing most of the gloom but it also showed up the room's dreariness in stark relief.

'You're up? I hope you're hungry.' Sophia forked out strips of bacon onto two plates.

'Yes, thank you.' Relieved she made it without encountering the furry beast, Aurora sat at the table. 'There was a rat in the bedroom.' She shivered in disgust.

'Huh, is there any wonder? This place is a haven for them I should imagine. I don't have time for cleaning it as much as it needs.' Sophia shrugged, using the back of her hand to swipe at her hair. She looked awful, her eyes watery and her nose red.

'Are you ill?'

'A slight cold.' Sophia turned away to bark out a cough that seemed to scrape at her chest.

'You should stay in the house today.'

'I can't. It's nothing. I got caught in the rain a few nights this week, that's all.'

'Well, go back to bed for a while before you start work.'

'I wish I could, but I'm doing Eddie's accounts for him regularly each morning now for extra money.'

'Oh.' Aurora blinked. She had no idea what Sophia did in the mornings before her shift started at three o'clock. 'I didn't hear you coughing in the night.'

'That's because I slept downstairs on the old sofa in the front room. I didn't want to disturb you.'

Astonished by her selflessness, Aurora stared. 'But it's freezing in there.'

'I was all right.'

'I beg to differ. Without adequate covering you would have been very cold and now you're sick.' Anger and guilt made her snap. She poured out two cups of tea, surprised to see milk in a small jar and sugar in a cracked bowl. 'You've been to the shops?'

'Not properly. Mrs Flannigan has been giving me odds and ends from the pub's kitchen until we can sort ourselves out.'

'This smells good.'

'I haven't been eating that much lately, didn't have an appetite. But I woke up this morning and was hungry. So, I went out early and bought a couple of things.' After putting the empty pan in the scullery, Sophia sat down on the opposite side of the small square table. Her dark hair was tied in a bun and she wore a brown skirt and cream blouse. She looked smart and tidy and Aurora frowned, she'd not been aware of the transformation. But then, she'd not been aware of anything for a long time.

Sophia cleared her throat, not meeting Aurora's gaze. 'I thought that if you were willing, we'd go and buy a few things. Make the house more livable.'

'I suppose we must if we are to live here.'

'You want to leave?' Sophia paused in cutting up her bacon. 'Of course I don't blame you for wanting to go home.'

'I'm not going home. I told you, I cannot return and hurt them. That part of my life is over. I can never go back. They are all better off without me.' A dull ache hit her chest whenever she thought of her family, of Reid.

'As you wish.' Sophia turned away to wipe her nose.

Thoughtful, Aurora stirred her tea. For some reason, perhaps it had something to do with the sunshine, she didn't know, but she knew she'd turned a corner in some respect. She couldn't continue sleeping the days away like she'd been doing. Although the prospect of living here made her quake, she knew there was no other option.

Pushing her half-finished breakfast away, Sophia left the table to blow her nose in the scullery. Aurora felt the stirrings of worry. She looked like Winnie did at Easter when she was ill. 'I think you should go back to bed,' she told Sophia when she came back into the room.

'I can't, not today. Big Eddie is away at the breweries this morning and we're expecting a delivery. I've got to go.' She took a last sip of her tea, ignored her food and reached for her brown coat lying on the back of her chair. 'I'll see you tomorrow.'

Aurora nodded and watched her leave the house. Someone in the street was singing and a baby cried in one of the houses, but Aurora felt dreadfully alone. She rose to go back to bed, but hesitated, knowing that she had to break this cycle. But what to do? The thought of going outside filled her with dread. Loud knocking on the front door made her jump.

'Aurora!'

Recognizing Lily's voice from number 10, she

hurried to open the door. Lily held Sophia in her arms, keeping her upright.

'What's happened?' She helped Lily to get Sophia inside.

'I don't know. I was sweeping me front step and saw her collapse at the corner. She was coughing badly.'

'I'm all right, really.' Sophia's face was a gray mask with a shiny red nose.

'No, you're not. You're going to bed and no arguments.' With Lily's assistance they started upstairs.

'I've got work to do.' Sophia's weak protest was followed by a bout of harsh coughing.

'Not today you don't. Eddie will understand and Mrs Flannigan will have to cope.' They got her onto the bed and Aurora took off her shoes and tucked her under the blankets. 'Rest now. I'll make you some tea.'

Downstairs, Aurora fiddled with the fire, hoping it had enough heat to boil the kettle. It didn't. She wrung her hands in despair.

'You've never looked after yourself before, have you?' Lily asked from the doorway.

Humiliation sent a blush up her neck to burn her cheeks. 'No.'

Lily gently pushed her aside and fed sticks to the fire and then when they were alight added small pieces of coal. 'Don't let the heat get down too low if you know you're going to cook on it later. Otherwise it takes a lot of coal to get the heat back up.' Lily went into the scullery and washed the teacup in the bucket. 'Coal is good to bank the fire with if you're going out to the

150

shops. It's much better and cheaper than wood, but it's also dirtier, which means we have to clean more.'

'I see.' Aurora nodded, praying she'd remember these facts. Simple tasks were suddenly overwhelmingly difficult.

'Get into the habit of going to the street tap every morning and filling two buckets of water. Me Dad does this for me before going to work. On Mondays when everyone is washing, there's a queue for water. Best bet is to go as early as you can.' Lily set out the tea things. 'Do you have a tray?'

'I've no idea.'

Hands on hips, her neighbor glared at her. 'Does Sophia take care of everything as well as go out to work?'

'I've been ill myself.' Shame and misery bowed her shoulders. 'No, that is not true. I've been hiding, wallowing in self-pity.'

'Why?'

'Because my life has become intolerable.'

'We don't all have perfect lives. I don't see what makes you so special you can use your mother this way. You should be grateful you have a mother.'

'I have two actually.'

Lily's eyes widened. 'Two?'

Sagging into a chair, Aurora told her briefly about her life.

'I thought you were a toff from the way you speak and your clothes. I told me Dad you were and he said I should stay away, as you'd not want to mix with the likes of us in this street.'

151

'I'm glad you haven't stayed away.' Aurora smiled and she meant it.

'I'm happy to be your friend, but the others might blow hot and cold on you. They wouldn't want someone in their lane looking down their noses at them.'

'I wouldn't.'

'Sometimes people like you can't help it. It's bred in.'

Aurora thought of Julia and nodded in understanding. Julia would rather die than talk to someone beneath her. As far as Julia was concerned the working class only existed to serve her. They were nameless and faceless people.

'So you can't go back home because you're to have a baby?'

'Yes, and please keep it to yourself. I'd bring disgrace to my whole family if they found out. I will not do that to them.'

Lily chuckled. 'I'm not likely to meet them, am I?'

'No, of course.' Aurora shook her head, feeling completely foolish. Once, not long ago she would have considered herself clever and educated in many ways, but within twenty-four hours of leaving home she knew she'd been mistaken. She knew nothing of the outside world. Oh, she knew how to speak French, play the piano, what were the countries of the British Empire, how to embroider a fine scene onto a tablecloth, how to treat guests and converse about mundane events in the social calendar, but she didn't know how to light a fire, cook a meal, wash clothes, buy food and the thousand other things needed to survive life without a wealthy father or husband to provide for her.

Lily poured the hot water from the kettle into the teapot. 'Well then, as I see it, you've got to make the best of what you have here.'

'It's not so easy.'

'Nonsense. If you look for excuses you'll find them, but that won't help you, will it?' She gave Aurora a cheeky smile. 'As they say, sink or swim isn't it?'

'I suppose so.'

'Take it from me, swimming and surviving is better than drowning. I can't swim a stroke but if I fell into the water I know I'd make it to land somehow. Sheer bloody mindedness probably.' Lily grinned and passed Aurora the cup. 'Take that upstairs and then we'll start cleaning this place up. And you should meet the women in the row. They're a nosy lot, but with hearts of gold.'

When Aurora returned downstairs after Sophia had fallen asleep, she found Lily, wearing an apron over her large stomach, washing up the breakfast things in the scullery, and felt instantly guilty. 'Leave that, Lily, please.'

'What, so they be left to pile up for Sophia when she comes back down. I don't think so.'

'No, no, I wouldn't do that.'

'But you have been, haven't you?' She wiped her hands on a bit of a rag that passed as a towel. 'I don't know how you've lived with yourself, letting her take care of you as if you were a bairn or an invalid or summat.'

'I know and I'm ashamed.' Aurora shrugged helplessly. 'I couldn't face it all. I wanted to die.'

153

Lily looked at her as if she spoke a foreign language. 'Die because you no longer have a nice home and fancy clothes?' She snorted with condescension. 'Welcome to how the rest of us live, Miss Pettigrew.'

'I'm sorry.'

'No good saying sorry.' Lily strode out of the scullery and into the kitchen. 'I'm happy to help you, but you've got to want to do it an' all.'

'I do.'

'Really?' Lily didn't hide her doubts.

'Yes.' Aurora gazed around the dingy kitchen that even the sunshine couldn't make pleasant and knew something had to change. 'Circumstances have forced me to lead this life and so I shall.' She squared up her shoulders, feeling better and more confident about the future than she had in weeks.

'Right then. Let's get scrubbing!' Lily paused in going back to the scullery. 'I don't suppose you have an apron?'

11

Although the bottom six inches of her skirt was wet and caked in grime, and her arms ached as though she'd been pulled by a horse all day, Aurora sat back on her heels and surveyed the sitting room with a good deal of satisfaction. While Lily worked in the kitchen, she had started in the front room. After sweeping cobwebs from the corners and ceiling, she'd washed the walls, scrubbing at the mould, before cleaning the window inside and out. She'd been amazed at how much dirt had accumulated in one room. With the window clean and open, extra light and fresh air filled the room. Lastly, on her knees, she had scoured the floorboards.

'My, that's a grand job.' Lily came in to stare at the difference. A smudge of dirt coated one of her cheeks and her white apron was now mucky and stained. 'Come, inspect the kitchen.'

Aurora followed her into the kitchen and it was her turn to stare at the transformation. The walls had been cleaned, so too the floor, the range was black-leaded, the window washed and the table set for the dinner that was cooking slowly on the stove.

'Oh, Lily.' Tears of gratitude rose and impulsively Aurora hugged her new friend to her side. 'Thank you so very much.'

'Nay, we've a long way to go yet.' Lily grinned,

155

adjusting the plain square tablecloth taken from her own home.

'We have some money.' Ideas sprang into Aurora's head. 'I mean Sophia has been saving for years, and she wanted to buy some things that we need.'

'Tomorrow we'll go shopping.' Lily nodded, frowning with thought. 'You've not got much at all.' She pulled out a chair and sat down, rubbing her back.

Seeing the action, Aurora felt full of remorse. 'I'm sorry that you've had to do this. You shouldn't have in your state.'

'Leave it out, I enjoyed it.' Lily laughed. 'Though I'll admit I'm ready for a bath and me bed!' She rose awkwardly, her stomach seemingly larger by the minute. 'Speaking of which, I'd best go and see to me Dad's meal or he'll be yelling the street down.'

'Thank you for everything.' Aurora stood on the front doorstep and watched Lily waddle across the cobbles to her own door. The sun was setting over the rooftops, but the day had been warm and the tepid heat remained.

'I'll see you in the morning, and remember to get your water!' Lily waved and closed the door.

'Good evening, Miss.'

Aurora turned. She hadn't noticed her immediate neighbor next door was leaving their house. 'Oh, good day.' She smiled at the young man, who she guessed was about eighteen.

'I'm Anthony Murphy.' He slapped down his flat cap over a tumble of black curls and hooked his thumb over his shoulder to indicate inside.

'Me mam said she'll come around tomorrow like, now you up an' about. She's been bad with her legs lately.'

His thick accent, a mixture of Irish and Yorkshire, made it hard for her to fully understand him, but she smiled anyway. 'Lovely. I'll look forward to it.' Though she didn't know how his mother knew about her, unless she saw her cleaning the window earlier. 'I'm Aurora.'

'Gawd, what a name, a right mouthful.' He laughed.

She blinked in surprise. 'You can call me Aurrie, if you want.'

'That's better.' He grinned boldly. 'Do you want extra water for t'night?'

'Oh, er . . . ' She kept forgetting about the water. What a nuisance it was to collect one's own water.

'I can get it for you, no charge this time since it's your first time needing it.'

'I thought the tap was turned off at night?'

'Aye, 'tis, but I know how to get more elsewhere. Though only for those who pay.' He touched his nose and winked. 'On the quiet, like.'

It took a moment for Aurora to understand his meaning. 'I see.'

'I usually charge those wanting me services, but for you I'll do it for nowt, since you an' your Mam have been ill.'

'That's very kind of you.' She wondered if the whole street knew her business.

He looked sheepishly up and down the street. 'Do you have a bath?'

She thought hard, did they? No, she didn't think so. 'Not yet. We need to buy one.'

'Leave it with me.' At that, he strode off down the lane whistling as carefree as a lark.

Aurora closed the door and went into the sitting room. How odd to be discussing water and a bath out on the street as if it was a natural thing to do. She added coal to the blazing fire. Despite the heat of the day, Lily said the fire would dry the place out a bit and take off the constant chill, which enveloped every room. As usual Lily had been right, for the fire was making this room much more habitable, even though Sophia's old horsehair sofa was the only piece of furniture in it.

After placing a wire mesh screen around the fire, one of the many things she had borrowed from Lily, Aurora then went into the kitchen to attend the soup simmering on the stove. The thought of cooking exhilarated and frightened her. She wished now she had joined Bettina and Harriet when they badgered Mrs Pringle into teaching them. Thinking of her sisters sent a sharp pain of longing into her heart. How she missed them and their chatter. She also missed her mother and father and wondered how they were coping without her. She'd have to write to them. Her thoughts turned to Reid, but she banished them. Thinking of him would only depress her and she couldn't afford to be brought down as low as she had been. Sophia needed looking after and, well, as Lily said, it was no good harping after something she couldn't have. Reid had to be put from her heart

158

and mind. Depriving herself of him was for his benefit, even if he didn't know it. He would marry Miss FitzGibbon and be happy, and what he felt for her would fade. She just hoped her own feelings would diminish as quickly too.

On the table was a list of all the things she needed to buy. She quickly added stationery to the list and then concentrated on ladling out some soup into a bowl. Lily had brought over her spare tray and set it up for Sophia's tea. With a slice of bread and a square of cheese joining the soup, Aurora carried the tray upstairs, wincing at how her body ached in ways she never thought possible. Who knew cleaning could be so hard and taxing? At home she had never given it a thought when Dotty, Fanny or Hilda cleaned. Now they had her sympathies.

Sophia was sitting up in bed, blowing her nose when Aurora entered the room. 'I've brought you up some food.'

'You cooked?' Sophia gasped, openly amazed.

'No.' She smiled self-consciously. 'Lily, the one who brought you home this morning, she made it.'

'How kind.'

'You must eat it all. You need to regain your strength.' Aurora studied the room with new eyes. Now she had experienced the pleasure of making a room fresh and fit for use, she was keen to subject each room in the house to a thorough clean. She'd not give any beastly rat an opportunity to feast near her again.

'I feel so bad about Big Eddie.' Sophia murmured between sips of soup. 'He relies on me.'

159

'I sent a note to him this morning. Well, Lily asked a lad, Arthur Filey from number 5, to run the message to Eddie.'

'Oh, good. That's better than not showing up at all.'

Aurora sat on the end of the bed. 'I'll call in and see him tomorrow, if you like, and explain.'

'I'll be up and about by the morning.'

'I doubt it.' She shook her head, feeling the need to take care of Sophia as she had taken care of her. 'Another day in bed is called for I think. You've no strength to go to work.'

'But — '

'No buts. I'll do it on my way to the shops.'

'Shops?' Sophia's eyes narrowed suspiciously, the last spoonful of soup halfway to her lips.

'Yes. Lily is coming with me. We require a great deal of things for this house if we are to have any comfort at all.'

'Don't spend all the money, Aurora.' Her tone hardened, sounded even scared. 'We must keep some back in case of emergencies. We have rent to pay and food and fuel. I won't live day to day as I have done in the past, not knowing if I'd be able to buy the next meal.'

'But I don't understand. You had money. Why did you go without when you had money in your trunk?'

'Only until recently did I have it. Not at the beginning. When I was . . . when I first left home I had nothing.' Sophia lifted her chin in defiance. 'After living hand to mouth for years I soon learned to save when I could. I refused to spend it unless I was in a dire situation.'

160

'Starving could be deemed dire,' Aurora said sarcastically. Living in Edinburgh Yard was a perfect reason to spend the money and get somewhere better.

'Big Eddie always allowed me to eat at the pub. I was never starving.'

'But why live in that awful place when you could have found somewhere decent.'

'Edinburgh Yard allowed me to save because of the low rent. Besides, I only slept there. I spent all my spare time visiting the library or galleries. I could stand living there as long as I knew that one day I would be free of it. I had plans of moving to the countryside.'

'And I ruined those plans.'

'No, not necessarily. We can always go to the country when we've saved some more. One day I'd like a small farm, or at least a cottage with some hens. My parents, your grandparents, always had a lovely home with a garden.'

Aurora thought of the farmland around home, the fields full of wheat and barley, lambs frolicking, the bellow of a cow, wildflowers and birds. She missed the openness of the countryside, of walking or riding Princess without seeing another soul for hours. She sighed, thinking of her lovely mare. Princess, like her family, had been another sacrifice for those few hours in the wood with Reid.

'What is it, Aurrie?' Sophia whispered. 'You look so dreadfully sad. Are you thinking of home?'

'I try my best not to, only sometimes it creeps up on me before I know it.'

161

'I understand. It took me a long time to adjust when I first left home. It is very hard to settle for this after living in a comfortable home.'

'Do you regret leaving them?'

'I had no choice. My father disowned me.' Sophia shrugged and fiddled with the edge of the sheet. 'But I always planned to get away from the city. I didn't care how long it took me. I just worked for the day when I'd leave York to go to the cottage in the country.'

'Then that is what we shall do. Buy a cottage, or a farm.'

Sophia laughed softly and rested back against the pillows. 'Rent a farm more like.'

'All right, rent then. But we need furniture for this place, so that will diminish the amount somewhat.'

'Yes. However once it is bought, we can save again.'

'And I will go out to work.'

'Oh no, Aurora.'

'Why not?'

'Because you've never done it before.'

'Neither had you at the start. I can learn just as you did. With both of us saving we can go that much sooner.'

'Yes, but you'll have the baby to consider.'

'It's not born yet.' Her thoughts raced ahead. 'And after it is, perhaps Lily will mind the baby, along with her own while I work. Or we can do shift work?'

'We'll see.' Sophia sounded skeptical and pushed the tray away. 'It's harder getting work than you can imagine, especially when you've

162

not done any before. I worked all sorts of dreadful jobs before I became a barmaid at Big Eddie's.'

Aurora rose, took the tray and headed for the door. 'I'm determined that we'll live out in the country. I don't want my baby growing up in the tenements.'

'So you're keeping it then?'

'I suppose I am.' She didn't really want to think about it, the baby. Until now she had successfully ignored thinking about the child growing in her womb. The whole prospect scared her witless. 'How much money is in the pouch?'

'About eighty pounds now.'

'That is a good sum.

'Yes, thanks to your Julia Sinclair.'

Aurora shivered, remembering Julia had paid for the information that led her to be here. 'Why did you reveal so much?'

'The money was a large temptation. I thought it would bring me closer to my cottage. I wasn't thinking straight. The money was all I wanted. I didn't care why someone wanted to know about me. Later I hoped it was Winnie or . . . even my father . . . I suppose I wanted to be found.'

'Your parents died when I was five.'

'Did they?' Sophia blinked, surprised. 'I didn't know.'

'You've not been in touch with Mother, with Winnie?'

'No.' Sophia glanced away. 'I had to make it a clean break or I wouldn't have survived it at all. I had to try and forget you, or at least only think of you as safe and happy.'

163

'I was.'

Sophia looked back at her. 'Then it was worth it.'

'Shall I leave you for a while to rest?'

'Yes.' Sophia turned her face away and Aurora knew she was thinking of her parents, of the life she once had, of the pain she had endured.

Downstairs, after eating a bowl of soup herself in the clean kitchen, Aurora filled the bucket with hot water from the kettle and washed the dinner things. When the scullery door opened, she nearly dropped the plates onto the stone floor.

'Hey there,' Anthony Murphy called out, lugging a tin bath through into the kitchen. 'Where d'you want this then?'

'You gave me a fright. Don't you know how to knock?'

'Sorry about that. Had me hands full, like.' He dumped the bath with a bang on the floor. 'I'll get the water.'

Aurora stared at the tin bath, suddenly eager to have a proper wash. She couldn't remember the last time she did. Her scalp itched.

Anthony brought in two buckets full to the brim of water. 'There's your lot, Miss.'

'Thank you very much.' Imagine being grateful for water. She couldn't believe it.

'Right, I'll be off then. Enjoy your bath. If you ever need owt, Tony Murphy's your man.' He gave her an exaggerated wink and, whistling loudly, left by the scullery.

Twenty minutes later, Aurora sat in the bath, a quarter filled with warm water. She'd used her own supply as well, nervously hoping she'd remember to get out of bed early to queue for more. Yet, nothing could take away the pleasurable feel of washing herself completely from head to foot. She washed her hair with a small knob of soap she found in Sophia's belongings. The lank greasiness of her long hair now felt lighter, her scalp tingled. Red blotches covered her body where fleas had bitten her, and she noticed how thin she'd become. She had no swell of pregnancy to remind her she was pregnant and worried if the baby had died. How would she know? For a moment she pondered on such a thing happening. No baby and she could go home! Then just as quickly she admonished herself for such horrid thoughts. For all the wrongs she'd done, she didn't want to kill her child.

When the water become too cold she hopped out and dried herself before the kitchen fire. She dressed in a clean chemise and nightgown, and wrapping Sophia's shawl about her shoulders, went into the sitting room to check the fire.

Sitting on the sofa, she dried her hair some more. It lay across her shoulders in long soft curls. The leaping flames were soothing and the bath had made her lethargic after a busy and hard working day. She placed her hand on her stomach and thought again about the growing child, or at least she hoped it was. How long did it take to become the size of Lily? This was the first time she had actually touched her stomach in protective reference to the baby inside and she was surprised by the loving warmth that she felt towards it. Her and Reid's child. She was determined to give this child the best life she could under the circumstances and that meant a good home. Tomorrow would be the start of a new beginning for her and the baby.

★ ★ ★

The following morning she woke as the black sky was turning gray and pink. After quickly dressing, she took two of the buckets and headed outside. A stream of women and men were doing the same, all heading to the tap at the end of the lane.

'Now then, lass, you're up and about?' One woman, with bright cheeks and dancing dark eyes gave her a wide grin.

'Aye, it's good to see you.' Another older woman nodded. 'We've been wondering who you were, like.'

'Your mam works in The Yellow Moon, don't she?' said an elderly man filling his bucket.

'Yes, she does.'

'Have you been poorly, lass?' another asked.

Aurora nodded, feeling as if every pair of eyes was on her.

'What's your name, lass?'

'Aurora.'

'My, that's a pretty name, ain't it, Jean?' A big loud woman nudged the smaller version beside her. 'I'm Dilys Potter and this here is me daughter, Jean. We live at number four.' She jerked her thumb over her shoulder to indicate the houses. 'That's Alfie O'Cleary, he's a widower and lives at number one.' She nodded

166

to the elderly man and then to a boy about ten years old. 'And that young lad, Cyril, belongs to the Harris family in number six. There's eight of them.'

'Pleased to meet you.' Aurora smiled, wishing they'd all go back into their houses. They weren't unkind, but she didn't want all this attention.

Dilys pointed to two women filling buckets. 'That's Hetty Barclay in the yellow dress and t'other is Jane Fulton. They're from numbers two and three. Jane's got five kids and her husband is away working on the railways.' She continued to introduce everyone else but Aurora soon forgot their names and which house they lived in. Was it the Fileys at number five and the Morrisons at number eight or the other way around? 'All who's missing is Lily Bradshaw and Noah Middleton and widow Mary Murphy.' Dilys finished with a chuckle.

'I've met Lily.' Aurora thankfully filled her buckets and headed back to her door.

'Aye, Lily said she'd helped you get the place knocked into shape. You should have called out, we'd have helped you. We allus pitch in to help each other in this lane.'

'Thank you. I'll remember that.'

'Drop in for a cuppa anytime you like, lass. We're a friendly lot,' Dilys called out. Aurora smiled in thanks and gratefully closed the door. She quickly boiled the kettle and reheated the leftover soup as there was nothing else to eat. She had to buy food today and learn to cook as well. After she ate, she took most of the money out of the leather pouch and hid it behind a loose brick in the scullery. The purse now held a few pounds. Loading the tea tray, she then took it upstairs to Sophia. Aurora was pleased to see her awake, although she didn't look any better. 'Here's your breakfast. I'm sorry it isn't much.' Actually, she was ashamed to serve such a dismal fare.

'I'm not that hungry, anyway.' Sophia struggled to sit upright. 'I'm so tired. I didn't sleep well.'

'Were you thinking of your parents?'

'Yes, though for what good it'll do me I don't know. What's done is done.'

'Stay in bed again today. I'm going to the shops with Lily, remember. So just sleep.'

'Don't forget to tell Big Eddie.'

'I won't. I'll be back later.' Back in the kitchen, Aurora drank some tea and from her small case used her brush to tidy her thick hair that was wild after its wash. In the end she tied it up with a black ribbon and pinned on a small black felt hat to control it as best she could.

'Hoo hoo!' Lily came down the passageway, wearing a green print dress and red shawl. 'Are you ready?'

'Yes.' She slipped the money pouch over her wrist. 'Lead the way.'

'I think Low Petergate is a good place to start,' Lily said as they left the lane and headed down George Street. 'Then maybe Coney Street for the better stuff.'

'I have to spend wisely,' Aurora warned.

'I know, but it'll be fun.' Linking her arm through Aurora's, Lily giggled. 'I'm going to enjoy spending your money.'

Four hours later, Aurora's feet throbbed and Lily's back ached as they sat drinking tea in the kitchen of number nine. To Aurora it seemed as though they had visited every shop in every street in York. 'I'll never be able to stand on my feet again,' she moaned, rubbing her toes.

'But we achieved so much.' Lily grinned, gazing around at the packages that filled the kitchen.

'And there's more to come when the deliveries start arriving this afternoon.' Aurora opened the nearest brown paper wrapped parcel and lifted up the white linen tablecloth and soft white towels. She had spent more than she should and was worried Sophia would be cross with her.

Lily opened another parcel to reveal curtains, a pair in rich green for the front room and two pairs in a soft rose for each of the bedrooms.

Despite her earlier forecast of never standing on her feet again, Aurora stood to put away the food they'd bought at the market, wincing with every step. The narrow pantry cupboard had looked bare and neglected, but now she filled it with pound bags of sugar, oats, tea and flour, jars of pickled onions and jam, as well as a small basket of eggs. She'd also bought vegetables and some fruit.

In the scullery, the coldest part of the house, she placed cheese, bacon, a parcel of sliced tongue and a pat of butter on the marble shelf in the corner.

Returning into the kitchen, she found the bread and the sponge cake she'd bought. She'd been surprised by the amount of pleasure she received when buying food. At home the only time she

169

dealt with food was sitting down to a meal in the dining room. Yet, today she learned the simple enjoyment of choosing what she needed, and with Lily's help, selecting the freshest produce.

Placing the bread on a wooden board, she smiled tiredly at Lily. 'I'll make a sandwich for Sophia. She'll be hungry.'

'Let me do that while you arrange everything else. I can make sandwiches sitting down.' Lily laughed, cutting the bread into slices. 'Tomorrow I'll teach you how to bake a cake. You can't go on buying that kind of stuff. It's cheaper to make your own.'

When a knock came at the door, Aurora went along to find the first of the deliveries had arrived. Bedroom furniture, including a new bed and mattress for Aurora to sleep on in the second bedroom, plus a small set of drawers. Also, a few things for the sitting room, a side table and a wooden chair with a padded seat upholstered in brown velvet and a round oak occasional table and a green velvet footstool. An extra indulgence had been a wing-backed chair in faded chintz, for the old sofa wasn't big enough for more than two people. She also purchased a large rug, decidedly worn in places, but still showing its swirl pattern in blue and brown. While she directed the men where to place everything, she was aware of the women standing on doorsteps watching with interest.

'Been shopping, have you lass?' Dilys stated the obvious as she crossed the cobbles. 'Let me give you a hand.'

'Oh, really, Mrs . . . er . . . ' Aurora blushed,

forgetting the woman's last name.

'Nay, lass, many hands an' all that.' Dilys barged inside. The other women and children in the street seemed to take this as a signal and all did the same. Aurora stood by the door lost for words as the house filled with the noise of furniture being moved and women's voices.

As she was about to close the door another horse and wagon drove down the lane, this from the ironmongers. In came boxes and crates of lamps, pots and pans, a foot warmer, two flat irons, a broom and several brushes, china crockery, extra cutlery, jugs and numerous other things Aurora didn't remember buying. However, one thing she was happy to see was paint. She couldn't wait to whitewash the entire house.

For a moment she panicked as strangers moved her things, touched and commented on what she'd bought. Her frustration grew into anger at their rudeness.

'They mean no harm, Aurora.' She turned to see Sophia coming slowly down the stairs, a handkerchief to her nose. 'This is their way. I know you aren't used to it. I wasn't either at first. But don't allow it to bother you, because the day may come when you need them.'

'You might be right, but I feel . . . ' She couldn't relay in words how she felt, except the word *invaded* hovered on her lips.

'It'll be all right. They'll leave soon, once their curiosity is sated.'

'I hope so.'

'I won't ask how much you've spent today. I dread the answer.'

Aurora felt her cheeks redden. 'I'm sorry. I'm not used to controlling how much money I spend. Father was always generous . . . '

'I can imagine. Never mind. What is done is done.'

She swallowed back another apology. 'Go back to bed. I'll bring you up some tea and a sandwich.'

'Will you cope?' Sophia's eyes mirrored her concern as she glanced towards the kitchen full of women and children.

'Yes, I'll have to, won't I?' She tried to keep the irritation from her voice.

'You'll have to make them all some tea.' Sophia sighed resignedly, climbing back up the stairs. 'Otherwise they'll talk about you being tight and unfriendly.'

'Oh, very well.' Aurora shoved her way through the milling women and small children underfoot and went into the kitchen where Lily sat pouring out cups of tea and handing around slices of cake. Lily was fast becoming a very good friend and she squeezed her shoulder lightly in thanks. Much later, with her tea quantities diminished and the cake completely gone, Aurora surveyed the downstairs rooms. She'd sent Lily home to lie down for a while before her father, Noah, came home, and with Sophia asleep upstairs, a comforting silence descended. The house seemed more welcoming now, not just because it had extra furniture, but because people had been here, there'd been laughter, and chatter and jokes. Neighbors, again some of whose names escaped Aurora, had washed up in

172

the scullery and wiped down the table as Dilys swept the little yard out the back while Jean black-leaded the range. Hetty Barclay and Jane Fulton proudly hung the curtains in the front room, but on hearing that Aurora forgot to buy lace net, they hurried to their homes and found some spare and put that up too. The warmth of the fire did plenty to diminish the gloom and chill of the growing evening. Aurora sat on the new chair and with a pen and paper drew up another list of things needed. Blankets headed the list, then a clock, a picture for the wall, a rug for the kitchen. Lost in her thoughts, she jerked when a loud tapping came at the kitchen window. Intrigued, she left the sitting room.

A stranger came in through the scullery. A small woman, no more than five foot and wearing all black tottered into the kitchen as if she'd been doing it for years. Aurora didn't know her, and her first thought was to get a new lock fitted to the scullery door. 'May I help you?'

'I'm Mary Murphy. I live next door.'

'How do you do.' Aurora smiled at Anthony's mother.

'I'm not so bad now I'm back up on me feet. Sure an' haven't I missed all the excitement of having new people in the row.'

'Oh yes, your son, Anthony, told me you've not been well.'

'Aye. There's times when it's difficult to walk. Me legs have always been the bane of me life, but sure an' I'm not complaining.' Her Irish lyrical voice affected Aurora in a way she never thought possible. This small, dainty woman before her looked as if a slight breeze would blow her down, but her voice was strong and so was the look in her clear green eyes. Aurora knew she would like Mary Murphy.

'Will you come into the sitting room and have some tea?'

'I wish I could, lass, but I'm to be getting back to me own kitchen and cook for me son. He's the only one left at home now and sure as I can't get used it. Eighteen I had and only one left.'

'Eighteen children?'

'Like shelling peas, lass, shelling peas.' Mrs Murphy laughed and went back into the scullery. 'But you're welcome next door whenever you like, an' if you're wanting anything, just give my Anthony a knock. There's not much that he can't find. God bless him.'

'Thank you, I will.' Aurora watched her leave by the back gate and then carefully added coals to the fire to heat up some hot chocolate for Sophie. She ached everywhere and didn't fight the huge yawn that escaped her. She gazed around the kitchen at the parcels and wrapping and boxes left from the shopping. What a day, the kind of which she never thought imaginable only a few months ago. But look at her now, stirring warm milk in a dark kitchen in the bowels of York. Her throat tightened with threatening tears and she gulped hard. How long would it take for her to think of this place as home and to accept that her family and Reid were lost to her forever?

12

'I really don't think this is a good idea.'

Aurora raised her eyebrows at Sophie as they sat in the kitchen eating porridge for breakfast. 'Why not? With us both working we can save more money for the cottage in the country.'

'I know, but you've never worked before.'

'Neither had you, but you managed it.'

'You are pregnant.

'So were you.'

Sophia tutted irritably. 'We can think about you going out to work after the baby is born.'

'But that is months away.' She pushed away her empty bowl. 'I cannot sit around here doing nothing. I'll go mad.'

'And I'll go mad with worry if you're out there.' Sophia took both bowls and placed them in a bucket then poured hot water from the kettle over them. 'We'll be fine with my wage.'

'We'll be better with two wages.' Aurora tidied the table. 'I will not be dissuaded on this.'

'Aurrie, please.' Sophia laid a hand on her arm. Aurora looked at it in surprise as they had hardly touched each other after the first night in Edinburgh Yard when Fred attacked her. Sophia released her. 'It's not as easy as you might think. You're different and you'll be mixing with others who will resent you.'

'I will not sit in the house all day while you go out to work. It's not right,' Aurora said, putting

175

on her coat. 'Just let me try, please.' She pinned on her hat and headed out the door. 'I'll see you later.'

In the lane, the women were washing windows, sweeping steps, or simply prattling to each other in the morning sunshine. Their children, those too young to go to school, played at their feet.

'Morning, Aurrie,' Dilys called, pausing in giving her front window a good clean. 'You're off shopping again?'

'No. I'm off to find work.' This statement had all the women scurrying to her, intent on giving her their opinion.

'Nay lass, you'll never stand it.' Hetty Barclay looked at the others to back up her comment. 'You're not made for it. A slip of a thing like you.'

'I can and I will, Hetty.' Aurora continued walking, more determined than ever.

'Call in and see Jim Thompson at his warehouse in Parliament Road, lass,' Dilys said. 'He might have something going.'

'Or try the market,' Jean added. 'I work there a couple of days a week on the fish stall.'

The other women called out various suggestions and wished her well.

'Thanks, I will do my best.' She waved and rounded the corner only to nearly bump into Mrs Murphy. 'Oh, I'm sorry!'

'No harm done, lass.' Mary Murphy smiled. 'Off to the shops then? Sure an isn't it the blight of our lives?'

'I'm looking for work.'

At once Mrs Murphy became serious. 'Are you really?' She glanced up and down the street as though weary of someone overhearing them. She stepped closer. 'Do you mind hard work?'

'I don't know. I've never worked before.'

'Nay, then forget it.' She stepped away.

'What were you going to say?'

'It don't matter. I doubt you're strong enough anyway.'

'I won't know until I try.'

'Listen, I know of a place. Ellerton's Eatery in Jubbergate. You can get kitchen work there. It's hard work, mind, standing on your feet all day. The money is good and higher than most places because the owners are the worst two bags of misery that you're ever likely to see and there's summat not right there.' She glanced up and down the street again. 'I hear Ellerton likes to walk on the other side of the law, but you didn't hear that from me.' The old woman tapped the side of her nose.

'Thank you for letting me know.' Aurora smiled.

'Don't thank me yet, lass. It's not the best place for you to go to, but keep it in mind if nothing else comes about.' Mrs Murphy, head down, hurried away.

Aurora spent the next two days walking the streets of York enquiring for work at everywhere she could think of. Most of the shopkeepers asked for her experience, and when they found out she had none, turned her away with a sympathetic refusal. The market holders shook their heads, and one even laughed openly at her, saying she couldn't make enough money to keep her family together, never mind pay someone. One factory foreman had immediately guessed she was a runaway and forcibly removed her from the entrance saying he wanted no trouble from her father.

Standing on Lendal Bridge, watching the murky water flow gently beneath it, Aurora was beginning to get depressed about her lack of success. All around her were industries, but the minute she opened her mouth and they heard the way she spoke, the owners sent her away with a flea in her ear about wasting their time. To a man they all told her to go home and stop playing silly beggars. One even mumbled that if she was his daughter she'd get a flogging for trying to take a job from someone who needed it more than her. Perhaps she should have borrowed clothes from Lily and not worn her best outfit of black silk, but at the time she had wanted to look her best. Foolishly, all she had done was drawn attention to herself.

The low horn of a boat sounded and she started. With a sigh, she turned away from the river and walked to the end of the bridge. Standing here wouldn't get her a job. Then she thought of the eatery Mrs Murphy told her about and decided to head there.

The outside of the teashop was painted a deep green with red window sills, the sign proclaiming it to be Ellerton's Eatery hung neat and tidy above the door. Aurora walked in and spoke to the waitress nearest to her.

'If you're looking for a job, go around the

back.' A young woman, dressed in black with a small white apron told Aurora the minute she said she didn't want tea but work.

Going through a narrow alley between the buildings and picking her way through the refuse coating the yard behind, Aurora made it to the back area of the eatery. A tawny cat watched her progress to the door from its advantage on top of a large pile of crates and barrels. She knocked on the door, listening to the fearful racket going on inside. Someone was screaming and yelling abuse and this was only stopped by the sound of a loud crash. Aurora stepped aside quickly as the door was flung open and a woman burst out, slapping on her flat hat. She turned back to the other larger woman standing in the doorway. 'You can stick your job where the sun don't shine, Ellerton, you stupid bitch! And you can tell that to your slimy husband an' all! The filthy swine.'

Aurora shrank back as the large woman, Ellerton, she supposed, turned purple with rage. 'Why, I'll have you, you dirty slut!' She shook her fist in the air and then spotting Aurora, peered at her. 'The entrance is around the front, Miss.' Her voice changed instantly into a false accent of superiority.

Aurora smoothed down her coat, which Sophia had pressed last night. Today she looked the best she had done since leaving home. 'Good day. Mrs Ellerton, is it?'

'Yes?' The woman's eyes narrowed suspiciously. 'What do you want?'

'I-I was looking for work.'

Ellerton looked at her for a long moment. 'You're not from around here are you?'

'No.'

'Are you married?'

'No.'

'On the run from the law?'

'No.'

'And you want work?'

'Yes.'

'I can tell from the look of you you've never worked a day in your life. Am I right?'

'Yes, that's true.' Aurora felt her spirit leave her as easily as Ellerton's false accent left her.

'Right, well, come in then.' Ellerton demanded. 'What's your name?'

'Aurrie Barton.' The name slipped out without thought, but she decided to go with it. Aurora Pettigrew was no longer real, simply a person who used to exist in another world.

'I want no troublemakers, understand? You do you work and shut you gob. It's hard graft, but I pay well for it. No one can accuse me of not paying what's right and decent.'

'Yes, of course.' Aurora followed her into a large scullery, and beyond a wide doorway she saw a busy kitchen full of people working. A tall man in a chef's hat swore in French at a serving girl.

'Hang your coat on that hook there.' Ellerton lifted her chin in the direction of the row or hooks on the wall. She smoothed down her red and black striped silk dress with its dainty black lace at the collar. The outfit was at total odds to her language and stern attitude. 'This 'ere is

180

Nancy, and that's Peggy.' She pointed to the two women bent over large stone sinks, their arms coated in gray soap suds. 'Yer start at seven every morning except Sundays, when we're closed. Yer finished at seven at night or when the work is done. Is that clear?'

Aurora nodded, slightly amazed. Ellerton was dressed like a lady but talked like a skivvy.

'Yer pay is two shillings a day. We pay well, as I said, but you have to earn it, understand? Slack off just once an' yer out.' She stepped to the kitchen door. 'Peggy, show 'er what's done.'

'I'm to start right away?' Aurora stared at her wide-eyed.

'Aye. What you waiting for?' Ellerton went into the kitchen and yelled at someone for not cutting the sandwiches neat enough. 'Do you want people to stop coming, you silly cow?'

All of Aurora's instincts told her to run from here, but before she could act, Peggy gave her a wide smile. 'Cheer up. We'll not see her in here again today. She's dressed to mingle with the customers out front.' Peggy grabbed a clean apron from a hook on the wall and passed it to Aurora. 'Mrs Ellerton usually stays out the front. She adopts a voice better than any toff's and sucks up to all her customers. This is the best teahouse in York, but if any of them lot came out the back here they'd soon see a different Mrs Ellerton.'

After tying on the apron, Aurora made no move, she just watched Nancy and Peggy wash pots, pans and china in a whirl of frenzied activity.

181

'Come on then. Get cracking. It'll pile up with just two of us now Viv's gone.' Peggy went to the back of the scullery to a large fireplace. Upon iron racks were heavy cauldrons of boiling water. Long wooden benches full of drying china and glassware stood on either side of the fireplace. 'Give us a hand.'

Aurora hurried to help her pour the water into the stone sink just as two young girls came in from the kitchen carrying a tray each filled with dirty cutlery.

Peggy used the back of her hand to push away strands of her sweat-soaked ginger hair. 'We wash everything that comes in from the kitchen. We've got to have the cauldrons full at all times and on the boil. We never wash with cold water. Under each sink are scrubbing brushes, soaps and pots of baking sodas. All that you need.' Peggy went back to her sink and poured the hot water in. 'We wash glassware first and then the china, but that's been done for today. Nancy and I will wash the cutlery now and then start on the pots and pans. If you stand on the other side of Nancy you can dry what we wash. You'll find there are containers for each type, spoons, forks and all that.' Peggy bent over the sink to work and Aurora went to stand beside Nancy.

'There's the towels,' Nancy murmured, pointing a wet gray-sludged hand to a rack above their heads filled with white towels. 'When you have a full tray place it on the stand by the door, someone will come and get it.'

Aurora smiled in thanks and reached for a towel. The women grew quiet as they worked.

Hot steam from the sinks caused them to sweat and Aurora's blouse stuck to her like a second skin, while strands of her wet hair lay against her forehead and face, irritating her.

'You're lucky to start so late in the day,' Peggy said, heaving a copper pot out of the water. 'You've missed most of the work.'

'I'll be here tomorrow,' Aurora replied with a determined nod.

★   ★   ★

The following morning, she arrived at the eatery as promised. She'd woken early, gone to fill the buckets at the tap, eaten a boiled egg for breakfast and left the house while Sophia still slept. Her back ached and her arms were sore to lift above her head, but she was resolved to work as others did. Money was needed and it didn't fall out of the sky. Earning it was the only way to get them out of the lane and into the clean countryside.

'Morning, Aurrie.' Nancy and Peggy chorused on seeing her. They both wore drab clothes of dark colors, their boots unpolished. 'Did you sleep like the dead?'

'I did, yes.' She grinned, forgetting about clothes and appearances. What people wore to work was hardly worth thinking about. Soon they'd be sweaty and mucky and although Aurora had taken care with tying up her hair and sponging her black skirt, she knew that here, she wasn't being judged and it felt rather liberating.

'Hurry up, Mademoiselles.' Claudio, the chef,

put his head around the doorway from the kitchen. 'My pans will not clean themselves.' He twirled the long ends of his very busy moustache. 'If you behave I might bring you in a pastry fresh from the oven!' He kissed the tips of his fingers and spun away.

Aurora donned her apron and wondered what their reaction would be if she suddenly spoke in French to Claudio. Her smile faded. Speaking French was in the past and wouldn't help her now, but just for a moment she forgot where she was, who she was and in her head spoke a few sentences of the chef's language.

'Come on, Aurrie,' Peggy called from the fire. 'Give us a hand.'

While they worked Peggy explained that Claudio and the kitchen staff came in before dawn to bake the tasty pastries and soft breads that had a reputation as the best in York. And which was why at only seven in the morning, the scullery was brimming with dirty pots, pans, trays, boilers, enamel bowls and numerous other utensils a busy kitchen needed to prepare for the day's trading ahead.

'Have you run away from home, or were you thrown out?' Peggy asked, scrapping sauce off a bowl.

Aurora blushed at her directness. 'I left, but it is complicated.'

'Well, it always is, isn't it? Still, you aren't the first and won't be the last.'

'You won't tell anyone, will you?' She looked from one to the other. 'I don't want anyone knowing about me.'

'It's none of our business, is it, Nancy?' Peggy answered for them both. 'Make sure you stay away from that toad Mervin Ellerton though. He likes the girls, if you know what I mean? And he likes the pretty ones like you even more.'

'Is he Mrs Ellerton's husband?'

'Aye, but he acts as though he's a single man. He's twelve years her junior do you know? And he's got his hands up more skirts than a dressmaker.'

Aurora stared as Peggy roared with laughter and made crude jokes.

Peggy, giggling and wiped her eyes and looked at Aurora. 'Don't worry, just keep him at arm's length and never go anywhere with him or your belly will be swelling before you know it.'

Swiftly ducking her head, Aurora didn't comment and concentrated on stacking piles of clean plates.

More trays were brought in and the three of them became too busy to talk any more. Within an hour, Aurora's back ached. By the time they had a short break four hours later, the ache was so violent she thought she'd never stand up straight again.

A kitchen girl brought in a tray holding three cups of tea and three plates of thick meat sandwiches and three jam tarts. Aurora copied Nancy and Peggy by grabbing her teacup, the plate and tart. She followed them out into the back courtyard, where they sat in the warm July sunshine on upturned crates.

'We sit out here when it's nice,' Peggy stated, sipping her tea. 'We can get a refill of tea, too, in case you're wondering. Claudio knows how hard we work and he turns a blind eye to it. Tomorrow we'll likely have soup and bread. We get whatever is served in the dining room, you see.'

'Despite the hard work, it seems a good place to work then?' Aurora asked, her sandwich of sliced beef and pickles quickly disappearing. She'd never been so hungry in her life.

'It's not so bad as long as Mervin keeps his distance,' Peggy told her between mouthfuls. 'Mrs Ellerton is a craggy old cow, a right tartar, but she runs a good business and makes plenty of money. Though Mervin adds to it in his own way.' She snorted in disgust.

'Oh?' She was yet to encounter the mysterious Mervin.

'Aye, he manages to . . . well, how can I say this . . . ' Peggy frowned. 'He has his own side business happening.'

Nancy grunted, revulsion on her small freckled face. 'It's a disgrace if you ask me. I wish I'd never found out about it.'

'It's York's worst kept secret true enough.' Peggy bit into her sandwich.

Genuinely puzzled Aurora stared blankly at her, but then remembered Mrs Murphy's warning that Ellerton might walk the wrong side of the law.

Peggy swallowed. 'He sells babies.'

'Pardon?' Aurora leaned closer, certain she'd misheard. 'What does he sell?'

'Babies.'

'I don't understand.'

Peggy swallowed a mouthful of tart down with a sip of tea. 'He gets girls in the family way. He enjoys preying on the girls who work here, and in the factories across the river, and has his way with them. Or he'll use sluts and sometimes even wives whose husbands are away with work. He also finds girls who are already in trouble and helps them get rid of the kids when their born.'

'Oh, my Lord.' Aurora screwed her face up in loathing. 'How is it possible for him to do such a thing?'

'He's a handsome chap, you see, and has all the right patter for the lasses.' Peggy shrugged her thin shoulders. 'If they're stupid enough to think he'll leave Mrs Ellerton for them, then they deserve being brought down.'

'Brought down?'

'Aye, he's in his element when they're with child. He gets his rocks off and makes a profit. You see, he persuades them to give him the baby and he sells the baby to good families.'

Aurora felt her mouth drop open. Peggy spoke so casually she thought she was imagining it all. 'He actually sells the babies? Are you sure?'

'Oh aye. Makes a good sum and all with them. I think he enjoys having all these kids running about that are his. He's mad.'

'That's appalling. Someone should tell the police.'

'There's a certain high up policeman who has one of the kids himself. His wife kept miscarrying.' Peggy finished her tart. 'Anyway, the girls don't want the babies, and there are good families in need of them. Farmers always want boys, you know, to carry on working the land. It's the same with the toff's, who need a boy child for the family business. There's the odd wealthy family in the district that have an Ellerton baby in their nest, you can believe that all right.'

'But he . . . I mean, it isn't right.'

'The girls shouldn't be so daft then, should they, and drop their drawers for him. He's not raping them, he has no need to. Lies roll off his tongue and they lap them up.'

'They still should have some protection from men such as him.'

'Protection?' Peggy laughed. 'You're not from around here, are you? You speak like you've been educated, but you're as green as grass about the real world.' She drained her cup and climbed off the crate. 'Come on, let's get back to it. We'll have another break at four o'clock. I wonder what we'll have to eat then?'

Aurora, slightly stupefied, plodded stiffly after Peggy and the quiet Nancy back into the scullery. How had she managed to end up working in a place such as this where a man was allowed to sell babies? She placed a hand on her own slight swell and promised it would never happen to her.

As the afternoon and evening wore on, she grew more exhausted and fell behind in her work. Desperate to avoid Mrs Ellerton's rage or even her appearance in the scullery, she tried valiantly to continue. At their four o'clock break, she was too tired to eat the baked potatoes or the egg custard and merely sipped at the tea, wishing with all her heart she had taken Sophia's advice and stayed at home.

A rough hand shook her shoulder and she opened her eyes to find she was sprawled across the crates and Peggy peering at her. 'Come on, it's time to go back.'

'I can't, Peggy,' Aurora's voice broke with tears.

'Don't be soft. You have to.' Peggy dragged her up by the arm. 'We've not long now. It'll be seven o'clock before you know it. In winter we shut at five. So there's something to look forward to.'

Somehow, she managed to walk and not crawl back into the building. The activity in the kitchen wasn't as insistent as during the morning, though Claudio was still issuing orders at a rapid rate.

With dogged determination, Aurora made it through to seven o'clock. If she hadn't been so worn out, she would have smiled with happiness of lasting out the first full day. Instead, she caught an omnibus to take her as far as Walmgate and then trudged down George Street and into the lane. She was aware of the women staring at her. Dilys called out something, but Aurora was too tired to acknowledge the greeting. She fumbled with the key and let herself in. The house was quiet and cool. Sophia was at work. Climbing the stairs, swaying with exhaustion, Aurora staggered into her room and collapsed on the bed and was asleep instantly.

Dilys crossed the cobbles and banged on the Murphys' door. Anthony came out already

189

tugging on his hat. 'Right lad, she's home, get yourself up to The Yellow Moon and let Sophia know.'

'Righto, Mrs Potter.'

Dilys found the door unlatched at number nine and went in. All was quiet downstairs and so she pulled herself up the stairs, cursing her weight, and stole into Aurora's room. The poor girl was lying on her side on the bed still wearing her coat and shoes. Her face pale and shadows of fatigue under her eyes.

Tutting as a mother would, Dilys took off Aurora's shoes and heaved the girl up to take off her coat before putting her under the blankets. 'Welcome to the real world, lass.'

13

Reid lifted his head from the paperwork on the desk and looked across at his father lying in the large double bed. The nurse they employed was down in the kitchen having a break and he was happy to take over her role for an hour.

His father's hand moved and Reid immediately went to his side. 'Can I get you something, Father?'

'Son . . . '

'It's Reid, Father.' He bent low, gripping his father's hand, willing him to recover. For months they thought he'd recuperate to his old self, and he'd even gone downstairs on a few occasions, but one set back after another in the last weeks had stripped away the robust intelligent man, the power head of the Sinclairs, and left a faded shell behind. 'Would you like some water?' His father's blue parched lips alarmed him. He poured a glass of water from the tray at the bedside and helped him up to sip at it. As always, his father's thin frame filled him with sorrow, a mere shadow of the healthy man he once was.

'Better.'

'Good.' Reid smiled, returning the glass to the tray. 'Do you need anything else?'

'More time . . . ' His father stared at him, his eyes clearer now than they had been for days. 'I didn't finish it all.'

'Finish what?'

'America.'

Nodding with understanding, Reid straightened the pillows slightly. 'I know, but I can do it. You trust me to set the businesses up and run them successfully, don't you?'

'You're the only one who . . . can.' He closed his eyes, the strength leaving him. 'So sorry, Reid . . . '

'Please, Father, you mustn't worry. I am known now to our partners in New York. They are sending me reports and the building of the new hotel will be finished by Christmas.'

His father's eyes popped open as though he'd just remembered something. 'Your mother . . . '

'I'll take care of her.'

'Don't let her bully you.' He took a shuddering breath. 'She is too strong for a woman . . . Lead your life . . . '

'Rest, Father.'

'I loved her from the first moment, too much so . . . Gave her a free rein.' He paused, his breath shallow. 'Wrong to do so.'

'Sleep now.' Reid crooned, silently begging his father to rest, to regain his strength, his health, his life.

'She loves you . . . all very much. Never forget that.'

'We know.' He patted his father's blue veined hand, amazed at how old it looked when at the beginning of the year it had been strong.

'I want her to be . . . happy, Reid.' His father licked his dry lips. 'She won't like being . . . a widow. It won't suit her.'

'Mother will be fine, I promise. I'll take care of her and the boys.'

'The boys . . . '

'I'll watch over them, Father, guide them the best I can, as you did me.'

'Proud of you.' They locked gazes until his father's eyelids drooped and he finally dozed off. Reid carefully placed his father's hand on top of the blankets and stood watching him for a moment. Satisfied his father slept comfortably, he went to the window and looked out over the Kensington Street. Below, people walked by, a carriage trundled past. Across the road, a maid opened the door to callers. All normal activities he felt removed from.

The July sun baked the capital and he wished he was in Yorkshire riding out along fields or even fishing beside a gurgling stream, but there was no hope of that for some time. He knew without the doctor's confirmation that his father wouldn't last much longer. He'd tried to prepare his family for it, but his mother blatantly refused to believe it. She tried to inject her own will of steel into her husband in the hope he'd rally. Whenever Reid tried to broach the subject of the future without his father, she refused to discuss it and would leave the room. He knew of her heartache, for he suffered it also. He was not only losing his father, but had already lost the woman he loved.

He leaned his shoulder against the window frame and, as always, his thoughts drifted to Aurora. What was she doing at this very minute? Shopping with her elderly Aunt? Reading? Perhaps strolling through a garden somewhere? He'd written to Winnie asking for an address to

193

write to Aurora, but received no reply.

He rubbed his chest as though to erase the ache that lingered there. Why had Aurrie turned from him? Why didn't she write back at least once? None of it made sense. Did she regret the night in the woods? He knew what courage it must have taken her to give herself to him, to cross that final barrier and he loved her all the more for it, not less. He'd written to her thanking her for the most precious gift she could give him. He again spoke of them getting married. Surely she wasn't ashamed, or doubted his intentions? Perhaps she did and he groaned with the agony of it. Did she understand why he remained in London and how the businesses, the family needed him more than ever?

His father gave a long sighing breath from the bed. Reid watched him, but his mind couldn't dismiss Aurora altogether. He couldn't rest until he had answers from her, but he couldn't find her until his father recovered or . . . died.

He bowed his head and rubbed his chest harder.

$\star \quad \star \quad \star$

Aurora wiped the perspiration from her forehead and plunged the pan back into the sink of hot water. She'd been working at the eatery for three weeks and, at the end of each day, she flopped into bed and pledged she wasn't returning. But the dawn would break the next morning and she'd stagger out of bed to go to work. She wasn't sure why she did it. Sophia begged her daily not to go, even the women of the lane said she was mad. However, something inside her forced her to go. She had to prove it to everyone that she could do it, but more than that, she had to prove it to herself. Women worked hard here and in the tenements around the lane. How could she not do the same and live amongst them? Her pride wouldn't allow her to do nothing.

'Ahh, my favorite girls in all the world.' Mervin Ellerton came up the back steps and through the open door into the scullery.

Aurora's flesh crawled at the mere sight of him, though she understood how others might be attracted to him. He had charm and good looks, in a dark swarthy way, and wore the best of clothes. His smile revealed large white teeth and when he spoke to you he looked you directly in the eyes and made you think he hung on your every word.

'Peggy, my dearest girl, do up your top buttons or you'll lead me to impure thoughts.' He grinned audaciously.

'Nay, it takes less than a few loose buttons to have you dropping your trousers, Merv Ellerton.' Peggy gave him a saucy look. 'Besides, it's too bloody hot in here. We're frying.'

'Then perhaps,' his voice lowered seductively, 'you should take your dress off altogether?'

'Oh aye, Mrs Ellerton would like that.' Peggy pushed him away with a gray soapy hand.

'Watch out!' Merv jumped back quickly and brushed at his dark brown suit with a slim white hand. 'This suit cost more than you could earn in six months.'

'Then I need a rise in me wages, don't I?'

'You're quick, my girl. I like that.' He laughed and then gave a long look at Aurora. 'Still with us I see, Aurrie.'

'As you see.' She turned her back on him, hating how his eyes would darken with desire whenever he looked at her. She knew, with an inborn woman's sense, he wanted her. She wished she could be bold towards him like Peggy, but it wasn't in her nature.

'One day I will have a smile from you, Miss Barton,' he spoke quietly from behind her.

'I wouldn't hold your breath,' she murmured low, head down.

When he'd gone through to the kitchen, Peggy sidled up to her. 'Don't cut him dead every time he speaks to you, Aurrie.'

'I can't help it. He's revolting.' She scrubbed vigorously at the pan with soda. 'I don't know how you can play up to him. He makes my skin crawl.'

'I do it to keep me job, simple as that. I told you to be careful around him, but if you keep cutting him dead when he merely looks your way will anger him and you'll be out on your arse.'

'There are other jobs.'

'Not paying this kind of money as you well know. Besides, no other job will give me food too, or these hours. Mrs Ellerton is as tough as nails, but she knows of me situation and turns a blind eye if I'm late sometimes. She knows I'll make it up to her tenfold.'

Aurora nodded. In the last few weeks she'd learned more about her co-workers. Peggy lived

196

with her invalid grandmother, who she cared for by herself, having no other family to help. By starting at seven in the morning, she had time to give her grandma breakfast and a wash before coming to work and her wage was enough for them both to survive on. Nancy lived in a tenement on the other side of York, with her thirteen brothers and sisters. She stayed at the eatery because food was scarce at home and here she had two meals a day, and after handing over most of her pay to her Ma, she still had a bit left over to buy the odd special treat.

Peggy began to sing, something she did often and which everyone enjoyed. She had a delightful voice, pure and sweet, which was at such odds to her sometimes bawdy behavior. Sometimes the kitchen staff would join in and at other times, they were content to listen. Aurora, who couldn't hold a note, was in awe of Peggy's talent and told her repeatedly she should be on the stage. But like a lot of the people she was beginning to know in this area, many had talents that would be never recognized due to poverty and the grinding neglect by those with power.

It made her more determined to live out in the country, where even if she was poor, her child would have clean air to breathe and not the choking smog of the polluted city.

The following day, being Sunday, the eatery was closed. After early church service Aurora spent the morning cleaning the house with Sophia.

'You know this being the Sabbath we should be devoted only to prayer?' Sophia joked, sweeping the stone flags of the little back yard.

'I'm sure God will turn a blind eye to us washing out our smalls and doing a bit of sweeping.' Aurora pegged another petticoat on the line strung between the house and the gate leading to the cut.

'My mother would be outraged that we aren't spending all of today inside a church.'

Aurora bent down to the basket and picked up a wet chemise. 'Grandmama was very religious?' She had faint memories of a small woman who smelt of cloves.

'Extremely. They both were, of course, Father especially. That's why I was shown the door when I was . . . when I found out about you . . .' Sophia swept forcefully. 'I don't blame them. I behaved wrongly. However, they could have dealt with it better, I think. I could have been sent away and returned later. But my father wouldn't hear of it. The moment he found out he said I was no longer his child.'

'My real father . . . who is he?'

Sophia stiffened. 'Nobody.'

'That's not fair.' She stood hands on hips. 'Why can't you tell me?'

'What good would it do now? He was a liar and in the end not a nice person.' Sophia swept out through the gate.

'He wouldn't marry you?' Aurora asked softly, pegging out a stocking.

'He couldn't, unless he became a bigamist.'

'He was married.' Aurora picked up the empty basket. Saddened by the news, she watched Sophia sweep. 'Did you know?'

'Not until it was too late.'

'Did he break your heart?'

'Oh, yes. He did that very well. I believed everything he said, but in the end he deserted me. Once, after I was shown the door by my father, I went to Alexander's home . . . yes, that's his name. From the road I saw his wife and baby enter a carriage while Alexander spoke to a groom.' She looked down at the pile of dirt she had swept. 'I knew from that day that I could never rely on anyone and only I could provide for myself.'

'I am sad that my real father is such a cad.'

'So am I.' Sophia glanced at her, a worried look in her eyes. 'You won't try to find him, will you?'

Aurora shook her head. 'No. I have no desire to see him.' She meant every word and hitched the basket up higher on her hip. 'Anyway, I think I have enough to deal with at the moment. I don't need a man such as him in my life.'

'I'm pleased to hear it.' Sophia gazed up to the clear blue sky. 'Shall we go for a walk down by the river? It's such a lovely day.'

An hour later they were walking alongside the River Ouse, casually watching the boats riding at anchor or the odd one plying the river. Many people were taking advantage of the warm sunny weather. Young couples strolled, concerned parents kept close watch on running children, old people sat under any shade available. A relaxed atmosphere filled the air as though the city was snoozing for a few hours.

'The father of your baby. Will you see him

199

again?' Sophia asked, as they ambled along a narrow path.

Aurora glanced at her from under the brim of her straw hat. She had wondered how long it would be before Sophia wanted details. 'I don't know.' Reid clouded her mind, making her chest ache with loss. 'It's all so difficult. I shouldn't hope that we will meet again. I need to let go of the past, but it's hard. No matter what I do or where I am, Reid lingers at the back of my mind and heart.'

'And there is no possible way you can be married?'

'No. Reid has a full life, an important life. I want him to do well, be successful, which he will be. He doesn't need me and my tainted history to bring him down. I couldn't be that selfish. It is better for me to forget him. He is likely to be engaged or even married now to Miss FitzGibbon and making his family happy.'

'What about your happiness?'

'I've done the right thing for my family. I haven't brought scandal to their door. I know Mother will have told our friends that I am holidaying in Europe or somewhere and my absence will not cause them harm. That eases my guilt. I ask for no more than that.'

'You cannot be on holiday forever though. One day they will have to tell people something else. Unless, you plan to return home at some stage in the future?'

'I don't see that happening for some years.' Aurora stared out over the water, thinking of her family, imaging what they were doing right now.

'I do like the thought of visiting them again one day. I miss them.'

'Yes, of course you do.'

'However, it cannot be for a while yet. At least not for a couple of years. Letters will have to suffice for now.'

'But you never put on your address for them to send a letter to you in return.'

'I will. When we're in the country.'

Sophia sighed deeply. 'Life is so very unfair at times.'

'How true.'

They walked on in silence for a few moments, each with their own thoughts.

'I would prefer it if you stopped working at the eatery, Aurrie. The work is too hard for you now.'

She placed a hand on the small swell of her stomach. 'I am hardly showing.'

'Nor will you be, working as hard as you do.' Sophia tutted. 'The baby is due in January, but you've hardly a stomach to show for it.' She stopped walking and stared hard at Aurora. 'You're not . . . not trying to kill it, are you?'

'Lord, no!'

'Then why do you continue working such a demanding job?'

They continued strolling, the sun hot on their backs. Thirsty, Aurora felt like a cup of tea. 'Jobs aren't so easy to come by when you have no skills. And as I've told you two wages will help towards the cottage in the country, and not only that but once the child is born, we'll only have your wage to live on. I need to do my bit while I can.'

'Everyone in the lane will find out about the baby shortly. Some will not tolerate you, unmarried and with child, to be living amongst them.'

'I know. I'll deal with that when it happens.'

'Do you want to move? We can go somewhere else and say you're a widow.'

'And start again?' The thought depressed her. 'It's taken weeks for us to make the house habitable. I can't do it all again so soon. I don't have the energy for it. No, we'll stay where we are.'

They came to the end of the path and had to turn up towards the city streets again. Sophia hesitated on the street corner, her eyes full of worry. 'You know that whatever happens, I will always be there for you.'

'Thank you.'

'This wasn't the life I wanted for you, that's why I gave you to Winnie, but now you are here, I don't think I could live without you being in my life again.' She ducked her head, her face red.

'It seems we are stuck with each other then.' Aurora smiled, touched by the words. She knew Sophia wanted a close relationship with her, but she still held back a little. Perhaps in time she would think of Sophia as a mother figure, but not yet. It was too soon and she felt disloyal to Winnie. She could manage the whole situation as long as she didn't think too hard about it and took one day at a time.

The sun disappeared behind the one lone cloud that had suddenly appeared and Aurora shivered for no reason as its shadow fell over them. 'Shall we go for a cup of tea somewhere?'

202

With the sun not yet peeking over the rooftops, Aurora stood behind Lily at the tap, who was filling her buckets. 'Why isn't your father doing it like he always does?''

Lily sighed and moved one full bucket away to place the empty one under the tap. 'He's asleep. We've had a bad night. He was up with a toothache and me, I had heartburn. So, I let him sleep in a bit since I couldn't get back to sleep. My back has been giving me hell this last week.'

'You've not long to go now, have you?'

Lily straightened and stared at her, frowning. 'Me dad told me last night that he knows you're having a baby.'

'He knows? How?' Aurora whispered, looking over her shoulder, but the lane was empty.

'I didn't tell him.' Lily glanced down at the filling bucket. 'Apparently Sophia told him in the bar.' She gave Aurora a queer look. 'You know they are very friendly with each other?'

'They are?'

'I think me dad is soft on her.'

'Sophia's not mentioned it before.'

Lily turned the water off and shifted her buckets away to allow Aurora to place her bucket beneath the tap. 'What do you think about it?'

She watched the water gurgle from the spout. 'I don't know to be honest. I never gave it any thought before. Sophia has remained single all this time.'

'Maybe she hasn't found the right man?'

203

'Perhaps.' Aurora nodded and swapped the buckets over.

'Are you annoyed about it?'

'Not annoyed, no . . . '

'What then?' Lily stood with her hands on her hips. 'Isn't he good enough then?'

'Don't be silly.' Though traitorously she blushed and she quickly bent her head to hide it. Noah was nice enough, but he was working class. Is that what Sophia wanted for life? But then what alternative did she have? Her own middle class society was closed to her, had been for over twenty years. A decent man like Noah was likely to be the best offer she'd ever have.

'Me dad's a good man. He's honest and loyal and hard working.'

'I know.'

'I can tell you're not happy about it.'

'It's not about Noah, Lily.' She straightened and looked at her. 'It's just that I didn't expect Sophia to form a relationship at this time.'

'Well I hardly think they'll be getting married next week.' She laughed.

'No.' Aurora forced a smile. In truth, she didn't like the idea that Sophia might give her attention and affection to another. It was self-centered, she knew, and she didn't particularly like herself for thinking such things, but selfishly she believed that she and Sophia would be together always, just the two of them, or the three of them when the child came. Now, she was painfully aware that Sophia was free and able to have an association with a man and maybe one day marry him.

Where did that leave her?

'Women in the lane have often asked why you call Sophia by her name and not mother.'

'What did you tell them?'

'That you were adopted and only recently found out about her. I hope that's okay?'

'It's close enough to the truth.'

Together they carried their buckets back towards their homes. Jane Fulton came out of her door and wished them a good morning, her tin pails clanking in the early morning stillness.

'I don't know how you're doing it.' Lily grinned.

'Doing what?'

Hands full, she nodded down towards Aurora's stomach. 'You're hardly showing. It'll be a small baby, I'll wager. Unlike mine.' Lily smiled ruefully and thrust out her big bump. 'It's a good thing you're not showing. It saves listening to them lot going on about it.' Lily tossed her head in the direction of the other doors in the lane. 'The time will come soon enough for their looks and whispers.'

'There is that I suppose.' Aurora paused as Mrs Murphy came out of her door carrying a bucket. 'Where's Anthony this morning?'

Mrs Murphy, pain in her eyes, hobbled towards them. 'He's away.'

'Your legs bad, Mrs Murphy?' Lily asked putting down her buckets.

'Sure an' it would be the worst time for them to do so with me boy gone.' The older woman sighed.

Aurora placed her full buckets by her own door and then took Mrs Murphy's empty one. 'I'll fill it for you.'

'Blessed be you're an angel sent straight from heaven, Aurrie Barton.' Mrs Murphy smiled, going back inside her door.

'I'll pop over after you've finished work, Aurrie,' Lily said, heading towards number 10. 'I'd best get me dad up before he's late.'

Aurora returned to Mrs Murphy's door with the filled bucket. Going inside she noticed the house was the same layout as her own and Lily's and probably all the houses in the lane. Religious pictures were hung in the hallway and through the open door into the front room Aurora saw Jesus on the cross above the fireplace.

'Come away in, lass.' Mrs Murphy called from the kitchen.

She carried the bucket down the hallway and into the kitchen, which was warm and cheery. The walls were papered in a dark pink print and a thick piece of blue swirl carpet was laid under the table. On the hob, bubbled a small pot of porridge and next to it in the frying pan was sizzling bacon.

'Care for some breakfast?' Mrs Murphy sat on a chair warming her legs before the fire. Her ankles were swollen and lumpy, reminding Aurora of lumps of uncooked dough.

'No, thank you. I have some waiting for me next door.' Aurora placed the bucket in the scullery.

'Thanks muchly for fetching me water, lass.' Mrs Murphy's shrewd eyes raked over her. 'You're as thin as a pikestaff, so you are. You're not eating enough.'

'I'm eating more than I was.'

'Well, double it, lass, for Ellerton will run you till you're nowt but skin and bone.'

'Will Anthony be gone long?'

'A week or so. Things got a bit too heated for him so he's lying low for a while, you know how it is.'

The diversion worked and Aurora raised her eyebrows in interest. 'Heated?'

'Big Eddie tipped him off that the polis were looking for him. 'Tis all over some illegal card games. My Tony knows nowt about them. 'Tis that spalpeen Roddy Doyle from Hope Street that's been organizing that. Jesus, Mary and Joseph, my lad is all I have left. How can I cope without him? But I'd rather he was away than in some stinking jail, so I do.'

Aurora nodded dutifully, but believed that Anthony probably had something to do with the card games. Lily had told her the Murphy lad was forever walking a narrow line where the law was concerned. She thought of the bath he'd given her. Was it stolen? What if the police came looking for stolen goods? Her skin prickled at the thought. Never in her wildest dreams did she imagine she would be living amongst thieves and petty criminals.

Mrs Murphy poured out some tea and added a dash of milk. Her white hair was in a tight bun at the back of her head and she wore the same black dress she always did. Her eyes were kind and gentle and wise. How would she survive without Anthony? On good days her legs could carry her as far as the little shop on the corner, but no further and on bad days she couldn't get out of bed. Compassion filled Aurora. 'If you need anything while Anthony is away, just knock on the wall and I'll come over.'

'To be sure you're an angel.' Mrs Murphy waved to the chair at the table. 'Sit yourself down, lass, or are you away to that job of yours?'

'Yes, I should be going or I'll be late.'

'You watch that randy ole Ellerton, won't you lass. Holy Mother of God he's a bad 'un as there ever was one. He'll be roasting that body of his in the fires of Hell one day, you mark my words. Him and that Roddy Doyle.' She stirred the porridge and lifted it off the heat. 'I'll say a prayer for them both at Mass, so I will.' She ladled out the gray sludge and Aurora repressed a shudder. Porridge without milk was hard to get accustomed to, but then wasn't everything like that in the lane?

'I must be going, Mrs Murphy.' Aurora edged for the doorway, conscious of the time ticking away. 'I'll call in again when I come home this afternoon.'

'Right you are, lass. Take care now.'

When Aurora arrived at the eatery, she found Peggy and Nancy already filling the sinks with hot water. 'I'm sorry to be late.'

'Never mind, you're here now.' Peggy smiled, then her smile froze as she stared at Aurora, who was reaching up to grab a new apron from the top rack. 'You have a bump.'

Aurora blushed, her hand going to her stomach in a tell tale sign. 'Yes.'

'Is that the real reason why you left home?' Peggy asked.

208

'Partly.'

'Why didn't you tell us?'

She looked from Peggy to Nancy and back again and felt ashamed. 'I was going to. Only, I find it difficult to talk about it.'

'That's all right. We understand, don't we, Nancy?' They both gave her a sympathetic smile.

'And I didn't want Mrs Ellerton to find out.'

'Find out what?' The domineering woman stood on the step leading into the kitchen. 'What you hiding?'

'That she was five minutes late, Mrs Ellerton.' Peggy turned back to the sink and started washing.

Ellerton peered at Aurora. 'Do it again and I'll dock you wages.'

Aurora nodded and hurried up to the other end of the kitchen. When Ellerton went back into the kitchen, Aurora glanced over her shoulder at the two girls. 'Thank you.'

'Think nothing of it.' Peggy shrugged. 'It's none of her business. She'd probably think it was Merv's anyway and get him to get rid of it.'

A wave of fierce protection came over her towards her unborn child. 'No one is touching my baby.'

14

Sophia finished wiping down the front bar and went into the little snug that catered for those wishing for a private area. Rinsing out her cloth in the bucket of hot soapy water, she hummed a jaunty tune. The mundane tasks allowed her mind to wander and she smiled thinking of Aurora. Last night they had taken turns in reading out pages of Charles Dickens' novel, *Great Expectations*. With each day that passed she was growing to love Aurrie more.

The thought of love made her think of Noah Middleton. He was a regular at the bar now when he knew she was working. Not that she minded. It was nice to be admired by a good man, one who didn't demand, who didn't tell her crude jokes or make suggestive comments. Noah treated her with respect, despite having known her for many years as simply a barmaid and seeing how she had behaved at times with other men. He had asked her to walk out with him, but so far she'd held off, not wanting to alarm Aurora, especially after the incident with Godfrey. Not that Noah was anything like Fred Godfrey. Noah was decent, kind, and if she was honest, worth giving her trust to, but if she accepted his courtship how would Aurrie react? Would she feel neglected? And did she want a relationship now when she still had to became closer to Aurora and gain her trust? Sophia sighed, confused by her thoughts. It was all so difficult to make everyone happy. Although if she married Noah it would be a relief to have someone look after her for a change, someone to share her worries with.

Dusting the shelf above the small fire in the corner, she paused, hearing Mrs Flannigan's raised shocked voice, and then a thump. Worried the older woman might have fallen, Sophia dropped her bucket and cleaning tools and ran down the passageway. 'Mrs Flannigan?'

She stopped abruptly in the kitchen. Framed in the doorway leading to the scullery, as though she had conjured him up from her thoughts, stood Fred Godfrey, looking wild with a straggly beard, his eyes glazed and his gaunt body covered with filthy clothes. Her heart smashed against her ribcage in fear. 'What do you want, Fred?'

'Revenge.' His lips curled back in a feral snarl. 'And I'm not stopping until I get it.' He lunged forward and she screamed. She turned and bumped straight into Big Eddie, who'd been working in his tiny office under the stairs.

'What the hell is going on here? Get out of here, Godfrey, you fool.' Big Eddie strode forward as if to swat him like a bothersome fly. Only they weren't prepared for Fred to flash a knife in his face. Eddie skidded to a stop. 'Now, calm down, Fred.'

'Calm down? After what that bitch did to me?' he sneered, jabbing the knife with each word. 'I nearly died because of her. I lost the lot, me job and me home all because of her! I was left for

211

dead, and then done over by some streets turds before I could gather me wits.' He lifted up his shirt to reveal a weeping red wound in his side. 'It won't heal.'

'I never did that!' Sophia gasped, horrified.

He grimaced with hatred. 'No, but you left me in the alley where some other bugger could though, didn't you? And for what? Me new boots and a few coppers in me pocket.'

Sophia took a step back. 'I didn't know! I'm sorry.'

Big Eddie crossed his arms over his broad chest. 'You've always had more enemies than friends with your double-dealing. It's no surprise you were been done over. Now, go home. There's nowt for you here.'

'I nearly died.' His voice came out on a harsh whisper. 'I wish I had because I lost everythin' and you're gonna pay, lassie.'

'Oh no, she isn't, Godfrey. You brought it upon yourself for attacking her lass. If Soph hadn't stopped you, you'd have done rape.'

'Aye, and enjoyed it too!' He spat onto the floor. 'Still, I'm not leaving until I've done some paying back of me own.'

'Go while you still can, Godfrey. I want you out of here before you cause any more trouble.' Big Eddie took a step ready to escort him out, but Fred pivoted sideways and plunged the knife into Big Eddie's chest.

Sophia screamed wordlessly, unable to believe her eyes as Big Eddie crumpled to his knees, a look of surprise on his face. Godfrey yanked the knife out of Eddie's chest and the big man fell forwards onto the floor.

Godfrey slowly lifted his head and stared with a smile at Sophia. 'Now to unfinished business.'

'Fred . . . no . . . ' Sophia walked backwards out of the kitchen and up the passageway. 'Please don't, Fred. I'll not tell anyone it was you . . . '

'If I'm going to be done for murder, I might as well make it two, or is it three?' He laughed like someone demented.

'Three?' she squeaked. Had he killed Aurora?

'The old woman back there.' He shrugged. 'Who knows?'

Oh my God, he'd killed Mrs Flannigan! 'We can talk about this, Fred. We'll work something out.'

'I've no wish to talk. It's all about actions now, lass. You will pay.' His quiet icy tone sent shivers down her back.

Sophia turned and ran into the bar room. He caught her at the front doors as she tried desperately to pull down the bolts on the locks. His first blow sent her sideways into a table. Her head rang like bells in a church tower.

She screamed as his fist came down and smacked her in the face, the force rolling her backwards over a bench seat and onto the floor. Opening her mouth to scream again she found his hands on her throat, cutting off her air. She flayed with her arms, her fingernails reaching and tearing at his face. When he cried with pain, his grip slackened on her throat and she kicked out. He ripped at her blouse, the material coming away easily in his rage. She cried out, but his fist hit her on the side of the head and sent her mind spinning in pain. His next blow struck her stomach, doubling her up in silent agony. She was dimly aware of her skirts being lifted up, of his cold hands on her legs. He punched her repeatedly in the stomach and ribs. She twisted away, frantic to escape the torture, but he was always there, his hands everywhere, hurting her. Another smack to her face sent the world black.

★　★　★

'Here's another tray for you.' Ollie, one of the eatery staff, placed a full tray of crockery on the side drainer and hurried back into the madness of the hot kitchen.

'Why is it so busy today?' Aurora panted, puffing upwards to shift her hair off her face. If she had a free hand she'd retie it, but to stop even for a moment wasn't possible.

'The Ellertons are havin' a private party or summat,' Nancy said, wiping sweat from her face. The heat from the hot August day outside and the busy kitchen seemed to meet and pool in the scullery.

'Not a good day for Peggy to miss.' Aurrie was desperate for a drink.

'No. Her Gran is poorly again.'

'Mrs Ellerton will dock her wages.'

'Aye, but she'll still keep her job.'

'That's because no one works as hard as Peggy and Mrs Ellerton knows it.' Aurora unloaded the tray, wishing the minutes would go by faster. They still had another four hours to go, and apart from her first week of work, over eight weeks ago, this day was proving the toughest yet. Her feet throbbed and she suspected her ankles had swollen. The cracks in her hands had started to bleed and her back seemed permanently bent. She stifled a cry as the soda seeped into the split skin in her fingers and not for the first time she wished she had listened to Sophia and stayed at home. Tiredness pulled at her bones. How she remained standing she didn't know.

'Ah, my girls.' Merv Ellerton sauntered into the scullery, running one finger along his thin moustache. 'I've come to say how well we appreciate you working so hard on our special day.'

Aurora turned away and placed the empty tray on a rack hanging on the opposite wall. She caught Nancy's blush and stiffened. She hoped the silly girl wasn't falling for Merv's patter. Thankfully, Merv's attentions to herself had waned soon after he learned of her condition, which now was clearly evident as the sweat soaked her clothes to her skin. However, every now and then, he still tried to charm her.

'Aurora, my dear, you should have a rest. Let me escort you outside for some air.' His smile seemed open and friendly but when she looked into his eyes and saw a hidden message there, she knew it was a falsehood.

'No, thank you. I have much work to do and we are one person short.'

'No, I insist.' He grabbed her hand and led her from the scullery and down the steps before she could reply. He turned back to Nancy. 'Dearest Nancy will cope for a moment won't you, my pet?'

Nancy simpered and nodded and Aurora wished Peggy was here, for she didn't stand any of his nonsense, and neither would Aurora. 'Really, Mr Ellerton, I'm — '

'Now, shush, Aurrie, I'm only thinking of you and your child.' He led her over to a crate and sat her down on it, before hunkering down beside her. 'What can I get you? Water? Tea?'

'I don't wish for anything, thank you.' She put a protective hand over her stomach, which despite Sophia's apprehension, had grown nearly double in size to a small neat bump.

'I adore the way you speak, Aurrie, so soft and gentle. A real lady. We don't have any of those here.' His took one of her booted feet and rested it on his knee. 'You aren't used to hard work, are you, but you've been a real soldier. Never complaining, staying out of trouble.'

She tried to take her foot off his knee but he held it firm, his fingers sliding over her short boot and up her stocking clad calf. 'I wish to return inside please, Mr Ellerton.'

'In a minute. First tell me about yourself. How did such a lady come to work here?' His hand reached her knee and she froze in horror. 'You know, I could make your life better than it is. I could return you to the comfort in which you were brought up.' His smile now matched the hunger in his eyes and he reminded her of a wolf, or a cunning fox.

'Please . . . I — '

'Come, Aurrie, tell me that you don't wish to be in a beautiful home again? I'm told you want to live in the countryside once more. You come

216

from the country, my dear?' His fingers kneaded her thigh, his gaze holding hers. 'I can do that for you. I can give you back all that you have lost. I can give you a house, a pony to ride, dresses and jewels. They can all be yours . . . ' He leaned in closer. 'As my mistress, you'd want for nothing, and I'd love you better than any man alive.' He leaned closer still. 'I'd love you like you deserve, Aurrie . . . ' His mouth was an inch from hers, his words hypnotizing. He smelt of the cigars he smoked and something else . . . not beer, but something stronger, brandy or whiskey . . . Her father had a whiskey bottle in the cabinet in his study. The thought of her father jerked her out of her exhausted stupor and she blinked.

'Aurrie, girl, say yes . . . ' Merv's mouth with that hideous moustache loomed closer and she reared back.

'Get away from me!' She pushed him hard and crouching as he was, he easily toppled backwards onto the dusty flags. She jumped off the crate and a wave of dizziness washed over her.

'Aurora, listen,' Merv pleaded, getting to his feet and dusting down his trousers. 'Let me explain . . . I want to take care of you. You're not the sort who should be working in a scullery. You're a lady and in trouble.'

'What I am is of no concern to you!' She marched into the scullery and untied her dirty, wet apron, ignoring Nancy's open-mouthed stare.

'I'm sorry, Aurrie,' Nancy muttered, her gaze darting past her to the yard beyond.

'For what?' Her stomach swirled queasily.

Nancy squirmed on the spot, her expression guilty.

Aurora stiffened. 'You've been talking about me to him?'

'He was only being kind,' she whined. 'He can be nice.'

'Don't be silly, Nancy. He's made a fool out of you.'

'He can send your baby to a good home, Aurrie, and then you can go back to your home if you want,' Nancy whispered, her hands dripping gray soapy water over the red flagstones. 'He'll look after you. He said so.'

'Don't be so blind, Nancy.' She wiped her sweat-soaked hair from her face. 'He's the kind who will only do what benefits him. You know the stories.'

'But he seemed . . . ' Nancy glanced down, shame-faced.

'He used you, Nancy, to get at me.' Aurora peered at her. 'You didn't . . . I mean he didn't . . . '

Nancy's head jerked up. 'No! I wouldn't do that. Me dad would kill me.'

Aurora sighed in relief. 'Don't ever give in, Nancy. Get married first. Find a good man who will take care of you.'

'Mr Ellerton said he'd take care of you. I thought I was doing the right thing.'

Merv came up the steps and stood in the doorway. 'I can help you, Aurora. Surely you need someone to take care of you.'

Aurora spun to face the monster, the heat of the day was nothing compared to the blaze of her anger. 'How dare you go through Nancy to get to me. How low can you be?'

'Now listen, you're getting all excited over nothing. I simply wanted to help.'

'And what do you want in return?' She flung the apron into the corner. 'You want me as your mistress.' She laughed, fighting the urge not to be sick. 'Does your wife know? Of course she doesn't.' She was aware of the kitchen staff watching her, but she didn't care, 'Well, I won't be your mistress, Mr Ellerton. Not you or anyone will take care of me. I can do that myself.' She barged past him, but stopped at the bottom of the steps. 'I will send someone for my wages. I will be paid up until the end of the week. If I am not, then I will go to the police about your little system of baby selling.' She hesitated and nodded wisely. 'No, bugger my wages. I'll go to the police anyway. You're vile and need to be locked up.'

He grabbed her arm cruelly, all trace of politeness and concern gone. 'You go to the authorities, bitch, and I'll do for you. Understand?'

She was too furious to be alarmed by his threat, but her mind worked. 'Then make sure there is enough money in the envelope to keep me quiet.'

His eyes widened. 'You're blackmailing me?'

'No, not at all. Merely advising.'

Mrs Ellerton barged out of the kitchen, hands on hips, her face ferocious with rage. 'You're not getting a penny, whore!'

Aurora wrenched her arm out of his hold. 'Then I'll see you both in court.'

'Court.' He laughed madly. 'You have the

money for such a case? Who will be your witnesses? No one will speak against me. I've given half the wealthy men in this county a family they couldn't provide themselves.'

'We'll see about all that, won't we? You forget, I too, have important associations. My father — '

Mrs Ellerton took a step closer, her top lip thin against her teeth. 'Stuck up little bitch. How dare you come here begging for a job and then threaten us. I'll see you dead in the gutter first and you whole family shamed!'

Merv laid a hand on his wife's arm. 'Save your breath. I'll tell the magistrate that the little tart was my mistress, that her baby is mine and I've turned her down and she's doing all this out of spite.'

Aurora recoiled as though he'd slapped her. 'They'll not believe you.'

'Do you want to drag your family into court to prove it?' His lips curved into a vicious grin.

'I hope you rot in Hell.' She marched down the yard, hot irate tears blurring her vision. She felt unclean, tainted. Pure fury got her half way home, but then suddenly the strength went from her legs and she collapsed against a shop window. She rested for a moment, praying she'd find the energy to continue. Her temper had nearly been her undoing. What if Ellerton made a noise about her and it got back to her family? No. She shook her head. He'd stay quiet and not want to draw attention to himself. But what if he didn't . . . Why had she been so stupid to try and blackmail him. Why couldn't she have just kept her mouth shut?

'Are you all right, luv?' The shopkeeper came out to help her upright.

'Fine, thank you.'

'You ought to get away home, and put your feet up a bit.' His anxiety made her want to cry.

'I'm going home now.'

'Aurrie?'

She turned to see Anthony Murphy crossing the road towards her.

'Here, lad.' The shopkeeper frowned, as though her collapse was Anthony's fault. 'Help her home, will you? She needs to be inside.'

'Course I will, what you take me for?' Anthony snapped, but then turned smiling eyes on Aurora. 'Come, Aurrie, lean on me.'

'Thank you, Anthony.' They walked several yards and Aurora found that she was leaning on him more and more. 'I'm so sorry. I don't seem to have any strength at all today.'

'Sure an' is it any wonder? Working all those hours at Ellerton's. Me mam says she wished she'd never told you about them.'

'The money was good.'

'Was?' He perked up. 'Yer mean you've left?'

'Yes.'

'Well, at least something good has happened today.'

She couldn't talk anymore and they lapsed into silence for the rest of the way home. The lane was deserted and Aurora was pleased. She didn't want the neighbors witnessing her struggle. However before she and Anthony reached number nine, they heard a jumble of voices and the moment they entered the hallway they were engulfed in a mass of heaving, fuming people spilling out from the sitting room.

'Ye gads, I never thought I'd see the day,' Dilys boomed, her eyes red from crying. 'Disgusted I am, disgusted!'

A little disorientated, Aurora, with Anthony's strong arms around her waist, pushed her way through the crowded room and found Lily, who sat on the sofa crying as though her heart would break. Opposite her, in the old wing backed chair, was Mary Murphy, frozen like a tiny marble statue.

'Oh Aurrie, lass!' Dilys, on realizing she was there, crushed her into her enormous breasts. 'We'll get the bastard, don't worry.'

'What . . . what?'

'Anthony, thanks for bringing her home.' Dilys slapped him hard on the shoulder.

'I don't understand?' Aurora unsteadily sat down beside Lily. 'What's happened, Lily?'

'Don't you know?' Lily's handkerchief was damp and limp in her hands. She looked at Anthony. 'What did you tell her?'

'Nothing. I didn't get the chance.'

Aurora braced for bad news. 'Tell me what?'

'Sophia.'

Aurora's heart seemed to somersault in her chest. 'What happened to Sophia?'

'Someone, a man, went into The Yellow Moon and went mad . . . ' A voice from the back spoke up.

'Not just some man, but Fred blasted Godfrey!' Old Alfie punched his gnarled fist into his other hand. 'The bastard!'

Dilys came forward. 'They've taken her to the hospital, lass. She'll be made right as rain there. Won't she now?' Dilys glared at the people hovering around as if to defy any of them to say something to the contrary.

'Me dad's gone to see her.' Lily sobbed. 'He's heartbroken.'

Aurora frowned, her head pounded terribly. 'Your dad?' Noah was heartbroken? Why? Had he done something? She couldn't make sense of it.

'Oh aye.' Lily nodded with a slight hiccup. 'I didn't understand how much he'd fallen for her either. I thought it was only friendship, but I was wrong, Aurrie.' Lily looked apologetic. 'He loves her.'

'He loves her?' Aurora couldn't think straight.

'And so he should. A person doesn't have to be single all their life once they become a widower.' Dilys stated, heaving her large bosom up with a forearm. 'Jean.' She pushed her daughter towards the door. 'Go put the kettle on. We could all do with a cuppa.'

'I'd just like someone to tell me what's going on.' Aurora murmured, fighting the nausea rising in her throat. She really didn't want to be sick on the new rug she'd bought.

'Tell her, Mary,' Hetty Barclay urged. 'You were there. Tell her what you told the polis.'

Mary Murphy blinked, the only sign she was alive. 'I went inter the pub to see Big Eddie. I wanted to thank him for sending Anthony home, now it's clear for him, you see. I found him dead on't floor . . . blood seeping out of his chest.

223

May God bless and keep him.' She crossed herself. 'Mrs Flannigan was out cold in't corner . . . ' Mary stared into the distance, not a facial muscle moving and Anthony hurried to put his arm around her and she glanced up at him. 'I heard scuffling, lad. I went into the bar an' there they were. He was . . . he was . . . ' She gulped and Anthony made a distressing sound in the back of his throat. Mary looked sadly at Aurora. 'Fred Godfrey has beaten you ma, lass. Beaten an' raped her. I couldn't do owt to stop him.'

The last words were barely heard as Aurora slipped off the sofa and onto the floor in a faint.

15

Every time Aurora walked through the doors of Doctor Peterson's private hospital, she felt herself grow smaller. Her whole body seemed to shrink in sufferance with the distressed people inside, room after room, row after row. And Sophia was one of them, but at least she was no longer at the large public hospital crammed in with hundreds of others. It had costs them a large slice of their carefully hoarded money, but Aurora felt it justified.

In the two weeks Aurora had been coming here, she'd become known to the nurses. Every day at ten o'clock she'd enter the building and smile at the woman at the front desk, before turning left and going up the stairs to the second floor. There, she'd go along the corridor to room number 5. Inside were two beds, one holding Sophia and the other holding Amelia Wilson, a patient whom had been in a coma for nearly a month, and who the doctors and staff had given up on ever returning to life.

As Aurora settled down on the chair next to Sophia's bed, she was determined that Sophia would be home by the end of the week. She bent over and kissed her cheek gently. The blue and purple bruising was fading to a garish green yellow. The cuts to her cheek, lips and above the eye were slowly healing. Her three broken ribs were mending too. The doctor was concerned about Sophia's mental health, wondering if she'd be able to cope with life outside the hospital. However, the news that Fred Godfrey had been found floating dead in the River Ouse had been a blessing. They would never have to worry about him coming after them again.

Sophia's eyes fluttered and then opened. 'I told you not to come every day.'

'And I told you I would, and I am.'

'You're late today then?' She gave a brief smile.

'Yes, sorry.' Aurora put her bag down on the floor and held Sophia's hand. The ordeal and aftermath of the attack had drawn them closer, Aurora couldn't help it. Seeing Sophia battered and bruised, near to death, had forced her to admit that she'd grown to love the woman who'd given birth to her, the one who'd also given her away for a better life. 'Now then,' she smiled with forced brightness, 'everyone sends their love. Noah will be along this afternoon, while I watch Lily. She's overdue, or so she thinks, but she's not entirely sure. She's ready to burst.'

'Poor love.'

'Yes, she's been bedridden for a week.' Aurora glanced around the pale, stark room, wanting to change the subject. Lily's never ending pregnancy and size alarmed Aurora. She prayed nightly to a God she didn't know if she believed in, hoping that if someone was up there watching over her that they'd not let her balloon to the size of Lily.

'And everyone in the lane is well?'

'Well, one of the Morrison's boys, Seth, I

226

think, was nearly run down two days ago by a hansom cab. Luckily a man pushed him out of the way in time. Seth was playing truant from school. We heard Mr Morrison giving him a good thrashing that night.'

'He deserved it, scaring his parents like that.'

'Oh, and old Alfie received a letter from a cousin in Canada. He was cock-a-hoop about that and insisted on going into each house and reading the contents to everyone.'

'How nice of him to share.'

'He asked me to help him write a letter in reply, because his handwriting is nigh impossible to understand. I'll do that tomorrow.'

'You are good.' Sophia smiled. 'I bet Dilys wanted to do it, to have her say.'

Aurora grinned. 'Most likely. Now, Mrs Murphy . . . ' She paused on mentioning Mary Murphy's name. The woman had been witness to Sophia's attack and blamed herself for not arriving at the pub sooner. Aurora had learned that Mrs Murphy fought Fred Godfrey off Sophia. She'd hit him repeatedly with whatever she found behind the bar until he'd had enough and run off. But Mary Murphy refused to talk about that day anymore. She'd said all she was going to. For the first time in her life she'd spoken to police, something she believed her late father, a petty criminal, would be turning in his grave over.

'Aren't the flowers nice?' Sophia glanced at the delicate wildflowers in a pottery vase on the windowsill. 'Noah picked them for me.'

'He's a good man.' Aurora nodded. Again the

227

attack had brought change into their lives in the form of Noah Middleton. Aurora had found it difficult to accept his attentions to Sophia at first, but gradually she grew to understand he loved Sophia very much, had secretly done so for a while, until that fateful day when he'd shown everyone exactly how he felt. Since then, he'd visited Sophia every evening after work and on the weekends. A quiet presence amongst their turmoil.

'Nothing will come of me and Noah, Aurrie, if you don't want it to,' Sophia said quietly. 'You will always come first with me.'

Aurora rose and went to the window to look out on the busy street below. Naturally, Noah wanted to marry Sophia when she had recovered, and the fact brought Aurora unease, because she'd be alone. Still, she would survive. Leaving home had taught her many things and one of those things was that she was stronger than she ever knew. She turned back to Sophia. 'I will never stand in your way of finding happiness.'

'I have happiness with you. I don't need a man.'

'I know, but he loves you and he is a good person.'

Sophia plucked at the sheet folded neatly over her waist. 'That is true. And perhaps one day you may find that living with me isn't what you want anymore, and leave, so at least I would have Noah.'

'This isn't about me leaving you, but about you marrying a good man.' She sat on the chair and sighed. 'Never mind that now. I want you to think about getting out of here and coming home.'

A spasm crossed Sophia's face. 'Of course.'

'What is it?'

'I don't know.'

'You do want to come home?'

'Well, yes . . . '

'But?'

'I suppose I'm frightened.'

Aurora took her hand and squeezed in reassurance. 'There's no need to be. Godfrey is dead.'

'It's not him, but everyone and everything else. I don't know if I can pick up the pieces again. I'm responsible for Big Eddie dying . . . Mrs Flannigan getting hurt and losing her job. It's all such a mess . . . '

'Godfrey is the one to blame, not you. You aren't responsible for another person's actions.'

Sophia turned her face away. 'I feel cheated.'

'Why?'

'When Fred knocked me out, he robbed me of the chance to fight back. I remember very little of the attack, of what he did to me.' Sophia glanced back to stare at her. 'I can't even find the strength of will to be really angry at him because I wasn't truly aware of what he did.'

'But the doctor told you. You bear the injuries.'

'I see the bruises, feel the aches, but I can't picture his face or the scene in the bar room. I am empty when I should be full of hate.'

'In time you'll feel better. I'm certain of it.' Aurora tried to inject hope into her voice. She was in out of her depth with this. She didn't know what to say or do to help Sophia.

'And Noah. What do I do about him?'

'What do you mean?'

'It's all very well us talking about me marrying him, but will he actually want to . . . to . . . touch me after Fred did what he did. Will I want him to?'

'Noah loves you. He wants to take care of you. How can you think him to be so shallow and weak that he would force you to do something you were comfortable doing?'

'Yes, of course. You are right.' Sophia sighed.

'All will be well, I promise. We'll get over this. Together. You trust me about that, don't you?'

Nodding, Sophia wiped at the tear which fell over her lashes. 'Forgive me. I'm not usually weepy.'

'You have every right to be.' Aurora again squeezed her hand affectionately.

'Can I ask you about something?'

'Absolutely.' Aurora bent down and opened the bag to take out her knitting. She'd been creating a pile of small clothes for the baby. She sat back and rested the knitting on her small mounded stomach. 'What do you wish to know?'

'Eddie's funeral . . . The inquest is over now.'

Taking a deep breath, she laid her knitting on her lap. 'How did you know about that?'

'Dilys told me. She visited me yesterday evening after leaving court.'

Fuming, Aurora would be hard pushed not to give Dilys a piece of her mind for worrying Sophia about it all. 'The inquest finished yesterday and Godfrey was found guilty.'

'Yes, Dilys said. So Big Eddie . . . ' What color Sophia had drained from her face. 'His funeral?'

'His aunt gave him a very nice burial this morning. We all went.'

'That's why you're late.'

'Yes.'

'I would like to send her a note, but I don't know what to say.'

Aurora nodded. 'When you're home we could write it together, yes?'

Sophia continually smoothed the folded sheet over her. 'Yes. And Mrs Flannigan?'

'She is well. Dilys found out that she's gone to live with her daughter in Lincolnshire.'

'One more thing.'

'Yes?' Aurora raised her eyebrows in anticipation, hoping the question wouldn't be too hard.

'What have the neighbors said about you?' Sophia's gaze dropped to Aurora's stomach, which she could no longer hide very well.

'They don't know, not yet. The cool change in weather has been helpful for that. I've been wearing my coat. No one has seen me without it and I keep the doors locked, preventing the likes of Dilys from barging in unannounced. However, for all that, I managed to buy one of those readymade skirts when I went into town. I got a larger sized waist.'

'We can't keep up the pretence forever.'

'I know. I'll deal with that when it happens. Now, I want to tell you that I've been to some of the land agents, to see if anyone knows of a cottage.'

Sophia's eyes brightened and she stopped

smoothing the sheet. 'You have? But do we have the money?'

'Well, one fellow I was talking to said the further away we go from the city the less expensive it is.'

'I see.'

'But do you want to live in some isolated spot?' Aurora was doubtful either of them could live in the middle of nowhere on some bleak wind-swept moor.

'I don't know . . . ' Sophia folded her hands over the top of the gray blanket. 'Although I do like the thought of being away from people.'

'We need to be close enough to a town to find some work though.'

'Yes, of course.'

'I'll visit some more agents tomorrow. I don't think it will be an easy task finding our cottage, but I won't give up.'

'I need to be home, Aurrie.' Sophia thrust the bedcovers aside and went to swing her legs out. 'I've been here long enough.'

'Wait. The doctor — '

'He can't keep me here. I'm better, much better. I need to go home. You mustn't be alone anymore. I've been selfish, wallowing in self-pity. How disgusting.'

'Stay right where you are.' Aurora grabbed her arm and made her stay in the bed. 'Let me find the doctor and we'll talk to him. Yes?'

Sophia held her stare. 'I need to be home, Aurrie, with you, and planning for our future.'

Standing, Aurora gave her a warm smile. 'I'll find the doctor.'

Within two hours, Sophia was ensconced in her bedroom in number nine. The doctor had allowed her to go home and he'd call in daily for another week. Aurora used the money from the pouch to pay his bill and then hired a hansom to take them home. It seemed the entire lane had turned out to welcome Sophia's return, even Lily had left her bed to see them. Aurora struggled to keep the women out of the house, but Lily said no one would rest until they'd come in and had a little chat with the patient.

Aurora gave them just a few minutes before herding them downstairs with the promise they could call in again tomorrow. Yet, they continued to knock on the front door for the next hour with offers of tureens of soup, a loaf of bread, old Alfie brought over his newspaper for Sophia to read, Dilys took in their washing and Anthony filled their buckets with water to save Aurora the trip to the tap in the morning. Despite them driving her nearly crazy sometimes with their fussing and inquisitiveness, she was grateful for their kindness and generosity.

The sun was slowly descending over the rooftops, casting the lane into golden shadows before their friends finally left them alone. Aurora was adding more coal to the sitting room fire when Sophia gingerly walked over to the sofa. 'What are you doing up? Get back to bed. How did you get down the stairs?' She fussed around her, arranging a blanket over her knees.

'I took my time and managed it fine.' Sophia smiled, though tiredness was etched around her eyes. 'I couldn't lie down for another minute.

233

I've been doing it for weeks. I wanted to talk to you.'

'I could have come up.' Aurora stood hands on hips, annoyed with her taking such a risk. After nearly loosing Sophia because of that madman Godfrey, she was deeply aware of how much she'd grown to care for her. Sophia was all she had in the world. She looked at her now, sitting on the sofa staring into the fire and couldn't imagine not having Sophia in her life. Sometimes she believed she had dreamt her other life, that all those other people had simply been made up by her imagination.

A knock on the door brought her out of her thoughts. She smiled wearily at Sophia. 'I bet that's Dilys again.' She went to the front door and opened it to reveal a smartly dressed woman wearing all black, behind her stood a male servant. 'May I help you?'

'I'm looking for Sophia Barton.' The woman was tall and thin with a proud bearing.

'May I ask who is calling?'

'Mrs Ethel Minton, Edward's aunt and owner of these terraces.' She gave the lane a stern glance as if she was displeased at the fact they belonged to her.

'Eddie's aunt? Do please come in.' Aurora opened the door wider for her to enter, and noticing Dilys peering from across the road, she waved before following Mrs Minton into the sitting room. The servant remained outside on the cobbles. 'Sophia, this is Eddie's aunt, Mrs Minton.'

'I am so pleased to meet you.' Sophia went to

stand, but Mrs Minton indicated for her to remain seated.

'I am not here on a social visit.' Mrs Minton gazed around the room. 'In fact I wish I wasn't here at all, but I had the need to see the woman who brought death to my door. The one who killed my nephew and gave me another loss I must bear.'

'I did not kill Eddie!' Sophia struggled to her feet and immediately Aurora was by her side helping her.

'Fred Godfrey may have plunged the knife into Edward but why was he there in the first place?' She sneered, her eyes narrowing with hate. 'Because of you.'

'Sophia had no idea this would happen,' Aurora butted in, ready to escort the woman out.

'She,' a bony finger was pointed in Sophia's direction, 'she is the one, the whore, who captivated my nephew.' Ethel Minton drew herself up even taller. 'I knew my nephew was soft on you. He was too soft by half where you were concerned.'

'There was nothing between Eddie and I. We were friends, good friends, nothing more.'

'Nothing more? Don't make me laugh. He got you into this house, didn't he? And you pay a lower rent. He gave you work as well. No man does that for a woman unless he expects some- thing in return.'

'That is not true.' Sophia's lips thinned in anger. 'If you knew your nephew at all, you'd not say such malicious things about him. He was decent and kind.'

'Oh, I knew my nephew, I knew he hankered after you because you were once a lady, but look at you now, a dirty whore with — '

'That's enough!' Aurora stepped in front of Sophia and pointed towards the door. 'Leave immediately.'

Ethel Minton laughed a dry cackle sound. 'Leave? My own house? Oh, no, that's where you are wrong. You two are leaving.' The older woman puffed out her chest in victory. 'I want you gone, but because I am not completely without honor, I'll give you two weeks to find somewhere else. If you aren't gone by that time, my men will throw you out onto the street. And in those two weeks the rent will be at the normal rate. You deserve no favors from me!' With a swish of her black skirts she was gone and in silence they heard the door bang shut behind her.

Astounded, Aurora stared at Sophia. 'We have to leave.' She couldn't believe it.

'In two weeks.' Sophia stepped backwards, feeling behind her for the sofa and gently sitting down. 'I'll have to get a job straight away.'

'You're not well enough. I will.'

'And you're pregnant.'

Sophia closed her eyes. 'I won't go back to Edinburgh Yard. I can't do it again.'

'No, not there.' Aurora shivered. 'I might be able to find light work somewhere. I'll go out first thing in the morning.'

'Even if you get something, we still have to move sooner than we expected.' Sophia's eyes filled with unshed tears. 'We're not ready.'

'We'll go to the country.'

'We haven't the money, not yet, and winter will be upon us shortly. Work is scarce in the country during the colder months.'

Another knock on the door made them jump and they looked at each other worriedly.

'She wouldn't come back,' Sophia said, glancing out of the window.

'I'll go.' Aurora once more opened the door, praying it was Lily or Dilys. Instead it was Noah Middleton. 'Oh, Noah.'

'Aurrie.' He nodded and slipped off his flat cap. 'Lily just told me you brought her home.'

'Yes. She was well enough to leave there.' She briefly smiled into his serious gray eyes. 'Come in.'

In the sitting room, Noah stood awkwardly with his back to the fire, gazing at Sophia. 'I'm so pleased you're home, lass.'

'I am too.'

'How you feeling?'

Sophia emitted a long sigh. 'Tired, Noah, dreadfully tired.'

He was instantly on his knees before her and Aurora's heart turned over at the loveliness of it. 'What can I get for you, lass?'

'A new home, Noah.' A single tear slipped over Sophia's lashes. 'We need a new home.'

16

Aurora walked along the streets of York, head down against the wind. The end of summer was proving difficult this year and warm days would be followed by squalls of rain and blustery winds such as today. Since Ethel Minton's visit six days ago, Aurora had gone out looking for work and new accommodation. Each day she had come home despondent on both issues. Without a wage they couldn't look at the better houses, and the poorer areas were the likes of Edinburgh Yard, which she and Sophia were adamant not to go back to. Noah and Lily had spoken as one offering their home to them, but Aurora was reluctant to agree as they'd be on top of each other, especially when the two babies came.

Aside from the anxiety of finding money and lodgings, she had become aware over the last few days of someone watching her. She couldn't define what made her so sure someone was, but instinct told her she didn't walk the streets alone. Then, last night, while closing the curtains a stranger lingered in the lane looking at her windows. As yet she hadn't mentioned it to Sophia, who after the attack was nervous enough and jumped at any loud bangs or sudden shouts. Perhaps she should mention it to Noah, ask him to keep an eye out, and just hope that she was imagining it all.

Her feet throbbed as she turned into Coney

Street. The baby kicked, a new sensation that Aurora marveled at in secret joy. She rubbed her stomach and hurried on. She needed to buy some buttons and thread, as Sophia was letting out all her skirts. She'd have liked to buy some linen material too, for a blouse, but every penny had suddenly become precious now neither of them was working.

She passed a tailor's shop and was bumped into by two men coming out of the doorway. She apologized, even though it wasn't her fault, at the same time the gentleman did too. Then she stopped and stared. Tom Sinclair stood gaping back at her, open-mouthed.

'Aurrie?' He frowned, puzzled.

She was the first to recover. 'How are you, Tom?'

'My God!' Tom enveloped her in a tight embrace and for a moment she relished being held by him. It'd been a long time since a man had held her, and Tom was as close as she would get to Reid. He stared at her in amazement. 'What are you doing in York?'

'Shopping.' She smiled brightly, acting as though them bumping into each other was an everyday occurrence. 'And you?'

'Oh this and that.' His gaze roamed over her and his grin faltered as he took in her appearance. He'd never seen her in anything but beautiful clothes and neatly groomed. She put a hand to her hair escaping from her felt hat and blushed. He'd noticed her faded clothes beneath her coat, which also needed a sponge and brush. Her shoes hadn't seen polish for weeks.

239

Tom turned to his companion. 'Hal, my friend, I'll meet you back at the hotel.'

Hal, a tall, healthy-looking young man winked, a devilish smile in his eyes. 'As you wish, my good fellow, but remember we leave on the evening train tomorrow.'

Aurora's blush deepened, imagining what Hal would think of her. 'You should have introduced me, Tom. He thinks the worst judging by that remark.'

'That's more exciting than the truth though, isn't it?' Tom's smile flashed, but the amusement in his eyes had vanished completely. 'There's a tearoom on the corner. Let's go.' He took her elbow and so shocked was she to see this serious side of him that she let him escort her into a small tearoom and assist her onto a wooden chair in the corner. He sat on the other side of the square table and lifted his hand to the passing waitress. 'Tea and a plate of-of cakes . . . er . . . food, sandwiches and the like.'

'Tom, I — ' The words dried in her mouth as she saw the agony in his eyes. 'What is it?'

'I cannot believe it.' He shook his head and looked as if he was going to cry.

Her heart leapt to her throat and she leaned forward. 'Good God, Tom, what?'

'What happened to you?' His voice came out on a whisper.

She sat back in her chair, again conscious of her appearance. 'You must be shocked.'

'Shocked?' he squeaked and then clearing his throat, he held his hands out as if in question. 'I thought you were travelling with your father's aunt? That's what your mother is telling everyone. Is this aunt without funds? Doesn't your father know — '

'Please, Tom, stop.' She rubbed her forehead, wondering how to tell him, whether she should tell him. 'I'm not with my father's aunt.'

'I don't understand.' He scratched his chin. 'Aurrie, dearest, you look like hell. You're so thin and . . . and shabby.'

She wanted to laugh at being called thin, especially when the front fastening corset she'd bought only two weeks ago no longer fitted her. The top button of her blue skirt was left undone and her white blouse strained across her breast, which she hid with her coat, but his expression of horror wiped the laughter from her instantly. Apart from the parts of her body concern with the child, the rest of her was thin, her hands and arms especially. 'It's a long story.'

'And I've got all day.'

'But I haven't.' She stood. 'I must go. It was nice seeing you again.'

'No.' He grabbed her wrist and forced her to sit down, causing the other customers to glance in their direction. 'Don't go, not yet.' He let go of her as she sat and the waitress brought over a tea tray, which she set out on the table. Tom watched Aurora the entire time and she knew he was full of questions. 'I want to hear it all, Aurrie.'

'Do you?' She pulled off her gloves, revealing her red and work-chapped hands and ignored his gasp of surprise at the sight of them. Dropping a cube of sugar into her cup, she then stirred it slowly with a teaspoon. 'I don't think you want to know, Tom, not really.' She gave him a sad smile, knowing his personality as one of fun and laughter, never taking anything seriously.

'I thought we were friends?'

'We were. When life was simple.'

'Aurrie, please. I can't bear to see you like this.'

'This?' She waved at her worn clothes. 'Good lord, Tom, this is a good day.' Her chuckle was brittle. 'We had enough water last night for a bath so I washed my hair . . . '

'We?' He leaned forward over the table, cradling his teacup in one hand and took her hand in his other.

'My mother, Sophia. We live together.'

'Your mother Sophia?' His eyes widened. 'Dearest, are you ill?'

'Mad you mean?' This time she did laugh. 'I wish I was, but alas I'm quite sane.' She bent over the table until their faces were nearly touching. 'Can you cope with knowing the truth, Tom Sinclair? The man who has never had a moment of responsibly in his life?'

He sat back. 'That's not fair.'

She shrugged, not caring. He didn't know anything about suffering, of hard work, of struggling to make a life from nothing.

'Something terrible has happened. I can gather that, Aurora. You don't have to tell me anything more if you don't want to.'

'You said you wanted to hear it.'

'Not if it upsets you.'

'I don't think anything could upset me now.

242

I'm immune to all.'

'Aurrie.'

She stared across the room, casually watching the other people at tables. The tearoom wasn't busy and had plenty of empty tables. The slim, dainty waitress returned with a plate of mixed sandwiches, a stand of delicate pastries and another small plate of slices of cake. Aurora fought the urge to wrap it all up and take it home for her and Sophia to eat later. They were economizing again, trying to save every penny for their uncertain future, and the basic food they ate was simply an energy intake, not a pleasurable pastime.

She studied Tom's immaculate army uniform for the first time. 'I forgot you had joined the army. You look very dashing. What are you doing in York?'

He sipped his tea. 'Visiting friends. Distancing myself from Mother.'

'Oh?'

'Since Father's funeral she has been unbearable.'

Aurora sat straighter. 'Your father died?'

'Yes. A week ago. His heart, you know.' He crumbled a triangle of stuffed pastry on his plate. 'We buried him in London yesterday. It's hit everyone hard. I couldn't deal with the whole situation and jumped on the first train north. I arrived here this morning.'

She closed her eyes at the thought of Reid suffering the loss of his dear father and she wasn't there to comfort him. 'I'm so sorry to hear of it. Mr Sinclair was a fine man.'

'Yes, he was. The best.' Tom glanced out of the window. 'We are all trying to comprehend the loss in our own way, but Mother is near insane with grief.'

'How sad.'

'Poor Reid cops the brunt of it all, unlucky sap.' Tom sniffed and sighed heavily. 'He's escaping to New York to get away. He was leaving this morning from Southampton and should be on the high seas by now. Mother has been driving us all demented, but him worst of all. She demands all of his time and energies. He must concern himself only with the family business, the estates, he must hurry up and marry and provide an heir. On and on she is at him. He's a saint to put up with it. I couldn't. I don't.' He gave a snort. 'I left the house as soon as I could. I wish the army hadn't given me leave. It is a coward I am, Aurrie, a blighted coward, who is now a solider sworn to fight for his country but one who runs from his own mother. Ironic, yes?'

Inside, she cried silently at the news Reid was so far away from her, crossing the Atlantic and living his life. Despite her heart beating a tattoo against her ribs at the talk of Reid, she squeezed Tom's hand, acknowledging his pain. 'Don't be too hard on yourself, Tom.'

'I have to be. No one else is and I need to be aware of who I truly am. I can have no false modesty, Aurrie, not anymore.' He crumbled more pastry. 'I am a father, don't you know. A few lines scribbled on a note told me so. A fine boy somewhere. My boy.'

'Oh, Tom.'

'Christ!' He thrust the plate away, scattering crumbs on the white linen tablecloth. 'Hark at me. I cannot even be a proper friend. Here we are with you in desperate need of . . . of some help and I talk about myself. I have more of Mother in me than I thought.' A look of disgust crossed his face. 'I am a useless person, Aurrie. But I think you already know this.'

'Oh stop it, Tom. I haven't the time to listen to you bleat about how unfair life has been to you. Have you run from home because you are bastard born? No. Did you find out that the person you loved and wanted to marry would be forever lost to you because his witch of a mother found out a family secret? No. Are you carrying a child that will be illegitimate like its mother? No!' She stopped abruptly; aware she'd raised her voice and was nearly shouting at him.

Tom's handsome face had lost all color. He stared at her. 'Oh God, Aurrie.'

Hands shaking, she picked up her teacup and sipped at it.

'You cannot be serious.'

'Of course I would lie about such things,' she said tartly.

'I want to know it all.' He took her hand and kissed it. 'None of these things make you any less in my eyes.' His gaze dropped to her stomach hidden under her coat.

'Yes, I am with child.'

'That's why you left home?'

'Yes.'

'Where are you living now?'

245

'Walmgate way,' she hedged, not wanting to fully divulge where she lived.

'Walmgate? In the slums?' He looked incredulous. 'I don't believe it.'

'Neither could I for a while.'

'Tell me about it.'

She nodded and taking a deep breath told him that she'd found out she was illegitimate, about running away, finding Sophia, moving to the lane, even told him about Big Eddie's murder and now the need for a new home. She took another deep shuddering breath, feeling a little better.

Tom sat back in his chair, absorbing all the details while she selected a beef sandwich and took a bite. 'It's all too amazing, Aurrie. I'm speechless.'

She shrugged and continued to eat, dreadfully hungry now.

'And your real mother, Sophia, she is a good person?'

'Oh yes. Very much so. She's like my mother ... like Winnie, just not as soft I suppose. Sophia's had to harden up to deal with what she's been through.'

'Who told you about her?'

Aurora swallowed and took a sip of tea, buying time.

'Can't you tell me?'

'I don't think I should.' She wiped her mouth. 'Actually, I should be going now.'

'Aurora.'

For a moment he sounded so much like Reid that she jerked in shock. Hot tears gathered behind her eyes and that angered her. She couldn't be weak and cry. There was no room in her life for tears. But every now and then Tom would look a certain way and remind her of Reid and it broke her heart all over again.

'Who told you and why?' Tom persisted, a steeliness coming into his eyes.

'You don't need to know.'

'I have a feeling that I do.'

'It doesn't matter now.'

'All the same, I need to know. You cannot tell half a story.'

'I must go, Tom.'

He leaned forward, his stare holding hers. 'Who are you protecting? Surely after such a revelation they don't deserve your honor.'

'The damage has been done. What is the point of causing more harm?'

'Harm?' His eyes narrowed. 'Harm to whom? You?'

'No.'

'Then your family?'

She swallowed, hating how he was winkling this out of her. She was doing her best to shield him, but he was like a dog with a bone. 'I am going home, Tom.'

'Tell me, Aurrie,' he whispered, his face softening with concern. 'I'll have no peace until you do.'

Her shoulders sagged in defeat. 'Your mother.'

'My mother?' His eyebrows nearly shot up to his hairline. 'What on earth!'

Aurora folded her napkin carefully, pressing down on the seam. 'She found out that Reid and I were . . . were . . . '

'You and Reid?' Tom shifted in his chair, his expression full of confusion. 'I don't understand.'

'I loved Reid.'

'I had no idea. None at all.' He glanced around the tearoom as though defying anyone to dispute his claim. 'How could this be?'

'Reid and I fell in love. I believe we had been for a while, but we only really acknowledged it last year. We planned to marry.'

'Christ Almighty.' Tom ran his fingers through his short hair. 'You and Reid. I cannot believe it.' Then his eyes widened. '*You* were the one he was talking about, the one he wanted to marry this summer!'

'Was I?' She shrugged. 'Perhaps at one time, but then I think he changed his mind and maybe Miss FitzGibbon grew in prominence in his life.'

'I don't believe that for a moment. If he wanted her they'd be engaged by now.'

It was her turn to be shocked. 'They aren't?'

'No. He has nothing to do with her, or any woman come to think of it. He was insufferable before father died and now I know why.' Tom stared at her. 'You ran away and he thought you'd gone travelling with an aunt. He didn't understand . . .'

'I had to go, Tom.'

'But why?'

'I couldn't hurt my family.' She placed a hand over her stomach.

Tom's eyes followed the gesture and his eyes widened. 'You're having *Reid's* baby?'

'You are quick,' she quipped, fighting the tears. 'But he can never know. I won't do that to him, Tom. You must promise to never tell him.'

'This is ridiculous, Aurrie. He would marry you in an instant. You said you loved him.'

'I do love him. I love him enough to want only the best for him. Don't you see? I'm bastard born. People, your mother especially, won't stand for it, not in your circle. I'd be a social pariah and Reid would lose friends, acquaintances, business deals.'

'No, you're wrong, so wrong, Aurrie.' He gripped both her hands in earnest. 'You have to come home. Tell him everything.'

She shook her head, knowing it was impossible. 'I won't turn up on the doorstep big with child, Tom. I won't do it to my family or yours. The scandal would be too much. I'm a bastard having a bastard. It would be social death for everyone. They don't deserve it. I must think of my sisters' future, my mother's happiness.' She lowered her gaze. 'To be honest, I don't think I could face my father and see disappointment in his eyes. And then there is your mother and her threats . . . '

'We'll get around that, I promise. Besides, Reid won't care about the scandal. He'd overcome all that. He'll want you above everything else.'

'But it's not just him it affects. He has to take care of your mother and your brothers until they are of age, which isn't for a few years yet. He has so much responsibility, the business, the inheritance, all the estates, everything. I won't add to his burden. I won't.'

'So you're sacrificing both of your happiness, his and yours?'

249

'I have to.'

'You're wrong, Aurrie. Very wrong. Reid will have you in a heartbeat. All the rest can be taken care of.'

'How? How do I explain Sophia to Reid's friends and business associates? I won't give her up now. She is a part of my family. And how do I explain walking down the aisle heavy with child?'

'The gossip will die down eventually.'

'But before it does it will do damage. I won't put anyone through that, not Reid, my parents, Sophia, my sisters, your brothers, no one.'

'And the child?'

'None of them will ever know about the baby. Sophia and I intend on moving away. I'll pretend to be a widow.'

'This is too much to take in.' Tom wiped a hand over his eyes. 'I'm stunned.'

'You must never speak of this. I hold you in confidence. Promise me!'

'You have my word, though I believe it to be a mistake.' He stood and she rose also. 'I need to get out of here and breathe.' He hurriedly paid the bill and taking her elbow escorted her outside.

The wind had died down a little and the sun poked out between white fluffy clouds. Exhausted, Aurora felt as though she'd fought a battle or run a mile. She was thankful Tom held her arm.

'Aurrie.'

'Yes.'

'I don't want to leave you. Can I take you home?'

'No, not today.' She smiled to soften the

words. 'I know you mean well, but I need some time alone.'

'I don't want to leave York without seeing you again. Can I call on you? Tomorrow morning?'

'I don't think so.' She shrugged helplessly. 'There's nothing more to be said.'

'I think there is.' His gaze dropped to her stomach again. 'I can't believe you're having Reid's baby. He finally lost control of himself and did something out of character.'

'What does that mean?'

'You know Reid as well as I do. Deflowering a virgin isn't something I'd believe he'd do.'

'Must you be so crass?'

He grinned. 'Sorry. I'm shocked that's all. Reid never shows us his softer side where women are concerned. He's never been a lady's man, never flaunted conquests before us.'

'He hasn't. You just happened to bump into me and for the first time see evidence.'

'True.'

They paused as the city's church bells pealed the hour. When able to speak again, Aurora gave his cheek a quick kiss and stepped away. 'It's been good to see you again, but try to forget me, Tom.'

His expression was strained. He glanced at the passing traffic. 'I could never forget you. You are the sister I never had.'

'Try to. It is for the best.' She pulled on her gloves.

'The regiment is in Africa, you know. I am not with them because father was dying and then there was the funeral. Being a Sinclair meant strings were pulled, you know how it is.' He shrugged one shoulder.

251

She nodded, but kept quiet.

'I leave for Africa very soon, but before I go I think we should be married.'

Robbed of breath, she stared at him.

17

Aurora nervously plumped up a thin red cushion on the sofa, checked the curtains hung straight and then gave the fire another poke.

'Aurrie, sit down, for heaven's sake.' Sophia twisted her hands on her lap. 'I'm becoming as jumpy as you.'

'I'm sorry.' She replaced the poker, and looked out the window. Tom was due to arrive any minute and her stomach rolled. 'I should never have agreed for him to come here.'

'You've nothing to be ashamed of. The house is the best in the lane, we've done all we could to make it decent.' Sophia smoothed her black skirt over her knees. 'You said he wouldn't judge us.'

'He won't, not really. I mean not intentionally.' Aurora swallowed, her tongue seemed too big for her mouth. She looked around the sitting room, noticing all its faults. The damp, the thin coat of whitewash, the cheap furniture. She felt her breakfast come back up and put a hand to her throat.

'Aurora, please.' Sophia stood and gently touched her arm. 'Sit and calm down.'

'You don't understand.' How could she explain to Sophia what she couldn't grasp herself? Marriage to Tom, a Sinclair? It was all wrong. Insane to even consider it. Yet, last night, it was all she could think about. This morning she had woken to a headache and despair eating her heart. She couldn't marry Tom, not even to give her baby a name and make him or her legitimate. It was like a betrayal to Reid. She couldn't do it. Once, all she wanted was to be a Sinclair, but not Mrs *Thomas* Sinclair. The irony was laughable, only she was far from laughing.

A shadow passed the window and she closed her eyes momentarily to summon the strength she'd need to reject Tom.

'I'll get the door.' Sophia went and answered the knock.

Aurora heard them talking, introducing themselves. A second later Tom was standing in the sitting room, which seemed a lot smaller than it was a minute ago.

'Good morning, Aurrie.' He smiled tenderly, as if knowing how delicate she felt.

She returned his smile. 'Thank you for coming, Tom.'

'Please sit down, Mr Sinclair. I'll get some tea.' Sophia said, waving him towards the chair and then disappearing into the kitchen.

Tom sat on the edge of the chair and Aurora had never seen him so unsure of himself. He wore an unreadable expression on his face. 'This is a lot different from home, Aurrie,' he murmured.

'Yes.'

'But not as bad as I imagined.'

'It was rather dreadful when we first arrived. It has taken us months to make it suitable.' She felt the heat from the fire through her skirts from standing so long in front of it. Sitting down on the sofa, she took a deep breath. 'Tom.'

'Aurrie.'

They spoke together and chuckled.

'May I go first?' Tom asked, his eyes hopeful.

'Please do.'

'I know what I asked you yesterday might have seemed impulsive, reckless even, but I meant it.'

'But Tom — '

He held a hand up. 'No, let me finish. I know you love Reid. I'm not asking you to love me, or to be a true wife to me in any respect.' He jerked to his feet and went to the fireplace. 'I sent a wire to my superior and got his permission.'

'Already?' Her eyes widened.

'Being a Sinclair has its advantages, as I told you yesterday.'

'But Tom — '

'I've done a lot of thinking during the night and this morning. I've weighed it all up in my mind and I know I want this.'

'Yes, maybe you do now, but what if you meet a lady and fall in love with her? If you're married to me you're not free to be with someone else.'

'Marriage has never been something I've coveted, Aurrie. I'll be honest in that. My mother has done nothing but parade suitable young ladies before our eyes from the minute we turned twenty, but none of them interested me beyond an evening of fun. I couldn't imagine having to be tied to one of them forever.'

'But by marrying me you will be tied to me.'

'Yet, that doesn't worry me at all. Perhaps it is because we will be two separate people still. I'll have no demands, no expectations from you, or you from me.'

She was beginning to understand his meaning. 'You don't know that one day you might meet the woman who you want to spend the rest of your life with, to have children with. I cannot take that from you.'

'The same could be said for you.' He raised one eyebrow in question. 'After all, you are young and beautiful. You could have anyone.'

'I will never have another man. Reid was . . .'

'Will you not reconsider contacting him?'

She shook her head. 'No. That past is past.'

'Are you sure?'

'Yes.'

'And what if you find another man?'

'There will never be another for me. But you, you are quite different. I will not rob you of the chance to be married to the one you love.'

He twirled the gold signet ring on his little finger. 'I have thought of that eventuality, not that I think it will happen, but I did think about it, and if such a woman was to come into my life then you and I could sort something out, divorce or whatever.'

'That's not so easy and again it would bring scandal, the very thing I'm trying to avoid.'

'But if that was to happen it wouldn't be anytime soon. It could be ten, twenty years away, or never!' He rested his arm along the mantelpiece and stared into the low fire. 'The honest truth is I don't see myself ever living a normal life, Aurrie. I don't want to stay in England, always at the beck and call of my mother. The army will do me for now, but I know later I will leave it and go my own way. I have a fancy to travel widely, go exploring, sail the seas.' He turned and grinned at her, one of his boyish grins she knew so well. 'Let me roam the world happy knowing I've done my bit. I've helped you and your child, my nephew, my blood. I can give you the support you need.'

'You make it sound so easy.'

'One small ceremony and you become my wife. That security is yours. I will set up an allowance for you and the child.'

'Oh no. No, Tom, not money.'

'I will not be swayed on this Aurrie. Whether you marry me or not, I have decided that your baby, my niece or nephew will have my support for life.' He swept his arm around the room. 'Do you think I would want you scraping a living amongst all this?'

'This is all I can expect, Tom. This is my life now and it will be my child's. I can work and earn money. I have Sophia's help. I can do it by myself.'

'Do you honestly think I would walk away from here and leave you with nothing?'

They both looked away, aware they had raised their voices.

'You are too proud, Aurrie.'

'And you are too good, Tom.'

He ducked his head and gave her a saucy look. 'I've never been called good, dearest.'

'That's because you're always so intent on being bad, just to shock people.'

'You know me too well.' He laughed. 'Where's that tea?'

Aurora rose to her feet. 'I'll go and see.' As she

257

went to leave, Tom grabbed her hand and brought it up to his chest. Seriousness replaced the humor. 'I know I am not Reid. I don't mean to take his place, but since you won't allow him the chance to be a father to his child, then please let me. He'd want to know I looked after the both of you in his stead.'

Aurora blinked back tears, her throat thick with emotion. 'I miss him, Tom, so very much. I gave him everything I had.'

'I know, dearest girl, I know.' He stroked her cheek. 'I could happily kill my mother for the damage she's caused.'

'So could I.' Her smile was watery. 'But what's done is done, and he doesn't have all the blame. I seduced him.'

Tom's mouth curved into a lopsided grin, so like Reid's. 'Then he's a lucky man.'

'And I was stupid to do so.'

'Being in love makes us do silly things.'

'Indeed. At least I have a part of Reid that she cannot take from me. And I am comforted by the knowledge that Reid will live his life fulfilling all the responsibilities his parents expect of him, that will compensate for any hurt I may have caused him.'

'None of that can replace you though, Aurrie.'

'Oh, he'll forget me in time when he's married with children.'

'Will he?' Tom frowned. 'I'm not so sure.'

She pulled away. 'I'll get the tea.'

'And you'll marry me and give the baby a name, its rightful name of Sinclair?'

'Will you let me think about it some more?'

258

'I leave tonight, Aurrie.'

'So soon?' She hated the thought of him going out of her life again. Being with him reminded her of home, of summer days gone by when her world was perfect and simple.

'The army calls, dearest.'

'Of course.' She nodded and left the room.

★ ★ ★

The sun burst out between clusters of clouds and drenched the little yard of number nine in bright sunshine. Aurora sighed, enjoying the warmth on her face for a moment before going back inside to finish packing. They'd begun packing after Tom left yesterday afternoon. They only had a week left remaining a number nine. There was so much to think about, Tom's proposal, moving, finding work. Her head swam with it all.

Sophia came out to find her, wiping her hands on a towel. 'There you are.'

'I stopped for a minute.'

'Stop a bit longer, it won't matter. Everything is about packed now that can be.' She sat on an upturned crate next to Aurora. 'Noah will take the last of the boxes over to his house this afternoon.'

'He won't take no for an answer, will he?''

'No.' Sophia lifted her face to the sun. 'What will you do about Tom?'

'I don't know. I'm so torn.'

'You should marry him.' Sophia turned her head and stared at her. 'For no other reason than to give the baby a name and allow it to be born on the right side of the blanket. Don't let the poor little blighter carry the shame we inflicted upon it. You have the chance to put it right.'

'But I worry about Tom and what he's giving up.'

'What is he giving up, for God's sake? He's told you repeatedly that he doesn't want a wife and children, a family home. He wants to travel, go on adventure. Give the man some credit for knowing what he wants.'

'He's escaping his mother.'

'Then let him. From all accounts she's a right witch. Let the man go and be free to please himself, knowing at least he's done right by you, his brother and his niece or nephew.'

'Can it be that simple though?'

'It can be whatever you make it, Aurrie.' Sophia stood on hearing the front door open. 'You'll be his wife in name only. We can still lead our lives.' She turned as Jean came running out of the scullery.

'Oh, you're both here, good.' She puffed.

'What's the matter?' Sophia frowned.

'Lily, her pains have started. She was calling for you. Come on.' Jean hurried back into the house.

Sophia looked at Aurora, her face worried. 'You don't have to go. I don't want you being scared of what to face when it's your own time.'

Aurora heaved herself up. 'Lily is my friend. If she wants me then I'll go to her. Besides, I need to know what I'll be enduring myself. Nothing is scarier than being ignorant.'

'But Tom is coming to say goodbye.'

'Not for hours yet.'

They washed and tidied themselves, with Aurora donning her coat to cover her stomach, then they crossed the cobbles to Lily's house. Old Alfie was sitting out on a chair reading his newspaper in the sun and they called good morning to him.

'Poor Lily is in for a hard day then?' he asked, a pipe drooping from the corner of his mouth.

'Yes. But worth it in the end,' Sophia replied.

'Is it? The poor fatherless scrap.'

Sophia paused on the step. 'The baby will have a grandfather and a loving mother, that's more than some.'

'Aye. Well, give her my best then.' Alfie lifted up his paper and went back to his reading.

Aurora rolled her eyes at Sophia when they found the house full of the gossiping women, sipping tea and eating cake.

'She's upstairs, lass,' Dilys said, pouring our more tea. 'Jean, take this out to Alfie, he'll dry out in this heat. What is with this weather, I ask you? Cold one minute and back to summer the next.'

Aurora and Sophia climbed the stairs. 'Dilys sure makes herself at home in other people's houses, doesn't she?'

'She's good hearted though,' Sophia whispered.

'Indeed, especially when she's eating someone else's food,' Aurora muttered, slowly opening the door to Lily's bedroom. Inside, they found Lily lying on the bed, pale and moaning as a contraction seized her. Rubbing her back was Mrs Murphy.

'Sure an' I'm glad to see you two here.' Mrs Murphy smiled.

'How's she doing?' Sophia asked, sitting on the side of the bed and tucking Lily's hair behind her ears.

'She's coming on a treat, aren't you, lass?' Mrs Murphy glanced up at Aurora. 'Come round this side, take over from me, I'll be needed at the other end soon.'

'Has the doctor been sent for?'

'Doctor?' Mrs Murphy scowled. 'And what would he be needed for? Jesus, Mary and Joseph. I'll have this little 'un out before the sun sets altogether.' As if to convince them of her worth, she got busy down the other end, tidying and sorting, before going to the door and yelling for more towels and fresh water.

'Aurora.' Lily opened her eyes and smiled. 'I was wondering where you were.'

'We didn't know until Jean came and fetched us.' Aurora held her hand. 'I'm sorry. I would have been here sooner.'

'I didn't tell anyone at first because I knew it would take a while. The pains started last night but they weren't much to bother about. They got stronger this morning after I sent me dad off to work and baked a cake. I started cooking a stew with some dumplings for me dad's dinner, but I had to stop.'

'Never mind any of that now.' Aurora stroked her cheek as Lily's eyes squeezed shut while another pain gripped her.

'That's a good girl,' Mrs Murphy crooned from the end of the bed. 'You push when you're ready, I'm here.'

'Oh no, Mrs Murphy,' Lily said, sucking in a breath, 'I'm fine . . . ' She put her chin on her chest and groaned loudly. 'Oh, dear God . . . help!'

'Go with it, lass. Do you need to push?'

'Yesss!' Lily strained, the veins popping out on her neck. She squeezed Sophia and Aurora's hands and Aurora tried hard not to whimper from the pain of it.

A minute later it was over and Lily relaxed slightly, but Aurora could tell she was bracing for another one. When it came again it was longer and stronger. Lily cried out from deep in her throat.

Sweat broke out on Aurora's forehead. 'Can we get some air in here?' She looked at the closed window. 'Shall I open it?'

'No,' Mrs Murphy snapped. 'It'll cause a draught on the mother and child. Take your bloody coat off.'

Sophia's eyes widened and she faintly shook her head. Heeding the warning, Aurora sat on the chair and patted Lily's hand. As well as being hot, she felt rather useless.

For the next hour, Aurora wondered if she could stand it anymore. Poor Lily suffered dreadfully, she hated seeing her in such pain, but now her own back was aching from all the bending and she was drenched in sweat. The room was like a furnace and even Mrs Murphy and Sophia were wilting in the oppressive atmosphere.

'Open the blasted window!' Lily screamed. 'I can't breathe!'

Aurora, ignoring Mrs Murphy ran to the window and pushed it up as high as it could go. She leaned into the fresh air, but there's wasn't a whimper of a breeze. Lily cried out again and Aurora rushed back to the bed just as the baby's head crowned. She stood staring at the tuff of hair, her eyes wide. Mrs Murphy murmured softly, coaxing Lily to be steady and not push too hard or she'd tear. Transfixed, Aurora watched Lily push and old hands swivel the shoulders. The baby slithered out in a rush of blood and fluid.

'There now, there now,' Mrs Murphy roughly wiped the baby over, clearing its puckered little face of white mucus. It let out a small wail. 'You've a lovely little lad, Lily,' she said. 'He's a good size too.' Mrs Murphy wrapped him up and then noticing Aurora so close, promptly put him in her arms. 'Here, have some practice, lass.'

Over the baby's head, Aurora stared at Mrs Murphy wordlessly. She knew!

'Sure, and I wouldn't be telling a soul, but them downstairs will guess soon enough. You can't hide behind a coat forever.' She turned away to deal with Lily and the afterbirth.

Aurora stepped closer to the bed. Sophia was wiping Lily's forehead with a cool cloth. 'Look, Lily, you have a son.' Aurora smiled down at the precious little person in her arms. He stared back at her, one hand free from the blanket. 'Welcome, little one, welcome to the world.'

'I'm calling him William Noah Bradshaw.' Lily sighed and gave a shiver as the afterbirth came away. She held out her arms for her son.

264

'A good name.' Sophia nodded as Aurora gave him to his mother and watched them together. 'I'll walk up to the ironmonger's and tell Noah he has a grandson.'

'You'll be all right, Lily?' Aurora asked.

'She'll be fine as soon as I've given her a bit of a wash.' Mrs Murphy spoke for her. 'She'll be tired and sore altogether, but nothing a bit of sleep won't put right.' She bundled a pile of bloodied clothes into a basket by the bed. 'I'll sit with her for a while and we'll have a cup of tea. Then Dilys has offered to sit up here until Noah finishes work.'

With that settled, Aurora and Sophia went downstairs and spent five minutes talking to the women about the baby. The excuse of going to Noah allowed them to escape the house and cross to their home.

'Aurora!' Tom hurried up the lane, his arm raised in greeting.

She put a hand to her hair, hoping she didn't look as awful as she felt. The August heat baked the cobbles. Tom joined them, bowed and enquiring after their health. She led him inside, but Sophia said she was going to Noah and left.

In the sitting room, Aurora sat on the chair and smothered a yawn. 'Oh, forgive me, Tom. My friend Lily just gave birth to a baby boy and anyone would think I'd done it I'm so tired.'

He stared around at the boxes. 'What are all these for?'

'We have to move by the end of the week.'

'That soon? Where will you go?'

'To Lily's for now. Her father is keen on

Sophia. I think they will marry one day.'

'But what about you?'

'I'll work that out as it comes. I can make it through each day if I only concentrate on one day at a time.'

'This is madness, Aurora, madness.' He slapped his thigh. She could see his mind working. 'You must marry me.'

'Yes.'

'I can take care of you, get you out of here. We'll find somewhere better for you and the baby and Sophia. I'm your best friend, damn it, let me take care of you. We can go to the church today to have the banns called and . . . ' his voice faded as he realized what she said. 'You'll marry me?'

'Yes.' She couldn't smile or be happy. She was doing it for her child. The baby that would soon be in her arms and depending on her for its very life. How could she not try to give it the best she could? Sophia had done it. Sophia had given her up for a better life. She wasn't about to give up her baby, but she could give him or her a name, its rightful name of Sinclair.

'Aurrie.'

She couldn't see him for the tears clouding her eyes. 'Tell me I'm doing the right thing, Tom.'

He crushed her into his arms. 'You are, dearest girl, you are.'

18

How are we going to hide you? I can't believe how big you've suddenly become.' Sophia gave Aurora a distressed glance as she paced the front room of number 10.

'You said it was about time I started to show properly.'

'I know, but Dilys knows something is going on. I'm certain of it.'

'If they find out then so be it.' Noah folded his newspaper. 'It's no one else's business.'

'Don't be foolish, Noah,' Sophia snapped. 'In this lane it's everyone's business what goes on.' She paused, a look of dismay on her face and she reached out her hand to him. 'I'm sorry.'

'Nay, I know you don't mean it.' He gave her a private smile and then turned to Aurora. 'Speaking of babies, I heard you have a cradle now?'

'Anthony found one for me.' Aurora grinned. 'You know what he's like. It was a little worn, and well, I would have liked a new one, but he spent a few days painting it and it's beautiful. He's keeping it in his room for now until we need it, as Mrs Murphy said it would be bad luck to bring it over here before the baby is born.' She glanced to Sophia. 'Mrs Murphy has knitted two sweet little bonnets. One for Will and one for my baby. The neighbors think they are both for Will.'

Sophia groaned. 'It'll get out, I tell you it will. Mrs Morrison won't stand for it. I know she won't. I heard that she once threw a stone and whatever muck she could find in the gutter at a girl in the next street who got with child before marriage.'

'Then she's a hypocrite.' Noah sucked on his pipe and finding it unlit, proceeded to fill the bowl with tobacco from a pouch in his pocket. 'I know when she came to this lane as a bride her waist was thick and their daughter was born only five months later.'

'Yes, but when you're already married it doesn't matter so much.' Sophia paced, worrying her thumbnail.

Aurora placed her knitting needles on her lap, the little jacket for her baby half finished. 'I'll keep inside a lot, at least for the next week and then it won't matter, I'll be married to Tom.'

Noah lit his pipe, squinting through the smoke. 'And soon we'll all be gone from here. So why should we give a toss to what any of them say?'

'Are you absolutely sure you want to come with us, Noah?' Aurora asked for the hundredth time.

'I told you, yes. Lily and I will follow you two where ever you go. There's nothing here for us if you leave the lane.'

'But the country is very different than the city. Some people can't take to it. They aren't used to the quiet and the space.'

'I'll be fine. I grew up in the country.'

'But Lily hasn't.'

'*Lily* will be fine also,' Lily said coming into the room, carrying baby Will. 'Please don't worry, Aurrie. I want to go to the country with you. It'll be a better life for Will. There he can grow up to be big and strong and have fresh air to breathe and good food. I won't deny him that.' She gave the baby to Sophia. 'I'll make us all a cup of tea.'

Knitting another row, Aurora dwelt on the happenings of the past days. Before Tom left for London to finalize his concerns, he had organized their wedding for Friday. She didn't know how he had managed it, although she believed he had paid the local vicar an enormous sum of money for them to be married without the three weeks reading of the banns. Instead they had only a one week banns and left it up to the vicar to explain the rest, apparently something along the lines of mixed communication or some such. Thankfully, he was a forward thinking man and muttered things about 'a man fighting for his country' and all that. After the ceremony, Tom would leave immediately for his ship to take him to his regiment in Africa.

After Sunday's banns reading, the women were agog with the news and crowded into number nine wanting to know all the facts. Aurora believed that most of the women knew she was pregnant. She had caught more than one of them on occasion looking at her thick waist and knew it was only a matter of time before one of them spoke their thoughts out loud.

Aside from the wedding plans and moving into number 10, Aurora had received a letter from

Tom in London. He had told her of a cottage and smallholding he owned near Hebden Bridge in West Yorkshire. It had been a part of his inheritance when he gained his majority, and he had signed the whole of it over to her. If she wished, she and Sophia could move there straight after the wedding. When Noah heard of this, he went quiet for days and Lily confided to Aurora that he wasn't going to ask Sophia to marry him now. He didn't want to make her choose, or give up the chance of living some-where nice away from the lane. Aurora instantly spoke to Sophia about it and together they decided to ask Noah and Lily to move to Hebden Bridge with them.

Tom's gift of the cottage meant more to Aurora than she could express. She wrote to Tom, explaining it was too much, that such a gift was unnecessary, but he'd refused her excuses. He wanted peace of mind while away, and with them living in the house he felt relieved. The security of having a home of her own lifted Aurora's spirits. Since agreeing to marry Tom, guilt plagued her about abandoning Reid. It was silly really. She couldn't have Reid and she wanted him to be happy in his life, so why couldn't she do the same for herself? The past had to be forgotten. Although it was easy to say, it was far less easier to do.

★ ★ ★

The next day, Aurora broke her promise to stay indoors and walked to the shops. She needed a

270

little peace and the cramped conditions at number ten didn't provide the solitude she wanted to think. So while Lily rocked Will to sleep upstairs and Sophia did the weekly washing in the scullery, Aurora wrapped a long shawl over her shoulders and across her stomach and left the house. Heavy dark clouds threatened rain, but she hoped they'd hold for an hour while she cleared her head.

Old Alfie was sitting on his chair outside his door and she crossed the cobbles to him. 'Good morning.'

'Morning, lass. You off out?'

'To the shops.'

'Don't be long, rain's coming.'

'I'll hurry then.' She paused. 'Do you need me to get you anything?'

'No ta, lass. I'm right. I walked down early and got me paper and some fish off the market. I like a nice piece of haddock for me supper.'

'Well, I'll be going then.' As she rounded the corner, she waved and smiled in greeting to Hetty Barclay, but not wanting to chat, she put her head down and kept going.

Ignoring the threat of rain for a while she meandered along the river, stopping every now and then to watch the men working on the boats. She liked to imagine each boat's destination and the goods they carried. Once, dreaming she was Reid's wife, she had envisioned sailing the oceans with him. Travelling to America and Italy, shopping in New York, listening to opera in Venice. There would be trips to France, Germany and Africa, maybe even the Orient.

271

She and Reid would dine and dance in exotic places, visit ancient ruins, sleep under the stars in tents on dry plains. Such girlish dreams. How long ago all that seemed. Another lifetime.

She turned away from the river towards the throbbing city and tried not to think of Reid, but it was difficult. Where was he right at this minute? Was he busy meeting interesting people in New York, or seeing fascinating places? Was he thinking about her as she was thinking about him? Sighing deeply, she put him from her mind.

Soon enveloped into the crowds of the busy York streets, she wandered aimlessly, content to window shop. She had a shopping list in her reticule but as yet felt uninclined to carry goods. With the baby's growth, she tired much easier now.

Turning into Goodramgate, she felt with prickly sensation of being followed. Stopping to look at a window display, she used the glass to see behind her. Over her left shoulder, across the road, a man wearing a black hat waited. To another person he seemed like a fellow with time on his hands, but as Aurora moved off, he also started walking. When she stopped again so did he. When she went into a shop, he loitered outside. How dare someone torment her this way? She was so tired of fighting for peace of mind. It must be Ellerton. Fury replaced her fear.

Coming out a glass and china shop, she hurried over to confront the man, taking him by surprise. 'You there! Why do you follow me?'

Taking a step back, the man glanced up and

down the street. 'I'm not.'

'Yes you are, so don't deny it.' She pointed a finger in his chest. 'Who sent you?'

'No one.'

'Liar!' She fought the urge to grab his labels and shake him. 'I'm tired of it, do you hear? Leave me alone.'

The fellow smirked, revealing a missing front tooth. 'I'm only doing what I get paid for, Miss.'

'Who is paying you?'

'That I can't tell you.'

'Well, you can tell him that if he doesn't leave me alone I'll go to the police.' She knew it must be Merv Ellerton behind this. Blast the man!

'I wouldn't advise that.' The fellow's eyes narrowed. 'Such an action would bring . . . unpleasantness to you and your loved ones.'

She sucked in a breath. He was threatening Sophia too? 'Just leave me alone.'

The man studied his dirty fingernails. 'Perhaps my boss could be persuaded.'

As quickly as the anger came, it now left her and her hands shook. 'I'm not interested in anything Ellerton has to say.'

'A foolish mistake.'

'Stay away from me.' She spun away and forced herself to stride down the road with her head high, although her insides felt as if they'd turned to water. The baby kicked hard against her ribs and she bit her top lip to stop crying out. She concentrated on getting home to Sophia and didn't look back. The sooner they left York the better.

* * *

By the morning of the wedding, everyone in number ten was a bundle of nerves. The house was packed up and looked bare, unloved. The furniture they were taking to the cottage had already left two days ago. After the wedding they were all going to the train station.

The women were in and out of each other's homes as they prepared for the ceremony, many were upset that there wasn't to be a celebration afterwards in the lane as usual when someone marries. Although, some remarked on the horse already bolting whenever they looked at Aurora's wide girth.

Out the front of the church, Aurora ignored the fussing of Sophia and Lily and Dilys. In her mind this wasn't her wedding day, the magical day she'd dreamed of with Reid. This was a simple occasion were she legalized her baby's future. Nothing more. Nothing less.

'Aurrie!' Peggy rushed towards her, with Nancy following behind. 'We couldn't miss your special day.'

'Thank you for coming.' Aurora squeezed Peggy's hand and noticing Nancy hesitancy she gave her a welcome smile. 'Thank you, both of you.'

'I hope you'll be happy, Aurrie,' Nancy murmured.

'Course she will.' Peggy laughed. 'She's caught herself a handsome chap and she's getting away from this place.'

Nancy stepped closer. 'Where will you go?'

274

'To the country,' Aurora hedged, not wanting any information to get back to Merv Ellerton. Nancy flushed and turned as Sophia came and introduced herself to them.

Peggy leaned closer. 'She's sorry, Aurrie, Nancy I mean. Merv can charm the birds out of the trees, you know that. She never meant to tell him anything. She's been in the doldrums ever since. Especially since the new girl, who took your place, is a right trollop. A real nasty piece of work and forever getting us in trouble over nothing.'

'I'm sorry to hear it, but I don't want to think of that place or Ellerton today.' She glanced over at Sophia and Nancy, who were deep in conversation.

'No, of course not.' Peggy nudged her. 'You've got better things to think about now. Imagine, a nice place out in the country. You're set, you are.'

'Yes. I'm very lucky.' Aurora wished Tom would hurry up and arrive. Her nerves couldn't take much more.

Five minutes late, Tom hurtled out of a hansom that had come straight from the train station and dashed to Aurora's side where she stood waiting by the church door with the others. Sophia ushered everyone inside to join the neighbors who'd gone in a few minutes before.

'So, Miss Pettigrew, are you ready to become a Sinclair?' Tom grinned, looking handsome in his stiff uniform.

She reached up and brushed a smut of coal off his shoulder. 'How was your journey from London?'

'Slept like a baby all the way.'

'Will you be in a lot of trouble for missing your ship?'

'Don't worry about that. It is a small hiccup. I sail on tonight's tide. A day won't make much difference.'

'But Tom, it is serious.'

'What can they do, shoot me?'

Her eyes widened. 'Well, yes.'

'I don't think so. Father went to school with most of my superior officers. They all wished they could have attended his funeral, but the troubles in Africa prevented it. I'll get told off, but I'll win them around . . . Besides, I'm a Sinclair with relations in many high places. Now enough of all that.' The laughter left his eyes for a moment and he took her gloved hand. 'Are you sure, Aurora?'

'Are you, Tom? I'm not losing my freedom as you are. It's this marriage or pretended widowhood for me, but for you . . . '

'I'm doing what I want to. I promise you. I never want you to feel guilty about me. Assure me you won't.'

She nodded and kissed his cheek. 'You're a good man, Tom Sinclair.'

'That's down to you, Aurrie. Without you, I am a rebel and a waster, and don't let anyone tell you different.' He grinned again and kissed her hand. 'Let's go get married.'

Noah walked her down the aisle and she fought tears, wishing it was her father instead. Anthony Murphy stood as best man to Tom and they were grinning like schoolboys as she joined them at the altar. To prevent gossip reaching his mother, Tom had told no one, not even his closest friends that he was getting married. Aurora hoped Julia would never find out, and prayed that Tom didn't let it slip one day in the future.

Afterwards, Aurora couldn't quite remember the ceremony. It was if her mind had closed down, all she felt was the cool gold band going onto her finger and that she was declared Mrs Sinclair.

They left the church to pealing of the bells and the calls of good wishes from some of the women, for only a few were going with them to the station. As Tom assisted her into the hansom cab, she looked across the road and saw the man, her silent shadow, watching. He tipped his black hat to her and smiled. When he walked away she took it as a sign the watching ordeal was over. Safely married, Ellerton obviously thought her as no longer a threat, and despite what he'd done, she was glad to have the whole sorry episode finished.

'Aurrie, are you all right?' Tom asked sitting in beside her. 'Your face is a little pale.'

'I'm fine.' She gave a brief smile and put the man and Ellerton from her mind.

On the platform, Aurora walked with Tom to the first class carriage and stood with him, knowing this would be the last time she'd see him for a long while. 'Thank you again, Tom.'

'Nonsense. I had to give my niece or nephew a good start in life didn't I?' He looked around at the milling crowds, for once his face serious, and then he gazed back at her. 'You'll write to me often, won't you, Aurrie. Let me know how you're getting on and everything. Your letters will be important to me out there.'

'Of course. I'll write every week.' She gripped his hands. 'You'll not be too reckless, promise me.'

He leaned down and kissed her softly on the lips. 'I am as I am, Aurrie, you know that.'

'I do, that's what worries me.'

'Don't worry over me.' He stared straight into her eyes. 'If you need anything get in contact with my solicitors in London. You have their address?'

'Yes.'

'Don't lose it. They have the deeds to the farm cottage. It's all yours. Also, there is the account which money will be deposited in for you each month.'

'Oh, Tom . . . It's too much.'

'No, it is what you deserve. It's your due. You'd have a lot more if Mother hadn't interfered and well . . . '

She knew what he was thinking and her heart thumped because of it. If Julia hadn't interfered she'd be married to Reid not Tom by now.

He handed her a small box. 'Give this to the baby.'

She opened the box to find a small silver pendant in the shape of horse nestled on a bed of white silk. 'It's beautiful.'

'Teach the baby to ride when it is old enough.' He peeked in at the box. 'Tell him or her of the rides we used to go on.'

'I will. Thank you.'

'Live a good life, Aurrie.'

'I will, Tom, thanks to you, but please don't make this a final goodbye. I want you to visit us one day. Promise me you will.' She flung her arms around his neck and kissed him passionately, not as a lover, but as a woman sending a man to war. It was a kiss of luck, of hope, a memory to take with him.

The train whistle blew and they sprang apart. Tom hugged her to him one last time and then abruptly turned away and went up the step into the train. Aurora watched the train pull slowly away, but Tom didn't lean out of the window and wave.

Sad at heart, she felt the presence of another and wasn't surprised that Sophia stood beside her. 'It's time to go, Aurrie. Our train departs in two minutes.'

'I'm coming.' Taking a deep breath, she forced a smile and went to join the others, who waited on the next platform. Dilys and Jean along with Mrs Murphy and Anthony had come to see them off.

'Now then, you'll not be forgetting us?' Dilys said hugging Sophia and then Aurora. 'My Jean can read and write so we'll be expecting letters, mind.'

'Yes, of course.' Aurora adjusted her blue hat and veil, which Dilys threatened to knock off with her exuberant hug. She tugged down the light blue jacket that matched the skirt and turned to Mrs Murphy and Anthony. 'Thank you both for your friendship. It has meant a great

279

deal to me. Please come and see us if you can.'

'I haven't been out in the countryside since I left Ireland forty years ago.' Mary Murphy patted Aurora's cheek. 'Take care of yourself now.' She leaned in closer so the others wouldn't hear. 'I wish I could be with you on your important day, but you're strong and have had good food all your life. You'll have no worries with that baby's birth.'

'I hope so, and I wish you could be there with me, too.'

'God keep you safe, lass.' She crossed herself.

'And you, too, Mrs Murphy.' Aurora then smiled at Anthony and squeezed his arm in farewell. 'Take care of your mother.'

He slipped off his flat hat and bowed. 'You know I will, Aurrie. Take care.'

'And you. Thank you for all your kindness.' She kissed his cheek and leaving him blushing like a girl, boarded the train behind the others.

Once they found their seats, Sophia linked her arm through Aurora's. 'We start another journey of our lives, Aurrie.'

'Yes. I wonder where this one will take us?'

Three hours later, and two train changes, one at Leeds station, which made Aurora dreadfully nervous in case she spotted someone she knew, they crammed into a hired carriage and made their way up the step sides of the Calder Valley away from the centre of Hebden Bridge. As they climbed, Aurora gazed at the silver ribbon of the river below and the formal lines of the canal which ran beside it.

'Where is the cottage then?' Lily asked,

breastfeeding Will in the corner of the carriage, her body and the baby hidden by a large blanket.

Aurora peeked out of the small window. 'Along Keighley Road the note says. The cottage is called Briar Rose Farm.'

'I can't believe I'm going to be living on a farm.' Lily's eyes widened in excitement. 'Imagine having fresh eggs laid at your door.'

'I hope all our furniture and bits and pieces are there,' Sophia said.

'Tell us again what animals are there, Aurrie,' Lily persisted.

'Well, I'm not sure. All Tom said was that the family who ran the farm had left last month to go to Australia because their grown up children emigrated there. One of the laborers was looking after the place until Tom's agent could advertise for a new farmer. Instead, Tom gave the farm to me.'

'I'm pleased we have a laborer.' Noah shifted in his seat next to Lily. 'I'm going to need some help. It's been years since I worked with animals.'

'Tom said it is only a small concern, Noah.' Aurora glanced out the window again as the carriage slowed. 'I doubt we'd have more than a few chickens, maybe a pig or something. I do hope there will be enough room for us all in the cottage.' She frowned as the carriage turned in between two black iron gates and trundled down a gravel drive. As the carriage swung around the bend in the drive Aurora stared at the house coming into view. 'Good Lord, I think the driver is lost.'

When the horses halted, Noah helped Aurora down so she could speak to the driver. They had stopped in front of a large two-story house built in gray stone. A low stonewall went off on either side of the house and before it was a neat garden. Aurora looked up at the driver. 'Briar Rose Farm is where we need to be.'

'And this is it, Madam.'

Aurora swung round to peer at the house again. 'There must be some mistake. It's a farm cottage with a few acres.'

'This is Briar Rose Farm.'

As she went to argue again a tall young man came through a gate in the wall and walked towards them. 'I thought I heard something. Welcome.' He held out his hand to Noah. 'I'm Jed Bromley. You must be Mr Middleton? And you must be Mrs Sinclair?' He shook Aurora's hand as well.

'This is Briar Rose Farm?'

'Yes, Mrs Sinclair.' Jed gave her a quizzical look as though she was a little slow in the head.

'Tom, my-my husband, told me the farm was small, with a cottage and a few acres.'

'We have thirty four acres, Mrs Sinclair. There is a cottage, where I live down the back, but this is the main house.'

Sophia and Lily climbed down from the carriage and stood staring at the house. Sophia gazed up at the windows above. 'If Tom thinks as this as a cottage I'd hate to wonder what he sees as a house.'

'I know.' Aurora agreed, none too pleased, glaring at the offending house, which compared to Sinclair Hall was indeed small, but even so, it wasn't the mere cottage she was expecting.

'How on earth will we heat it and keep it clean?' Lily whispered, half afraid.

'Shall I show you inside?' Jed looked from one to the other, sensing their unease. 'I've lit some fires and removed the dustsheets.' He swallowed and led the way to the dark brown front door. This door opened into a black and white tiled square entry with a hallway disappearing down past the dark timbered staircase. 'You've got a front room, small parlor, dining room and a little room the former family used as the master's study. Down the hallway are the kitchen, storerooms and scullery. There's also a large cellar.'

'Upstairs?' Aurora asked, entering the front sitting room, which was well lit from the large window overlooking the drive and another window on the far side wall. The room was wallpapered in light blue and white stripes. The carpet was patterned in a darker blue and red pattern. The furniture, aside from their own, was big and heavy, but not out of place and all very useful. A roaring fire blazed in the large fireplace with its white painted stone mantelpiece.

'Upstairs are four bedrooms, Mrs Sinclair. Plus a small landing and linen cupboard.' Jed said, placing another log on the fire. 'We've had fine weather all month but today's been a bit chilly. We might have rain by the week's end.'

'I never expected such a house, Aurora,' Sophia said quietly. 'It reminds me of the house I grew up in.'

'Will you show Mr Middleton and myself

outside, please?' Aurora and Noah followed Jed down the hallway and into the service areas of the house. The kitchen was enormous and Aurora fought the anger swelling up in her chest. Blast Tom. She didn't ask for any of this. He'd allowed her to believe he was giving her a small cottage, but this-this *house* demanded respect and no doubt afforded the family living here an image of social responsibility that she wouldn't be able to ignore.

'At the moment the farm is down on the amount of animals we usually keep because I'm on my own.' Jed told them as they walked across a flagged yard towards the outbuildings, again all built in the same gray stone as the house. In the distance, beyond the buildings, the green fields gently sloped up and down stretching out in the direction of Wadsworth Moor.

'What animals do you keep here?' Noah asked, as they went past one long building and through a gateway into another big square yard surrounded on three sides by low outbuildings.

'We have sheep, cows, pigs, hens, and geese mainly.' Jed opened a barn door. 'I've got old Bessie here.' He walked towards the mare in the stall. 'She pulls the cart.' He gave her a slap on the neck and rubbed her ears. 'Mr Sinclair said that I was to talk to you about what you wanted to do. The previous farmer made a good living and I'm sure it can happen again.'

'Mr Sinclair was here?' Aurora's eyes widened in surprise. 'When?'

'Er . . . about two weeks ago.' Jed escorted them outside again.

Aurora glanced at Noah. 'He never mentioned a word to me.'

'Mr Sinclair told me you might not want to have it as a working farm.'

'We do, don't we, Aurrie?' Noah asked, scratching his chin.

'Yes, it would be a shame to waste such land.' She sighed resignedly. 'We will depend on you entirely Jed. Do you have help?'

'In the summers of past years the former master hired local lads to work about six months. But as I mentioned before, the farm isn't full now so I'm on my own.'

'But we can buy stock and fill the yards again, can't we, Aurrie?' Noah asked, glancing around.

'Yes. This will be a working farm again.' She looked at Jed. 'Will you and Noah be enough to do the work, or do I need to employ another man.'

'Actually,' Jed rubbed the back of his neck. 'My brother, Dickie, is fifteen and in need of a job. Our Ma made him stay on at school and then apprentice with the undertaker in Hebden, but he doesn't like it and prefers working with animals.'

'Right then, he can start here. I'll leave you to sort it out, Jed, and make sure your mother is happy about it.'

'Thank you, Mrs Sinclair.'

Aurora gazed around at the buildings. Her shock was receding and germs of ideas replaced her anger at Tom. He had said this was hers, the deeds in her name. She turned to stare at the back of the house, her mind accelerating. A solid

285

house, land, animals, an income. A home. She nodded to herself, liking her thoughts. A home for her and Reid's child. Security. Perhaps, her future wasn't going to be as bleak as she imagined it to be.

19

'You are aware we will have to entertain,' Aurora said to Sophia as they stocked the larder with goods bought that morning from Hebden Bridge market. 'Did you see people lend an ear every time we spoke to someone at the market?'

'Yes, they were all interested in the newcomers.'

'I didn't want it to be so.'

'Nor I.' Sophia dragged a sack of potatoes into the corner. 'A quiet life is what I want. It's been too many years since I last had to pay calls. Mother used to take Winnie and I with her to the most tedious church tea parties. I didn't like it then and I shan't like it now. Sometimes there's a lot to be said for being friendless.' She grinned, hanging a net of onions on a hook suspended from the ceiling beam.

'My confinement will buy us some time.' Aurora placed the last of the jars of preserves on the larder shelf.

'Well, only having two decent dresses to my name, I dare not show my face at anything fancier than a market.'

Aurora sighed. 'Don't speak of clothes. I have nothing that fits and I loathe buying large garments that I will not wear again after the baby is born.'

'We'll take them in, never mind that.' Sophia studied her. 'That isn't the reason you've put off

287

ordering new clothes is it?'

Sitting at the scrubbed kitchen table, Aurora twirled the teapot around in readiness to pour out the tea. 'No. Oh, I don't know. I used to enjoy wearing the latest fashion and purchasing nice materials for the dressmaker to make up, but I did all that with Bettina and Harriet and . . .'

'And your mother.' Sophia pulled out the next chair and sat down. 'You can talk of them, Aurrie.'

'I didn't want to pain you, or make you think I regret finding you.'

'Winnie is my sister, I love her, ever more so for taking my darling baby and giving you a good home. She saved us both because I know I would have perished, and you too, if she hadn't taken you. We must talk of them, Aurrie, otherwise we're not being honest with each other and that could start to cause problems later.'

'Why didn't you go with them, when they took me?'

'I had to make a clean break and besides, I knew Father would cut Winnie out of his and Mother's life if she took me in. From what you've told me they never really forgave her for taking you.'

'Which is why we didn't see them hardly at all.'

'It was their choice,' Sophia shrugged. 'You must write to your parents again. One letter since you ran away isn't enough. They'd be worried dreadfully.'

'I will write tonight.'

'Aurrie, Sophia,' Lily came into the kitchen. 'A

fancy looking fellow has just arrived. He's talking to Dad out the front.'

Whisking off her apron, Aurora turned to Sophia. 'So it begins?'

Sophia groaned. 'We'll need to buy some good china then.'

'And you some dresses.' She laughed and tiding her hair went down the hallway to the front door. Outside on the drive, she walked towards Noah and Jed who were standing talking to a large man with an impressive round stomach. He looked more pregnant than Aurora did and she hid a smile.

'Ah, Aurrie, we have a visitor.' Noah indicated to the smiling man with the florid cheeks. 'This is Mr Bart Blackwell from Pecket Well.'

Aurora's smile threatened to erupt into a wide grin at the man's name rhyming with his village. She hoped he wasn't a simpleton.

'How do you do, Madam?' He held out a big meaty hand and clamped down on Aurora's fingers. With his other hand he doffed his black hat. He wore an elaborate embroidered green waistcoat and his jacket, when flapping open, revealed a lining of dark purple silk beneath. 'Bart Blackwell, local councilor, at your service.'

'Good day, sir. Pecket Well? Is that close by?'

'Just down the road, Madam.' He took a step closer. 'My home is on the other side of the village, but my businesses are in Hebden Bridge and other nearby towns.'

'Oh, I see.' All humor left her as she sensed something threatening about the man, and took a step back.

'I hear tell you have married Mr Tom Sinclair. Around here we thought of him as a bachelor for life.' His small dark eyes, at such odds with his massive stature, held her stare. 'But when faced with such a beauty as yourself why wouldn't a man want to give up his freedom?'

Aurora cringed. 'Indeed, Mr Blackwell. You knew my husband well?'

He thrust his thumbs into the narrow pocket slits in his waistcoat and rocked on his heels. 'Not as well as we'd all like, I'm sure. Mr Sinclair was notable *because* of his appearance a few weeks ago. This farm here has been rented many years and the Sinclairs have been absentee landlords.'

'Perhaps they trusted their tenants and had no need to visit?'

'Pah, that's no way to run businesses.' He looked her up and down as though she was a prized mare at a horse show.

'I doubt the fortunes of the Sinclairs rested on this one farm, Mr Blackwell.'

'That is as may be, Mrs Sinclair, but I believe the local people deserve to see who it is they work for from time to time. I hope as a member of the family you will now do your share and be a prominent citizen within the district.'

'I own a farm, sir, not a castle. Why on earth would I want to force myself among the local people?'

He frowned and stopped rocking. 'Come now, don't be modest.'

'Modest?'

'Surely your husband has spoken of the

influence his family could have in this area?'

Aurora's mouth went dry. 'No, he has not.'

A gleam of satisfaction widened Blackwell's tiny eyes. 'You married the second son, did you not?'

'That's correct.'

'Then perhaps this is all he has of what the Sinclair's own in this part of Yorkshire.' He sniffed and drew himself up to his full imposing height. 'The Sinclair heir must have the lot of it then.'

She felt the warmth drain from her face. 'You know of the-the eldest son?' If he said he knew Reid she'd just die.

'No, not at all. He is like his forbearers and hasn't shown his face to us.' A look of disgust crossed his broad features.

She sagged in relief. 'I am sorry to disappoint you, Mr Blackwell, but I shall not be in the habit of making a presence of myself in the area. I wish for a quiet life.' She was thankful of Sophia's words coming to help her.

'I am indeed disappointed, Madam. I know I speak for many when I say we had hoped the Sinclair family would concern themselves within this vicinity.'

'But why?'

'Because in some form or another, the Sinclairs either employ or house a good number of people around here.'

'They do?' She felt faint.

'The Sinclair family owns two mills, a glassworks, terraced housing and rent out four shop premises. Apart from this farm, there are another two sheep farms, one beyond Wadsworth Moor and another across the way towards Erringden.'

'You seem to know a great deal about the Sinclair's, Mr Blackwell.' Noah spoke up, glancing anxiously at Aurora.

'Why I course I do, I make it my business as a councilor of this district council.' He smiled widely and started rocking on his heels again as though waiting for them to gush appropriate comments of his status. His smile soon waned when none were forthcoming.

'I would welcome you inside for refreshment, Mr Blackwell, but we only arrived three days ago and I am afraid the house isn't in order as yet.' It wasn't strictly true, but she didn't feel capable of making polite talk to this man over cups of tea, not today, not after the shock he'd given her.

'Understandable, my dear Mrs Sinclair. I will, however, on behalf of my wife and myself offer you and your family the invitation to dine at our home. I will send my wife over to see you.' He dug out of his pocket his card and handed it to her. 'Will Mr Sinclair be returning home soon?'

'My husband is on his way to South Africa. He's a captain in the army.'

'A fighting man, hey? Capital! If you should be in need of anything, anything at all, Mrs Sinclair, please don't hesitate to contact me.'

'Thank you, Mr Blackwell.'

'Until we meet again, Mrs Sinclair.' He bowed to her and touched the brim of his hat to Noah.

They watched him drive his dogcart down the drive in silence. Jed had wondered off to continue the job he and Noah were doing before Blackwell interrupted them.

'Well, Aurrie. What do you make of that?' Noah asked, taking his flat cap off and scratching his gray hair.

'I felt a fool, Noah. I didn't know any of that. The Sinclairs own so much in this area.'

'To my way of thinking Mr Sinclair should have told you what to expect.'

'It's a good thing Tom is on his way to Africa, otherwise I wouldn't be responsible for my actions!'

Noah grinned. 'Yes, and he's not going to suffer dinner at the Blackwell's either.' He pulled his cap down low. 'I'd best get back to chopping wood.'

Aurora returned inside to find Sophia waiting for her in the front sitting room. 'Who was he?'

She handed over his card and rubbed her eyes with shaky fingers. 'I don't know what Tom thought he was doing bringing me here.'

'Come, sit down and tell me what happened.'

After Aurora had filled her in on what Blackwell said, she sighed deeply, staring at the low fire nestled in the grate. 'Why would Tom send me here, knowing his family owned so much in the area?'

'If Mr Blackwell is correct, the Sinclairs don't come to Hebden Bridge anyway, so you have nothing to worry about.'

'And what if one day Reid does decide to come and view his properties, what then?'

'You may not ever run into him.'

'And what if I do?'

293

'You'll just have to deal with that if or when it happens.'

'I can't. I can't live here with that hanging over my head.'

'Don't be silly. It might never happen. If they haven't visited before now, I doubt they ever will. And doesn't Reid spend most of his time in London or America now. Maybe that's why Tom gave you this house, knowing you wouldn't meet any Sinclairs here. Perhaps his other houses were in areas that Reid visits.'

The information of the Sinclairs owning a good deal of property around the area made Aurora uneasy for weeks and took the shine off her happiness in the new home. Summer was over for another year and as the gales roared down from the moors and across the open fields of the farm, she waited for replies to her numerous letters she sent Tom. Sophia had talked her out of leaving, which within the first week was all she wanted to do. Staying where Reid might find her was out of the question, but finally commonsense prevailed and she knew she'd be foolish to uproot herself again, especially since she'd not find a home as nice as Briar Rose farm so easily.

Not only that, but people depended on her now. Sophia, Noah and Lily and baby Will, were relying on her for the roof above their heads and food in their mouths. And soon her baby would arrive and she needed to be prepared.

★   ★   ★

Reid escorted his mother down from the carriage and nodded to Tibbleton, the Pettigrew's butler, who held the carriage door open for them. 'How are things, Tibbleton?'

'Good, thank you, sir.' Tibbleton bowed. 'Good day, Madam. The mistress is in the garden, sir, taking tea. If you'd kindly follow me.' He led the way across the drive and onto the manicured lawns.

'Taking tea in the garden? In October? How ridiculous to do such a thing at this time of year,' Julia tutted.

'It is not cold, Mother. The day is very pleasant.' Reid gazed around at the sun-baked garden. Surprisingly the weather had changed again and returned to calm days that still hinted of the summer just gone. It had been many months since his last visit home. The only things that had altered were the seasons. Autumn cooled the night air now and tinted the leaves on the trees colors of amber and gold, crimson and rust, but apart from that everything remained the same, except Aurora wasn't here or was she? His heart skipped thinking that she might be only yards away.

His mother glared at him. 'I don't wish to take tea.' She lowered her voice. 'Why couldn't we have gone straight home first? I would have called on Winnie tomorrow. It is insensible to call here first when our home is only beyond those trees!'

'I fancied some company and none of our friends know we are back in the country. We haven't seen the Pettigrews for a long time.' He couldn't admit aloud that he was tired of his mother's exhausting presence already and longed for news of Aurora and for some gentler company.

'It could have waited,' she snapped. 'There are things at the Hall which need my attention.'

'After being away for months, there is nothing that is so urgent it cannot wait another half hour. Humor me.' He spied Winnie sitting with her daughters at the white wrought iron setting beneath the dappled shade of a beech tree. His stomach lurched painfully when he noticed Aurora was missing from the group. He'd hoped by now she had returned from travelling. How much longer would he have to wait for her? This time he was determined to get some answers from Winnie.

Winnie looked up and Reid saw the flash of anxiety on her features before she carefully schooled her expression into a false smile. Insight told him their company wasn't wanted and he wondered why. He studied Winnie as she focused on his mother and weariness entered her eyes, or was it wariness? He knew immediately she didn't like his mother, but good manners made her perform the functionary role of hostess and friend.

'Winnie, my dear, are you mad to sit outside in this weather? You'll catch your death.'

'Nonsense, Julia.' Winnie accepted Julia's air kiss beside her cheek and then pulled her shawl closer over her thin shoulders. 'We might as well enjoy what is left of the fine weather while we can. I'm tired of sitting indoors day after day. We found this sun trap and intend to use it for an hour before the warmth fades.' She turned to Reid and quickly slipped the letter she held under her green skirt, but not before he saw the writing on it. Aurora's writing. Bitter rejection filled him. 'How are you, Reid. You look in good health after your voyage to New York.'

He bent over her hand. 'I am indeed well, Mrs Pettigrew. And you?'

'We are all in fine health. More tea for our guests, please, Tibbleton.' Winnie smiled at the butler. She turned back to Julia, who sat opposite, eyeing the fashion pages Bettina and Harriet were studying. 'This is a nice surprise, Julia. I thought you'd stay in London now until next summer, or go to your property in Kent for the winter.'

'Oh, we aren't staying here long.' Julia adjusted her wide brimmed hat, which overflowed with dark purple feathers and artificial white silk roses. 'I no longer find the Northern climate suitable. Also the North is rather dull, don't you agree? Most of our friends are in London.'

Reid groaned inwardly at his mother's crassness. Sometimes he wished she wouldn't open her mouth. He glanced from his mother to Winnie and made comparisons for the first time. Each woman looked exactly as their status required. His mother wore her wealth and breeding like a well-fitted glove. Her lavender gray dress was expensive and her perfume was bought in Paris only last week. A maid had worked for an hour on her hair this morning. Whereas Winnie appeared comfortable as a woman of moderate means and

297

respectability, something about her gave him the impression she didn't care for nor need the air of sophistication his mother possessed. Her dark green gown had little adornment, her hair was neat and put up, but her shoulders sagged, giving her a look of polite despair.

'Did your trip to America go well, Reid?' Winnie asked.

'Yes, thank you. The travelling can become tiresome, but it is such an interesting place. They have immense developments there. It's as though the whole country is in a race, competing with each other to be the first at something. Whether it be constructing tall buildings, fancy resorts, the best restaurants, or — '

'Reid is always successful, aren't you, dear?' His mother cut in and he gave her an irritated stare. Why did she behave as though he was still in short pants and not a grown man?

'Your hat is very lovely, Mrs Sinclair,' Bettina spoke quietly.

'Thank you, dear girl.' Julia preened like a peacock. 'I acquired it in Paris. I've just returned from there, you know. They have the most exquisite milliners. They quite overshadow London's offerings.'

'Why aren't you still in mourning, Julia?' Winnie asked.

His mother's eyes narrowed at the slight. 'My darling John asked me to not wear them for long and to regain my life as soon as I felt able to. He was always annoyed with our queen for her overwhelming display of widowhood. John begged me not to do the same.' The girls gasped

298

at the comment but Julia carried on unperturbed, smoothing down her skirt of lavender. 'This is the first week I have worn color. I couldn't help myself while I was in Paris. I was rather tired of black after several weeks.'

While Bettina and Harriet drew Julia into fashion discussions, Reid ignored the way his stomach churned at his mother's lack of respect. His shock at seeing her out of her black mourning only eight weeks after his father's death had caused them to have words in London and on the journey north. He thought the trip to Paris might have made her see sense and she'd buy some Paris designs for mourning, but the plan had backfired. He didn't understand his mother, and increasingly he felt the need to distance himself from her. Only, guilt made him admonish these thoughts. He promised his father to watch over the family and so he would.

He leaned closer to Winnie. 'I couldn't help but notice that your letter has Aurora's writing on it. Is she well? It has been so long since she was home. I would like to write to her, if I may.'

Winnie's hand slipped the letter further under her skirt, her gaze darting to Julia. 'She is extremely well, thank you.'

'Is she returning home soon?' He ached to snatched the letter and run off with it. He missed Aurora beyond words. It was as though half of him was gone, dead. He'd give years off his life for a glimpse of her and felt pathetic.

'I don't think she will for some time yet.'

His heart dipped at the news.

Julia turned her shoulder to the girls and

stared hard at Winnie and himself. 'What is this you are speaking of?'

Reid watched Winnie, what color she had in her cheeks paled and pity welled in him. His mother could be impossible, but he loved her because she was his mother. However, to others who didn't have that bond of family, he knew she could be overpowering and indeed at times rude and self-absorbed. This startling revelation alerted him to the fact he'd been blind to her faults all his life, and he wondered what else he didn't know, or care to admit.

He leaned back in his chair as Tibbleton approached with a maid following, and they set down two trays of tea things and plates of cakes. Again he watched his mother and Winnie. His mother's eyes hardened and he became aware of how it robbed the beauty from her. Winnie looked like a rabbit caught in a trap. His compassion for her deepened.

'You have gone rather pale, Winnie.' Julia gloated. 'Has something happened?'

'Not at all, Julia.' Winnie dismissed the servants and poured the tea.

His mother cocked her head to one side. 'Is everything all right with Josiah?'

'Absolutely. Why wouldn't it be? Sugar?'

'We all know how easily fortunes can rise and fall if one isn't careful.' Julia's cold tone stilled them all.

'Unless you have information I don't know about, Julia, then I can assure you our *fortune* is quite secure.'

'One can never be too careful, Winnie. Josiah

hasn't dealt with money and business as long as the Sinclairs have. It can be a very *unstable* life.'

Reid clenched his teeth. His mother was not only being rude but offensive as well. How long had she treated the Pettigrews like this? And why hadn't he ever been aware of it. He accepted his teacup from Winnie and felt the tension from her and the two girls opposite. He turned to his mother and smiled brightly. 'We were talking of Aurora actually, Mother.'

Julia stiffened. Her mouth became a thin tight line. 'Really?'

'Yes. I was asking after her.' He forced himself to relax and settle the strain of the group, but the flash of disdain in his mother's eyes wasn't lost on him. His mind worked overtime. Something was wrong here. The friendship between the two families wasn't as close as he always thought. The pretence gave him a sick feeling in his gut. How had he missed it? Why did her expression freeze at the mention of Aurora?

'And how is your eldest daughter, Winnie?'

'She is excellent, thank you Julia.'

'We received a letter from her only this morning,' Harriet said, sipping her tea. 'She is married.'

'Harriet!' Winnie snapped.

Reid sat unmoving. Unable to breathe or think, he gripped his teacup and saucer wondering if he had heard correctly.

'Married?' Julia laughed delightedly. 'How marvelous. Who is the lucky beau? Why were you not invited to the nuptials? Is she still abroad? Dear lord, she hasn't married a foreigner has she?'

He glared at his mother's happiness, but ignoring her he concentrated on Winnie and silently begged her to refute the information. Harriet had misunderstood, that's all. Only the truth was in Winnie's eyes, her face, the way her hands shook slightly holding the plate of tiny tarts she'd been about to pass around.

'We are not yet acquainted with Aurora's husband. She sent a telegram,' she glanced sharply at her daughters, 'and the telegram was very brief.'

Reid noted Bettina's blush and Harriet's puzzled stare at Winnie. The telegram was a lie. Beneath Winnie's skirts was a letter, Aurora's letter, not a simple telegram.

'I am so thrilled for you all, Winnie.' Julia beamed at each one of them. 'Aren't you happy to hear such news, Reid? I look forward to meeting the happy couple. I suppose by next year you'll be a grandmother, Winnie. How exciting.'

Reid jerked, spilling the tea he didn't want. Aurora married. Aurora loving another. Aurora carrying some man's child. Aurora allowing a man's touch on her body, to be kissed and caressed by another. Some fellow other than him would lead her to bed, undress her, see her naked, waiting for him . . .

He lurched to his feet, nearly dropping the teacup. He couldn't stand the pain encircling his chest. Without care he placed the teacup and saucer on the tray and spun away. He had to leave before he did or said something irrational, like swear and throw his chair across the lawn, but some part of his brain performed sensibly and he focused on breathing.

'I apologize, Mrs Pettigrew, but I've suddenly remembered a very important appointment I have in Leeds. Do forgive me,' he spoke with a calmness he thought was beyond him. He moved normally, grabbing his mother's elbow and lifting her from her chair.

'Come, Mother, I am in a hurry.' He ignored her bewildered look and bowed to the women seated. 'Good day, ladies.'

His grip tightened on his mother's elbow as he hurried them across the lawns to the drive and the waiting carriage.

'Reid, please, slow down, you'll ruin my shoes.'

Once in the carriage, he closed his eyes against the images of Aurora and her faceless husband in bed. Where his heart lay was a pain so acute he wanted to die from it. He hoped to die, needed to die, for living with the knowledge that the one woman he had always loved was gone from him was too much to bear.

'Reid — '

'Don't speak please, Mother. My head is pounding from a dreadful headache.' He huddled in the corner, staring out of the window as they made the short journey to their own drive.

'Never mind, my dear, I was more than ready to leave anyway,' she muttered smugly. 'Winnie is such a dull friend at times.'

Her conceitedness made him want to rage at her. He thought he'd be sick all over her expensive gown. More than that, he wanted to cry. No, not just cry, but wail and roar. He banged the roof of the carriage and had opened the door before the driver applied the brakes. 'I need some air. I'll take a walk.' He jumped down from the carriage as it halted and then leapt across the ditch by the side of the road. Within seconds he'd climbed over the stonewall and was running across the harvested fields.

He fell once, stumbled up and kept running until he made the woods on the estate's boundary. Collapsing against a tree, he slid to the ground and purged himself of the tears, the anger and the pain inside.

20

Aurora closed the shop door on the battering gale that carried sleet in it, stinging exposed skin. The warmth of the shop was a comfort and she intended to linger amongst the cheery Christmas goods to thaw out her cold hands.

'Ah, Mrs Sinclair. What brings you out on such a day?' The shopkeeper, Mrs McTavish smiled from the other side of the counter.

'I must be mad, mustn't I? Aurora returned her kind smile. 'Jed had to come into town and I decided to go with him. We are short of thread and a few other things. It could have waited but I was bored of being in the house.'

Mrs McTavish wiped down the already clean countertop. 'When I was having my bairns, I felt the last few weeks were longer than all the previous months together.' She laughed.

Aurora rubbed her rounded belly beneath her coat. 'At home I'm not allowed to do anything. My family keeps feeding me every time I sit down.'

'A pregnant woman knows how caged animals feel, I believe. We're just waiting for the release.'

'Too true.'

'You are due at Christmas?' She began weighing out colorful boiled sweets into small brown paper bags, which she tied with red string. The shop was full of treats for the festive season purchases.

'After the New Year, I think.'

Mrs McTavish frowned and paused in her weighing. 'Lord, lass, you're not very big then. We'll be celebrating the new century in just two weeks.'

Placing her hand over her stomach, she felt the baby kick. Lily had been enormous when she was having Will, but Aurora was rather thankful she wasn't as large as she expected. She was happy with her bump, but Sophia said she wasn't big enough for someone close to term and was forever forcing her to eat hearty meals and the egg puddings Lily made.

'I expect it's worrying over that good husband of yours, being out over the water in that foreign land.' Mrs McTavish tipped the scales with sweets once more. 'It's not looking too good out there, is it?'

Aurora's good humor sank. The newspapers were full of battles, especially the battle of Ladysmith, a town with a lovely name, but which, at the moment, was under siege. She had no idea if Tom was involved and cowardly didn't want to know. She refused to read the newspapers articles mentioning the war. If he was involved in the siege or any other battle she'd only worry even more, if that were possible. His letters were scarce and the last one she received mentioned only the antics of his fellow men, the heat and dreadful army food and nothing about the war at all.

Another customer entered the shop and diverted Aurora's thoughts. Mrs Digby, a small woman and wife of a local lawyer, waved her hand. 'Mrs Sinclair. I am pleased to see you. It saves me the journey out to your home.'

'Good day, Mrs Digby.' She dutifully inclined her head, but wished she hadn't run into this particular woman. Since their arrival eight weeks ago, she had been inundated with requests to join different ladies societies and received callers almost daily. Their hands of friendship were welcome, but Aurora found the routine of paying back those calls tiring and a little tedious. She had done enough of that at home in Leeds and desperately wished to be left alone here.

'Mrs Sinclair, we at the Ladies Committee wish to know if you'd like to join us tomorrow night at Mrs Pope's home? We are making up parcels to send to the brave men, like your husband, in Africa, fighting for the Empire.'

Before Aurora could answer, the shop door opened again and in walked Bart Blackwell and his thin, quiet wife, Gertrude, whom Aurora had met previously at a long and boring dinner party hosted by them.

'Mrs Sinclair and Mrs Digby.' Blackwell bowed to them while his wife gave them a wane smile.

Mrs Digby bustled forward. 'Mrs Blackwell, I was just telling Mrs Sinclair about tomorrow night.'

'I'm afraid I must decline, Mrs Digby.' Aurora broke in, aware of Bart Blackwell walking closely behind her.

'Oh, but the cause is so close to your own heart. You must want to do your bit for our boys.'

Aurora strove for patience. 'Indeed I do, but

my time is getting near and I'll not be venturing out at night now winter is upon us.'

'Oh, yes of course.' Mrs Digby patted Aurora's hand before she turned back to Gertrude Blackwell, took her to the counter and continued talking without letting up to her and Mrs McTavish.

'Will your husband's family be attending the birth, Mrs Sinclair?' Blackwell murmured close to her ear.

Affronted at his closeness, Aurora stepped back annoyed. 'No, they will not.'

'We've not seen any of the family since you moved here.' His slimy tone grated on her nerves. He was forever moving too close to her, whispering low, trying to force an intimacy she didn't care for.

'Are you spying on my home, sir?'

He laughed loudly, making the other women stare in his direction. 'Indeed, Mrs Sinclair, you are a whit.'

'Excuse me, I have to go.' She was tired of seeing the man, which happened to be weekly at present. Never more than seven days went by without him driving to the farm and taking tea with her and Sophia. Each Sunday at church he would leave his wife and waylay Aurora as she left after the service. Last Sunday when the first banns had been read for Sophia and Noah's wedding, he'd been the first to shake their hands and gush how wonderful it was to have a Christmas wedding.

'Have you heard from your husband recently?' He rocked on his heels, a habit Aurora found extremely irritating. 'Does the African climate suit him?'

'I doubt it, Mr Blackwell, since to enjoy the climate one must enjoy being shot at too.' She didn't try to hide the sarcasm, knowing that he was too thick-headed to heed it anyway.

'His family would be proud of him though.'

She stared at him, his flabby long jowls covered in graying whiskers disgusted her. 'I'm sure they are.'

'You sound as if you aren't certain,' he probed. 'Do you not get along with them?'

Aurora stiffened, her lip curling in a sneer. 'What I do regarding my husband's family is none of your concern, Mr Blackwell.'

He held up his hands as if in surrender. 'Take no offence, my dear Mrs Sinclair. I let my tongue run away with me. I shouldn't have spoken my thoughts out loud, but with you not having family visitors for the birth, I assumed — '

'I believe you'd be better off not assuming anything at all.'

'Forgive me, please.' He had the grace to flush crimson. 'I am dreadfully curious by nature, you see.'

'I'm sorry, but I really must be going.'

'I would like us to become great friends, Mrs Sinclair,' he murmured, stepping his large bulk closer to her. 'I could be very generous and helpful to those who are *true* friends.' He glanced at his wife before displaying his crooked teeth in a wide smile. 'Your husband is away and I am sure you missing his company. Once your child is born I would find it my utmost pleasure to give you any *assistance* you might need. I am widely respected hereabouts, and well, your little farm could find itself improved greatly with me as a benefactor, if you know what I mean.'

She blinked, speechless at what he was offering. She too glanced at the chatting women and assured they were busy talking she turned back to Blackwell and gave him her brightest smile. 'Let me try to understand you, sir. You're saying that for my friendship, a special friendship once my child is born, you would be willing to stock my farm?'

'Yes,' he whispered excitedly. 'You're a fine woman, Mrs Sinclair. I would be happy to not only stock your farm, but help raise it to a standard as great as my own.'

She fought a chuckle and instead pulled her bottom lip in between her teeth, her expression thoughtful. 'I see, but I have money of my own, Mr Blackwell, I do not need you to stock the farm. I can do it myself.'

He floundered a little. 'But Mrs Sinclair, it's more than a simple case of buying beasts. It's knowing the right people, breeders, produce agents, the markets, you know? I have the contacts. Money can easily be wasted if all the stages aren't done correctly and a farm can go bankrupt within two seasons.'

'And you think I am incapable of making my farm pay?'

'You're a lady, of course it would be difficult, and your soon to be father-in-law hasn't much knowledge in the area either.'

'But my husband has.'

'He is not here.' His innocent expression was at odds with the hunger in his eyes. 'And his family doesn't seem to be interested in your welfare as far as I can see.'

'And you are?'

He grasped her hand in both of his large paws. 'Oh, my lady, indeed I am, very much. If only I could show you how much.' His eyes flickered to her stomach. 'But all in good time, my dear.'

'Mr Blackwell,' she raised her voice so the ladies at the other side of the shop could hear her. 'Mr Blackwell, I would rather eat broken glass than whore myself to you for a few beasts. Good day!' She stomped from the shop and out into the snowy gale, which nearly took her hat off her head.

'Mrs Sinclair!' Jed pulled the cart in close to her and then jumped down to assist her up onto the seat.

'Oh, Jed, we need to get home. It was silly of us to venture out in this weather. I'll not come into town again until after the baby is born.'

'We'll be home soon enough, I promise. Wrap that blanket around you, Madam.'

Aurora did as he bid, but couldn't help looking back at the shop as the horse pulled away. Blackwell stood at the window staring with a thunderous face and she shivered more due to him than the cold. She should not have said what she did. Oh why couldn't she have kept her temper? It was like the Ellerton situation all over again. Why couldn't they leave her alone!

Tom finished shaving and, wiping the towel around his jaw and neck, he studied his reflection in the small square mirror hanging on a nail above the sink. Was that a gray hair above his right ear? Surely not at his age. He grinned at his vainness and then listened to the drone of music as the regimental band rehearsed across the street for the Christmas concert tonight. He hoped the bar would be open. Spending two hours listening to other fellows ruin classical pieces wasn't the most splendid of ways to celebrate the season.

A fly buzzed about his head. He swiped at it. Cursed things. Flies irritated him. They had no respect for rank. In the corner of the mirror, he spotted his writing desk behind him and the sheets of blank paper sitting on top.

He threw the towel onto the rail and missed, then went and sat at the desk, reached for his pen and inspected the nib. Finding it in good repair, he pulled a sheet of yellow paper from his stationary stack and began to write.

December 23rd 1899
Ladysmith
Dear Aurrie,
I should have written 'Happy Christmas' to you earlier, in my last letter, and it is silly to do so now as by the time you receive this it'll be months from now, if at all. The natives will do favors for money and the army does it best to get messages out, but whether this letter gets to you remains to be seen. Nevertheless, I hope it is/was a joyous occasion for you all.

When I sat down to write this letter I was thinking of some humorous incidents to tell you.

But I stopped myself from putting them down on paper. To you of all people I won't lie to, as I do to the rest of my family. To them I write queer little letters of interesting things happening, but I cannot do that with you. I will not pretend to you that being in the army is all fun and laughter. It is not. Oh, it is the adventure I sought, but it isn't one of enjoyment and good entertainment. There are times when my fellow officers make me laugh and we can spend an evening in harmony. However, since arriving in this accursed land I've seen some things that I thought at the time would make me never laugh again. Only, time goes on and images lose their sharpness, they have to or we'd be all lunatics.

You may have heard back home that Ladysmith is surrounded? Isn't it ironic that me, the one who never expected to be a fighter as a youngster, is now the one fighting for his life? Despite it all, I'm a good officer, Aurrie. Does that surprise you? It does me. I get along well with the men and they don't mind my lack of experience, for they know I'm the first one to stand with them when it counts. How did I become so brave, Aurrie? Or am I still the reckless one my mother despairs over?

We're holding out here well enough. Please don't worry. I am well. Food is getting awfully expensive for the town's people and rations are short for the soldiers. There will be no Christmas pudding for us, which is disappointing, as I like a good pudding. Water is running out like everything else, except the enemy's shells. The roof of my little house was holed last week. *It'll need fixing before we get rain.*

This morning while I was on duty, the odd Boer shell landed in the town and killed a horse. For some reason this angered me far more than anything that has gone on before. An innocent, hard working horse killed and for what, I ask you? The animals are in a sorry state, the cows don't give enough milk, the oxen but skin and bones. Dysentery is killing so many good men, Aurrie, it breaks your heart to see it.

December 24th 1899
Forgive me for not finishing the above. News came that the Relief were coming for us, but it proved to be a false rumor sadly.

Sorry, I had to break off again, Aurrie, I've managed to hear of a runner going out this evening. I'll not have time to finish this letter and am hurrying now so forgive my hand. Please give my kind regards to Sophia and the others. By the time you receive this letter your baby might be born, and I hope him or her are in good health.

To you dearest, Aurrie, I give you my love. Keep well and happy, dearest, I live knowing that via you I have done some good in the world and I am content.
Farewell, my wonderful friend,
Yours etc,
Tom Sinclair.

He put done the pen and hurriedly folded the letter into the envelope and left the bedroom. In the kitchen of the little house he shared with two fellow officers, he gave the letter to a subordinate with instructions on where to take it and watched him go. He let out a breath of longing that always gripped him when he thought of home. He didn't know which part of home he wanted. It wasn't just one thing he wanted, but a collection that to him, made up 'home'. He wanted to laugh with his friends, ride with his brothers, and listen to his mother make plans for Christmas. He wanted his room at the Hall, a snowy day, to go pheasant shooting, drink at his father's gentleman's club in Belgravia, visit his tailor and admire pretty girls at a ball. All these things made up home for him.

Across the dusty, dirt street, a lieutenant he knew waved in greeting. 'Happy Christmas to you.'

'And you.' Tom smiled with a nod. 'May our present be the Relief!'

The whine of an incoming shell went unnoticed by the pair of them as it was a common enough occurrence, but within a moment they knew the whine was aiming for them. Tom turned and looked up at the blue sky.

21

'Happy Christmas!' Sophia raised her glass at the table.

'Happy Christmas to all.' Aurora added hers to the others raised, which included Jed, who'd quickly become a member of the family. They sat in the dining room eating the sumptuous meal Sophia and Lily had prepared with the fire ablaze as snow drifted on the breeze outside the frosted window. Yesterday, on Christmas Eve, Sophia and Noah had been quietly married after the Sunday service. They had celebrated with a small family party and this morning Aurora had blushed on seeing how happy and in love Sophia and Noah were on coming down to breakfast.

'Our first Christmas as a real family,' Lily said, her eyes filling with tears. 'So much has happened to us all in one short year.'

Aurora's throat grew tight. What a year it had been. She thought back to other Christmas days with her parents and sisters and the ache of missing them grew larger. She'd sent them another letter with loving Christmas messages enclosed to each of them, but it wasn't enough. She longed to see them.

Lily passed the gravy pot across to Sophia. 'I know you'll be having your own grandchild soon, but I would be honored if you'd allow Will to call you grandma too.'

Sophia's smile nearly split her face. 'Thank

you, Lily, I think that is the best Christmas present I could have.' She grinned over at baby Will lying in his cradle by the fire, and then leaned over to kiss Noah's cheek. 'I never thought I'd be so blessed.'

Later, as darkness crept across the land and the animals were bedded down for the night, Aurora retired early, leaving the others to sing carols and play cards.

Lying in bed, watching the half moon through the window, she wallowed in thinking of Reid. What was he doing now? Where was he, at the London townhouse, the Hall in Leeds, or still across the sea in New York? Was he happy?

A lone tear trickled down her cheek and fell onto the pillow. She rubbed her belly in comfort, wishing the baby was born, giving her a part of Reid to love and cherish as she could never do with him.

★ ★ ★

Reid swallowed a mouthful of brandy, savoring the way it burned down to the pit of his stomach. If he kept drinking enough it would burn out his memories too. Memories of the beautiful Aurora, *his* Aurora, who was now married. Why? Why had she done it? Why had she rejected him? For days he'd tried to work out why Winnie had lied about the letter, saying it was a telegram, and although he presumed Winnie didn't want to reveal more details to his mother, the whole situation mystified him and left a ghastly taste in his mouth.

317

Muted laughter drifted through from the other rooms. He looked out of the library window at the half moon and cursed his mother and her friends who partied in the drawing room. He hated his mother's parties, which were become more and more frequent. Why she had to encircle herself with people all the time he didn't know. His father had been able to put up with it, but he couldn't. Christmas was meant to be spent with family. Yet, here he was, surrounded by a house full of people he didn't care much about. James and Edward had remained in London, his father gone, and barely mourned by those who should do it most sincerely, and Tom . . . Tom was in Africa. Not just anywhere in Africa, but Ladysmith.

Closing his eyes, he leaned his forehead against the icy cold windowpane. Poor bloody stupid Tom. The man's craziness had landed him in the hottest hellhole on earth. Still, he was one brave fool and Reid admired him for it. In truth, he envied him. Tom was away from all this nonsense. Tom didn't have to make polite chat with strangers. Tom didn't have their mother watching him every day, expecting something from him, but what he didn't know.

He heard the door open behind him and knew who it was instantly. His mother's perfume reached him before her words.

'There you are, dearest. What are you doing in here?'

'Getting drunk. No, I should say staying drunk.' He didn't look at her. Didn't want to see the censure in her face. He was so tired of doing the right thing by the family. Where had it got him? Yes, he was wealthy beyond his wildest dreams, he'd done all what his father had asked and more, but he was alone, lonely. Putting his family before Aurora had cost him dearly, and he wasn't certain the price had been worth it.

His mother tutted loudly. 'This will not do, Reid. For weeks you've been neglecting the Sinclair businesses, coming home stinking of drink. It's so unlike you that I'm beginning to worry. Tonight you drank more at the dinner table than anyone else. People noticed. It cannot continue.'

Slowly turning around, he once more felt the growing dislike of the woman who only months before he loved devotedly. Since the afternoon tea with Winnie, he'd seen his mother in a new light, one that didn't shine but was tarnish in the extreme. He now noticed the arrogant way she treated anyone she believed to be beneath her, whether that be servants or friends and acquaintances. She was selfish and extravagant. Although he felt she had loved his father and did mourn him, her anguish of losing her husband wasn't as acute as it should be, unless she was a superb actress and hid it well, but he didn't think she was that good at play acting. All too quickly she had shed her widow's blacks and gone abroad to Italy and Paris, where new friends wouldn't be able to comment on her lack of grief. No, he saw through her now and didn't like what he saw.

'Reid?'

He blinked back to the present. 'Mother.

Leave. Me. Alone.' He gulped the last of the brandy and promptly poured another.

'Reid, stop this nonsense.'

He waved the glass at her. 'Go away.'

'It's Christmas and we — '

'How do you think Tom is celebrating Christmas, Mother? Have you even thought about him today? Do you care?'

Surprised at the attack, she straightened her shoulders, her magnificent ruby gown shimmering in the gaslight. 'Of course I care.'

'Why? So you can boast of having a solider son to your useless friends.'

'That is enough, Reid. You are seriously displeasing me tonight.'

'And you seriously displease me, Mother.' He took another large swallow, firing his throat and gut.

'I've done nothing to warrant your disapproval! I've tried to make this Christmas, the first without your father or your brothers, into a pleasant time. I filled the house with people so it wouldn't seem so empty. Was that wrong?'

'Yes! Because I don't care a fig about any of them in there. I wanted us to feel the silence of those missing from the table.'

'Why be so morbid for God's sake?'

'Because it makes you not take them for granted.'

'Such twaddle, Reid.' She tossed her head in disgust. 'James and Edward preferred to stay in London with friends, rather than come here and be with us. What does that tell you?'

'It tells me they couldn't stand being holed up

in the house with you!' He finished the glass in one gulp and poured some more.

'What a shameful thing to say to me. I have done nothing wrong.'

'No? Where are your widow gowns, Mother? Why aren't you mourning our father, your husband?'

'Because your father told me not to. He said to me that he didn't want me to be depressed and unhappy, that I must live for him too.'

'Yes, he would have said that, he was that kind of man, respectable, loving, and generous.'

'I'm following his commands.'

He swayed. 'You are indecent.'

She gasped, her hands going to her mouth. 'What has happened to you? You'd have never said such a thing to me before.'

He raised an arrogant eyebrow and took another gulp of his drink. 'Perhaps I see you more clearly than ever before?'

'I'm going back to my friends.' She turned away.

'What battalion is Tom in?' He added more drink to his glass.

Her step faltered. 'I won't play your silly games.' She quickly made for the door. 'I'm returning to my guests.'

'You don't know or care, do you? Well, I'll tell you shall I? The King's Royal Rifle Corps, Mother, did you hear that.'

'I think you should retire for the night,' she snapped.

He drank the rest of the drink in one swallow and poured out some more in the balloon glass.

His movements grew heavy and slow. 'Do-do you know your son is under . . . under s-s-siege, Madam?'

Her hand twisted the doorknob but didn't open it. 'I am not completely without sense.'

'So you've read the papers then?' He blinked, his eyelids felt as though weights sat on them. He drank some more. He blinked again to focus. 'You know then that while . . . while you are entertaining your guests, your second son is trap-trapped in a town under shellfire. He is low on food and . . . water in an area that is hot and dry as any desert.'

'Be quiet.'

'That-that s-sickness, dys-dysentery and the like, is killing more men than the shells exploding around them.'

'Enough Reid.'

'Why? Don't you want to hear what your son is going through? Will it ruin your lovely p-par-party, your Christmas?' He swayed and had to hold onto the back of a chair to stay upright.

'Go to bed immediately,' his mother's furious voice reached through the fog engulfing his head.

'Or is it because you don't . . . care for him as you should? You-you care for the Sinclair name,' he hiccupped, 'and as the first . . . first born you care for me because I control the family weal-weal . . . money now, but,' he waved his glass at her, 'the three other sons you bore don't warrant your concern, do they? Why is that, M-mother?'

'I said that is enough!' Two spots of angry

color brightened her cheeks better than the expensive rouge she'd applied hours earlier.

'How would you feel if all your four sons joined the army?' He laughed, finding the notion very funny. 'With luck we might all get sh-sh-shot too. Then you could boast of your brave dear dead boys.'

'You are insensible with drink. Go to bed, Reid. I don't want to see you again tonight!' She slammed the door behind her and it echoed in the silent room.

He crashed down onto a nearby chair, his vision blurred. 'And I don't want to see you again ever, Mother.'

22

Reid sat at the breakfast table alone, his plate of eggs, bacon, mushrooms and toast half eaten. His mother had a tray in her room each morning and never came down to breakfast unless they had guests. Thankfully, in the last few days the houseguests lingering on from the Christmas and New Year celebrations had slowly gone home and the Hall rang with the silence. Once the snow had receded he planned on leaving too, back to London, or if his mother decided to return to London he would go elsewhere, a friend's house perhaps. No, he shook his head. He wasn't fit company for friends. Yet he couldn't stay here either. The Hall and especially the Pettigrews across the way held too many memories of Aurora.

He flicked the newspaper and read the articles about the war in South Africa while sipping his tea. Since that disastrous night of getting so drunk that he'd woken up the next morning on the library floor, he'd not touch alcohol again. The mere thought made his bile rise.

'Your mail, sir.' Denning, the footman handed him a silver platter with several envelopes on.

'Thank you.' Reid lifted the top envelope and saw it was from George Bolton in Lancashire, an old friend. The next envelope was from his solicitor in London, another from his steward at the Sinclair estate in Kent and lastly a letter whose name or handwriting he didn't recognize. Slitting open the pale envelope, he scanned the letter, but bewildered by the contents, he started again from the top.

Mr Reid Sinclair
Dear Sir,
I am writing to you on behalf of the good people of Hebden Bridge who I represent in the office of councilor.
It has come to our notice that having a close member of your esteemed family now living within our environs it would be beneficial to offer you the hand of friendship and open communication in respect of your concerns in our town.
As a valued member of the business community, my fellow councilors and I send you this letter as a way of invitation for your presence to one of our council meetings at your convenience.
A gentleman of your prominence would be warmly welcomed and your advice at such a meeting would be highly valuable.
Your humble servant,
Bartholomew Blackwell.
Councilor.
Pecket Well.
Yorks.

He read the letter twice more and was still puzzled. A close member of the family? He searched his memory for some distant relative who'd be living there and couldn't think of one. He knew a little of Hebden Bridge. After his father's death he'd been made aware of all the properties scattered around the country, belonging to the Sinclairs. He knew there were several properties they owned in the Hebden Bridge area, but they were small tidings and a trusted agent took care of them, so he'd not bothered visiting them as he had with other larger Sinclair holdings.

'Would you care for more tea, sir?' Denning asked, holding the teapot aloft.

'No, thank you.' Reid scooped up his mail and pushed back his chair. 'Have the carriage ordered, will you? I need to go to the station.'

'Yes, sir.' Denning left the room but bowed at the doorway as his mistress walked in. 'Good morning, Madam.'

Reid hesitated as his mother strolled to the table. They had said very little to each other in recent days.

'Oh, you have finished already?' She pouted.

'Yes, I'm heading out to Leeds.'

'In this weather? It's snowed all night.'

'I have business to attend to.' He tucked his mail into the inner pocket of his jacket. 'Do we know anyone in Hebden Bridge, family perhaps?'

His mother frowned and rubbed her head, this morning she looked her age for the first time. Deep lines were around her eyes and mouth no matter how much night cream she applied to them. 'Where is this place?'

'Near Halifax.'

'Good lord, no. Why would we know anyone there? We'd hardly have family in a mill town, would we?' She sat down on the chair and waved away a scurrying maid.

'You never know. Textile is a wealthy industry and the Sinclair's do own mills in other parts of Yorkshire.'

'My family would never live in such a town. I doubt my father went any further north than Nottingham in his life. London or India were our homes.' She rolled her eyes. 'Halifax indeed.'

'There is nothing wrong with Halifax, Mother.'

'Well, why ask me such a question then? Your father's people could be scattered everywhere for all we know.' Her tone grew bored. She poured herself a cup of tea, but stopped when Denning returned.

'Your carriage will be out the front shortly, sir.'

'Very good. I need to pack some clothes for two or three days. Will you see to it now? I'm in a hurry.' Reid finished his tea as the footman left.

'Where are you going that will keep you away two days?' His mother asked lightly, trying not to appear too interested but he could see the cold calculation in her eyes.

'On business.'

'Can't it wait? The roads will likely be blocked.'

'We'll get through. I'll be taking the train from Leeds.'

'The trains might be stopped also.'

'You should hope not or you'll not be travelling to London on Friday.'

'If you're not going to be home I might as well go today,' she snapped.

'As you wish.' He shrugged and turned for the door. 'I'll be back by the end of the week if you're still here.' Her presence constantly irritated him now. He wondered how he had stood it before. Ignorance was bliss in this case. How did his father love her so devotedly for so many years?

'As if you care where I'd be?' she said sarcastically.

He ignored her and walked to the front door where Matthews helped him with his coat and gloves. His mother's suffocating attention had increased beyond words since his father's death. At times he felt he couldn't breathe from it.

Denning descended the stairs with a small portmanteau and opened the door for him. A blast of cold hit Reid and he shivered. 'Thank you, Denning.' He turned to Matthews. 'I'll leave everything in your capable hands.'

'Very good, sir.'

Climbing into the carriage he gave the driver instructions to take him to Leeds railway station and settled back on the seat. With luck the roads wouldn't be too bad and the trains running on time. By this afternoon he wanted to be in Hebden Bridge, snow or no snow.

'Mr Sinclair, sir,' the driver called down, 'there's a carriage coming down the drive. Do you want to wait for it?'

'Is it one of my mother's friends?' Reid called back. He had no wish to stay for them. Though in truth, none of her acquaintances would call before eleven o'clock, never mind just gone nine.

'Nay, sir, I think it is a hired vehicle.'

'Hired?' Reid climbed down from the carriage and watched the transport stop behind them on the drive and a well-dressed gentleman stepped

328

out. Reid didn't know of him and held out his hand. 'Welcome to Sinclair Hall. I'm Reid Sinclair. May I help you?'

'Ah, Mr Reid Sinclair? Reid Charles Phillip John Sinclair?'

'Yes, that's right.' Reid frowned. Only a solicitor would use a full name as means of identification.

The older man, who only came to Reid's shoulders, and seemed as wide as he was short nervously took off his black hat and wiped his forehead vigorously as if to erase the creases lining there. 'My name is Lawrence Waters-Smith, from Waters-Smith Solicitors, London. I'm your brother, Thomas Sinclair's, solicitor.' He shook Reid's hand with a flourish, but his eyes wore a haunted expression.

'Please, come inside.' Reid ushered his guest into the Hall, where they both divulged themselves of hats and outer coats, before going through to the drawing room. 'Tom is not here.' He indicated for the fellow to sit, apprehension creeping up his spine.

'I know that, sir. He is in South Africa.' Waters-Smith glanced around the room, holding his leather satchel in both hands.

'Did Tom instruct you to come see me?' Reid crossed his arms, wondering what nonsense Tom had gotten involved in now. 'Has he not paid your bill, sir?'

'Oh, no, nothing like that, Mr Sinclair, I assure you.'

'He's not in trouble with the law, is he? Or the army?'

'Reid, did we have a visitor?' His mother sailed

329

into the room on a cloud of perfume. 'Oh, I see we still have.'

'Mother this is Mr Waters-Smith, a solicitor from London.'

'Indeed?' Julia allowed the man to lightly bow over her hand before she sank onto a nearby sofa with a look of vague interest on her face. 'A solicitor from London.'

'Tom's solicitor.'

Her plucked arched eyebrows lifted. 'Lord, he isn't in trouble is he? I thought the army would pull him into line. Is it gambling? Or a girl in a delicate way again? I despair over that boy, really I do.'

'Mother, please.' Reid gave her a warning stare and turned his attention to Waters-Smith. 'How may I help you, sir?'

Waters-Smith opened the satchel. 'First, let me say how sorry my partner, Mr Roberts, and I am to learn — '

'I knew it.' Julia scowled. 'What has he done this time? Broken the law, hasn't he? Has the army court marshaled him? They haven't shot him have they?'

'Mother!' Reid wanted to shake her silly.

Flustered, Waters-Smith drew out a sheath of papers. 'I came as soon as I could after receiving the correspondence from the army superiors.' He glanced worried at them. 'Again my deepest sympathies.'

Reid stiffened. 'You are sounding as though my brother is dead, sir?'

Julia gasped, her eyes widened. 'But he isn't. We would know.'

Waters-Smith paled and nearly dropped his satchel. 'Sir, Madam, I'm afraid he is. Haven't you been notified?'

'Nonsense!' Reid barked, wanting to throttle the man. 'Are you sure you have the right Tom Sinclair?'

Shuffling the papers, the solicitor reached inside his jacket and found his wire glasses, which he thrust onto his nose. He scanned the top sheet. 'Captain Thomas Gordon Francis Sinclair, of Sinclair Hall, Leeds.'

'Yes, that's my brother, but he isn't dead. I haven't been notified.' Reid gave the man a bemused look. 'There has been some mistake.'

'I received the notice myself, sir, from his regiment's chief at their headquarters in London.'

His mother gasped and stared at him in horror. Reid felt as if his mind was retreating, slowing down and he had to work hard to talk sense. 'Mr Waters-Smith, I would know if my brother was dead.'

'Of course he would.' Julia jumped to her feet, irritation altering her expression. 'We would be listed as Tom's next of kin, either myself as his mother, or Reid as his eldest brother and head of the family.'

'Mother, please.' He gestured for her to sit down, for she towered over the small man who seemed to have shrunk under her attack. 'Sir, can you show me what evidence you have of my brother's death, since this is the first we've heard of it and quite frankly we refuse to believe this information.'

'Your brother came to see me at my office several times before he departed for Southern Africa. He gave me strict instructions on what I was to do should he be . . . should he . . . ' The fellow swallowed, his Adam's apple jerking over his stiff white collar. 'In the case of Mr Sinclair's death, his wife would be — '

'Ah! There, you see?' Julia pounced on him again. 'My son wasn't married. So you're wrong and misinformed! It is some other Tom Sinclair.'

Sweat beaded the solicitor's forehead. 'Your son did marry, Madam.'

Reid blanched and his mother gripped his arm, her eyes wide with disbelief. 'Tell him he's wrong, Reid.'

'Madam, forgive me, but I have the marriage certificate in my safe keeping.'

'Who?' Julia tensed, her tone cutting and Reid saw her transform from her moment of weakness back to the woman of steel he knew. 'What slut did my stupid son marry?'

'Quiet mother, that is not important.' Reid stepped forward as the enormity of the situation finally dawned on him. Tom was dead. He clenched his teeth, striving for control against the biting pain this news brought. 'Sir, you are certain my brother, in Africa, is dead?'

'Yes, Mr Sinclair.' He flushed out a yellow document and gave it to Reid. 'This is from the regiment's London office. Your brother was killed by a shell exploding at Ladysmith on December 24th 1899.'

'Why weren't we told!' his mother shrieked.

'Because we weren't listed as next of kin,

332

Mother,' Reid replied, his grip on the document made the edges fold. He couldn't read a word on the paper, not even a letter.

'But surely one of your father's friends would have come to us?'

'Madam,' the little man coughed politely. 'The town is under siege, not much communication is getting in or out and from what I was told only those who are listed or who are within the army are alerted to our terrible loses over there. The newspapers try to keep the nation abreast of events, but it is a never ending tide of bad news.'

'I still don't believe it. I won't believe it. I want more proof.'

Watching his mother wring her hands, Reid sought to find words to console her, but couldn't. Not so long ago he would have held her, comforted her in such a time, but not now. He didn't want to offer comfort or receive it in return. It was as though he no longer occupied his body, but watched the scene from a great height.

Waters-Smith was again searching in his bag. With a triumphant snort he pulled out an envelope and gave it to Reid. 'Mr Sinclair told me to give this to you should he be killed, sir.' His harried gaze darted to Julia but she had her back to them, and was staring out of the front window.

Slitting open the envelope, his hands shaking, Reid opened the brief letter.

Reid, dear brother.
If you are reading this, then the worst has

happened and I'm never coming home again. I know this will be a great shock to you, but I am in a better place now, or perhaps I'm not. Who knows? I could be dining with the Devil.

Nonetheless, my time is done, but my life hasn't been totally wasted. I have a son, as you know, in Oxford. I've left him a small legacy and I hope you will take the details of his whereabouts from Waters-Smith and visit the boy one day.

Also, I have secretly married. Does this surprise you? Probably not. You know me well enough. What may astonish you though is to whom. Last summer I found a lady down on her luck, without a home or a husband for her baby. I provided both things.

Do not think me weak, brother, I would not have been so hasty if the circumstances involved anyone else other than this lady, whom I loved most dearly as a sister.

Reid, I married Aurora Pettigrew.

Reid jerked, his breath caught in his throat ready to choke him. He stifled a moan, but his mother was beside him in an instant.

'What is it? What does it say!'

He held up his hand, not trusting himself to speak. Slowly, bracing for the hurt to split him asunder, he continued to read.

Aurora is pregnant, Reid, not with my baby, but with yours. I treated her as a sister, or more importantly as a sister-in-law. The baby needed a name, the Sinclair name, and so I provided it in your stead. I hope you forgive me and her,

334

and in time understand I behaved in the way I thought was best for all concerned. You must claim her, Reid. Don't let pride stand in the way, hers or yours.

Your son or daughter will need you, but more than that, Aurora loves you.

Go to her.

I wish you a lifetime of happiness, brother.

Tom.

It was impossible for him to read the letter again. Tears blurred his vision and he coughed to clear his tight throat. Mr Waters-Smith looked on with sympathy and Reid straightened, having forgotten the man's presence.

'Reid?' His mother stood beside him, glancing from the letter to his face. 'Well?' She gripped his arm. 'Speak. Oh, I can't stand it!' She collapsed onto the sofa, crying hysterically and calling out Tom's name.

He walked to the door and beckoned the solicitor to follow. In the hallway entrance he asked Denning to dismiss the carriage waiting for him, and to send Gavet to her mistress. Then he went down the hallway to his study and waited for Waters-Smith to enter.

A twisting knot of misery had hold of his insides and his throat ached from being denied the release of tears, but he had to stay in control. One slip and he would be smashed to pieces as easily as driftwood was broken up on the beach. To pretend that the letter he still held in his hand was about a stranger was the only way he could function. He flinched away from thinking about it so he could survive the next minute, the next hour.

Waters-Smith remained standing. 'Sir, I will not trespass on your grief for any longer. It will take only a moment more of your time for me to read the Will.'

'My brother's wife, she was next of kin?'

'Yes, sir.'

'Shouldn't she be here?' His throat convulsed. Oh my love, Aurrie . . .

'I called on Mrs Sinclair yesterday, as she is unable to attend this meeting due to her present condition.'

'There are provisions for her?' His voice came out on a croak and he slipped his finger inside his collar and pulled at it to get air. She carried his baby . . .

'Oh, yes, sir, handsome provisions. Mr Sinclair has left her a farm and cottage and all holdings tied to it. Also there is a good sum of money from investments.' Waters-Smith read from another sheet of paper the list of items Tom had left to his younger brothers, a property each that he himself had inherited on his majority a year and half ago, plus small personal items. To Reid he left two things, his chestnut horse stabled here at the Hall and a silver and ivory penknife that Reid had bought him for his twenty-first birthday. However, the penknife was with Tom's other belongings in South Africa, but they would be sent on as soon as possible.

After finishing the reading, Waters-Smith gathered up his papers and prepared to leave.

'I thank you for your time,' Reid said, shaking

the man's hand and seeing him to the door.

'I wish it had been on happier terms, Mr Sinclair. My details are on the letterhead if you or your brothers wish to contact me. Good day, sir.' He gave him several sheets of documents and made his farewell out to the hired cab.

Reid hesitated in the hall, not knowing what to do or where to go next. He felt numb all over. Two maids scuttled past, giving him shy looks.

Dry-eyed, all though her eyelids were puffy from recent crying, his mother stood in the doorway of the drawing room. 'My son has truly gone then?'

He nodded and barging past her went to the drink's cabinet and poured out a large brandy.

'I'll have one too, please.'

He splashed some of the golden liquid into another balloon glass and handed it to her, then took a deep swallow of his own.

His mother sipped her drink, her face gray. 'We will have a memorial for him. In London. We must arrange a plaque to go alongside your father's on the tomb.' She took another sip. 'I cannot believe I won't see him again. He always brightened a room, didn't he?' her voice caught. 'Oh, he was naughty at times, I know that. On certain occasions he drove me to distraction, but he was my boy. My handsome happy son, who people liked and respected. He filled a cloudy room with sunshine. And now he is gone, like his father . . . '

Reid stared out of the window, seeing nothing, feeling even less.

'Whom did he marry?' His mother's voice was

low, rumbling in her chest like a wolf's growl. 'Was it that whore from Oxford, the one who gave him a child? The young man she married died of fever, you know, within a month of marrying her. I've been worried that Tom would do something rash. I was hoping he'd never find out. I paid the chit enough money to keep her quiet and not contact him. Yet, you never know with these people.'

'No. It isn't her.' He finished his drink, silently begging for her to be quiet. Every word she spoke was as sharp as a knife piercing his gut.

'I suppose it is some other tramp?'

'You know her.' Oh yes, they all knew her, but she had gone, run from them all.

'God lord.' A nerve twitched in her left eyelid. 'Stupid boy to keep it a secret. Is she high or low?'

'Depends on your perspective.' He had to go to Aurrie, to see her, to hear her voice say she loved him. Only fear stopped him. Did she love him? Did she hate him, forcing a child upon her, making her leave home, all that she's known? Yes, she must loathe him. He bowed his head in shame.

'Stop playing games, Reid!' His mother's nostrils flared. 'Who is it?'

'Mother, please, leave it alone for now.' He had to get out of this room. He needed air.

She jerked to her feet. 'I will not! Why should I? I am his mother. I have a right to know. Why do you boys insist on keeping secrets from me?'

'Perhaps because you behave this way? Because you are always interfering in our lives.

Look at what you did last week with James. He wants to join the navy, Mother, but you refuse to give him your permission.'

'The navy is dangerous. I'm keeping him safe. This is just a whim of his.'

'No it isn't. James doesn't have whims. A commission in the navy was what he has been wanting for years. He talked to Father about it and Father agreed to it. So, why do you go back on his word?'

'Have you seen what the navy spits out? Maimed men. Young men sent home without arms or legs, or not sent home at all, but dropped to the sea depths. They are away from home for years, cooped up with other men and things, filthy things, happen!' She shook her head wildly. 'I know as a lady I shouldn't be aware of these occurrences, but I am. I listen, I find out facts.'

'Mother — '

'No, Reid. I won't let him go. The army has taken Tom. Do you honestly believe I would allow James to go now? He stays home. In England and I won't be dissuaded on that.'

'Then you are a selfish woman.'

'I am his mother.' Her eyes flashed her rage at him. 'He stays where I can watch over him.'

'You're keeping him close to you so you can be in command over his every decision. It's not normal. They have to make their own mistakes and learn from them.'

'What? Like Tom?' She glared at him. 'What I do is for the betterment of you all.'

'It is so you can keep in control of us, Mother, don't deny it.'

'That is a shameful thing to say.'

'Yet, the truth.'

She turned away and fiddled with the jeweled rings on her fingers. 'Today is not the day to argue. We've had a shock. A terrible tragedy has happened.'

'Yes. I'm sorry.' He took a deep breath, wishing he was miles from here.

'Whom did Tom marry?' She faced him, proud and defiant as always, but he saw the tense way she held her shoulders.

'Aurora Pettigrew.' There, he had said her name out loud, but he kept as still as possible, feeling the violence swelling up in him.

His mother closed her eyes briefly and when she opened them again they were full of hate, but a treacherous smile hovered on her lips. 'The bitch has struck back. How interesting,' she whispered.

'Pardon?'

'Nothing, darling.' She left the room and also left him feeling cold. What on earth did she mean? A sick feeling swirled in the pit of his stomach. He shook his head. He couldn't deal with her right now. Aurora filled his mind and the fact that he was going to be a father.

23

A biting wind carried snow so thick it blurred the landscape, concealing recognizable features and filling the void in a white sheet. Outside the world was silent, even the blizzard made no noise.

In her bedroom, Aurora panted, hot and sweaty. Sophia had banked the fire up so much that it sent out a red hot blaze and no one could stand within four feet of it. She watched tiredly as Lily rinsed the cloth in a bowl of cool water. At the end of the bed Sophia paced, her eyes worried, her hair in disarray. Aurora knew what they both thought. The midwife or doctor would never get here through the snowdrifts. They were alone to bring this baby into the world.

As her body tensed for another contraction, Aurora held her breath.

'No breathe, Aurrie, don't hold it,' Lily said, bending over her holding the blissfully cool cloth to her forehead.

'Every five minutes.' Sophia stood at the end of the bed, rubbing Aurora's bent leg. 'Good girl. You're doing well.'

'I'm not!' She let go of a gasp as the contraction peaked and then ebbed away slowly. She was about to speak again when abruptly the sensation of water gushing from her made her gasp. 'I've wet the bed!'

'Your waters have broken.' Lily glanced at Sophia in alarm.

'Is that good?' Aurora panicked.

'Yes, it's just the next stage. Progress.' Sophia smiled with reassurance. 'Rest if you can.'

Aurora closed her eyes and relaxed against the pillows. She'd been in labor for eight hours, most of the day. Her first pains had started before dawn after a sleepless night thinking about Tom.

Poor Tom. Her chest felt heavy with sorrow. Reading the telegram telling her of Tom being killed had been one of the most wretched things she'd ever done. She had contacted the solicitor in London that same morning and three days later, yesterday, he arrived at the cottage. His visit reaffirmed all that Tom had spoken of before he left. The farm was hers. She wished she could cry for Tom, he deserved her tears, but the grief in her chest gently simmered with no relief.

Tightening encircled her stomach once more and she hunched her shoulders to deal with the coming contraction. While the pain tightened her insides like a vice, the world beyond the bed grew dim and unfocused. Lily and Sophia's encouragement sang in her ears. Gradually, the pain waned and she rested, dozing a little.

As the night drew in, turning the white countryside to gray and silver, Aurora struggled to keep awake. The contractions had slowed down and at one point she didn't have a pain for an hour. She was aware of Sophia's quietness and Lily's anxious concern, but the tiredness defeated her and she slept for a while until another dull pain woke her.

'Aurrie, darling, we need you to stay awake and get this baby out.' Sophia pulled up the sheet and opened Aurora's legs wider. 'Do you feel the need to push?'

'No.'

'You might on the next pain.'

'Where's Lily?' Aurora looked around the empty bedroom.

'Feeding Will.' Sophia gently raised Aurora up from the pillows. 'Come on, out you get. You're going to walk. Lily said Mrs Murphy told her to do that.'

Every muscle ached as she swung her legs over the edge of the bed. 'I wish Mrs Murphy was here now.'

'So do I.' Sophia's smile was grim. 'I'm no midwife, that's for sure. Bloody snow.'

'Swearing, Mrs Middleton?' Aurora joked as they shuffled around the room. 'I wouldn't let Mr Blackwell hear you speak like that. You'll not be invited to any of the council balls.'

'Mr Blackwell can go to Hell.' Sophia grunted. 'Nosy old goat in a fancy waistcoat.'

Aurora's chuckle turned into a moan as a pain sent her to her knees. Her groin grew heavy as if a lead weight was hanging from her hips.

'Good, they've started again.' Sophia helped her up. 'Let's keep going.'

'I'd rather not.' She panted, bent over. 'It's like someone is gripping my insides and pulling them out with a rope.'

'That's how I remember it, too.' Sophia guided her around the room. 'We want this baby born soon, dearest. I'm losing beauty sleep and I need all I can get.'

'Drivel.' Aurora gave her a wry smile. 'Do you

think it'll be born by morning?'

'Yes, I hope so.'

'Dawn isn't too far away now, is it?'

Sophia glanced out the window. They hadn't bothered to draw the curtains. 'A few hours. Do you know that you were born at dawn?'

'Really?'

'Aurora means dawn. I read it somewhere and thought it a good fitting name.'

'It's different.'

Sadness changed Sophia's expression. 'It's all I could give you.'

'No, that's not true.' Aurora paused in walking. 'You gave me to people who loved me, who gave me a wonderful life where I wanted for nothing.'

'I did the right thing then?'

'Yes.' She smiled, only to grimace as a twinge became a tearing pain. Abruptly more liquid gushed from between her legs. 'I'm wet. My God, it's blood.' Her knees buckled again and she held onto Sophia tightly as something pounded her low down. 'Got to sit.'

Sophia aided her over to the bed, but as Aurora lifted her leg over the edge, she felt a stinging force push through her pelvis.

'Oh good heavens! It's the head.' Sophia pushed Aurora backwards. 'Lie down, quickly.'

Frightened, Aurora gripped the sheets in her hand and pushed hard, unable to stop the urge. In a moment the pressure eased as a wet slithery body flushed from her.

Sophia cried out, catching the slippery baby. 'God help me. Aurora help! It's out. Oh my

Lord, what do I do? It's so small,' she gabbled.

Sitting up to see better, Aurora stared at the tiny blue bloodied body, its pulsing cord attaching it to her. 'Is it alive?'

'I don't know. Hold it.' Sophia thrust the baby onto Aurora's stomach and she grabbed it instinctively, but warily, while Sophia rushed to whip the warming towel off the rack before the fire. She hastily bundled the baby and then tied off the cord before struggling to cut it with sewing scissors. 'There. It's done.'

'It's not crying.' Aurora gazed down at the quiet tiny baby who lay passive in her arms. 'Is it breathing?' She stiffened in panic, pushing the baby towards Sophia, whose face lost all color. 'Is it breathing!' she screamed.

Uncovering the baby, Sophia placed two fingers on its little chest and the baby squirmed, but made no sound. 'I think it is.' She blew on the baby's face and it opened its mouth, an arm moved. 'Cry for us sweetheart, please,' Sophia begged.

Aurora felt the blood drain from her face. Her baby was dying. 'It's too small. It won't live.'

'No, it's . . . ' Sophia glanced down the body, 'it's a girl and she breathing. Look.' She held help the baby up from the towel, its tiny legs thrashed.

'Why won't it cry then?'

Sophia tapped the little bottom and the baby's face screwed up and emitted a short wail.

Relief washed over Aurora in waves, she turned her head and vomited over the side of the bed, her body protesting painfully. She lay back

345

gasping, holding her aching stomach and drawing in air.

Sophia wrapped the baby up again. 'There we are, little one, Grandmama has you. Yes, she does, darling, and everything is going to be all right.'

Lily hurried into the room, her eyes wide. 'Oh, I missed it!'

Sophia smiled, cuddling the baby in her arms, tears flowing unchecked down her cheeks. 'Be glad you did, lass, be glad you did.'

⋆   ⋆   ⋆

Reid stood at the gate dividing the acres of gardens between the Hall and the Pettigrew's home. He'd spent the morning writing correspondence in regards to planning Tom's memorial. Tonight he and his mother were leaving for London. His heart constricted at going away. The only place he should be travelling to was wherever Aurora was, but he had a duty to perform first. He owed that to Tom. Silently though, he vowed that when that was finished he would go to Aurora and beg for her forgiveness. After today, she would always come first.

The cold from the snow-thick ground seeped through his boots. He pushed open the gate and walked through the trees towards the Pettigrew house. In the distance, he saw the gardener and his lad shoveling snow off the drive. His footsteps faltered as he crossed the lawn area, past sweeping flowerbeds all dormant and hidden beneath their soft cloak of white. When he rounded the front of the house a maid was sweeping the front step. He smiled. 'Is Mrs Pettigrew home?'

'Yes, Mr Reid, er, Mr Sinclair, in the drawing room.' She bobbed a curtsey and held the door open for him just as Tibbleton came out and told her to attend to another task.

Tibbleton ushered him in and took his black coat. 'Cold day, sir.'

'Very much so.'

Tibbleton coughed. 'I'm sorry to hear about Mr Tom, sir. On behalf of all the staff I give you our condolences.'

'Thank you, Tibbleton. I appreciate that.' Reid nodded in thanks and entered the drawing room.

Winnie looked up from writing at her secretary in the corner. 'Reid, dear boy.' She stood and held her hands out to him. 'I thought you had immediately returned to London.'

'We go this evening.' He kissed her cheeks, glad to see she looked a little better than she did during the summer. 'How are you?'

'In good health.' She gestured for him to sit and then turned to Tibbleton who stood in the door. 'Tea, please, and some of Mrs Pringle's stuffed dates.' And then gave her attention back to Reid. 'How does your mother fare?'

'I think she is in shock.' He shrugged, not knowing what to say. After the initial outburst she had remained calm and controlled, like himself.

'We grieve for dear Tom. He was so uplifting. Josiah thought very well of him.'

347

'I'm happy to hear it. Many despaired over Tom and his wildness. Myself included. But I am glad Mr Pettigrew thought Tom had potential beyond his craving for doing the wrong thing.' Reid hung his hands between his knees and stared into the fire. 'I have learned recently that my brother was more sensitive than I gave him credit for. For my shame I just wish I had known earlier.'

'Death does that, Reid, teaches us lessons we never thought to learn.' She smiled kindly and looked over to watch Dotty and Tibbleton bring in the tea tray. Once they had gone, closing the door behind them, she poured out the tea.

'Are the girls home?' Reid asked, accepting his cup and saucer.

'Bettina and Harriet are in the study with their German tutor. They won't be down for an hour yet.' She watched him carefully and he flushed under her scrutiny. 'Is there something you want to discuss with me?'

'Yes.' He put the cup and saucer back on the tray and walked over to the fireplace. He watched the flames leaping around the wood, but didn't feel the heat.

'What is it, Reid?'

'I know that Aurora ran away.'

Winnie gasped. 'How? What do you know?'

'I also know who Aurora married and why.'

'You do?' Winnie's hand went to her throat and tears filled her eyes. 'But who? We don't know ourselves. She never mentioned his name. We've been thinking all sorts of things.'

'She married Tom.'

348

'Tom who?'

'My brother, Tom.'

'Your Tom?' Her mouth gaped open and she blinked in shock. 'But — '

'I love Aurora, Mrs Pettigrew, I do most dearly.' He suddenly knelt at her knee and gripped her hands, unable to bear the hideous burden crushing his chest. 'I love her more than anything in the world.'

Tears ran down her cheeks and she squeezed his hands. 'How did Tom come to marry my daughter then if you love her?'

'I think, no, I know she ran away from here because . . . because she was carrying my child. At least that is what Tom wrote in a letter.'

'A child?' Winnie's throat convulsed and she bit her lip as a moan escaped. 'She was in trouble. Oh Aurora . . . '

'I'm sorry. Desperately sorry.'

'That was not the only reason why she left, Reid.' Winnie bowed her head. 'Oh, my dearest girl.'

'It wasn't?' His heart seemed to dip down to his boots and back up again to lodge painfully in his chest.

'She found out that I am not her real mother, and that my sister is the one who gave birth to her.'

He reared back, staring at her in astonishment. He couldn't believe it. 'My God. That means she — '

'That means she had a lot to deal with all at the same time.' Winnie finished for him, fumbling for a handkerchief and wiping her eyes.

'When she left we found a note from her saying she was going to look for her real mother. Josiah and I have no idea how she found out. No one knew but our parents, who are dead, and ourselves. We moved to Leeds away from everyone once Sophia, my sister, gave us Aurora, so it wouldn't cause speculation amongst our friends. By the time we saw them again, they assumed Aurora was ours.'

He got to his feet and went back to the fire, resting his arm along the mantelpiece. 'I cannot believe it.'

'She had no money, Reid, or very little. Josiah dreads to think how she has survived. We've had two letters. One not long after she left, saying she was well and then another, the day when you and your mother called, saying she was married.' As though thankful for finally being able to speak of this matter, Winnie hurried on. 'The first letter was stamped in York and the second in Halifax. Josiah has had men searching, he hired people to find her, but with no luck so far and then when she said she had married we didn't have her husband's name to use to further the search. But my husband is a stubborn man, Reid, and won't give up. He's now having church records searched for banns and the wedding registers, but he cannot visit every church in England. We thought it would take years!' Tears sprang from her eyes again and she dabbed at them ineffectually. 'I can't believe she married Tom. At least it was someone who would know how to take care of her and treat her properly.'

'You mentioned Halifax? She sent a letter

from Halifax?' Reid thought to the letter he'd received from the fellow in Hebden Bridge. 'I think I might know where she is.'

'Oh Reid.' She hunched over in her chair and cried broken-heartedly and he comforted her in his arms. After a while, she rose and crossed to her secretary. From a drawer, Winnie pulled out a crumbled piece of paper and gave it to Reid. 'One of the maids found this some months ago. I didn't know what it meant really. I didn't know the handwriting or who it was addressed to, but now I think Aurora had dropped it. Will you read it and tell me what you think?'

He nodded and puzzled, took the note. He blinked in surprise on seeing his own handwriting.

My darling,
Soon, it will be possible for us to be together. There are things I must do, arrangements I've made in haste, which have now prevented me from declaring myself fully to your father.
Be patient my dearest Hermione . . .

It took some moments for him understand the implications of the contents. Hermione . . . He jerked and stared at Winnie. 'This is my letter to Aurora, but I . . . this . . . ' He knocked the paper with the back of his hand. 'I never wrote Hermione's name. That name isn't in my handwriting. This letter was meant for Aurora not Hermione. You must believe me.'

'It's what Aurora believed, Reid, that's important.'

351

'How did she get it?' His mind whirled. 'Do you have the envelope?'

'No.' Winnie's chin wobbled and fresh tears flowed. 'You must have felt so betrayed by us all.'

As naturally as breathing, he moved to comfort her, wondering why he could easily hold this woman in his arms but to do such a thing with his mother was impossible. 'I'll go to her once I've returned from London.'

'Tom was like a brother to her, she always said that.'

'And he married her to protect her, like a brother. He wanted her child to have a name, to have the rightful name of Sinclair, as it should. He did it for me as well.' He shrugged, emotion filling his throat. 'We'll soon know the whole story.'

'So if she has married Tom, he must have provided her with a home, money? She wouldn't be on the street?'

'She has a home and money, yes.'

'Oh, thank God.' She bowed her head and cried some more.

'I am so sorry for my part in this, I promise you I did not know of her condition. She stopped writing to me and the next thing I knew she had gone. It made no sense to me. I've been mad with worry like yourself. If only she had come to me. I would have married her as we planned.'

'You had planned to marry?'

'Yes, but with my father being ill . . . ' He sucked in a breath. 'I should have controlled myself.' He clenched his teeth, frustrated, angry

352

and aching for the truth. 'I'm sorry.'

'She must have been ashamed, Reid, on both accounts, about her child and parentage.' Winnie wiped her eyes again, her handkerchief sodden and limp. 'Josiah will be so thankful for this news. We have worried nonstop for so long.'

'I'll make it right, I promise you.' He stepped towards the door. 'I must go, but I'll be back soon, with Aurora.'

Winnie, crumbled handkerchief in her hands, rose and walked with him to the door. 'Bless you, bring back my girl, I beg you. Tell her we love her. All is forgiven.'

'Soon you can tell her yourself.' He smiled, feeling lighter of heart now he had a purpose.

24

Gently easing the baby off her nipple, Aurora smiled at the tiny head, the delicate eyelids, and the sweet snub of her nose. A dibble of milk ran out of her mouth and Aurora wiped it away with the corner a linen cloth. 'There, my sweet girl,' she crooned, adjusting her blouse with one hand, 'that should keep you satisfied for an hour or two.'

The bedroom door opened and Sophia came in, her eyes soft with love as she gazed at the baby. 'All finished? Shall I put her down?'

'Please.' Aurora handed over her nine day old daughter, Olivia, and rose from the chair. 'Did I hear the post?'

'Yes, sorry I should have brought them up with me, but I was putting Will down for a nap for Lily, who is making dumplings.' Sophia tucked the baby into the cradle and gazed down at her. 'You know, I see you in her as a baby.'

'Really? I see Reid. She has his shaped eyes. I wonder if they will be blue like his or brown like mine.'

Sophia bent and kissed her granddaughter softly on the head. 'She'll be beautiful whatever she has.'

Aurora waited for Sophia and leaving the door open so they could hear the baby, they went downstairs to the warmth of the sitting room. From the kitchen came Lily's singing. 'What's she singing?'

'Some tune Jed taught her.' Sophia collected the mail from the side table and passed them to Aurora. 'They got on very well together.'

Aurora raised her eyebrows. 'How interesting.'

'Thinking of doing some match-making are you?' Sophia laughed. 'I don't think you need to. It looks as if it's happening all by itself.'

'Jed's a good man.'

'Yes.' Sorting through the envelopes, Aurora yawned behind her hand. 'They're mainly bill accounts.'

'You look tired. Did Olivia keep you awake much last night?'

'She woke at three and then again at six.' Aurora glanced at the carriage clock on the mantelpiece. It was now just after ten in the morning. Tiredness stung her eyes. She couldn't believe how exhausting it was to take care of a baby. 'Are Noah and Jed outside?'

'Yes. The farrier came early and after he left, they decided to mend the roof over the chicken pen. Jed said he saw a fox in the home field yesterday. He's set a trap. He's worried it might take down one of the pregnant ewes as well as steal the odd hen.'

Aurora gazed out of the window at the snow-covered fields beyond the drive. 'It will be good to have spring arrive.'

'Yes, we can sit the babies out in the sun.' Sophia added more wood to the blazing fire. 'And plant flowers and vegetables.' Using the iron poker she adjusted a log and then replaced the poker in its stand. 'I'll go make us a cup of tea.'

'That'll be nice.' Aurora nodded, aware of Sophia's transformation since her marriage to Noah. It was as though she had regained her self-respect. Sophia wore nice clothes, her hair was neatly held in a bun, she stood tall and straight, laughter danced in her eyes and a happy smile hovered on her lips. Noah, the babies and this house gave her a purpose. She was forever coming up with plans, ideas to decorate the rooms and discussing the future of the farm with Noah and Jed. Sophia was adjusting to her new life with vigor. She was putting down roots.

Staring around the room, Aurora tried to summon the enthusiasm to do the same. After all, this farm was hers, not Sophia's, but she couldn't feel at home here. It was proving difficult to think ahead. And wearing black mourning clothes for dear Tom didn't help her mood either.

Sighing, she picked up her needlework from her basket, but returned it almost immediately. Since the baby arrived she couldn't concentrate on anything.

Resting back in the chair, her thoughts wondered. The security of having her own house gave her peace of mind, but not happiness. On first arriving, she been excited to be here, away from the tenements in the lane, away from the filth and poverty. However, try as she might, she couldn't settle. She felt an impostor, or a guest at someone's house. She thought of the place as Sophia's domain. Ever since she'd given birth a restlessness had overcome her. The future stretched out before her in dull understanding that this was all she would have.

She jerked up from the chair and went to stand before the fire, admonishing herself for her selfishness. She should be grateful to have a roof over her head, an income, people who cared for her, but it wasn't enough and she hated feeling that way. Each time she looked at her baby girl she saw Reid's features and her heart ached for him. Was she going to spend the rest of her life wanting a man she couldn't have?

Movement on the drive caught her attention and she moved to the window to watch the carriage crunch through the thin coating of fresh snow. She turned for the door to go upstairs. She didn't want visitors today. She'd let Sophia entertain them. Listening to the women of Hebden Bridge gossiping was the last thing she needed.

She met Sophia, carrying a tea tray, at the doorway. 'Someone has come, but I'm not ready for social calls. Can you see to them?'

'Of course.' Sophia put the tray on a side table. 'I'll make your excuses and hopefully they won't stay long.'

Aurora was half way up the stairs when knocking came at the door. She hurried up to the landing and peeked over the banister as Sophia opened the door.

'Good day, Mr Blackwell. How may I help you?'

'Ah, Mrs Middleton. You are looking in splendid health, if I may say so.'

'Thank you.'

'I've come to pay my respects to Mrs Sinclair. We've heard the wonderful news that she is safely delivered of a daughter.'

'That is correct, Mr Blackwell, but unfortunately Mrs Sinclair is not receiving visitors as yet.'

'I quiet understand.' He entered the hall and Sophia shut the door on the cold day. 'However, I was wishing to talk to her about another matter, concerning her husband's family.'

Aurora held her breath.

'I'm sure it can wait, Mr Blackwell,' Sophia said politely. 'Or perhaps you can send a letter?'

'Hmm . . . ' Blackwell rubbed his chin. He looked up the staircase and Aurora jerked back out of sight. 'No need for a letter. If you'll pass the massage on?'

'Of course,' Sophia murmured.

'If you could inform Mrs Sinclair that I've written to her brother-in-law, Mr Reid Sinclair of Sinclair Hall, Leeds, and I've invited him to a council meeting. Since the Sinclair's own properties in this area, I thought it would be beneficial to have a man of his experience to attend a meeting and share his knowledge.'

Aurora gripped the banister to keep herself upright. Blackwell contacted Reid?

'And has Mr Sinclair sent a reply?' Sophia's voice came out hard and short.

'Not as yet, but I believe the invitation would be welcomed, given that he has family here to visit as well. Mrs Sinclair and your good self, madam, should expect invitations to dinner at my house when Mr Sinclair arrives. I am trying to plan a ball at the Assembly rooms to coincide with his stay.'

'Thank you, Mr Blackwell. I will let my daughter know.' Sophia opened the door and gave him a stiff smile.

Blackwell again glanced up the staircase. 'Well ... er ... yes, yes, indeed. Good day, Mrs Middleton.'

'Good day.' Sophia closed the door on him and hurried up the stairs. 'Are you all right?'

Aurora nodded, but felt quite the opposite.

Sophia's lips thinned into a line of annoyance. 'We are cursed with that man. Stupid Blackwell. Always interfering.'

'So Reid will know I am here,' Aurora whispered, numb with shock. 'The one thing I have been trying to avoid all this time and Blackwell has unraveled it all with one letter.'

'Come sit down.' Sophia held her close and guided her into the bedroom where they sat on Aurora's bed. The baby slept peacefully in the cradle at the end.

'I will have to leave.' Aurora said, woodenly, her heart heavy in her chest.

'No!' Sophia stared at her. 'No, we'll work something out.'

'I cannot face Reid. It's impossible. Too much time has gone by.'

'We must think clearly. You have said that Reid travels a lot. He could be in America as we speak. He may not see Blackwell's letter for months. We have time to work something out. Make plans.'

'Tom's solicitor came here a week ago. With Tom's death, Reid would be in the country. Julia would have sent for him. What if Reid has read the letter and is on his way here right now?' Panic flooded her. She stood, ready to pack and run. 'Would he know I've married Tom? Oh God. He wouldn't understand why I did that.'

'Calm down.' Sophia rose and hugged her. 'It'll be all right.'

'No, no it won't.' Aurora gazed at her baby daughter, Reid's daughter, and her heart flipped. 'What am I going to do? Blackwell did this to punish me for what I said in the shop that day. I humiliated him and now he's trying to do the same to me. He knows I have nothing to do with Tom's family. He wants to cause trouble.' She gripped her hands together and held them under her chin. 'I wish we had never come here.'

'Don't say that. It's a good place. We have a nice home. Blackwell is the fly in the soup. He has spoilt things. He is to blame.'

'I cannot stay here, waiting to see if Reid knocks on the door. I'll go crazy with it.'

'Very well, and I do understand, believe me.' Sophia paced the floor, worrying her thumbnail as she always did when stressed. 'Let's go downstairs and with everyone discussing it, we'll work something out.'

Aurora sadly shook her head. 'I'm leaving.'

'What? No.'

'Help me pack.'

'Running away isn't the answer, Aurrie.' Sophia grabbed her hands. 'Dearest, listen to me.'

'Don't you see? I cannot face Reid. I know it's cowardly to run, but I have no option. I cannot have him and to see him, knowing that I have to

360

say goodbye to him all over again will surely kill me this time.'

'You only gave birth days ago. You can't possibly travel, and not with a new baby, and its winter. Besides, where will you go?'

'I'm not sure.'

'There, that's my point. Running away won't solve this.'

Hot tears gathered behind her eyes. 'I'm sorry, but I'm going.'

'Then I'll come with you.'

'No. You're married now. You're Noah's wife. Anyway, I need you to stay and look after this place for me.'

'You won't be able to manage.'

'I have money this time. The account Tom opened for me will allow me to live well. I'll even hire a nursemaid to help me.'

'I don't like it. You shouldn't be alone at this time.'

'I'll manage. I don't want to leave you, but I must go . . . '

Different emotions flittered across Sophia's face for a moment before she finally nodded. 'I'll help you pack.'

'Once I've found somewhere I'll write and you can come see me.' Aurora pulled a small trunk out from under the bed. 'I'll stay in a hotel for a couple of weeks until I find somewhere more permanent. You can come and see me there.'

'Were will you go first?'

'Scotland.'

'Scotland?' Sophia looked aghast as though Aurora had said the Far East.

'I've never heard Reid mention going to Scotland before. I won't meet him up there.'

The doorbell rung and they both froze. The strength left Aurora's legs and she crumbled onto the edge of the bed. 'Please, Lord don't let that be him.'

'I'll go down.'

Aurora strained to listen as Sophia left the room and walked downstairs. Faint voices drifted up, but she couldn't make sense of them. She jumped when the door was thrust opened and Sophia's smiled in reassurance. 'It's Peggy.'

'Peggy?'

'Peggy from York.' Sophia nodded. 'She's in the parlor. I'll stay up here and start packing for you and watch the baby.'

Aurora hurried downstairs and into the parlor. Peggy stood in front of the fire, holding her hands out to the blaze. Beside her on the rug was a small carpetbag. 'Peggy!'

'Aurrie.' They held each other tight for a moment before separating. 'I'm sorry I didn't give you warning of my coming.' Peggy straightened her black felt hat.

'I'm so surprised to see you.' Aurora indicated for her to sit down.

Peggy grinned and looked pointedly at Aurora's stomach. 'You've had the baby then?'

'Yes. A little girl. She's perfect.'

'Wonderful.'

'How long are you here for?'

'Well, that depends.'

'Oh?'

A wave of sadness altered Peggy's face. 'Me

362

grandmother died two weeks ago.'

'I'm sorry to hear it. You must be dreadfully upset.'

'And I've left Ellerton's.'

'Really? Why?'

'Merv got Nancy pregnant.' She shrugged. 'I couldn't take it anymore.'

Aurora's eyes widened in surprise. 'Nancy? But she hated what he did.'

'Aye, but he paid her attention, you see, and gave her money to buy nice things. She says she loves him. Idiot.'

'Poor Nancy. Silly fool.'

'Aye. I was so cross. I slapped her when she told me. All these years I've looked out for her, and she goes and gives in to him. She was like me little sister.'

'How tragic. I never thought she'd fall for into his trap.'

'When you left and me Gran became sicker . . . Nancy said she felt abandoned by us. She was lonely. Twaddle that is, pure twaddle. How can she be lonely in her family? There's over a dozen of them still at home!'

'I suppose I should have seen it coming. He sweet-talked her into revealing information about me. She protested that he was only trying to help. He had got to her back then. Why didn't I realize?'

'I didn't see it either.' Peggy sighed and stared into the fire. 'Nancy cried when I left, but I couldn't stay. After burying Gran I just felt lost. Then I found your address from the letter you sent me at Christmas. I simply hopped on a train. And here I am.'

Aurora smiled. 'And here you are.'

'But there is something I have to confess to.'

'Oh?'

'Before I left Ellerton's . . . Well, I gave them a piece of my mind, kind of like you did.' Peggy took a deep breath. 'Anyway, I think I might have put you in danger, and meself too.'

'How so?' Aurora swallowed back her apprehension.

'I threatened Merv, like you did. I told them all in the kitchen that I was going to the authorities to report him.'

'What happened?'

'He threatened me, saying he'd do me in. I ran.'

'Ran here?'

'I went back to me rooms first and got together some things. I was as quick as I could manage. It was hard leaving me Gran's things and the neighbors kept coming in . . . ' Peggy twisted her hands in her lap. 'I didn't think anything of it as I was in such a hurry, but well, a man got on the train the same time I did and watched me every now and then on the journey here. He got off at Hebden Bridge too.'

'What did he look like?'

'Average height. Black hat. Nasty looking character. He seemed to be watching me every move.' Peggy shuddered. 'Oh, and he smiled at me as we got off the train and he had a missing front tooth.'

'Oh good lord.' Aurora thought her heart would stop. 'It sounds like the same man.'

364

'What man?'

'The man Merv had following me before I left.'

'Why didn't you say owt?'

'I was marrying Tom and moving away. I didn't think I would have to. I thought Merv would forget about me as long as nothing happened and I didn't go to the police like I said I would.'

What color Peggy had left her face. 'Gawd, I'm sorry, Aurrie, really I am.'

They both turned as Lily brought through a tea tray and Sophia followed her carrying Will. Lily's eyes were red from crying and Aurora guessed that Sophia had told her the news of her leaving. For a while they sat drinking tea and chatting about nothing much important. Then, unable to put it off any longer, Aurora told Sophia about the man in the black hat.

'You should never have kept that from me,' Sophia admonished, handing Will to Lily. 'You were in danger.'

'I know. I'm sorry.'

Lily hitched Will higher on her lap. 'Me dad won't let any man near us. We'll be safe with him and Jed watching out for us.'

'We cannot hide forever, Lily.' Aurora sighed, feeling trapped and utterly useless.

'If this Merv Ellerton thinks you're going to the authorities, then you might as well do so,' Sophia muttered, pouring out more tea. 'If he's arrested then we have nothing else to fear.'

'But what if he's not arrested? What if he pays off the police and others?' Sipping her tea,

Aurora listened for a cry from upstairs. Her head pounded. 'Besides, I'm leaving anyway. I think I should just do that and hopefully the shadow man will not follow.'

Peggy straightened. 'Anyway, what can one man do? He's probably only reporting back to Merv and nothing else. If we stay away from the police, he'll leave us alone.'

'You know I just had a thought, Aurrie.' Sophia glanced at them all. 'Perhaps Peggy could go with you to Scotland?'

Peggy's eyes brightened. 'I'll go anywhere, Aurrie. I've got no home or family.'

They spent the rest of the day packing and making plans. Noah and Jed were to drive them in the cart down to the train station at three o'clock; they'd catch the evening train to Scotland. While Lily and Peggy prepared a hamper for them to take on the train, Sophia sat on Aurora's bed holding the baby while watching Aurora pack the last minute things.

Aurora adjusted the straps on the carpet bag. She looked up at Sophia. 'How will I cope without you?'

'You'll manage. You're strong. Like me.' Sophia grinned, and then leaned down to kiss the baby. 'The truth is I don't know how I'll cope without you.'

'I'll write often.'

Sophia nodded. 'Yes, do, for I will miss you terribly.'

A slight tap on the bedroom door preceded Lily. 'Sorry, Aurrie, but there's a woman downstairs. She says she wishes to see you.'

'You go. I'll listen out for Olivia if she wakes up,' Sophia said, as they went downstairs. 'I'll be in the kitchen with Lily if you need me.'

Frowning with puzzlement at who her visitor could be, Aurrie paused in parlor doorway. All warmth left her face when Julia Sinclair turned from the fire. She glanced around the room looking for Reid and disappointment hit her hard to find him not there. Why did she think he would be? Had he sent his mother in his place?

'Ah, Aurora.' Dressed entirely in black, Mrs Sinclair smiled her feline smile.

Old hurt and suspicions clamored up inside Aurora. 'Why are you here?'

'That is a fine welcome.'

'You expected more?' Aurora snorted. 'So, why are you here?'

'Well, should it be a crime for me to visit my daughter-in-law?'

'So, you know.' Aurora cringed and stepped into the room. 'We have nothing to say to each other.'

'Come now, Aurora, that is hardly so. Much has happened since we last saw each other.'

Pushing back her shoulders, Aurora pasted a smile on her face. 'I am sorry, Julia, but I'm in a hurry. I'm leaving for a holiday today and I really must finish my packing.'

'Spending my son's inheritance I see?'

'If you'll excuse me.' Aurora bowed her head and turned away.

'How rude! I haven't come all this way to be ignored by you!'

Aurora let out a breath and faced her

mother-in-law. 'I do not know why you came here, nor do I care. I'm sure it has something to do with you trying to hurt and belittle me, but frankly *Julia*, I don't care. I have my own life to lead and you don't have the power to cause me pain anymore.'

A nerve twitched in Julia's eye. 'I want answers. Why did you marry Tom? Was it to escape the slums of York?' Julia's triumph lit her face. 'Oh, yes. I know all about your time in York. I made it my business to find out. I am amazed by your resilience, but, my dear, you've made an enemy. One who was quite happy to talk to me.'

Aurora stiffened, a slender finger of anxiety trickled down her back. 'I have nothing to say to you.'

'You don't have to. Merv Ellerton was more than pleased to tell me everything.' Julia glided around the room as graceful as a panther and just as deadly. 'The poor man is worried you'll squeal like a stuck pig to the authorities. I assured him you wouldn't, but he wasn't convinced.'

'Why are you so sure I wouldn't go to the police?'

'And draw attention to yourself, I don't think so. Am I right?' Julia raised an elegant eyebrow, her expression arrogant.

Fear clutched at Aurora's innards. 'What do you want from me? My silence? You have it. Do you want my promise never to be in contact with the Sinclair family again? You have it.'

'Yes, I want all that and more.'

'I have nothing more to give. You've taken everything. Good bye Julia.'

'Wait.'

'What?' Her fist clenched, Aurora strove for patience.

'May we try to be civilized with each other?' Julia walked to the window and moved aside the lace curtain. 'Do you want to know about Tom's memorial?'

'I'm sure it was very beautiful and moving.'

Julia continued to stare out of the window. 'I never expected to lose two people I loved in one year. I refuse to lose anymore of my family.'

'That choice isn't yours to make. It is something that, for once, you cannot control.'

'How true. And I do not like it.' She gave Aurora a glimpse of a smile. 'You are looking well. The time spent in the slums doesn't seem to have affected you?'

Aurora cocked her head, wary of such small talk. 'Wouldn't you like to know?'

'Not really.' Julia glanced out the window and then quickly slipped on her gloves. 'I doubt we'll see each other again. There is nothing that connects us now Tom is dead.'

'You are quite right.' Aurora refused to ask about Reid. Julia hadn't mentioned him and neither would she.

'It is best if our families stay apart from now on. Don't you agree?'

Disgusted that Julia was still trying to force her to bend to her will, Aurora simply glared at her. 'Good afternoon, Mrs Sinclair. I'm sure you can see yourself out.' She walked out of the room and spotted Sophia coming down the hall from the kitchen.

Sophia embraced her. 'Are you all right? Who is it?'

'Julia Sinclair. Will you see her out to her carriage?'

Sophia nodded and was ready to march into the parlor, but Julia had come out and headed for the front door. Aurora left Sophia to deal with her for she didn't have the strength. She leaned against the wall feeling so tired she thought she'd fall.

Lily came out of the kitchen, wiping her hands on her apron. 'Everything all right, Aurrie?'

'It will be.'

'You look done in. Why don't you go up and sleep for an hour. You'll be no good to Olivia if you're bone tired.'

'I think I might once the packing is done.'

'We've got everything under control here. Peggy's finished the hamper.'

Aurora nodded and squeezed Lily's arm in thanks before carrying on upstairs to finish her packing. Reaching her room on shaky legs, she opened the door and went to the cradle. For a moment she stared, not comprehending the empty space where her baby should be laying. Then, thinking Lily had her, she hurried back downstairs to the kitchen.

'Lily, do you . . . ' her voice dried up as Lily turned from the oven with a tray of bread loaves in her hands. Baby Will gurgled in his bassinet by the back door, but he was alone. Peggy came in from the scullery carrying a bottle of ginger beer.

'What is it, Aurrie?' Lily asked, placing the tray on the table.

'Where's Olivia?'

'Asleep upstairs, isn't she?'

'No.' Aurora turned as Sophia came into the kitchen.

'There, Mrs Sinclair has gone. Uppity witch.'

'Olivia. Where is she?' Aurora pleaded, gripping the back of a chair. 'She's not upstairs. Did you put her somewhere else? In your room?'

Sophia blinked, surprised. 'No. I left her in your room. She was asleep in the cradle when I came down.'

'She's not there!' Aurora raced out the kitchen and back upstairs with Sophia and Peggy hard on her heels. In a frenzy, they rushed into each bedroom but the baby wasn't to be found.

Back downstairs, Aurora, with the help of the others, searched all the rooms and then went outside to find Noah and Jed, praying that one of the men had taken the baby for a walk.

However, as she skidded to a halt inside the stables and saw Jed and Noah cleaning and mending harness she knew that searching for her baby would do no good. Olivia was gone.

25

Long into the night, and hours after the police had gone, Aurora paced the parlor floor. She couldn't think straight. Thoughts and images whirled through her mind like a merry-go-round. Her breast, full of milk for Olivia, ached, but the tears she wanted to cry wouldn't fall. Her baby. Stolen. It seemed too bizarre to be real. Somehow, Julia had managed to strike at her heart once more.

A log shifted in the fireplace and Sophia left the sofa to poke it back into place. Lily had gone to bed with Will, but Peggy, Jed and Noah had left with the police. Jed and Peggy were going to York to search for Merv Ellerton or find out any information on his whereabouts, while Noah had gone to Leeds on the off chance Julia had returned to the Hall.

Aurora had wanted to go with them, but the police asked her to remain home. They needed to have her where they could reach her should any news come through.

'If only I had walked to the carriage with her, instead of staying on the steps.' Sophia murmured for the umpteenth time since the police were called.

'If only I had realized that Julia hadn't been alone.' Aurora stared out of the window at the night sky. 'How were we to know that while talking to me, her henchmen were creeping through the

372

house looking for my baby? I understand now why she looked through the window the whole time, she was waiting for them to climb back into the carriage with Olivia . . . ' her voice cracked and she gulped in air.

'The bitch.'

'I wondered why she hadn't mentioned Reid.' Aurora watched the flames dance. 'You know, I felt superior. For once I felt I had the upper hand. I had her grandchild, Reid's daughter, and she knew nothing about it. Or so I thought. But as always she was ahead of me. She knew about Olivia. And she took her. I must have nothing of the Sinclair family.'

Sophia jerked to her feet. 'God, I can't stand not being able to do anything.'

'I know.' Aurora gazed down at the plain gold wedding band on her finger. She slid the ring off her finger and calmly threw it into the fire. She never wanted to see a Sinclair again.

★   ★   ★

Reid yawned and wiped a hand over his tired eyes. He'd arrived from London only an hour ago after preparing Tom's memorial and dealing with business demands. He'd also helped James secure a commission in the navy, which he would join after his exams in the spring and all without their mother's knowledge. Edward was still content to continue at Oxford and so with his brothers happy, he could now concentrate on his own future. A future with Aurora. Tomorrow he would see her.

The Hall groaned and creaked as night settled on the countryside. He found it odd that the noises of the house never frightened him, even as a boy. The Hall, every room, nook and cranny was his home and he loved it. Leaning back in the leather chair, he gazed around the study. The corners were in shadows where the candlelight didn't reach, however, he knew every detail of the oak-paneled room. He always thought of this room as his father's, but now it was his.

Picking up a sheet of paper from the desk, he studied the figures written. To improve the Hall would cost a lot of money, thankfully he had it, but the thought of workmen trudging through the house, making noise and a mess, filled him with dread. Ten years ago, his father had introduced gas lighting into the lower rooms of the Hall, but now he had inherited, he wanted the entire house fitted with gas lighting. It would be an enormous undertaking, but no more than having hot water piped upstairs. The summer would see changes, lots of them, and not just in the house, which he wanted to be perfect for Aurora, but with him personally. He wanted to be married, have children and grow old with Aurrie. Was he asking too much?

Tomorrow he was travelling to Hebden Bridge to visit Aurora. With luck, she'd agree to see him and he hoped he could start to correct the damage done. Would she forgive him?

A knock heralded Matthews, the butler. 'Sorry to disturb you, sir.'

'That's quiet all right.' Reid placed the paperwork away in a drawer.

'Your unpacking is finished, sir, and I have repacked for your trip in the morning. I've lit a fire in your bedroom. It's a cold night.'

'Thank you.'

'Mrs Sinclair has arrived and gone to her rooms. Shall I lock up now?'

Reid rose from his chair. 'My mother has arrived? She wasn't expected.' He frowned and headed for the door. His mother had left London for Paris three days ago, after the memorial, or so she had told him.

He took the stairs two at a time and strode down the gallery to his mother's suite of rooms on the west end of the hall. He tapped lightly on the door, but not waiting for her acceptance, walked in. The sitting room was littered with travel baggage, but his mother wasn't in attendance, nor was her maid, Gavet. Stepping through into the bedroom he noticed the bed was covered with clothes and shawls.

Talking came from the dressing room, but before he could enter it a baby's cry shattered the silence and he froze.

A baby?

In his mother's dressing room?

Intrigued, he silently opened the door. His eyes widened as his mother crooned to a baby in her arms while Gavet was folding small garments.

'Mother?' he croaked.

She spun towards him, astonishment making her mouth gape. 'Reid. I didn't think you were here. I thought you to be still in London.'

He advanced into the room. 'I arrived less than an hour ago. Why do you have a baby?'

'It is nothing.' She waved him away and gave the baby to Gavet before linking her arm in his and making for the door.

He dug his heels in. 'I beg to differ. It isn't nothing to have a baby in your room. Whom does it belong to?'

'Gavet.' His mother announced. 'Gavet has had a baby. We didn't want the news to be made public so I offered her my help.'

The way her gaze couldn't quite meet his and the awkward way Gavet held the child heightened his suspicions. 'Again. I ask you. Whom does this baby belong to? The truth now.'

'Me.' His mother smiled, raising her head proudly as though she had just given birth herself.

'You?'

'Yes. I have adopted the child.'

'Why?'

'Because I wanted a daughter.' She let go of his arm and walked past him into the bedroom. 'My sons act as though they don't care for me, or listen to my judgment, so I thought I would start again and this time with a daughter.'

For a moment he thought she had lost her reason. 'You aren't serious?'

'Terribly serious. People do it all the time.'

'They do?'

'Oh yes. In fact, I made an acquaintance recently, who helps good families obtain children they couldn't have themselves. I decided I would do the same and adopt a child.'

'Don't you think you are a little old for such an undertaking?'

'Nonsense. I'm not in my dotage yet, dear

boy.' She sat at her dressing table and began pulling off her jeweled rings. 'I will let you know that I'm going away tomorrow. Probably to the continent for a few months. Somewhere warm.'

'I see.' The baby cried again and it raised the fine hairs on the back of his neck. 'Why didn't you go to Paris like you had arranged in London?'

'I changed my mind.'

He nodded, thinking hard. 'You have never mentioned this desire for a baby before.'

'Well, with Tom's death it all suddenly made sense to me. Then meeting that man . . . I felt the time was right.'

'Who is this man?'

'A gentleman from York. He's provided for all the good families in the district. Though of course it is all hushed to prevent any scandals.' She took out one earring and stared at him through the mirror. 'I hope you will miss me when I'm abroad.'

'Indeed.' His smile was brittle. 'Is it wise for you to travel with a baby in cold weather? It was snowing again this evening.'

'I'm sure it'll be all right.' She smiled at him in the mirror and took out her other earring.

'Still, I would like to spend some time with my new sister, if I may? Can you delay your departure?'

'You? Spend time with a baby? Whatever for? She's tiny and cannot do anything.'

He struggled to find a reasonable excuse, but something nagged at him. 'Just a few days perhaps, until the weather clears.'

'I'll think about it.' She rose from the stool.

377

'Now, if you'll excuse me. It's been a long day and I wish to retire.'

'Of course.' He bowed. 'Good night, Mother.' He left the room. But the uneasy feeling stayed with him as he went to his own bedroom. His mother wasn't insane; she was as clear-headed as anyone he knew. No, this adoption was well thought out. She'd argued the point well. Many women her age took on wards, or guided young ladies through their first season, but they were of an age to be interesting and molded. But a baby, and a very young baby at that? It just didn't seem right. His mother wasn't the patient type. He couldn't see her taking care of a child for years. She'd be in her seventies before the child had grown to adulthood.

He sat on the edge of his bed, waiting for Gilbert, his father's elderly valet to come in and take his boots off. Where was the man? He reached up to pull the bell rope just as the door opened. 'Ah, there you are, Gilbert.'

'I apologize, sir.' Gilbert stood there dithering.

'What is it, man?' Reid sighed. What was wrong with the house tonight?

'Sir, I don't know how to say this . . . ' Gilbert pulled at his starched collar and checked over his shoulder.

'Close the door.' Reid stood, alarmed by this diligent old man uneasiness. Gilbert, who'd started his service in Grandfather Sinclair's time, was as trustworthy as they came. 'Now tell me.'

'Sir, as you know my habit is to have a walk after supper before I come upstairs to attend to my duties.'

'Yes, I know this.' Reid narrowed his eyes. 'Has someone stopped you from doing this?'

'No sir. You see, it was while I was out walking, I came across a fellow. He was skulking in the bushes near the drive.'

'A vagrant?'

'No, sir.' Gilbert scratched his gray stubbly chin. 'At first he wouldn't say who he was, but he asked me if the mistress was at home.'

'My mother?'

'Yes, sir.'

'Did he say anything else?'

'I didn't reply to his question, but asked him his name. I said if he told me his name I would tell him if the mistress was at home.'

Tired and a little fed up, Reid ran his fingers through his hair. 'Is there some point to this, Gilbert? I'm awfully tired.'

'I'm sorry, sir. The man's name is Noah Middleton.'

'Noah Middleton.' Reid searched his memory for any recognition. 'No, I don't know the name, Gilbert. Should I?'

'I don't rightly know, sir. Only that he wanted to know if the mistress had arrived home and whether she had a baby with her.'

Reid jerked in surprise. 'A baby?'

'Yes. I told him of course the mistress didn't have a baby with her. The very thought of it. Perhaps the man is simple? Although he didn't look like it.'

'Where is he now?'

'I'm not sure, sir. I told him that he'd best be on his way and I came inside.'

Reid walked to the door and yanked it open. 'Stay here, Gilbert, and tell no one of what you just told me.'

'Yes, sir.'

On the landing, Reid saw Matthews in the hall below, checking the front door locks and turning down the gas candelabra on the side table. 'Matthews!' Hurrying down the stairs, Reid pointed to the doors. 'Open them.'

Matthews did as he was told. 'Can I help you, sir?'

'Yes, come with me, quickly now. There's a man in the grounds. I want him found.'

'A poacher?' Matthews grabbed Reid's coat and flung it around his master's shoulders.

'No. He mustn't be harmed. Go and get some men from the stables and have my carriage brought around.'

'Yes, sir.' While Matthews ran off around the corner of the house, Reid took off down the drive, the snow crunching beneath his feet.

'Mr Middleton! Sir, I need to speak with you,' he called through cupped hands. An owl hooted, but other than that the grounds were cloaked in white silence. 'Mr Middleton, you are in no danger. Are you there?'

He ran all the way down to the big black iron gates and opened one enough to slip out and onto the road leading to Leeds. The moon went behind a scud of cloud, darkening the shadows to nearly black. 'Mr Middleton!'

'I'm here.' A voice spoke in the night gloom and ahead a dark figure loomed out of the trees at the side of the road. He jumped a small

380

snowdrift and stood in the middle of the road. 'And who may you be?'

'Reid Sinclair.'

'Ah, Aurrie's man,' said the shadowy figure, coming closer.

'Aurora?' Reid's heart seemed to somersault. 'You know of Aurora Pettigrew?'

'She's Aurrie Sinclair now. I'm her stepfather, Noah.'

The man stopped within five feet of him, and with his eyes adjusted to the murkiness, Reid could see the details of a well-dressed man of about fifty years. 'Did Aurora send you? Do you have news of her?'

'Not good news, I'm afraid. Her baby was stolen today.'

'Her baby was stolen?' The air left Reid's lungs in a whoosh, which had him reeling. His mother!

'Yes. A woman, your mother I'm led to believe, visited our home today and while she was there someone took the baby. We believe your mother is involved with the kidnap. The police will likely be here in the morning to talk to her, if she was stupid enough to return home. Or did she give the child to that monster in York? Do you know?'

'Sorry, what?' Reid shook his head mindlessly. 'A monster in York?'

The fellow sighed despondently. 'I've come here to find Aurrie's baby. If she's not here then I must be going. I've a train to catch to York. I can't tarry. The hired cab wouldn't stay for me. Bastard.'

'The baby is here.' The words came out

381

clipped, as though chipped from ice.

'Thank God.' Middleton lifted his head sharply. 'You are involved?'

'No! Definitely not. I only just found out a short time ago that a child was in the house.' Reid's legs were wobbly as he stepped towards the gates. How was any of this possible? Did his mother really have Aurrie's baby upstairs, and if she did, it meant that child was also his! He cleared his dry throat. 'Please, come with me. I'll take you to her.'

Unable to speak further for the emotion clogging his throat, Reid led the silent man up the drive and to the house. Matthews stood on the front steps, issuing several men with lanterns as the carriage came out of a side archway. 'Matthews, send the men to bed, but I'll still need the carriage.'

'Yes, sir.' The butler eyed Middleton curiously, but did as ordered.

Reid turned to Middleton, who, now standing in the gaslight, could be seen more clearly. Reid liked the decent look of the man, a man who you knew you could instantly trust, and wondered why such thoughts came into his head at this crucial time. 'Come this way.'

They went upstairs silently as the clock chimed the half hour of ten o'clock. The long corridor to the west wing seemed eternal to Reid. With every step his heartbeat slowed until he thought it would stop altogether.

Without knocking, he opened the door and walked into his mother's sitting room, Middleton was right behind him. Going through into the

382

bedroom, he noticed his mother asleep in the bed, and the door to the dressing room stood open. A low burning gas wall lamp set above a small range of drawers broke the darkness. In the corner of the dressing room was a carved wooden cradle, one he knew used to belong in the nursery. Gavet slept on her trundle bed beside the cradle.

Middleton pushed past him, bent down and lifted the sleeping child into his arms. His eyes were full of hate towards Reid. 'She's nowt but newly born. 'Tis a disgrace,' he whispered harshly, and headed for the door.

Reid quickly followed him out and they left his mother's room without waking either woman. 'Wait.'

Not slowing down, Middleton dashed ahead towards the staircase. 'I'm taking her home before owt else happens. Aurrie's beside herself with worry. Your mother should be hanged for taking an innocent babe.'

'Listen to me. I have my carriage waiting. I'll come with you.'

Halfway down the staircase, Middleton stopped and faced him. 'I thank you for your help, but its best you not come with me. Your mother has caused enough worry and I don't think your presence will help matters. All Aurrie needs is her baby.'

Reid looked down at the precious bundle in the man's arms. From within the white wrappings he could only see a soft curve of a small cheek. 'She's my daughter, too.'

The other man's eyes narrowed. 'She belongs

to Aurrie. I'm taking her home.'

'This is her home.'

Middleton straightened his back, his face hardened ready to fight. 'I said, I'm taking her home to her mother. And if you are a decent enough fellow, you'll let me.'

Reid nodded, tears hot behind his eyes. 'Yes, take her to Aurrie.' He followed Middleton down the stairs and out to the carriage. 'Matthews, is there a blanket on the seat?'

'Yes, sir, two, and a hot brick for your feet.'

'I'm not going, but this gentleman is.' Reid held the door while Middleton climbed into the carriage and sat down, the baby held close to his chest. 'Hebden Bridge is it?'

'Aye.' Middleton nodded.

He directed the driver where to go and then turned back to Middleton. 'Tell Aurrie I . . . I . . . Tell Aurrie . . . ' As he faltered, one of the horses snorted loudly into the night air and pawed the frozen ground. The cold seeped into Reid's bones. He closed the door and stepped back as the carriage lurched forward. 'Tell Aurrie I'm sorry,' he whispered.

26

Reid read over his father's will once again to make certain he wasn't going against his wishes. Content, he folded the document and put it in the bottom drawer of the desk before locking it with a key.

Taking a deep breath, he added his signature to several other documents on the desk and then sat back and waited. The rising sun streaked through the window, glinting off the snow and blinding those foolish enough to stare outside.

Matthews entered the study, carrying a breakfast tray, which he placed on the corner of the desk. 'Shall I pour, sir?'

'Please.' Reid reached over and took a plate of warm buttered toast and ate without thought to the food. He wasn't even hungry but he knew his body would need fuel for the day ahead. 'Will you have my mail sent out first thing?'

'Yes, sir.' Matthews passed him the cup and saucer. 'Anything else, sir?'

'My mother will require the second carriage today. See that is ready for her.'

'Yes sir.'

'Has Forthby returned from his journey last night?'

'I believe he has, sir. He's having his breakfast as we speak.'

'Good. Have him write down the address where he dropped the man off last night, will you? And I'll need the carriage to take me to the station in an hour.'

'Very good, sir.' Matthews bowed and left the room.

Reid finished his breakfast, still waiting for the inevitable. Then, as he was about to pour a second cup of tea and the clock struck six o'clock, he heard the commotion. Within minutes his mother was hurrying through the house calling his name. When she finally entered the study she was wearing her dressing gown and slippers, her dark hair straggling about her shoulders.

'Good morning, Mother.'

'Reid, something horrible has happened. The baby is gone!'

'Stolen?' He was all mock innocence.

'Yes. Taken in the night.' She looked distraught but he remained unmoved.

'Who would do such a thing?' He held up the teapot. 'Tea?'

'Don't be absurd, we must find her. The baby — ' She stopped mid-sentence, her eyes widening as she understood he wasn't in the least worried. 'You have the baby?'

'No, I don't.'

Her lips thinned in irritation. 'But you know where she is?'

'My daughter is back with her mother.'

'Oh!' She gasped, fumbling for the nearby chair. 'You had no right!'

He leapt to his feet, thumping his fist onto the desk. 'No right? You steal a baby and you tell me I have no right to give her back? Are you mad?'

'Reid, the child is better off with us. Don't you see?'

'How did you know Aurora was pregnant with my child? Did you go through my papers? Did you find that letter from Tom explaining why he married Aurora?'

She raised her chin, her eyes narrowing with spite. 'How else could I know? As always you keep everything from me. You make me snoop through your things like a criminal.'

He couldn't believe what he was hearing. 'You are incredible.'

'That baby is your daughter, my granddaughter. She needs to be with us. She's yours! A Sinclair.'

'Yes, but unlike you, Mother, I won't simply take without giving something back.'

Two red spots of rage blemished her cheeks. 'You are too soft. Be a man and go and get what is yours. That little slut thinks she's won, but I won't allow it.'

'Oh, I will go and get what is mine, but I don't mean just the baby, I mean Aurora, too. I want to make her my wife, as I should have done last year.'

'No.' His mother shook her head. 'No, not that. Pay her off and bring the child back. The Pettigrews will never know she is Aurora's. We'll go abroad, to America.'

He shook his head. 'You aren't listening to me. You never do. I love Aurora. I want her as my wife.'

'Please, no, Reid, don't do this.' Shakily, his mother perched herself on the edge of the chair, she looked old.

'Why are you so against Aurora?'

'She's bastard born. She's not good enough for you, for this family.'

He stared at her, the pieces falling into place. 'You were the one who told Aurora about her birth. You made her run away. Why? Why hurt her in such a manner? The Pettigrews are supposed to be your friends.'

'They think themselves to be better than they are!' she scoffed. 'I'll not have some jumped up trades people associated with our family. Aurora whored herself to you to trap you so you'd marry her. She knew I wanted better for you than her lowly family.'

'You're wrong. She didn't whore herself to me. I loved her and she loved me. I was going to marry her anyway. But then her letters stopped and she went away . . . ' The warmth seeped from his face. 'Tell me you didn't take her letters also. Is that how you knew about us?'

'I had to do something to make you see sense!'

He jerked towards her, ready to strangle the life from her. She stifled a scream, terror in her eyes, and he pulled back just in time. Fist clenched, hatred in his heart, he turned away, unable to look at her.

'Reid, I-I . . . Please understand I was only doing what I thought best.'

'It is indeed a shame that my own mother has no idea of what is best for me.' He laughed hollowly, staring blindly out of the window at the sun-dazzled white drive. 'Your scheming caused me only pain. Does that please you?'

'Absolutely not. It wasn't my intention. I

thought you might be a little hurt at first, but that you'd soon get over her.'

'But I haven't.' He kept staring out the window. One of the gardeners was shoveling snow off the path. The scraping sound grated on him. He turned back to his mother, who sat huddled in her chair, defeated, though it gave him no joy.

She gazed at him, tears in her eyes. 'I am sorry for the hurt I caused you. I didn't think Aurora was good enough for you.'

'No, Mother, she's too good for me,' he said softly. 'I will never be happy with anyone else, but her. Can you not understand that?'

'You'll be the laughing stock of all your friends.'

'How little faith you have in our class, Mother.' He picked up the documents from the desk and held it out to her. 'If Aurora agrees to marry me, I'll bring her home to the Hall. If you cannot be civil and welcoming then you are to leave here today. I've made provisions for you to live in the dowager house on the Kent estate, or buy a townhouse in London. The decision is yours.'

Devastation was written across her pale features. She ignored the proffered papers and turned away, her head lowered. 'So I have lost you.'

'Again, that is your choice, Mother. You can accept Aurora and be included in our lives, or be banished to Kent or London or Paris, wherever you wish to go. I care not.'

'I cannot live without my boys,' she whispered. 'You are all I have.'

'Then you must learn to live with us, accept

our decisions. We are men now, Mother. Let us go or we will grow to hate you.'

She nodded slightly, a shuddering sigh escaping her. 'Go to her then. I will try to accept her as your wife.'

★ ★ ★

Snow drifted on the breeze, giving the landscape a fresh coat of white. Aurora held Olivia close, rocking slightly as she gazed out of the bedroom window. Although Olivia had fallen asleep over twenty minutes ago, she was loathed to put her down and leave her. Since Noah returned in the middle of the night, she'd kept the baby in her arms, not allowing her out of her sight, letting her suckle until she was full and fell asleep on the nipple.

Her mind drifted to Reid and the details of the night before as Noah had relayed them to her. Reid had given back their daughter. He'd gone against his mother. And she knew with certainty that soon he would knock on the front door. But her thoughts went no further than that.

She turned and smiled when Sophia walked into the room. 'This little Miss is so full her tummy is like a barrel.'

'Unlike her mother then.' Sophia gave her a hard look. 'Will you come down and have some of the lovely meal Lily has cooked? You need to eat for your strength and milk supply.'

'I know, and I will have the meal. But she's coming down too.'

Sophia held out her arms for the baby. 'I'll sit

beside you with her, while you eat. How about that?'

'Thank you.' Aurora passed Olivia over and they left the bedroom to go downstairs.

In the warm kitchen, Lily ladled out the midday meal onto the waiting plates. Noah was outside seeing to the animals, and Jed and Peggy had returned from York an hour ago with the news that after the police chief questioned him, Ellerton had fled abroad somewhere and no one knew where. They were delighted to find Olivia home, safe and well. Sophia had sent them to bed after their sleepless night of travelling.

'I want to see you eat all of that up,' Lily warned, handing Aurora a plate full of bacon, eggs, mushrooms and toast.

'Thank you, Lily.' Her stomach rumbled at the delicious aroma and she hungrily tucked into the meal while Sophia sat beside her holding Olivia.

'I'll keep some aside for Peggy and Jed. They'll be hungry when they wake.' Lily smiled.

'Jed has an appetite the largest I've ever seen,' Sophia joked.

'He works hard,' Lily defended and then blushed when Sophia grinned at her. 'Well, he does!'

Aurora relaxed in their friendly banter and finished her meal before Noah came in through the back door, shaking the snow off his boots and hat as he did so. 'A hired carriage has just pulled up.' He looked at Aurora. 'It's him.'

Her heart banged in her chest like a threshing machine. He'd arrived sooner than she thought.

'I'll go and let him in, will I?' Lily gave a

391

nervous smile and hurried out of the kitchen.

Pushing back her chair, Aurora stood and smoothed down her black skirt. She gazed at Olivia and then at Sophia. 'Will you watch her for me?'

'Yes, she'll not leave my arms, but do you not want to see him? I can send him away if you wish.' Sophia's eyes searched her face. 'I'll do whatever you ask.'

Closing her eyes, Aurora fought for composure. So many emotions curses through her, elation, dread, wanting, fear, hope and despair. 'What could he want?' she whispered. 'Olivia?'

'Hopefully both of you, my dear girl.'

'But what if he doesn't?' her voice rose on a touch of hysteria.

'Then we'll deal with that too.' Sophia reached out and softly squeezed her arm. 'Hold your head up, you're a Barton and we are strong.' She released her and pushed her gently towards the door. 'Go now.'

Taking each step slowly, carefully, one at a time, Aurora went along the hallway. In the entrance hall, she paused, licked her dry lips and straightened her shoulders back. Lifting her chin, she walked into the sitting room.

Reid stood before the fire, his head bowed, hands clasped behind his back. He hadn't heard her enter and she stared hungrily at him, absorbing every detail, the profile of his handsome regal face, the breadth of his bowed shoulders, the cut of his trousers, the polish of his boots. Reid Sinclair. The man she loved with every breath of her body.

He raised his head and turned to stare at her. His blue eyes softened with love and longing. He held out one hand to her and she stepped closer to take it. His warm grip went straight to her heart. 'I had to come.'

'Yes.'

'I'm sorry, Aurrie.' He held his hands out helplessly. 'Sorry for everything that has happened. If I had that time back again I would change so much.'

'Me too.'

'Will you forgive me? I didn't know any of it until Tom . . . ' his voice broke.

She nodded, her throat too tight to speak.

'I never stopped loving you. Not for a minute.'

'Nor I you,' she whispered.

His chin wobbled and he took a deep breath. 'I'll not let you leave me again. Even if I have to court you for years to win back your love and respect, I'll do it. I'll do whatever you want me to, but I won't allow you to leave me again.'

'I don't want to.'

He closed his eyes and a tear escaped from one corner. Aurora threw herself into his arms and he crushed her against his chest. She couldn't breathe, but that didn't matter. She was in his arms where she belonged and that's all she cared about. He slackened his hold enough to press his lips to hers and then he leaned back to cup her face in his hands, his eyes wet with tears. 'I love you.'

'I love you, always and forever.' She kissed him hard, desperately, grasping handfuls of his jacket in her need to be near him. This was where she belonged, she'd always known it. And despite everything, if she had to do it all again, experience the heartache and the pain she would, if it meant she'd end up in his arms.

A baby's cry broke them apart and he stiffened.

Aurora stared into his face, searching for clues to his thoughts. 'Our daughter. You gave her back to me.'

'She should never have been taken from you.'

The past pushed its way between them, shifting the mood, spoiling the precious moment.

'We have much to discuss, Aurrie.' Reid ran his hands down her arms, but she moved away. A log fell in the grate, sending sparks of red and orange up the chimney.

'I did what I thought was right at the time, Reid.'

'I know, darling.'

'There are things you need to know.'

'I know about your parentage and it doesn't matter, not to me. How could you think it would?'

'Your mother is very persuasive and I was too shocked to think clearly then.'

'I'm sorry you went though it all alone.' He was beside her instantly and when she went to move away he caught her hand. 'No, don't distance yourself from me anymore. I love you. We'll be married as soon as I can arrange it. I won't let anything part us ever again.'

'How will it work between us when your mother hates me so much that she pays for someone to investigate my family? She stole my baby!'

'I'm so sorry for that and I've dealt with her.'

'You have?' She couldn't help sounding skeptical.

'Yes. I cannot exile her from my life altogether, I promised my father I would take care of them all, but she will never come between us again. I promise you that on my life.' He sighed heavily. 'I have learned that the mother I loved as a boy is not the woman she is now. I don't know when or why she changed, but as we, my brothers and I, grew up she became controlling, and Father indulged her. That's no excuse, believe me, and I didn't realize how impossible she had become until recently.' He shook his head, as though bewildered he'd missed it. 'Tom saw it much sooner than me.'

'Tom saw many things clearer than most. I miss him.'

'So do I. Very much.'

'If we marry . . . '

'We *will* marry!' He gripped her hands. '*You* are the most important person in my life. I would die for you.'

'Your mother said something similar to me about you.' She allowed him to lead her to the sofa.

He held her gaze. 'Do you trust me?'

She took a deep breath. 'Yes.'

He smiled wryly. 'You don't sound convincing, sweetheart.'

'Trust has to be earned, Reid. I saw you with a girl at Tom's party. I know now that it was just folly, but — '

He frowned, remembering. 'That girl was

nobody. I was letting off steam, having some fun, but it went no further than a few kisses.'

He rubbed his hand over his face. 'It meant nothing. Drunken silliness, that's all it was. I'll never ever do such a thing again. I promise you that.'

'I believe you.' And she did. The devastated look on his face convinced her it was indeed nothing.

'But I have been through a lot, Reid. It'll take time to repair our relationship.'

'I know, my love, and I'd give anything to have spared you from any of it. Things should never have gone the way as they did.'

She thought of the lane, of Mrs Murphy, Anthony, Dilys, the Ellertons and closer to home, of Lily and Noah, and of course Sophia. So many people and experiences, a life so very different to everything she'd ever known. How could she explain any of it to him? 'I am not the same person you once knew.'

'Then allow me to get to know you again. We have a lifetime to talk, Aurrie.' His smile seemed unsure and her resistance dissolved like puddles on a summer's day.

'I need you to love me for who I am, where I came from, who my family are.'

'I do and I will for the rest of my life.'

She stared down at their joined hands. 'I missed you.'

'Oh my darling.' He crushed her into his arms, kissing her with an abandonment that she gloried in. 'I love you. I love you.'

'Never let me go,' she cried into his neck.

'Never. I promise.'

The baby's crying came from the kitchen and Aurora's breast tingled with the release of milk. She stood, her hands in his. 'I need to go to her.' She gazed down at him. 'Would you care to see your daughter?'

'My daughter.' His throat worked and he smiled, rising to his feet. In the hall, Aurora saw Sophia disappearing up the stairs and so she led Reid up to the bedroom.

Sophia stood by the window gazing out, rocking the baby and humming. She stopped on seeing them and looked from one to the other.

'This is Reid Sinclair,' Aurora made the introductions. 'Reid, this is my mother, Sophia Middleton.'

'I'm glad to finally meet you, Mr Sinclair.' Sophia gave him a piercing look before handing the baby to Aurora and leaving the room.

'There, my darling, Mama is here,' Aurora crooned, kissing the tiny soft cheek.

'She's so small.'

'Yes. Too small really. The midwife says I must feed her often as possible to build her strength up, but she's a fighter. I can tell.'

'Like her mama.' Reid kissed the top of the baby's head.

'Here, hold her.' Aurora handed the baby over to him and she seemed even smaller in his arms. She watched Reid lift the baby closer for him to kiss her again and her heart swelled with love at the sight of them both.

'What's her name?' he whispered.

'Olivia Winifred Sophia Sinclair.'

His chest expanded and adoration lit his eyes as he gazed at his baby. 'Olivia Sinclair, I'm your papa.'

Epilogue

As the carriage trundled through the gates and up the drive, Aurora nervously held Olivia tighter. The baby's arm twitched but she didn't wake up. Aurora glanced up at Reid, who sat beside her and he returned her smile. She then looked across at Sophia and Noah sitting opposite and Sophie's answering expression was as nervous as her own.

Everything had happened so fast. Within three days of Reid knocking on the door at the farm cottage she was preparing to return home. Reid hadn't stayed at the farm, but gone back to the Hall so he could speak to her parents and ask her father's permission to marry her, which was silly really with her being a widow, but Reid wanted to do it properly and she'd agreed. He was the man she always meant to marry. It also gave him the opportunity to speak to her parents about all that had happened, before she saw them.

They had also discussed Merv Ellerton and Reid promised that he'd make sure that when the man returned from his bolt hole, he would be quietly *advised* to stop his illicit business or face the consequences.

All too soon the carriage stopped and the door was opened by Tibbleton. 'Welcome home, Miss Aurora, I mean, Mrs Sinclair.'

'Thank you, Tibbleton. It is good to see you again.' She waited for Reid to descend from the carriage first and take the baby from her before giving her hand to Tibbleton who helped her down. He did the same to Sophia with Noah following last.

Aurora looked up the house, at the windows above and then around the snow covered garden and lawns. Tears blinded her. She was home. Turning back to the front door, she stopped on seeing her mother coming out to stand on the top step. Winnie opened her arms and Aurora ran into them, crying.

'My darling girl, you're home.'

'I'm sorry for everything,' Aurora mumbled, her mother's soft fragrance of rose and jasmine filled her senses.

'As I am, my dearest one.' Winnie kissed her cheek, holding her tight. 'But all will be well now. This is a new beginning.'

'May I have a turn?' Josiah stood behind and Bettina and Harriet, both crying silently, were standing behind him.

Aurora rushed into his arms, happiness flowing out of her like water from a burst dam. Her father's strong arms held her fiercely before he allowed her sisters to come forward and embrace her too.

Amidst crying and talking, Aurora turned to see Sophia walk up to Winnie, for them to smile shyly at each other and then hold each other close, their tears mingling.

Reid cleared his throat. 'Might we not go inside? I have precious cargo.'

At once they were all fussing and smiling at the baby and each other. Reid was ushered inside first with the baby and everyone crowded into the drawing room after him. He reluctantly handed Olivia over to Winnie, who kissed and cried over her granddaughter, while Bettina and Harriet fought over who was to hold her next.

'You've made me a very happy man, Aurrie dear,' her father said, coming up beside her and taking her hand and kiss it. 'This house hasn't been the same since you left.'

'I'm sorry, Father, for everything. For the worry I caused, the gossip . . . '

'Enough of that. What is done is done and not all of it can be laid at your feet.' He stared down at their joined hands. 'No, your mother and I did wrong to not tell you, or prepare you for the truth.'

'You weren't to know it would come out.' She glanced over at Reid, who was busy boasting to Winnie about his clever daughter. 'Julia had no right to meddle in what didn't concern her.'

Her father followed her gaze. 'Ah, but she always will if it is in regards to her sons. You must be prepared for that. Some women will fight to the death for their offspring, like animals in the wild.'

'That is what worries me, what stops me from being completely happy with Reid. I'm always wondering what Julia will do next.'

'You mustn't let her ruin your future, Aurrie, she nearly did it once.'

'I know.' She linked her arm through his. 'I know Reid has told you a little about the Ellertons and — '

He patted her hand. 'Forget them. It'll all be

taken care of, I promise. That man will not be in business for long, of that I am certain.'

'Thank you.' Relieved, she rested against his side.

He smiled, his eyes warm. 'When will you be married?'

'In three weeks. The first banns were read yesterday in church at Hebden Bridge.'

'And that is where you'll stay until you marry?'

'Yes.'

He frowned. 'You aren't coming home?'

'No, Father, I'm sorry.' She smiled sadly in apology. 'I'm staying at the cottage until I marry Reid. I think it is for the best, but you will give me away, won't you?'

'Of course, my dearest girl.' He patted her arm in reassurance. 'And then?'

She took a deep breath. 'Then we return to Sinclair Hall.'

He looked surprised. 'So you'll be close by?'

Aurora lifted her chin. 'Just across the lawns.'

Later, after feeding Olivia and leaving her in the company of her doting aunts, Aurora went downstairs and into the drawing room. Her mother and Sophia were sitting before the fire, sipping tea.

Sophia glanced up with a smile. 'Is Olivia settled?'

Aurora sat beside her on the sofa. 'I don't think she'll sleep, Bettina and Harriet are singing to her.'

'Dear heaven, the poor babe,' her mother muttered, pouring Aurora a cup of tea.

'Where are the men?'

'Reid has gone back to the Hall, he says for you to join him when you're able.' Her mother passed the teacup over to her. 'Josiah and Noah have gone to the stables to check on a mare. They've talked non-stop about farming practices for an hour. We shooed them away.'

'I'm sorry Noah is taking up Josiah's time, Winnie,' Sophia passed Aurora a plate of shortbread. 'He's determined to make Aurora's farm the best in Yorkshire.'

'I wanted to talk to you about that.' Aurora bit into the shortbread. No one made it as good as Mrs Pringle.

'What about the farm?'

'I'm signing it over to you and Noah, and in turn it will go to Lily and Will.' The two women stared at her as she ate more shortbread.

'But Aurrie, Tom left you the farm. It's your security.'

'I won't need it once I'm married to Reid.'

Winnie nodded. 'That's true.'

Sophia shook her head. 'We can't take it.'

'Why?' Aurora put her plate down and wiped crumbs from her mouth. 'It makes perfect sense. I want you to have it.'

'I don't deserve it,' Sophia whispered, her eyes filling with tears.

'Don't speak so.' Aurora took her hand in a fierce grip. 'I want you to be happy and secure. You didn't have to take me in when I found you. You took care of me instead of sending me on my way.'

Winnie dabbed her wet eyes with her handkerchief. 'It's very fitting, Soph. For years

I've worried how you are. Now I can be happy knowing you are married to a good man and have a home of your own.'

'And Hebden Bridge isn't far. We can visit often.' Aurora selected another shortbread.

'Thank you, Aurrie.' Sophia kissed her cheek. 'You don't know what this means to me. Noah will be as happy as a dog with two tails.'

'You're my mother. I love you. Do you think I would stop seeing you once I marry Reid?'

Sophia froze. 'That's the first time you've said that to me.'

Aurora paused from taking another bite. 'What?'

'That you love me. You've never admitted to it in front of me.'

'I'm sure I have.'

'No.' Sophia's bottom lip trembled. 'I never thought you would love me as your mother because you already have a mother.'

She looked from Sophia to Winnie. Both these women meant a lot to her, they both loved her, wanted the best for her. Too much had happened for her to pick one over the other, not that she ever would. She needed them both in her life. 'I am a very lucky person. I have *two* wonderful, beautiful mothers and I love you both very much.'

Leaving Winnie and Sophia to talk of old times and discuss new ones, Aurora donned her coat and boots, scarf and mittens and left the house to walk across to the Hall. Snow crunched under her feet, the only sound in the silent gardens. Unlatching the gate, she gazed at the bare trees, their branches dusted with white, their bud tips swelling with new growth, readying for the coming spring.

Deciding to enter the Hall from a side door, she stepped into the conservatory, a glass domed room full of warmth and light. Cream furniture and leafy green potted plants gave the room a tropical feel and Aurora pulled off her mittens and tucked them into her coat pocket. She had always liked the simple spaciousness of the conservatory compared to other rooms of the Hall, which were stamped with Julia's extravagances.

Voices drew her out into the hallway and towards the front of the house. Before reaching the main reception rooms she turned left into a smaller tiled hallway that led to the study, billiard room and at the end the library.

At the study's closed door, Aurora hesitated, hearing raised voices from within. She closed her eyes on recognizing Julia's voice. Despite Reid's assurances, she couldn't help but feel anxious about seeing Julia again. Aurora quickly knocked on the door, determined to get it over with.

'Come in,' Reid called.

Aurora opened the door and entered. She smiled at him and lifted her cheek for his kiss as he joined her. She then turned her attention to Julia, whose appearance surprised her. Dressed expensively as always, Julia wore a skirt and short waist jacket in severe black, but she looked old. 'Good day, Mrs Sinclair.'

'Aurora.' Julia inclined her head like a duchess.

Aurora, feeling Reid's tension through his body, stepped forward. Something had to be done. For them to belong in the same family there had to be a truce or some sort. 'Julia, can we not start again?'

After flicking a glance at Reid, she nodded. 'Yes. I believe we must.'

Aurora slipped her hand through Reid's arm, hating the tense atmosphere and wishing she was back home with her family. But this house, and the people in it, was her future and she had to make a stand now or forever be in Julia's shadow. 'I know you love your sons, Julia. I know how much you adore Reid, how proud you are of him. I am too. His happiness means the world to me. That's why I left in the first place, so he could free of me and my family associations, but don't you see? It's never as easy as that. Neither of us can be truly happy without the other.'

'That's romantic nonsense.' Julia didn't look at her but continued to stare at the white world beyond the curtains.

'I don't agree.' Aurora sighed deeply. 'Perhaps we will never be friends, but whether you like it or not, Reid and I will marry in three weeks time and my place will be beside him, wherever he is.'

'You said you would accept Aurora as my wife, Mother,' Reid added, a warning threat in his tone.

'And I will.'

'Then mean it. You've been wrong on many accounts and due to your actions I have suffered, and Aurora and her family have suffered. You should beg for their forgiveness.'

'No.' She glared up at him, her eyes wide with horror. 'Never could I do that. Me? Beg? Are you mad?'

'Then I will thank you to leave this house at once and reside in the dowager cottage in Kent. You will never see Olivia or your future grandchildren we shall have.'

Julia's face paled, the well-known strength of spirit she owned fled and her shoulders sagged. 'You are to truly banish me from your life?'

Aurora, unable to cope with anymore, pulled at Reid's arm. 'No, Reid, not like this. I won't be the reason for more scandal. Disowning her will be the talk of drawing rooms for years and we'd never be free of it.' She reached up and kissed his cheek. 'I'll be back shortly.'

Reid frowned. 'Where are you going?'

'I'll be back. Stay here.' She ran from the room, from the Hall and across the gardens. Donaldson, her father's gardener raised his hand in salute as she ran passed him and ran into the kitchen, where Mrs Pringle dropped a spoon into the pot she was stirring at Aurora's sudden appearance.

Taking the stairs as fast as her skirts allowed, she went up to her old room and only stopped once she was in her bedroom. In the corner near the low fire, Olivia slept in the cradle all the Pettigrew girls had slept in.

Bettina, sitting on a chair beside the cradle, jumped at the interruption. 'Oh, Aurrie, it's you. She's sleeping. I was just watching her.'

'Thank you.' Aurora kissed her sister's cheek. 'I have to take her for a short while.'

'Where?' Bettina stood, scowling like a petulant nursemaid being relieved of her charge.

'To the Hall. I won't be long.' Aurora carefully scooped up her bundled daughter and nestled her close to her chest. 'Pass me that other blanket, will you? I'm going outside.'

'Outside?' Bettina was aghast. 'It's too cold.'

Aurora hurried to the door. 'Tell Mother I'll be an hour or so.' She made the return journey back to the hall, this time a little slower and more studiously so she wouldn't skid in the slippery conditions. Once in the Hall she went straight to the study and found Reid standing staring into the fire and his mother sitting on a chair by the window, each had their back to the other.

Reid turned, his eyes full of questions as he watched her walk across the carpet to his mother.

'Julia,' Aurora said softly, and when the other woman glanced up at her, Aurora placed the baby in her arms. 'Meet your granddaughter, Olivia Sinclair. I believe she will have your blue eyes.'

Julia sat stiffly in the chair, the child held away from her body. Olivia sniffled and snuffled, now disturbed from her sleep she opened her eyes and stared into the face of her grandmother. She yawned and blinked once and then as babies often did for no reason, she smiled lopsidedly.

Julia whimpered and brought the precious bundle closer to her chest. With one finger, she traced the delicate shape of Olivia's cheek and then lifted the baby closer so she could kiss her little head.

Aurora grinned as Reid hugged her to him and kissed her temple. They watched devotedly as the newest Sinclair tamed the oldest one.

We do hope that you have enjoyed reading this large print book.

Did you know that all of our titles are available for purchase?

We publish a wide range of high quality large print books including:
Romances, Mysteries, Classics
General Fiction
Non Fiction and Westerns

Special interest titles available in large print are:
The Little Oxford Dictionary
Music Book
Song Book
Hymn Book
Service Book

Also available from us courtesy of Oxford University Press:
Young Readers' Dictionary
(large print edition)
Young Readers' Thesaurus
(large print edition)

For further information or a free brochure, please contact us at:
Ulverscroft Large Print Books Ltd.,
The Green, Bradgate Road, Anstey,
Leicester, LE7 7FU, England.
Tel: (00 44) **0116 236 4325**
Fax: (00 44) **0116 234 0205**

Other titles published by Ulverscroft:

A LUCKY SIXPENCE

Anne Baker

It's 1937 and for sisters Lizzie and Milly Travis there's nothing quite like the thrill of the funfair at New Brighton. Amid the bright lights and whirling rides, Lizzie wins a lucky sixpence on a stall — as well as the heart of a handsome stallholder. Ben McCluskey isn't the type of man Lizzie's respectable parents had in mind for her, nevertheless the young couple embark on a whirlwind romance. Lizzie's mother worries that history will repeat itself when Ben introduces her daughter to a world she never knew existed. And, as war looms, Milly realises that her sister's luck can't last for ever . . .

A MOTHER'S LOVE

Katie Flynn

Liverpool, 1940. There comes a moment in every child's life when they must learn to stand on their own two feet. For 15-year-old Ellie Lancton, that time has come all too soon. The death of her mother and the increase in air raids leaves Ellie alone and in grave danger. It's not long before she is forced to leave her beloved Liverpool behind and cross the Mersey to seek refuge in the countryside. But as the war takes comforts away, so too does it bring new opportunities; for work, new friendships, and perhaps a little love . . .